RED QUEEN

RED QUEEN

VICTORIA AVEYARD

An Imprint of HarperCollins*Publishers*

HarperTeen is an imprint of HarperCollins Publishers.

Red Queen
Copyright © 2015 by Victoria Aveyard
Scarlet Guard symbol and King's Crest symbol © & ™ 2014 Victoria Aveyard
Endpapers illustrated by Amanda Persky.
All rights reserved. Printed in the United States of America. No part of this book may be used or reproduced in any manner whatsoever without written permission except in the case of brief quotations embodied in critical articles and reviews. For information address HarperCollins Children's Books, a division of HarperCollins Publishers, 195 Broadway, New York, NY 10007.
www.epicreads.com

Library of Congress Control Number: 2014952542
ISBN 978-0-06-231063-7 (trade bdg.) — ISBN 978-0-06-236271-1 (int. ed.)

Typography by Torborg Davern
16 17 18   PC/RRDH   40 39 38 37 36 35 34 33 32 31

First Edition

To Mom, Dad, and Morgan, who wanted to know what happened next, even when I didn't.

RED QUEEN

ONE

I hate First Friday. It makes the village crowded, and now, in the heat of high summer, that's the last thing anyone wants. From my place in the shade it isn't so bad, but the stink of bodies, all sweating with the morning work, is enough to make milk curdle. The air shimmers with heat and humidity, and even the puddles from yesterday's storm are hot, swirling with rainbow streaks of oil and grease.

The market deflates, with everyone closing up their stalls for the day. The merchants are distracted, careless, and it's easy for me to take whatever I want from their wares. By the time I'm done, my pockets bulge with trinkets and I've got an apple for the road. Not bad for a few minutes' work. As the throng of people moves, I let myself be taken away by the human current. My hands dart in and out, always in fleeting touches. Some paper bills from a man's pocket, a bracelet from a woman's wrist—nothing too big. Villagers are too busy shuffling along to notice a pickpocket in their midst.

The high, stilt buildings for which the village is named (the Stilts, very original) rise all around us, ten feet above the muddy ground. In the spring the lower bank is underwater, but right now it's August, when dehydration and sun sickness stalk the village. Almost everyone looks forward to the first Friday of each month, when work and school end early. But not me. No, I'd rather be in school, learning nothing in a classroom full of children.

Not that I'll be in school much longer. My eighteenth birthday is coming, and with it, conscription. I'm not apprenticed, I don't have a job, so I'm going to be sent to the war like all the other *idle* ones. It's no wonder there's no work left, what with every man, woman, and child trying to stay out of the army.

My brothers went to war when they turned eighteen, all three of them sent to fight Lakelanders. Only Shade can write worth a lick, and he sends me letters when he can. I haven't heard from my other brothers, Bree and Tramy, in over a year. But no news is good news. Families can go years without hearing a thing, only to find their sons and daughters waiting on the front doorstep, home on leave or sometimes blissfully discharged. But usually you receive a letter made of heavy paper, stamped with the king's crown seal below a short thank-you for your child's life. Maybe you even get a few buttons from their torn, obliterated uniforms.

I was thirteen when Bree left. He kissed me on the cheek and gave me a single pair of earrings for my little sister, Gisa, and me to split. They were dangling glass beads, the hazy pink color of sunset. We pierced our ears ourselves that night. Tramy and Shade kept up the tradition when they went. Now Gisa and I have one ear each set with three tiny stones to remind us of our brothers fighting somewhere. I didn't really believe they'd have to go, not until the legionnaire in his polished armor showed up and took them away one after another. And this fall, they'll come for me. I've already started saving—and stealing—to buy Gisa some earrings when I go.

Don't think about it. That's what Mom always says, about the army, about my brothers, about everything. *Great advice, Mom.*

Down the street, at the crossing of Mill and Marcher roads, the crowd thickens and more villagers join the current. A gang of kids, little thieves in training, flutters through the fray with sticky, searching fingers. They're too young to be good at it, and Security officers are quick to intervene. Usually the kids would be sent to the stocks, or the jail at the outpost, but the officers want to see First Friday. They settle for giving the ringleaders a few harsh knocks before letting them go. *Small mercies.*

The tiniest pressure at my waist makes me spin, acting on instinct. I grab at the hand foolish enough to pickpocket me, squeezing tight so the little imp won't be able to run away. But instead of a scrawny kid, I find myself staring up at a smirking face.

Kilorn Warren. A fisherman's apprentice, a war orphan, and probably my only real friend. We used to beat each other up as children, but now that we're older—and he's a foot taller than me—I try to avoid scuffles. He has his uses, I suppose. Reaching high shelves, for example.

"You're getting faster." He chuckles, shaking off my grip.

"Or you're getting slower."

He rolls his eyes and snatches the apple out of my hand.

"Are we waiting for Gisa?" he asks, taking a bite of the fruit.

"She has a pass for the day. Working."

"Then let's get moving. Don't want to miss the show."

"And what a tragedy that would be."

"Tsk, tsk, Mare," he teases, shaking a finger at me. "This is supposed to be fun."

"It's *supposed* to be a warning, you dumb fool."

But he's already walking off with his long strides, forcing me to almost trot to keep up. His gait weaves, off balance. *Sea legs*, he calls them, though he's never been to the far-off sea. I guess long hours on his master's fishing boat, even on the river, are bound to have some effect.

Like my dad, Kilorn's father was sent off to war, but whereas mine returned missing a leg and a lung, Mr. Warren came back in a shoe box. Kilorn's mother ran off after that, leaving her young son to fend for himself. He almost starved to death but somehow kept picking fights with me. I fed him so that I wouldn't have to kick around a bag of bones, and now, ten years later, here he is. At least he's apprenticed and won't face the war.

We get to the foot of the hill, where the crowd is thicker, pushing and prodding on all sides. First Friday attendance is mandatory, unless you are, like my sister, an "essential laborer." As if embroidering silk is essential. But the Silvers love their silk, don't they? Even the Security officers, a few of them anyway, can be bribed with pieces sewn by my sister. Not that I know anything about that.

The shadows around us deepen as we climb up the stone stairs, toward the crest of the hill. Kilorn takes them two at a time, almost leaving me behind, but he stops to wait. He smirks down at me and tosses a lock of faded, tawny hair out of his green eyes.

"Sometimes I forget you have the legs of a child."

"Better than the brain of one," I snap, giving him a light smack on the cheek as I pass. His laughter follows me up the steps.

"You're grouchier than usual."

"I just hate these things."

"I know," he murmurs, solemn for once.

And then we're in the arena, the sun blazing hot overhead. Built ten years ago, the arena is easily the largest structure in the Stilts. It's nothing compared to the colossal ones in the cities, but still, the soaring arches of steel, the thousands of feet of concrete, are enough to make a village girl catch her breath.

Security officers are everywhere, their black-and-silver uniforms standing out in the crowd. This is First Friday, and they can't wait to watch the proceedings. They carry long rifles or pistols, though they don't need them. As is customary, the officers are Silvers, and Silvers have nothing to fear from us Reds. Everyone knows that. We are not their equals, though you wouldn't know it from looking at us. The only thing that serves to distinguish us, outwardly at least, is that Silvers stand tall. Our backs are bent by work and unanswered hope and the inevitable disappointment with our lot in life.

Inside the open-topped arena is just as hot as out, and Kilorn, always on his toes, leads me to some shade. We don't get seats here, just long concrete benches, but the few Silver nobles up above enjoy cool, comfortable boxes. There they have drinks, food, *ice* even in high summer, cushioned chairs, electric lights, and other comforts I'll never enjoy. The Silvers don't bat an eye at any of it, complaining about the "wretched conditions." I'll give them a wretched condition, if I ever have the chance. All we get are hard benches and a few screechy video screens almost too bright and too noisy to stand.

"Bet you a day's wages it's another strongarm today," Kilorn says, tossing his apple core toward the arena floor.

"No bet," I shoot back at him. Many Reds gamble their earnings on the fights, hoping to win a little something to help them get through another week. But not me, not even with Kilorn. It's easier to cut the bookie's purse than try to win money from it. "You shouldn't waste your money like that."

"It's not a waste if I'm right. It's *always* a strongarm beating up on someone."

Strongarms usually make up at least one-half of the fights, their skills and abilities better suited to the arena than almost any other Silver. They seem to revel in it, using their superhuman strength to toss other champions around like rag dolls.

"What about the other one?" I ask, thinking about the range of Silvers that could appear. Telkies, swifts, nymphs, greenys, stoneskins—all of them terrible to watch.

"Not sure. Hopefully something cool. I could use some fun."

Kilorn and I don't really see eye to eye on the Feats of First Friday. For me, watching two champions rip into each other is not enjoyable, but Kilorn loves it. *Let them ruin each other,* he says. *They're not our people.*

He doesn't understand what the Feats are about. This isn't mindless entertainment, meant to give us some respite from grueling work. This is calculated, cold, a message. Only Silvers can fight in the arenas because only a Silver can *survive* the arena. They fight to show us their strength and power. *You are no match for us. We are your betters. We are gods.* It's written in every superhuman blow the champions land.

And they're absolutely right. Last month I watched a swift battle a telky and, though the swift could move faster than the eye could see, the telky stopped him cold. With just the power of his mind, he lifted the other fighter right off the ground. The swift started to choke; I think the telky had some invisible grip on his throat. When the swift's face turned blue, they called the match. Kilorn cheered. He'd bet on the telky.

"Ladies and gentlemen, Silvers and Reds, welcome to First Friday, the Feat of August." The announcer's voice echoes around the arena, magnified by the walls. He sounds bored, as usual, and I don't blame him.

Once, the Feats were not matches at all, but executions. Prisoners and enemies of the state would be transported to Archeon, the capital, and killed in front of a Silver crowd. I guess the Silvers liked that, and the matches began. Not to kill but to entertain. Then they became the Feats and spread out to the other cities, to different arenas and different audiences. Eventually the Reds were granted admission, confined to the cheap seats. It wasn't long until the Silvers built arenas everywhere, even villages like the Stilts, and attendance that was once a gift became a mandatory curse. My brother Shade says it's because arena cities enjoyed a marked reduction in Red crime, dissent, even the few acts of rebellion. Now Silvers don't have to use execution or the legions or even Security to keep the peace; two champions can scare us just as easily.

Today, the two in question look up to the job. The first to walk out onto the white sand is announced as Cantos Carros, a Silver from Harbor Bay in the east. The video screen blares a clear picture of the warrior, and no one needs to tell me this is a strongarm. He has arms like tree trunks, corded and veined and straining against his own skin. When he smiles, I can see all his teeth are gone or broken. Maybe he ran afoul of his own toothbrush when he was a growing boy.

Next to me, Kilorn cheers and the other villagers roar with him. A Security officer throws a loaf of bread at the louder ones for their trouble. To my left, another hands a screaming child a bright yellow piece of paper. 'Lec papers—extra electricity rations. All of it to make us cheer, to make us scream, to force us to watch, even if we don't want to.

"That's right, let him hear you!" the announcer drawls, forcing as much enthusiasm into his voice as he can. "And here we have his opponent, straight from the capital, Samson Merandus."

The other warrior looks pale and weedy next to the human-shaped hunk of muscle, but his blue steel armor is fine and polished to a high sheen. He's probably the second son of a second son, trying to win renown in the arena. Though he should be scared, he looks strangely calm.

His last name sounds familiar, but that's not unusual. Many Silvers belong to famous families, called houses, with dozens of members. The governing family of our region, the Capital Valley, is House Welle, though I've never seen Governor Welle in my life. He never visits it more than once or twice a year, and even then, he *never* stoops to entering a Red village like mine. I saw his riverboat once, a sleek thing with green-and-gold flags. He's a greeny, and when he passed, the trees on the bank burst into blossom and flowers popped out of the ground. I thought it was beautiful, until one of the older boys threw rocks at his boat. The stones fell harmlessly into the river. They put the boy in the stocks anyway.

"It'll be the strongarm for sure."

Kilorn frowns at the small champion. "How do you know? What's Samson's power?"

"Who cares, he's still going to lose," I scoff, settling in to watch.

The usual call rings out over the arena. Many rise to their feet, eager to watch, but I stay seated in silent protest. As calm as I might look, anger boils in my skin. Anger, and jealousy. *We are gods*, echoes in my head.

"Champions, set your feet."

They do, digging in their heels on opposite sides of the arena. Guns aren't allowed in arena fights, so Cantos draws a short, wide sword. I doubt he'll need it. Samson produces no weapon, his fingers merely twitching by his side.

A low, humming electric tone runs through the arena. *I hate this part.* The sound vibrates in my teeth, in my bones, pulsing until I think something might shatter. It ends abruptly with a chirping chime. *It begins.* I exhale.

It looks like a bloodbath right away. Cantos barrels forward like a bull, kicking up sand in his wake. Samson tries to dodge Cantos, using his shoulder to slide around the Silver, but the strongarm is quick. He gets hold of Samson's leg and tosses him across the arena like he's made of feathers. The subsequent cheers cover Samson's roar of pain as he collides with the cement wall, but it's written on his face. Before he can hope to stand, Cantos is over him, heaving him skyward. He hits the sand in a heap of what can only be broken bones but somehow rises to his feet again.

"Is he a punching bag?" Kilorn laughs. "Let him have it, Cantos!"

Kilorn doesn't care about an extra loaf of bread or a few more minutes of electricity. That's not why he cheers. He honestly wants to see blood, Silver blood—*silverblood*—stain the arena. It doesn't matter that the blood is everything we aren't, everything we can't be, everything we *want*. He just needs to see it and trick himself into thinking they are truly human, that they can be hurt and defeated. But I know better. Their blood is a threat, a warning, a promise. *We are not the same and never will be.*

He's not disappointed. Even the box seats can see the metallic, iridescent liquid dripping from Samson's mouth. It reflects the summer sun like a watery mirror, painting a river down his neck and into his armor.

This is the true division between Silvers and Reds: the color of our blood. This simple difference somehow makes them stronger, smarter, *better* than us.

Samson spits, sending a sunburst of silverblood across the arena.

Ten yards away, Cantos tightens his grip on his sword, ready to incapacitate Samson and end this.

"Poor fool," I mutter. It seems Kilorn is right. *Nothing but a punching bag.*

Cantos pounds through the sand, sword held high, eyes on fire. And then he freezes midstep, his armor clanking with the sudden stop. From the middle of the arena, the bleeding warrior points at Cantos, with a stare to break bone.

Samson flicks his fingers and Cantos walks, perfectly in time with Samson's movements. His mouth falls open, like he's gone slow or stupid. *Like his mind is gone.*

I can't believe my eyes.

A deathly quiet falls over the arena as we watch, not understanding the scene below us. Even Kilorn has nothing to say.

"A whisper," I breathe aloud.

Never before have I seen one in the arena—I doubt anyone has. Whispers are rare, dangerous, and powerful, even among the Silvers, even in the *capital*. The rumors about them vary, but it boils down to something simple and chilling: they can enter your head, read your thoughts, and *control your mind*. And this is exactly what Samson is doing, having whispered his way past Cantos's armor and muscle, into his very brain, where there are no defenses.

Cantos raises his sword, hands trembling. He's trying to fight Samson's power. But strong as he is, there's no fighting the enemy in his mind.

Another twist of Samson's hand and silverblood splashes across the sand as Cantos plunges his sword straight through his armor, into the flesh of his own stomach. Even up in the seats, I can hear the sickening squelch of metal cutting through meat.

As the blood gushes from Cantos, gasps echo across the arena. We've never seen so much blood here before.

Blue lights flash to life, bathing the arena floor in a ghostly glow, signaling the end of the match. Silver healers run across the sand, rushing to the fallen Cantos. Silvers aren't supposed to die here. Silvers are supposed to fight bravely, to flaunt their skills, to put on a good show—but not *die*. After all, they aren't Reds.

Officers move faster than I've ever seen before. A few are swifts, rushing to and fro in a blur as they herd us out. They don't want us around if Cantos dies on the sand. Meanwhile, Samson strides from the arena like a titan. His gaze falls on Cantos's body, and I expect him to look apologetic. Instead, his face is blank, emotionless, and so cold. The match was nothing to him. *We* are nothing to him.

In school, we learned about the world before ours, about the angels and gods that lived in the sky, ruling the earth with kind and loving hands. Some say those are just stories, but I don't believe that.

The gods rule us still. They have come down from the stars. And they are no longer kind.

TWO

Our house is small, even by Stilts standards, but at least we have a view. Before his injury, during one of his army leaves, Dad built the house high so we could see across the river. Even through the haze of summer you can see the cleared pockets of land that were once forest, now logged into oblivion. They look like a disease, but to the north and west, the untouched hills are a calm reminder. *There is so much more out there.* Beyond us, beyond the Silvers, beyond everything I know.

I climb the ladder up to the house, over worn wood shaped to the hands that ascend and descend every day. From this height I can see a few boats heading upriver, proudly flying their bright flags. *Silvers.* They're the only ones rich enough to use private transportation. While they enjoy wheeled transports, pleasure boats, even high-flying airjets, we get nothing more than our own two feet, or a push cycle if we're lucky.

The boats must be heading to Summerton, the small city that springs to life around the king's summer residence. Gisa was there today, aiding the seamstress she is apprenticed to. They often go to the market there when the king visits, to sell her wares to the Silver merchants and nobles who follow the royals like ducklings. The palace itself is known as the Hall of the Sun, and it's supposed to be a marvel, but I've never seen it. I don't know why the royals have a second house, especially since the capital palace is so fine and beautiful. But like all Silvers, they don't act out of need. They are driven by want. And what they want, they get.

Before I open the door to the usual chaos, I pat the flag fluttering from the porch. Three red stars on yellowed fabric, one for each brother, and room for more. *Room for me.* Most houses have flags like this, some with black stripes instead of stars in quiet reminder of dead children.

Inside, Mom sweats over the stove, stirring a pot of stew while my father glares at it from his wheelchair. Gisa embroiders at the table, making something beautiful and exquisite and entirely beyond my comprehension.

"I'm home," I say to no one in particular. Dad answers with a wave, Mom a nod, and Gisa doesn't look up from her scrap of silk.

I drop my pouch of stolen goods next to her, letting the coins jingle as much as they can. "I think I've got enough to get a proper cake for Dad's birthday. And more batteries, enough to last the month."

Gisa eyes the pouch, frowning with distaste. She's only fourteen but sharp for her age. "One day people are going to come and take everything you have."

"Jealousy doesn't become you, Gisa," I scold, patting her on the head. Her hands fly up to her perfect, glossy red hair, brushing it back into her meticulous bun.

I've always wanted her hair, though I'd never tell her that. Where hers is like fire, my hair is what we call river brown. Dark at the root, pale at the ends, as the color leeches from our hair with the stress of Stilts life. Most keep their hair short to hide their gray ends but I don't. I like the reminder that even my hair knows life shouldn't be this way.

"I'm not jealous," she huffs, returning to her work. She stitches flowers made of fire, each one a beautiful flame of thread against oily black silk.

"That's beautiful, Gee." I let my hand trace one of the flowers, marveling at the silky feel of it. She glances up and smiles softly, showing even teeth. As much as we fight, she knows she's my little star.

And everyone knows I'm the jealous one, Gisa. I can't do anything but steal from people who can actually do things.

Once she finishes her apprenticeship, she'll be able to open her own shop. Silvers will come from all around to pay her for handkerchiefs and flags and clothing. Gisa will achieve what few Reds do and live well. She'll provide for our parents and give me and my brothers menial jobs to get us out of the war. Gisa is going to save us one day, with nothing more than needle and thread.

"Night and day, my girls," Mom mutters, running a finger through graying hair. She doesn't mean it as an insult but a prickly truth. Gisa is skilled, pretty, and sweet. I'm a bit rougher, as Mom kindly puts it. The dark to Gisa's light. I suppose the only common things between us are the shared earrings, the memory of our brothers.

Dad wheezes from his corner and hammers his chest with a fist. This is common, since he has only one real lung. Luckily the skill of a Red medic saved him, replacing the collapsed lung with a device that could breathe for him. It wasn't a Silver invention, as they have no need for such things. They have the healers. But healers don't waste their time saving the Reds, or even working on the front lines keeping soldiers alive. Most of them remain in the cities, prolonging the lives of ancient Silvers, mending livers destroyed by alcohol and the like. So we're forced to indulge in an underground market of technology and inventions to help better ourselves. Some are foolish, most don't work—but a bit of clicking metal saved my dad's life. I can always hear it ticking away, a tiny pulse to keep Dad breathing.

"I don't want cake," he grumbles. I don't miss his glance toward his growing belly.

"Well, tell me what you *do* want, Dad. A new watch or—"

"Mare, I do not consider something you stole off someone's wrist to be *new*."

Before another war can brew in the Barrow house, Mom pulls the stew off the stove. "Dinner is served." She brings it to the table, and the fumes wash over me.

"It smells great, Mom," Gisa lies. Dad is not so tactful and grimaces at the meal.

Not wanting to be shown up, I force down some stew. It's not as bad as usual, to my pleasant surprise. "You used that pepper I brought you?"

Instead of nodding and smiling and thanking me for noticing, she flushes and doesn't answer. She knows I stole it, just like all my gifts.

Gisa rolls her eyes over her soup, sensing where this is going.

You'd think by now I'd be used to it, but their disapproval wears on me.

Sighing, Mom lowers her face into her hands. "Mare, you know I appreciate— I just wish—"

I finish for her. "That I was like Gisa?"

Mom shakes her head. Another lie. "No, of course not. That's not what I meant."

"Right." I'm sure they can sense my bitterness on the other side of the village. I try my best to keep my voice from breaking. "It's the only way I can help out before—before I go away."

Mentioning the war is a quick way to silence my house. Even Dad's wheezing stops. Mom turns her head, her cheeks flushing red with anger. Under the table, Gisa's hand closes around mine.

"I know you're doing everything you can, for the right reasons," Mom whispers. It takes a lot for her to say this, but it comforts me all the same.

I keep my mouth shut and force a nod.

Then Gisa jumps in her seat, like she's been shocked. "Oh, I almost forgot. I stopped at the post on the way back from Summerton. There was a letter from Shade."

It's like setting off a bomb. Mom and Dad scramble, reaching for the dirty envelope Gisa pulls out of her jacket. I let them pass it over, examining the paper. Neither can read, so they glean whatever they can from the paper itself.

Dad sniffs the letter, trying to place the scent. "Pine. Not smoke. That's good. He's away from the Choke."

We all breathe a sigh of relief at that. The Choke is the bombed-out strip of land connecting Norta to the Lakelands, where most of the war is fought. Soldiers spend the majority of their time there, ducking in trenches doomed to explode or making daring pushes that end in a massacre. The rest of the border is mainly lake, though in the far north it becomes tundra too cold and barren to fight over. Dad was injured at the Choke years ago, when a bomb dropped on his unit. Now the Choke is so destroyed by decades of battle, the smoke of explosions is a constant fog and nothing can grow there. It's dead and gray, like the future of the war.

He finally passes the letter over for me to read, and I open it with great anticipation, both eager and afraid to see what Shade has to say.

Dear family, I am alive. Obviously.

That gets a chuckle out of Dad and me, and even a smile from Gisa. Mom is not as amused, even though Shade starts every letter like this.

We've been called away from the front, as Dad the Bloodhound has probably guessed. It's nice, getting back to the main camps. It's Red as the dawn up here, you barely even see the Silver officers. And without the Choke smoke, you can actually see the sun rise stronger every day. But I won't be in for long. Command plans to repurpose the unit for lake combat, and we've been assigned to one of the new warships. I met a medic detached from her unit who said she knew Tramy and that he's fine. Took a bit of shrapnel retreating from the Choke, but he recovered nicely. No infection, no permanent damage.

Mom sighs aloud, shaking her head. "No permanent damage," she scoffs.

Still nothing about Bree but I'm not worried. He's the best of us, and he's coming up on his five-year leave. He'll be home soon, Mom, so stop your worrying. Nothing else to report, at least that I can write in a letter. Gisa, don't be too much of a show-off even though you deserve to be. Mare, don't be such a brat all the time, and stop beating up that Warren boy. Dad, I'm proud of you. Always. Love all of you.
  Your favorite son and brother, Shade.

Like always, Shade's words pierce through us. I can almost hear his voice if I try hard enough. Then the lights above us suddenly start to whine.

"Did no one put in the ration papers I got yesterday?" I ask before the lights flicker off, plunging us into darkness. As my eyes adjust, I can just see Mom shaking her head.

Gisa groans. "Can we not do this again?" Her chair scrapes as she stands up. "I'm going to bed. Try not to yell."

But we don't yell. Seems to be the way of my world—*too tired to fight*. Mom and Dad retreat to their bedroom, leaving me alone at the table. Normally I'd slip out, but I can't find the will to do much more than go to sleep.

I climb up yet another ladder to the loft, where Gisa is already snoring. She can sleep like no other, dropping off in a minute or so, while it can sometimes take me hours. I settle into my cot, content to simply lie there and hold Shade's letter. Like Dad said, it smells strongly of pine.

The river sounds nice tonight, tripping over stones in the bank as it lulls me to sleep. Even the old fridge, a rusty battery-run machine that usually whines so hard it hurts my head, doesn't trouble me tonight. But then a birdcall interrupts my descent into sleep. *Kilorn.*

No. Go away.

Another call, louder this time. Gisa stirs a little, rolling over into her pillow.

Grumbling to myself, hating Kilorn, I roll out of my cot and slide down the ladder. Anyone else would have tripped over the clutter in the main room, but I have great footing thanks to years of running from officers. I'm down the stilt ladder in a second, landing ankle-deep in the mud. Kilorn is waiting, appearing out of the shadows beneath the house.

"I hope you like black eyes because I have no problem giving you one for this—"

The sight of his face stops me short.

He's been crying. *Kilorn does not cry.* His knuckles are bleeding too, and I bet there's a wall hurting just as hard somewhere nearby. In spite of myself, in spite of the late hour, I can't help but feel concerned, even scared for him.

"What is it? What's wrong?" Without thinking, I take his hand in mine, feeling the blood beneath my fingers. "What happened?"

He takes a moment to respond, working himself up. Now I'm terrified.

"My master—he fell. He died. I'm not an apprentice anymore."

I try to hold in a gasp, but it echoes anyway, taunting us. Even though he doesn't have to, even though I know what he's trying to say, he continues.

"I hadn't even finished training and now—" He trips over his words. "I'm eighteen. The other fishermen have apprentices. I'm not working. I can't *get* work."

The next words are like a knife in my heart. Kilorn draws a ragged breath, and somehow I wish I wouldn't have to hear him.

"They're going to send me to the war."

THREE

It's been going on for the better part of the last hundred years. I don't think it should even be called a war anymore, but there isn't a word for this higher form of destruction. In school they told us it started over land. The Lakelands are flat and fertile, bordered by immense lakes full of fish. Not like the rocky, forested hills of Norta, where the farmlands can barely feed us. Even the Silvers felt the strain, so the king declared war, plunging us into a conflict neither side could really win.

The Lakelander king, another Silver, responded in kind, with the full support of his own nobility. They wanted our rivers, to get access to a sea that wasn't frozen half the year, and the water mills dotting our rivers. The mills are what make our country strong, providing enough electricity so that even the Reds can have some. I've heard rumors of cities farther south, near the capital, Archeon, where greatly skilled Reds build machines beyond my comprehension. For transport on land, water, and sky, or weapons to rain destruction wherever the Silvers might need. Our teacher proudly told us Norta was the light of the world, a nation made great by our technology and power. All the rest, like the Lakelands or Piedmont to the south, live in darkness. We were lucky to be born here. *Lucky.* The word makes me want to scream.

But despite our electricity, the Lakelander food, our weapons, their numbers, neither side has much advantage over the other. Both have Silver officers and Red soldiers, fighting with abilities and guns and the shield of a thousand Red bodies. A war that was supposed to end less than a century ago still drags on. I always found it funny that we fought over food and water. Even the high-and-mighty Silvers need to eat.

But it isn't funny now, not when Kilorn is going to be the next person I say good-bye to. I wonder if he'll give me an earring so I can remember him when the polished legionnaire takes him away.

"One week, Mare. One week and I'm gone." His voice cracks, though he coughs to try to cover it up. "I can't do this. They—they won't take me."

But I can see the fight going out of his eyes.

"There must be something we can do," I blurt out.

"There's nothing anyone can do. No one has escaped conscription and lived."

He doesn't need to tell me that. Every year, someone tries to run. And every year, they're dragged back to the town square and hanged.

"No. We'll find a way."

Even now, he finds the strength to smirk at me. *"We?"*

The heat in my cheeks surges faster than any flame. "I'm doomed for conscription same as you, but they're not going to get me either. So we run."

The army has always been my fate, my punishment, I know that. But not his. It's already taken too much from him.

"There's nowhere we can go," he sputters, but at least he's arguing.

At least he's not giving up. "We'd never survive the north in winter, the east is the sea, the west is more war, the south is radiated to all hell—and everywhere in between is crawling with Silvers and Security."

The words pour out of me like a river. "So is the village. Crawling with Silvers and Security. And we manage to steal right under their noses and escape with our heads." My mind races, trying my hardest to find something, anything, that might be of use. And then it hits me like a bolt of lightning. "The black-market trade, the one *we* help keep running, smuggles everything from grain to lightbulbs. Who's to say they can't smuggle people?"

His mouth opens, about to spout a thousand reasons why this won't work. But then he smiles. And nods.

I don't like getting involved with other people's business. I don't have time for it. And yet here I am, listening to myself say four dooming words.

"Leave everything to me."

The things we can't sell to the usual shop owners we have to take to Will Whistle. He's old, too feeble to work the lumberyards, so he sweeps the streets by day. At night, he sells everything you could want out of his moldy wagon, from heavily restricted coffee to exotics from Archeon. I was nine with a fistful of stolen buttons when I took my chances with Will. He paid me three copper pennies for them, no questions asked. Now I'm his best customer and probably the reason he manages to stay afloat in such a small place. On a good day I might even call him a friend. It was years before I discovered Will was part of a much larger operation. Some call it the underground, others the black market, but all I care about is what they can do. They have fences, people like Will, everywhere. Even in Archeon, as impossible as that sounds. They transport illegal goods all over the country. And now I'm betting that they might make an exception and transport a person instead.

"Absolutely not."

In eight years, Will has never said no to me. Now the wrinkled old fool is practically slamming shut the doors of his wagon in my face. I'm happy Kilorn stayed behind, so he doesn't have to see me fail him.

"Will, *please*. I know you can do it—"

He shakes head, white beard waggling. "Even if I *could*, I am a tradesman. The people I work with aren't the type to spend their time and effort shuttling another runner from place to place. It's not our business."

I can feel my only hope, Kilorn's only hope, slipping right through my fingers.

Will must see the desperation in my eyes because he softens, leaning against the wagon door. He heaves a sigh and glances backward, into the darkness of the wagon. After a moment, he turns back around and gestures, beckoning me inside. I follow gladly.

"Thank you, Will," I babble. "You don't know what this means to me—"

"Sit down and be quiet, girl," a high voice says.

Out of the shadows of the wagon, hardly visible in the dim light of Will's single blue candle, a woman rises to her feet. Girl, I should say, since she barely looks older than me. But she's much taller, with the air of an old warrior. The gun at her hip, tucked into a red sash belt stamped with suns, is certainly not authorized. She's too blond and fair to be from the Stilts, and judging by the light sweat on her face, she's not used to the heat or humidity. She is a foreigner, an outlander, and an outlaw at that. *Just the person I want to see.*

She waves me to the bench cut into the wagon wall, and she sits down again only when I have. Will follows closely behind and all but collapses into a worn chair, his eyes flitting between the girl and me.

"Mare Barrow, meet Farley," he murmurs, and she tightens her jaw.

Her gaze lands on my face. "You wish to transport cargo."

"Myself and a boy—" But she holds up a large, callused hand, cutting me off.

"*Cargo*," she says again, eyes full of meaning. My heart leaps in my chest; this Farley girl might be of the helping kind. "And what is the destination?"

I rack my brain, trying to think of somewhere safe. The old classroom map swims before my eyes, outlining the coast and the rivers, marking cities and villages and everything in between. From Harbor Bay west to the Lakelands, the northern tundra to the radiated wastes of the Ruins and the Wash, it's all dangerous land for us.

"Somewhere safe from the Silvers. That's all."

Farley blinks at me, her expression unchanging. "Safety has a price, girl."

"Everything has a price, *girl*," I fire back, matching her tone. "No one knows that more than me."

A long beat of silence stretches through the wagon. I can feel the night wasting away, taking precious minutes from Kilorn. Farley must sense my unease and impatience but makes no hurry to speak. After what seems like an eternity, her mouth finally opens.

"The Scarlet Guard accepts, Mare Barrow."

It takes all the restraint I have to keep from jumping out of my seat with joy. But something tugs at me, keeping a smile from crossing my face.

"Payment is expected in full, to the equivalent of one thousand crowns," Farley continues.

That almost knocks the air from my lungs. Even Will looks surprised, his fluffy white eyebrows disappearing into his hairline. "A *thousand?*" I manage to choke out. No one deals in that amount of money, not in the Stilts. That could feed my family for a year. *Many years.*

But Farley isn't finished. I get the sense that she enjoys this. "This can be paid in paper notes, tetrarch coins, or the bartering equivalent. Per item, of course."

Two thousand crowns. A fortune. Our freedom is worth a fortune.

"Your cargo will be moved the day after tomorrow. You must pay then."

I can barely breathe. Less than two days to accumulate more money than I have stolen in my entire life. *There is no way.*

She doesn't even give me time to protest.

"Do you accept the terms?"

"I need more time."

She shakes her head and leans forward. I smell gunpowder on her. "Do you accept the terms?"

It is impossible. It is foolish. *It is our best chance.*

"I accept the terms."

The next moments pass in a blur as I trudge home through the muddy shadows. My mind is on fire, trying to figure out a way to get my hands on anything worth even close to Farley's price. There's nothing in the Stilts, that's for sure.

Kilorn is still waiting in the darkness, looking like a little lost boy. I suppose he is.

"Bad news?" he says, trying to keep his voice even, but it trembles anyway.

"The underground can get us out of here." For his sake, I keep myself calm as I explain. Two thousand crowns might as well be the king's throne, but I make it seem like nothing. "If anyone can do it, we can. We *can*."

"Mare." His voice is cold, colder than winter, but the hollow look in his eyes is worse. "It's over. We lost."

"But if we just—"

He grabs my shoulders, holding me at an arm's length in his firm grip. It doesn't hurt but it shocks me all the same. "Don't do this to me, Mare. Don't make believe there's a way out of this. Don't give me hope."

He's right. It's cruel to give hope where none should be. It only turns into disappointment, resentment, rage—all the things that make this life more difficult than it already is.

"Just let me accept it. Maybe—maybe then I can actually get my head in order, get myself trained properly, give myself a fighting chance out there."

My hands find his wrists and I hold on tight. "You talk like you're already dead."

"Maybe I am."

"My brothers—"

"Your father made sure they knew what they were doing long before they went away. And it helps that they're all the size of a house." He forces a smirk, trying to get me to laugh. It doesn't work. "I'm a good swimmer and sailor. They'll need me on the lakes."

It's only when he wraps his arms around me, hugging me, that I realize I'm shaking. "Kilorn—," I mumble into his chest. But the next words won't come. *It should be me.* But my time is fast approaching. I can only hope Kilorn survives long enough for me to see him again, in the barracks or in a trench. Maybe then I'll find the right words to say. Maybe then I'll understand how I feel.

"Thank you, Mare. For everything." He pulls back, letting go of me far too quickly. "If you save up, you'll have enough by the time the legion comes for you."

For him, I nod. But I have no plans of letting him fight and die alone.

By the time I settle down into my cot, I know I will not sleep tonight. There must be something I can do, and even if it takes all night, I'm going to figure it out.

Gisa coughs in her sleep and it's a courteous, tiny sound. Even unconscious, she manages to be ladylike. No wonder she fits in so well with the Silvers. She's everything they like in a Red: quiet, content, and unassuming. It's a good thing she's the one who has to deal with them, helping the superhuman fools pick out silk and fine fabrics for clothes they'll wear just once. She says you get used to it, to the amount of money they spend on such trivial things. And at Grand Garden, the marketplace in Summerton, the money increases tenfold. Together with her mistress, Gisa sews lace, silk, fur, even gemstones to create wearable art for the Silver elite who seem to follow the royals everywhere. The parade, she calls them, an endless march of preening peacocks, each one more proud and ridiculous than the next. All Silver, all silly, and all status-obsessed.

I hate them even more than usual tonight. The stockings they lose would probably be enough to save me, Kilorn, and half the Stilts from conscription.

For the second time tonight, lightning strikes.

"Gisa. Wake up." I do not whisper. The girl sleeps like the dead. "*Gisa.*"

She shifts and groans into her pillow. "Sometimes I want to kill you," she grumbles.

"How sweet. Now *wake up*!"

Her eyes are still closed when I pounce, landing on her like a giant cat. Before she can start yelling and whining and get my mother involved, I clamp a hand on her mouth. "Just listen to me, that's all. Don't talk, just listen."

She huffs against my hand but nods all the same.

"Kilorn—"

Her skin flushes bright red at the mention of him. She even giggles, something she never does. But I don't have time for her schoolgirl crush, not now.

"Stop that, Gisa." I take a shaky breath. "Kilorn is going to be conscripted."

And then her laughter is gone. Conscription isn't a joke, not to us.

"I've found a way to get him out of here, to save him from the war, but I need your help to do it." It hurts to say it, but somehow the words pass my lips. "I need you, Gisa. Will you help me?"

She doesn't hesitate to answer, and I feel a great swell of love for my sister.

"Yes."

It's a good thing I'm short, or else Gisa's extra uniform would never fit. It's thick and dark, not at all suited to the summer sun, with buttons and zippers that seem to cook in the heat. The pack on my back shifts, almost taking me over with the weight of cloth and sewing instruments. Gisa has her own pack and constricting uniform, but they don't seem to bother her at all. She's used to hard work and a hard life.

We sail most of the distance upriver, squashed between bushels of wheat on the barge of a benevolent farmer Gisa befriended years ago. People trust her around here, like they can never trust me. The farmer lets us off with a mile still to go, near the winding trail of merchants heading for Summerton. Now we shuffle with them, toward what Gisa calls the Garden Door, though there are no gardens to be seen. It's actually a gate made of sparkling glass that blinds us before we even get a chance to step inside. The rest of the wall looks to be made of the same thing, but I can't believe the Silver king would be stupid enough to hide behind glass walls.

"It isn't glass," Gisa tells me. "Or at least, not entirely. The Silvers discovered a way to heat diamond and mix it with other materials. It's totally impregnable. Not even a bomb could get through that."

Diamond walls.

"That seems necessary."

"Keep your head down. Let me do the talking," she whispers.

I stay on her heels, my eyes on the road as it fades from cracked black asphalt to paved white stone. It's so smooth I almost slip, but Gisa grabs my arm, keeping me steady. Kilorn wouldn't have a problem walking on this, not with his sea legs. But then Kilorn wouldn't be here at all. He's already given up. *I will not.*

As we get closer to the gates, I squint through the glare to see to the other side. Though Summerton only exists for the season, abandoned before the first frostfall, it's the biggest city I've ever seen. There are bustling streets, shops, cantina bars, houses, and courtyards, all of them pointed toward a shimmering monstrosity of diamondglass and marble. And now I know where it got its name. The Hall of the Sun shines like a star, reaching a hundred feet into the air in a twisting mass of spires and bridges. Parts of it darken seemingly at will, to give the occupants privacy. Can't have the peasants looking at the king and his court. It's breathtaking, intimidating, magnificent—and this is just the *summer* house.

"Names," a gruff voice barks, and Gisa stops short.

"Gisa Barrow. This is my sister, Mare Barrow. She's helping me bring some wares in for my mistress." She doesn't flinch, keeping her voice even, almost bored. The Security officer nods at me and I shift my pack, making a show of it. Gisa hands over our identification cards, both of them torn, dirty things ready to fall apart, but they suffice.

The man examining us must know my sister because he barely glances at her ID. Mine he scrutinizes, looking between my face and my picture for a good minute. I wonder if he's a whisper too and can read my mind. That would put an end to this little excursion very quickly and probably earn me a cable noose around my neck.

"Wrists," he sighs, already bored with us.

For a moment, I'm puzzled, but Gisa sticks out her right hand without a thought. I follow the gesture, pointing my arm at the officer. He slaps a pair of red bands around our wrists. The circles shrink until they're tight as shackles—there's no removing these things on our own.

"Move along," the officer says, gesturing with a lazy wave of the hand. Two young girls are not a threat in his eyes.

Gisa nods in thanks but I don't. This man doesn't deserve an ounce of appreciation from me. The gates yawn open around us and we march forward. My heartbeat pounds in my ears, drowning out the sounds of Grand Garden as we enter a different world.

It's a market like I've never seen, dotted with flowers and trees and fountains. The Reds are few and fast, running errands and selling their own wares, all marked by their red bands. Though the Silvers wear no band, they're easy to spot. They drip with gems and precious metals, a fortune on every one of them. One slip of a hook and I can go home with everything I'll ever need. All are tall and beautiful and cold, moving with a slow grace no Red can claim. We simply don't have the time to move that way.

Gisa guides me past a bakery with cakes dusted in gold, a grocer displaying brightly colored fruits I've never seen before, and even a menagerie full of wild animals beyond my comprehension. A little girl, Silver judging by her clothes, feeds tiny bits of apple to a spotted, horselike creature with an impossibly long neck. A few streets over, a jewelry store sparkles in every color of the rainbow. I make note of it but keeping my head straight here is difficult. The air seems to pulse, vibrant with life.

Just when I think there could be nothing more fantastic than this place, I look closer at the Silvers and remember exactly who they are. The little girl is a telky, levitating the apple ten feet into the air to feed the long-necked beast. A florist runs his hands through a pot of white flowers and they explode into growth, curling around his elbows. He's a greeny, a manipulator of plants and the earth. A pair of nymphs sits by the fountain, lazily entertaining children with floating orbs of water. One of them has orange hair and hateful eyes, even while kids mill around him. All over the square, every type of Silver goes about their extraordinary lives. There are so many, each one grand and wonderful and powerful and so far removed from the world I know.

"This is how the other half lives," Gisa murmurs, sensing my awe. "It's enough to make you sick."

Guilt ripples through me. I've always been jealous of Gisa, her talent and all the privileges it affords her, but I've never thought of the cost. She didn't spend much time in school and has few friends in the Stilts. If Gisa were normal, she would have many. She would smile. Instead, the fourteen-year-old girl soldiers through with needle and thread, putting the future of her family on her back, living neck-deep in a world she hates.

"Thank you, Gee," I whisper into her ear. She knows I don't just mean for today.

"Salla's shop is there, with the blue awning." She points down a side street, to a tiny store sandwiched between a pair of cafés. "I'll be inside, if you need me."

"I won't," I answer quickly. "Even if things go wrong, I won't get you involved."

"Good." Then she grabs my hand, squeezing tight for a second. "Be careful. It's crowded today, more than usual."

"More places to hide," I tell her with a smirk.

But her voice is grave. "More officers too."

We continue walking, every step bringing us closer to the exact moment she'll leave me alone in this strange place. A thrum of panic goes through me as Gisa gently lifts the pack from my shoulders. We've reached her shop.

To calm myself, I ramble under my breath. "Speak to no one, don't make eye contact. Keep moving. I leave the way I came, through the Garden Door. The officer removes my band and I keep walking." She nods as I speak, her eyes wide, wary and perhaps even hopeful. "It's ten miles to home."

"Ten miles to home," she echoes.

Wishing for all the world I could go with her, I watch Gisa disappear beneath the blue awning. She's gotten me this far. Now it's my turn.

FOUR

I've done this a thousand times before, watching the crowd like a wolf does a flock of sheep. Looking for the weak, the slow, the foolish. Only now, I am very much the prey. I might choose a swift who'll catch me in half a heartbeat, or worse, a whisper who could probably sense me coming a mile away. Even the little telky girl can best me if things go south. So I will have to be faster than ever, smarter than ever, and worst of all, *luckier* than ever. It's maddening. Fortunately, no one pays attention to another Red servant, another insect wandering past the feet of gods.

I head back to the square, arms hanging limp but ready at my sides. Normally this is my dance, walking through the most congested parts of a crowd, letting my hands catch purses and pockets like spiderwebs catching flies. I'm not stupid enough to try that here. Instead, I follow the crowd around the square. Now I'm not blinded by my fantastic surroundings but looking beyond them, to the cracks in the stone and the black-uniformed Security officers in every shadow. The impossible Silver world comes into sharper focus. Silvers barely look at each other, and they *never* smile. The telky girl looks bored feeding her strange beast, and merchants don't even haggle. Only the Reds look alive, darting around the slow-moving men and women of a better life. Despite the heat, the sun, the bright banners, I have never seen a place so cold.

What concern me most are the black video cameras hidden in the canopy or alleyways. There are only a few at home, at the Security outpost or in the arena, but they're all over the market. I can just hear them humming in firm reminder: *someone else is watching here.*

The tide of the crowd takes me down the main avenue, past taverns and cafés. Silvers sit at an open-air bar, watching the crowd pass as they enjoy their morning drinks. Some watch video screens set into walls or hanging from archways. Each one plays something different, ranging from old arena matches to news to brightly colored programs I don't understand, all blending together in my head. The high whine of the screens, the distant sound of static, buzzes in my ears. How they can stand it, I don't know. But the Silvers don't even blink at the videos, almost ignoring them entirely.

The Hall itself casts a glimmering shadow over me, and I find myself staring in stupid awe again. But then a droning noise snaps me out of it. At first it sounds like the arena tone, the one used to start a Feat, but this one is different. Low and heavier somehow. Without a thought, I turn to the noise.

In the bar next to me, all the video screens flicker to the same broadcast. Not a royal address but a news report. Even the Silvers stop to watch in rapt silence. When the drone ends, the report begins. A fluffy blond woman, Silver no doubt, appears on the screen. She reads from a piece of paper and looks frightened.

"Silvers of Norta, we apologize for the interruption. Thirteen minutes ago there was a terrorist attack in the capital."

The Silvers around me gasp, bursting into fearful murmurs.

I can only blink in disbelief. Terrorist attack? On the Silvers?

Is that even possible?

"This was an organized bombing of government buildings in West Archeon. According to reports, the Royal Court, the Treasury Hall, and Whitefire Palace have been damaged, but the court and the treasury were not in session this morning." The image changes from the woman to footage of a burning building. Security officers evacuate the people inside while nymphs blast water onto the flames. Healers, marked by a black-and-red cross on their arms, run to and fro among them. "The royal family was not in residence at Whitefire, and there are no reported casualties at this time. King Tiberias is expected to address the nation within the hour."

A Silver next to me clenches his fist and pounds on the bar, sending spider cracks through the solid rock top. *A strongarm.* "It's the Lakelanders! They're losing up north so they're coming down south to scare us!" A few jeer with him, cursing the Lakelands.

"We should wipe them out, push all the way through to Prairie!" another Silver echoes. Many cheer in agreement. It takes all my strength not to snap at these cowards who will never see the front lines or send their children to fight. Their Silver war is being paid for in Red blood.

As more and more footage rolls, showing the marble facade of the courthouse explode into dust or a diamondglass wall withstanding a fireball, part of me feels happy. The Silvers are not invincible. They have enemies, enemies who can hurt them, and for once, they aren't hiding behind a Red shield.

The newscaster returns, paler than ever. Someone whispers to her offscreen and she shuffles through her notes, her hands shaking. "It seems that an organization has taken responsibility for the Archeon bombing," she says, stumbling a bit. The shouting men quiet quickly, eager to hear the words on-screen. "A terrorist group calling themselves the Scarlet Guard released this video moments ago."

"The Scarlet Guard?" "Who the hell—?" "Some kind of trick—?" and other confused questions rise around the bar. No one has heard of the Scarlet Guard before.

But I have.

That's what Farley called herself. Her and Will. But they are *smugglers*, both of them, not terrorists or bombers or whatever else the broadcast might say. *It's a coincidence, it can't be them.*

On-screen, I'm greeted by a terrible sight. A woman stands in front of a shaky camera, a scarlet bandanna tied around her face so only her golden hair and keen blue eyes shine out. She holds a gun in one hand, a tattered red flag in another. And on her chest, there's a bronze badge in the shape of a torn-apart sun.

"We are the Scarlet Guard and we stand for the freedom and equality of all people—," the woman says. I recognize her voice.

Farley.

"—starting with the Reds."

I don't need to be a genius to know that a bar full of angry, violent Silvers is the last place a Red girl wants to be. But I can't move. I can't tear my eyes away from Farley's face.

"You believe you are the masters of the world, but your reign as kings and gods is at an end. Until you recognize us as *human*, as *equal*, the fight will be at your door. Not on a battlefield but in your cities. In your streets. In your homes. You don't see us, and so we are everywhere." Her voice hums with authority and poise. "And we will rise up, Red as the dawn."

Red as the dawn.

The footage ends, cutting back to the slack-jawed blonde. Roars drown out the rest of the broadcast as Silvers around the bar find their voices. They scream about Farley, calling her a terrorist, a murderer, a Red devil. Before their eyes can fall on me, I back out into the street.

But all down the avenue, from the square to the Hall, Silvers boil out from every bar and café. I try to rip off the red band around my wrist, but the stupid thing holds firm. Other Reds disappear into alleys and doorways, trying to flee, and I'm smart enough to follow. By the time I find an alleyway, the screaming starts.

Against every instinct, I look over my shoulder to see a Red man being held up by the neck. He pleads with his Silver assailant, begging. "Please, I don't know, I don't know who the hell those people are!"

"What is the Scarlet Guard?" the Silver yells into his face. I recognize him as one of the nymphs who was playing with children not half an hour ago. "Who are they?"

Before the Red can answer, a spray of water pounds against him, stronger than falling hammers. The nymph raises a hand and the water rises up, splashing him again. Silvers surround the scene, jeering with glee, cheering him on. The Red sputters and gasps, trying to catch his breath. He proclaims his innocence with every spare second, but the water keeps coming. The nymph, wide-eyed with hate, shows no signs of stopping. He pulls water from the fountains, from every glass, raining it down again and again.

The nymph is drowning him.

The blue awning is my beacon, guiding me through the panicked streets as I dodge Reds and Silvers alike. Usually chaos is my best friend, making my work as a thief that much easier. No one notices a missing coin purse when they're running from a mob. But Kilorn and two thousand crowns are no longer my top priority. I can only think about getting to Gisa and getting out of the city that will certainly become a prison. *If they close the gates . . .* I don't want to think about being stuck here, trapped behind glass with freedom just out of reach.

Officers run back and forth in the street—they don't know what to do or who to protect. A few round up Reds, forcing them to their knees. They shiver and beg, repeating over and over that they don't know anything. I'm willing to bet I'm the only one in the entire city who had even *heard* of the Scarlet Guard before today.

That sends a new stab of fear through me. If I'm captured, if I tell them what little I know—what will they do to my family? To Kilorn? To the Stilts?

They cannot catch me.

Using the stalls to hide, I run as fast as I can. The main street is a war zone, but I keep my eyes forward, on the blue awning beyond the square. I pass the jewelry store and slow. Just one piece could save Kilorn. But in the heartbeat it takes me to stop, a hail of glass scrapes my face. In the street, a telky has his eyes on me and takes aim again. I don't give him the chance and take off, sliding under curtains and stalls and outstretched arms until I get back to the square. Before I know it, water sloshes around my feet as I sprint through the fountain.

A frothing blue wave knocks me sideways, into the churning water. It's not deep, no more than two feet to the bottom, but the water feels like lead. I can't move, I can't swim, *I can't breathe.* I can barely think. My mind can only scream *nymph*, and I remember the poor Red man on the avenue, drowning on his own two feet. My head smacks the stone bottom and I see stars, *sparks*, before my vision clears. Every inch of my skin feels electrified. The water shifts around me, normal again, and I break the surface of the fountain. Air screams back into my lungs, searing my throat and nose, but I don't care. *I'm alive.*

Small, strong hands grab me by the collar, trying to pull me from the fountain. *Gisa.* My feet push off the bottom and we tumble to the ground together.

"We have to go," I yell, scrambling to my feet.

Gisa is already running ahead of me, toward the Garden Door. "Very perceptive of you!" she screams over her shoulder.

I can't help but look back at the square as I follow her. The Silver mob pours in, searching through the stalls with the voracity of wolves. The few Reds left behind cower on the ground, begging for mercy. And in the fountain I just escaped from, a man with orange hair floats facedown.

My body trembles, every nerve on fire as we push toward the gate. Gisa holds my hand, pulling us both through the crowd.

"Ten miles to home," Gisa murmurs. "Did you get what you needed?"

The weight of my shame comes crashing down as I shake my head. There was no time. I could barely get down the avenue before the report came through. *There was nothing I could do.*

Gisa's face falls, folding into a tiny frown. "We'll figure out something," she says, her voice just as desperate as I feel.

But the gate looms ahead, growing closer with every passing second. It fills me with dread. Once I pass through, once I leave, Kilorn will really be gone.

And I think that's why she does it.

Before I can stop her, grab her, or pull her away, Gisa's clever little hand slips into someone's bag. Not just any someone though, but an escaping Silver. A Silver with lead eyes, a hard nose, and square-set shoulders that scream "don't mess with me." Gisa might be an artist with a needle and thread, but she's no pickpocket. It takes all of a second for him to realize what's happening. And then someone grabs Gisa off the ground.

It's the same Silver. There are *two* of them. *Twins?*

"Not a wise time to start picking Silver pockets," the twins say in unison. And then there are three of them, four, five, six, surrounding us in the crowd. *Multiplying. He's a cloner.*

They make my head spin. "She didn't mean any harm, she's just a stupid kid—"

"I'm just a stupid kid!" Gisa yells, trying to kick the one holding her.

They chuckle together in a horrifying sound.

I lunge at Gisa, trying to pry her away, but one of them pushes me back to the ground. The hard stone road knocks the air from my lungs, and I gasp for breath, watching helplessly as another twin puts a foot on my stomach, holding me down.

"Please—," I choke out, but no one's listening to me anymore. The whining in my head intensifies as every camera spins to look at us. I feel electrified again, this time by fear for my sister.

A Security officer, the one who let us inside earlier this morning, strides over, his gun in hand. "What's all this?" he growls, looking around at the identical Silvers.

One by one, they meld back together, until only two remain: the one holding Gisa and the one pinning me to the ground.

"She's a thief," one says, shaking my sister. To her credit, she doesn't scream.

The officer recognizes her, his hard face twitching into a frown for a split second. "You know the law, girl."

Gisa lowers her head. "I know the law."

I struggle as much as I can, trying to stop what's coming. Glass shatters as a nearby screen cracks and flashes, broken by the riot. It does nothing to stop the officer as he grabs my sister, pushing her to the ground.

My own voice screams out, joining the din of the chaos. "It was me! It was my idea! Hurt me!" But they don't listen. They don't care.

I can only watch as the officer lays my sister next to me. Her eyes are on mine as he brings the butt of his gun down, shattering the bones in her sewing hand.

FIVE

Kilorn will find me anywhere I try to hide, so I keep moving. I sprint like I can outrun what I've done to Gisa, how I've failed Kilorn, how I've destroyed everything. But even I can't outrun the look in my mother's eyes when I brought Gisa to the door. I saw the hopeless shadow cross her face, and I ran before my father wheeled himself into view. I couldn't face them both. *I'm a coward.*

So I run until I can't think, until every bad memory fades away, until I can only feel the burning in my muscles. I even tell myself the tears on my cheeks are rain.

When I finally slow to catch my breath, I'm outside the village, a few miles down that terrible northern road. Lights filter through the trees around the bend, illuminating an inn, one of the many on the old roads. It's crowded like it is every summer, full of servants and seasonal workers who follow the royal court. They don't live in the Stilts, they don't know my face, so they're easy prey for pickpocketing. I do it every summer, but Kilorn is always with me, smiling into a drink as he watches me work. *I don't suppose I'll see his smile for much longer.*

A bellow of laughter rises as a few men stumble from the inn, drunk and happy. Their coin purses jingle, heavy with the day's pay. *Silver money*, for serving, smiling, and bowing to monsters dressed as lords.

I caused so much harm today, so much hurt to the ones I love most. I should turn around and go home, to face everyone with at least some courage. But instead I settle against the shadows of the inn, content to remain in darkness.

I guess causing pain is all I'm good for.

It doesn't take long to fill the pockets of my coat. The drunks filter out every few minutes and I press against them, pasting on a smile to hide my hands. No one notices, no one even cares, when I fade away again. I'm a shadow, and no one remembers shadows.

Midnight comes and goes and still I stand, waiting. The moon overhead is a bright reminder of the time, of how long I've been gone. *One last pocket*, I tell myself. *One more and I'll go.* I've been saying it for the past hour.

I don't think when the next patron comes out. His eyes are on the sky, and he doesn't notice me. It's too easy to reach out, too easy to hook a finger around the strings of his coin purse. I should know better by now that nothing here is easy, but the riot and Gisa's hollow eyes have made me foolish with grief.

His hand closes around my wrist, his grip firm and strangely hot as he pulls me forward out of the shadows. I try to resist, to slip away and run, but he's too strong. When he spins, the fire in his eyes puts a fear in me, the same fear I felt this morning. But I welcome any punishment he might summon. I deserve it all.

"Thief," he says, a strange surprise in his voice.

I blink at him, fighting the urge to laugh. I don't even have the strength to protest. "Obviously."

He stares at me, scrutinizing everything from my face to my worn boots. It makes me squirm. After a long moment, he heaves a breath and lets me go. Stunned, I can only stare at him. When a silver coin spins through the air, I barely have the wits to catch it. *A tetrarch. A silver tetrarch worth one whole crown.* Far more than any of the stolen pennies in my pockets.

"That should be more than enough to tide you over," he says before I can respond. In the light of the inn, his eyes glint red-gold, the color of warmth. My years spent sizing people up do not fail me, even now. His black hair is too glossy, his skin too pale to be anything but a servant. But his physique seems more like a woodcutter's, with broad shoulders and strong legs. He's young too, a little older than me, though not nearly as assured of himself as any nineteen- or twenty-year-old should be.

I should kiss his boots for letting me go *and* giving me such a gift, but my curiosity gets the better of me. It always does.

"Why?" The word comes out hard and harsh. After a day like today, how can I be anything else?

The question takes him aback and he shrugs. "You need it more than I do."

I want to throw the coin back in his face, to tell him I can take care of myself, but part of me knows better. *Has today taught you nothing?* "Thank you," I force out through gritted teeth.

Somehow, he laughs at my reluctant gratitude. "Don't hurt yourself." Then he shifts, taking a step closer. *He is the strangest person I've ever met.* "You live in the village, don't you?"

"Yes," I reply, gesturing to myself. With my faded hair, dirty clothes, and defeated eyes, what else could I be? He stands in stark contrast, his shirt fine and clean, and his shoes are soft, reflective leather.

He shifts under my gaze, playing with his collar. I make him nervous.

He pales in the moonlight, his eyes darting. "Do you enjoy it?" he asks, deflecting. "Living there?"

His question almost makes me laugh, but he doesn't look amused. "Does anyone?" I finally respond, wondering what on earth he's playing at.

But instead of retorting swiftly, snapping back like Kilorn would, he falls silent. A dark look crosses his face. "Are you heading back?" he says suddenly, gesturing down the road.

"Why, scared of the dark?" I drawl, folding my arms across my chest. But in the pit of my stomach, I wonder if I should be afraid. *He's strong, he's fast, and you're all alone out here.*

His smile returns, and the comfort it gives me is unsettling. "No, but I want to make sure you keep your hands to yourself for the rest of the night. Can't have you driving half the bar out of house and home, can we? I'm Cal, by the way," he adds, stretching out a hand to shake.

I don't take it, remembering the blazing heat of his skin. Instead, I set off down the road, my steps quick and quiet. "Mare Barrow," I tell him over my shoulder, and it doesn't take much for his long legs to catch up.

"So are you always this pleasant?" he prods, and for some reason, I feel very much like I'm being examined. But the cold silver in my hand keeps me calm, reminding me of what else he has in his pockets. *Silver for Farley. How fitting.*

"The lords must pay well for you to carry whole crowns," I retort, hoping to scare him off the topic. It works beautifully and he retreats.

"I have a good job," he explains, trying to brush it off.

"That makes one of us."

"But you're—"

"Seventeen," I finish for him. "I still have some time before conscription."

He narrows his eyes, lips twisting into a grim line. Something hard creeps into his voice, sharpening his words. "How much time?"

"Less every day." Just saying it aloud makes my insides ache. *And Kilorn has even less than me.*

His words die away and he's staring again, surveying me as we walk through the woods. *Thinking.* "And there are no jobs," he mutters, more to himself than me. "No way for you to avoid conscription."

His confusion puzzles me. "Maybe things are different where you're from."

"So you steal."

I steal. "It's the best I can do," falls from my lips. Again, I remember that causing pain is all I'm good for. "My sister has a job though." It slips out before I remember—*No she doesn't. Not anymore. Because of you.*

Cal watches me battle with the words, wondering whether or not to correct myself. It's all I can do to keep my face straight, to keep from breaking down entirely in front of a complete stranger. But he must see what I'm trying to hide. "Were you at the Hall today?" I think he already knows the answer. "The riots were terrible."

"They were." I almost choke on the words.

"Did you . . . ," he presses in the quietest, calmest way. It's like poking a hole in a dam, and it all comes spilling out. I couldn't stop the words even if I wanted to.

I don't mention Farley or the Scarlet Guard or even Kilorn. Just that my sister slipped me into Grand Garden, to help me steal the money we needed to survive. Then came Gisa's mistake, her injury, what it meant to us. What I've done to my family. What I have been doing, disappointing my mother, embarrassing my father, stealing from the people

I call my community. Here on the road with nothing but darkness around me, I tell a stranger how terrible I am. He doesn't ask questions, even when I don't make sense. He just listens.

"It's the best I can do," I say again before my voice gives out entirely.

Then silver shines in the corner of my eye. He's holding up another coin. In the moonlight, I can just see the outline of the king's flaming crown stamped into the metal. When he presses it into my hand, I expect to feel his heat again, but he's gone cold.

I don't want your pity, I feel like screaming, but that would be foolish. The coin will buy what Gisa no longer can.

"I'm truly sorry for you, Mare. Things shouldn't be like this."

I can't even summon the strength to frown. "There are worse lives to live. Don't feel sorry for me."

He leaves me at the edge of the village, letting me walk through the stilt houses alone. Something about the mud and shadows makes Cal uncomfortable, and he disappears before I get a chance to look back and thank the strange servant.

My home is quiet and dark, but even so, I shudder in fear. The morning seems a hundred years away, part of another life where I was stupid and selfish and maybe even a little bit happy. Now I have nothing but a conscripted friend and a sister's broken bones.

"You shouldn't worry your mother like that," my father's voice rumbles at me from behind one of the stilt poles. I haven't seen him on the ground in more years than I care to remember.

My voice squeaks in surprise and fear. "Dad? What are you doing? How did you—?" But he jabs a thumb over his shoulder, to the pulley rig dangling from the house. For the first time, he used it.

"Power went out. Thought I'd give it a look," he says, gruff as ever.

He wheels past me, stopping in front of the utility box piped into the ground. Every house has one, regulating the electric charge that keeps the lights on.

Dad wheezes to himself, his chest clicking with each breath. Maybe Gisa will be like him now, her hand a metallic mess, her brain torn and bitter with the thought of what could have been.

"Why don't you just *use* the 'lec papers I get you?"

In response, Dad pulls a ration paper from his shirt and feeds it into the box. Normally, the thing would spark to life, but nothing happens. *Broken.*

"No use," Dad sighs, sitting back in his chair. We both stare at the utility box, at a loss for words, not wanting to move, not wanting to go back upstairs. Dad ran just like I did, unable to stay in the house, where Mom was surely crying over Gisa, weeping for lost dreams, while my sister tried not to join her.

He bats the box like hitting the damn thing can suddenly bring light and warmth and hope back to us. His actions become more harried, more desperate, and anger radiates from him. Not at me or Gisa but the world. Long ago he called us ants, Red ants burning in the light of a Silver sun. Destroyed by the greatness of others, losing the battle for our right to exist because we are not *special*. We did not evolve like them, with powers and strengths beyond our limited imaginations. We stayed the same, stagnant in our own bodies. *The world changed around us and we stayed the same.*

Then the anger is in me too, cursing Farley, Kilorn, conscription, every little thing I can think of. The metal box is cool to the touch, having long lost the heat of electricity. But there are vibrations still, deep in the mechanism, waiting to be switched back on. I lose myself in trying to find the electricity, to bring it back and prove that even one small thing can go right in a world so wrong. Something sharp meets my fingertips, making my body jolt. An exposed wire or faulty switch, I tell myself. It feels like a pinprick, like a needle spiking in my nerves, but the pain never follows.

Above us, the porch light hums to life.

"Well, fancy that," Dad mutters.

He spins in the mud, wheeling himself back to the pulley. I follow quietly, not wanting to bring up the reason we are both so afraid of the place we call home.

"No more running," he breathes, buckling himself into the rig.

"No more running," I agree, more for myself than him.

The rig whines with the strain, hoisting him up to the porch. I'm quicker on the ladder, so I wait for him at the top, then wordlessly help detach him from the rig. "Bugger of a thing," Dad grumbles when we finally unsnap the last buckle.

"Mom will be happy you're getting out of the house."

He looks up at me sharply, grabbing my hand. Though Dad barely works now, repairing trinkets and whittling for kids, his hands are still rough and callused, like he just returned from the front lines. *The war never leaves.*

"Don't tell your mother."

"But—"

"I know it seems like nothing, but it's enough of something. She'll think it's a small step on a big journey, you see? First I leave the house at night, then during the day, then I'm rolling around the market with her like it's twenty years ago. Then things go back to the way they were." His eyes darken as he speaks, fighting to keep his voice low and level. "I'm never getting better, Mare. I'm never going to *feel* better. I can't let her hope for that, not when I know it'll never happen. Do you understand?"

All too well, Dad.

He knows what hope has done to me and softens. "I wish things were different."

"We all do."

Despite the shadows, I can see Gisa's broken hand when I get up to the loft. Normally she sleeps in a ball, curled up under a thin blanket, but now she lies on her back, with her injury elevated on a pile of clothes. Mom reset her splint, improving my meager attempt to help, and the bandages are fresh. I don't need light to know her poor hand is black with bruises. She sleeps restlessly, her body tossing, but her arm stays still. Even in sleep, it hurts her.

I want to reach out to her, but how can I make up for the terrible events of the day?

I pull out Shade's letter from the little box where I keep all his correspondences. If nothing else, this will calm me down. His jokes, his words, his *voice* trapped in the page always soothe me. But as I scan the letter again, a sense of dread pools in my stomach.

"*Red as the dawn . . .*" the letter reads. There it is, plain as the nose on my face. Farley's words from her video, the Scarlet Guard's rallying cry, in my brother's handwriting. The phrase is too strange to ignore, too unique to brush off. And the next sentence, "*see the sun rise stronger . . .*" My brother is smart but practical. He doesn't care about sunrises or dawns or witty turns of phrase. *Rise* echoes in me, but instead of Farley's voice in my head, it's my brother speaking. *Rise, red as the dawn.*

Somehow, Shade knew. Many weeks ago, before the bombing, before Farley's broadcast, Shade knew about the Scarlet Guard and tried to tell us. *Why?*

Because he's one of them.

SIX

When the door bangs open at dawn, I'm not frightened. Security searches are normal, though we usually only get one or two a year. This will be the third.

"C'mon, Gee," I mutter, helping her out of her cot and down the ladder. She moves precariously, leaning on her good arm, and Mom waits for us on the floor. Her arms close around Gisa, but her eyes are on me. To my surprise, she doesn't look angry or even disappointed with me. Instead, her gaze is soft.

Two officers wait by the door, their guns hanging by their sides. I recognize them from the village outpost, but there's another figure, a young woman in red with a triple-colored crown badge over her heart. *A royal servant, a Red who serves the king*, I realize, and I begin to understand. This is not a usual search.

"We submit to search and seizure," my father grumbles, speaking the words he must every time this happens. But instead of splitting off to paw through our house, the Security officers stand firm.

The young woman steps forward and, to my horror, addresses me.

"Mare Barrow, you have been summoned to Summerton."

Gisa's good hand closes around mine, like she can hold me back. "W-What?" I manage to stammer.

"You have been summoned to Summerton," she repeats, and gestures to the door. "We will escort you. Please proceed."

A summons. For a Red. Never in my life have I heard of such a thing. So why me? What have I done to deserve this?

On second thought, I'm a criminal and probably considered a terrorist due to my association with Farley. My body prickles with nerves, every muscle taut and ready. I'll have to run, even though the officers block the door. *It'll be a miracle if I make it to a window.*

"Calm down, everything's settled after yesterday." She chuckles, mistaking my fear. "The Hall and the market are well controlled now. *Please proceed.*" To my surprise, she smiles, even as the Security officers clench their guns. It puts a chill in my blood.

To refuse Security, to refuse a *royal summons*, would mean death—and not just for me. "Okay," I mumble, untangling my hand from Gisa's. She moves to grab on to me, but our mother pulls her back. "I'll see you later?"

The question hangs in the air, and I feel Dad's warm hand brush my arm. *He's saying good-bye.* Mom's eyes swim with unshed tears, and Gisa's trying not to blink, to remember every last second of me. *I don't even have something I can leave her.* But before I can linger or let myself cry, an officer takes me by the arm and pulls me away.

The words force themselves past my lips, though they come out as barely more than a whisper. "I love you."

And then the door slams behind me, shutting me out of my home and my life.

They hasten me through the village, down the road to the market square. We pass by Kilorn's run-down house. Usually he's awake by now, halfway to the river to start the day early when it's still cool, but those days are gone. Now I bet he sleeps through half the day, enjoying what little comforts he can before conscription. Part of me wants to yell good-bye to him, but I don't. He'll come sniffing around for me later, and Gisa will tell him everything. With a silent laugh I remember that Farley will be expecting me today, with a fortune in payment. She'll be disappointed.

In the square, a gleaming black transport waits for us. Four wheels, glass windows, rounded to the ground—it looks like a beast ready to consume me. Another officer sits at the controls and guns the engine when we approach, spitting black smoke into the early-morning air. I'm forced into the back without a word, and the servant barely slides in next to me before the transport takes off, racing down the road at speeds I had never even imagined. *This will be my first—and last—time riding in one.*

I want to speak, to ask what's going on, how they're going to punish me for my crimes, but I know my words will fall on deaf ears. So I stare out the window, watching the village disappear as we enter the forest, racing down the familiar northern road. It's not so crowded as yesterday, and Security officers dot the way. *The Hall is controlled*, the servant had said. I suppose this is what she meant.

The diamondglass wall shines ahead, reflecting the sun as it rises from the woods. I want to squint, but I keep myself still. I must keep my eyes open here.

The gate crawls with black uniforms, all Security officers checking and rechecking travelers as they enter. When we coast to a stop, the serving woman pulls me out of the transport and past the line and through the gate. No one protests, or even bothers to check for IDs. She must be familiar here.

Once we're inside, she glances back at me. "I'm Ann, by the way, but we mostly go by last names. Call me Walsh."

Walsh. The name sounds familiar. Paired with her faded hair and tanned skin, it can mean only one thing. "You're from . . . ?"

"The Stilts, same as you. I knew your brother Tramy, and I wish I didn't know Bree. A real heartbreaker, that one." Bree had a reputation around the village before he left. He told me once that he didn't fear conscription as much as everyone else because the dozen bloodthirsty girls he was leaving behind were far more dangerous. "I don't know you though. But I certainly will."

I can't help but bristle. "What's that supposed to mean?"

"I mean you're going to be working long hours here. I don't know who hired you or what they told you about the job, but it starts to wear on you. It's not all changing bedsheets and cleaning plates. You have to look without seeing, hear without listening. We're objects up there, living statues meant to serve." She sighs to herself and turns, wrenching open a door built right into the side of the gate. "Especially now, with this Scarlet Guard business. It's never a good time to be a Red, but this is very bad."

She steps through the door, seemingly into the solid wall. It takes me a moment to realize she's going down a flight of stairs, disappearing into semidarkness.

"The job?" I press. "What job? What is this?"

She turns on the stairs, all but rolling her eyes at me. "You've been summoned to fill a serving post," she says like it's the most obvious thing in the world.

Working. A job. I almost fall over at the thought.

Cal. He said he had a good job—and now he's pulled some strings to do the same for me. I might even be working with him. My heart leaps at the prospect, knowing what this means. *I'm not going to die, I'm not even going to fight. I'm going to work and I'm going to live. And later, when I find Cal, I can convince him to do the same for Kilorn.*

"Keep up, I don't have time to hold your hand!"

Scrambling after her, I descend into a surprisingly dark tunnel. Small lights glow on the walls, making it just possible to see. Pipes run overhead, humming with running water and electricity.

"Where are we going?" I finally breathe.

I can almost hear Walsh's dismay as she turns to me, confused. "The Hall of the Sun, of course."

For a second, I think I can feel my heart stop. "Wha-what? The palace, the actual palace?"

She taps the badge on her uniform. The crown winks in the low light.

"You serve the king now."

They have a uniform ready for me, but I barely notice it. I'm too amazed by my surroundings, the tan stone and glittering mosaic floor of this forgotten hall in the house of a king. Other servants bustle past in a parade of red uniforms. I search their faces, looking for Cal, wanting to thank him, but he never appears.

Walsh stays by me, whispering advice. "Say nothing. Hear nothing. Speak to no one, for they will not speak to you."

I can hardly keep the words straight; the last two days have been a ruin on my heart and soul. I think life has simply decided to open the floodgates, trying to drown me in a whirlwind of twists and turns.

"You came on a busy day, perhaps the worst we will ever see."

"I saw the boats and airships—Silvers have been going upriver for weeks," I say. "More than usual, even for this time of year."

Walsh hurries me along, pushing a tray of glittering cups into my hands. Surely these things can buy my freedom and Kilorn's, but the Hall is guarded at every door and window. I could never slip by so many officers, even with all my skills.

"What's happening today?" I dumbly ask. A lock of my dark hair falls in my eyes, and before I can try to swish it away, Walsh pushes the hair back and fastens it with a tiny pin, her motions quick and precise. "Is that a stupid question?"

"No, I didn't know about it either, not until we started preparing. After all, they haven't had one for twenty years, since Queen Elara was selected." She speaks so fast her words almost blur together. "Today is Queenstrial. The daughters of the High Houses, the great Silver families, have all come to offer themselves to the prince. There's a big feast tonight, but now they're in the Spiral Garden, preparing to present, hoping to be chosen. One of those girls gets to be the next queen, and they're slapping each other silly for the chance."

An image of a bunch of peacocks flashes in my head. "So, what, they do a spin, say a few words, bat their eyelashes?"

But Walsh snorts at me, shaking her head. "Hardly." Then her eyes glitter. "You're on serving duty, so you'll get to see for yourself."

The doors loom ahead, made of carved wood and flowing glass. A servant props them open, allowing the line of red uniforms to move through. And then it's my turn.

"Aren't you coming?" I can hear the desperation in my voice, almost begging Walsh to stay with me. But she backs away, leaving me alone. Before I can hold up the line or otherwise ruin the organized assembly of servants, I force myself forward and out into the sunlight of what she called the Spiral Garden.

At first I think I'm in the middle of another arena like the one back home. The space curves downward into an immense bowl, but instead of stone benches, tables and plush chairs crowd the spiral of terraces. Plants and fountains trickle down the steps, dividing the terraces into boxes. They join at the bottom, decorating a grassy circle ringed with stone statues. Ahead of me is a boxed area dripping with red and black silk. Four seats, each one made of unforgiving iron, look down on the floor.

What in hell is this place?

My work goes by in a blur, following the lead of the other Reds. I'm a kitchen server, meant to clean, aid the cooks, and currently, prepare the arena for the upcoming event. Why the royals need an arena, I'm not sure. Back home they are only used for Feats, to watch Silver against Silver, but what could it mean here? This is a palace. Blood will never stain these floors. Yet the not-arena fills me with a dreadful feeling of foreboding. The prickling sensation returns, pulsing under my skin in waves. By the time I finish and return to the servant entrance, Queenstrial is about to begin.

The other servants make themselves scarce, moving to an elevated platform surrounded by sheer curtains. I scramble after them and bump into line, just as another set of doors opens, directly between the royal box and the servants' entrance.

It's starting.

My mind flashes back to Grand Garden, to the beautiful, cruel creatures calling themselves human. All flashy and vain, with hard eyes and worse tempers. These Silvers, the High Houses, as Walsh calls them, will be no different. *They might even be worse.*

They enter as a crowd, in a flock of colors that splits around the Spiral Garden with cold grace. The different families, or houses, are easy to spot; they all wear the same colors as each other. Purple, green, black, yellow, a rainbow of shades moving toward their family boxes. I quickly lose count of them all. *Just how many houses are there?* More and more join the crowd, some stopping to talk, others embracing with stiff arms. This is a *party* for them, I realize. Most probably have little hope to put forth a queen and this is just a vacation.

But a few don't look to be in the celebrating mood. A silver-haired family in black silk sits in focused silence to the right of the king's box. The patriarch of the house has a pointed beard and black eyes. Farther down, a house of navy blue and white mutter together. To my surprise, I recognize one of them. Samson Merandus, the whisper I saw in the arena a few days ago. Unlike the others, he stares darkly at the floor, his attention elsewhere. I make a note to myself not to run into him or his deadly abilities.

Strangely, though, I don't see any girls of age to marry a prince. Perhaps they're preparing elsewhere, eagerly awaiting their chance to win a crown.

Occasionally, someone presses a square metal button on their table to flick on a light, indicating they require a servant. Whoever's closest to the door attends to them, and the rest of us shuffle along, waiting for our turn to serve. Of course, the second I move next to the door, the wretched black-eyed patriarch slaps the button on his table.

Thank heavens for my feet, which have never failed me. I nearly skip through the crowd, dancing between roving bodies as my heart hammers in my chest. Instead of stealing from these people, I mean to serve them. The Mare Barrow of last week wouldn't know whether to laugh or cry at this version of herself. *But she was a foolish girl, and now I pay the price.*

"Sir?" I say, facing the patriarch who had called for service. In my head, I curse at myself. *Say nothing* is the first rule, and I have already broken it.

But he doesn't seem to notice and simply holds up his empty water glass, a bored look on his face. "They're toying with us, Ptolemus," he grumbles to the muscled young man next to him. I assume he is the one unfortunate enough to be called Ptolemus.

"A demonstration of power, Father," Ptolemus replies, draining his own glass. He holds it out to me, and I take it without hesitation. "They make us wait because they can."

They are the royals who have yet to make an appearance. But to hear these Silvers discuss them so, with such disdain, is perplexing. We Reds insult the king and the nobles if we can get away with it, but I think that's our prerogative. These people have never suffered a day in their lives. What problems could they possibly have with each other?

I want to stay and listen, but even I know that's against the rules. I turn around, climbing a flight of steps out of their box. There's a sink hidden behind some brightly colored flowers, probably so I don't have to go all the way back around the not-arena to refill their drinks. That's when a metallic, sharp tone reverberates through the space, much like the one at the beginning of the First Friday Feats. It chirps a few times, sounding out a proud melody, heralding what must be the entrance of the king. All around, the High Houses rise to their feet, begrudgingly or not. I notice Ptolemus mutter something to his father again.

From my vantage point, hidden behind the flowers, I'm level with the king's box and slightly behind it. Mare Barrow, a few yards from the king. What would my family think, or Kilorn for that matter? This man sends us to die, and I've willingly become his servant. It makes me sick.

He enters briskly, shoulders set and straight. Even from behind, he's much fatter than he looks on the coins and broadcasts, but also taller. His uniform is black and red, with a military cut, though I doubt he's ever spent a single day in the trenches Reds die in. Badges and medals glitter on his breast, a testament to things he's never done. He even wears a gilded sword despite the many guards around him. The crown on his head is familiar, made of twisted red gold and black iron, each point a burst of curling flame. It seems to burn against his inky black hair flecked with gray. How fitting, for the king is a burner, as was his father, and his father before him, and so on. Destructive, powerful controllers of heat and fire. Once, our kings used to burn dissenters with nothing more than a flaming touch. This king might not burn Reds anymore, but he still kills us with war and ruin. His name is one I've known since I was a little girl sitting in the schoolroom, still eager to learn, as if it could get me somewhere. *Tiberias Calore the Sixth, King of Norta, Flame of the North.* A mouthful if there ever was one. I would spit on his name if I could.

The queen follows him, nodding at the crowd. Whereas the king's clothes are dark and severely cut, her navy and white garb is airy and light. She bows only to Samson's house, and I realize she's wearing the same colors as them. She must be their kin, judging by the family resemblance. Same ash-blond hair, blue eyes, and pointed smile, making her look like a wild, predatory cat.

As intimidating as the royals seem, they're nothing compared to the guards who follow them. Even though I'm a Red born in mud, I know who they are. Everyone knows what a Sentinel looks like, because no one wants to meet them. They flank the king in every broadcast, at every speech or decree. As always, their uniforms look like flame, flickering between red and orange, and their eyes glitter behind fearsome black masks. Each one carries a black rifle tipped with a gleaming silver bayonet that could cut bone. Their skills are even more frightening than their appearances—elite warriors from different

Silver houses, trained from childhood, sworn to the king and his family for their entire lives. They're enough to make me shiver. But the High Houses aren't afraid at all.

Somewhere deep in the boxes, the yelling starts. "Death to the Scarlet Guard!" someone shouts, and others quickly chime in. A chill goes through me as I remember the events of yesterday, now so far away. How quickly this crowd could turn. . . .

The king looks ruffled, paling at the noise. He's not used to outbursts like this and almost snarls at the shouts.

"The Scarlet Guard—and all our enemies—are being dealt with!" Tiberias rumbles, his voice echoing out among the crowd. It silences them like the crack of a whip. "But that is not what we are here to address. Today we honor tradition, and no Red devil will impede that. Now is the rite of Queenstrial, to bring forth the most talented daughter to wed the most noble son. In this we find strength, to bind the High Houses, and power, to ensure Silver rule until the end of days, to defeat our enemies, on the borders, and within them."

"Strength," the crowd rumbles back at him. It's frightening. "Power."

"The time has come again to uphold this ideal, and both my sons honor our most solemn custom." He waves a hand, and two figures step forward, flanking their father. I cannot see their faces, but both are tall and black-haired, like the king. They too wear military uniforms. "The Prince Maven, of House Calore and Merandus, son of my royal wife, the Queen Elara."

The second prince, paler and slighter than the other, raises a hand in stern greeting. He turns left and right, and I catch a glimpse of his face. Though he has a regal, serious look to him, he can't be more than seventeen. Sharp-featured and blue-eyed, he could freeze fire with his smile—he despises this pageantry. I have to agree with him.

"And the crown prince of House Calore and Jacos, son of my late wife, the Queen Coriane, heir to the Kingdom of Norta and the Burning Crown, Tiberias the Seventh."

I'm too busy laughing at the sheer absurdity of the name to notice the young man waving and smiling. Finally I raise my eyes, just to say I was this close to the future king. But I get much more than I bargained for.

The glass goblets in my hands drop, landing harmlessly in the sink of water.

I know that smile, and I know those eyes. They burned into mine only last night. He got me this job; he saved me from conscription. He was one of us. *How can this be?*

And then he turns fully, waving all around. There's no mistaking it.

The crown prince is Cal.

SEVEN

I return to the servants' platform, a hollow feeling in my stomach. Whatever happiness I felt before is completely gone. I can't bring myself to look back, to see him standing there in fine clothes, dripping with ribbons and medals and the royal airs I hate. Like Walsh, he bears the badge of the flaming crown, but his is made of dark jet, diamond, and ruby. It winks against the hard black of his uniform. Gone are the drab clothes he wore last night, used to blend in with peasants like me. Now he looks every inch a future king, Silver to the bone. To think I trusted him.

The other servants make way, letting me shuffle to the back of the line while my head spins. He got me this job, he *saved* me, saved my family—and he is one of them. Worse than one of them. A prince. *The* prince. The person everyone in this spiral stone monstrosity is here to see.

"All of you have come to honor my son and the kingdom, and so I honor you," King Tiberias booms, breaking apart my thoughts as if they were glass. He raises his arms, gesturing to the many boxes of people. Though I try my hardest to keep my eyes on the king, I can't help but glance at Cal. He's smiling, but it doesn't reach his eyes.

"I honor your right to rule. The future king, the son of my son, will be of your silverblood, as he will be of mine. Who will claim their right?"

The silver-haired patriarch barks out in response. "I claim Queenstrial!"

All over the spiral, the leaders of the different houses shout in unison. "I claim Queenstrial!" they echo, upholding some tradition I don't understand.

Tiberias smiles and nods. "Then it has begun. Lord Provos, if you would."

The king turns on the spot, looking toward what I assume is House Provos. The rest of the spiral follow his gaze, their eyes landing on a family dressed in gold striped with black. An older man, his gray hair shot with streaks of white, steps forward. In his strange clothes he looks like a wasp about to sting. When he twitches his hand, I don't know what to expect.

Suddenly, the platform lurches, moving sideways. I can't help but jump, almost knocking into the servant next to me, as we slide along an unseen track. My heart rises in my throat as I watch the rest of the Spiral Garden spin. Lord Provos is a *telky*, moving the structure along prebuilt tracks with nothing but the power of his mind.

The entire structure twists under his command, until the garden floor widens into a huge circle. The lower terraces pull back, aligning with the upper levels, and the spiral becomes a massive cylinder open to the sky. As the terraces move, the floor lowers, until it stops nearly twenty feet below the lowest box. The fountains turn into waterfalls, spilling from the top of the cylinder to the bottom, where they fill deep, narrow pools. Our platform glides to a stop above the king's box, allowing us a perfect view of everything, including the floor far below. All this takes less than a minute, with Lord Provos transforming the Spiral Garden into something much more sinister.

But when Provos takes his seat again, the change is still not done. The hum of electricity rises until it crackles all around, making the hairs on my arms stand up. A purple-white light blazes near the floor of the garden, sparking with energy from tiny, unseen points in the stone. No Silver stands up to command it, like Provos did with an arena. I realize why. This is not some Silver's doing but a wonder of technology, of electricity. *Lightning without thunder.* The beams of light crisscross and intersect, weaving themselves into a brilliant, blinding net. Just looking at it hurts my eyes, sending sharp daggers of pain through my head. How the others can stand it, I have no idea.

The Silvers look impressed, intrigued with something they can't control. As for us Reds, we gape in complete awe.

The net crystallizes as the electricity expands and veins. And then, as suddenly as it came, the noise stops. The lightning freezes, solidifying in midair, creating a clear, purple shield between the floor and us. Between us and *whatever* might appear down there.

My mind runs wild, wondering what could require a shield made of lightning. Not a bear or a pack of wolves or any of the rare beasts of the forest. Even the creatures of myth, great cats or sea sharks or dragons, would pose no harm to the many Silvers above. And why would there be beasts at Queenstrial? This is supposed to be a ceremony to choose queens, not fight monsters.

As if answering me, the ground in the circle of statues, now the small center of the cylinder floor, opens wide. Without thinking, I push forward, hoping to get a better look with my own eyes. The rest of the servants crowd with me, trying to see what horrors this chamber can bring forth.

The smallest girl I've ever seen rises out of darkness.

Cheers rise as a house in brown silk and red gemstones applauds their daughter.

"Rohr, of House Rhambos," the family shouts, announcing her to the world.

The girl, no more than fourteen, smiles up at her family. She's tiny in comparison to the statues, but her hands are strangely large. The rest of her looks liable to blow away in a strong breeze. She takes a turn about the ring of statues, always smiling upward. Her gaze lands on Cal—I mean the prince—trying to entice him with her doe eyes or the occasional flip of honey-blond hair. In short, she looks foolish. Until she approaches a solid stone statue and sloughs its head off with a single, simple slap.

House Rhambos speaks again. "Strongarm."

Below us, little Rohr destroys the floor in a whirlwind, turning statues into pulverized piles of dust while she cracks the ground beneath her feet. She's like an earthquake in tiny human form, breaking apart anything and everything in her way.

So this is a pageant.

A violent one, meant to showcase a girl's beauty, splendor—and strength. *The most talented daughter.* This is a display of power, to pair the prince with the most powerful girl, so that their children might be the strongest of all. And this has been going on for hundreds of years.

I shudder to think of the strength in Cal's pinkie finger.

He claps politely as the Rhambos girl finishes her display of organized destruction and steps back onto the descending platform. House Rhambos cheers for her as she disappears.

Next comes Heron of House Welle, the daughter of my own governor. She's tall, with a face like her bird namesake. The destroyed earth shifts around her as she puts the floor back together. "Greenwarden," her family chants. *A greeny.* At her command, trees grow tall in the blink of an eye, their tops scraping against the lightning shield. It sparks where the boughs touch, setting fire to the fresh leaves. The next girl, a nymph of House Osanos, rises to the occasion. Using the waterfall fountains, she douses the contained forest fire in a hurricane of whitewater, leaving only charred trees and scorched earth.

This goes on for what feels like hours. Each girl rises up to show her worth, and each one finds a more destroyed arena, but they're trained to deal with anything. They range in age and appearance, but they are all dazzling. One girl, barely twelve years old, explodes everything she touches like some kind of walking bomb. "*Oblivion*," her family shouts, describing her power. As she obliterates the last of the white statues, the lightning shield holds firm. It hisses against her fire, and the noise shrieks in my ears.

The electricity, the Silvers, and the shouts blur in my head as I watch nymphs and greenys, swifts, strongarms, telkies, and what seems like a hundred other kinds of Silver show off beneath the shield. Things I never dreamed possible happen before my eyes, as girls turn their skin to stone or scream apart walls of glass. The Silvers are greater and stronger than I ever feared, with powers I never even knew existed. How can these people be real?

I've come all this way and suddenly I'm back in the arena, watching Silvers display everything we are not.

I want to marvel in awe as a creature-controlling animos calls down a thousand doves from the sky. When birds dive headfirst into the lightning shield, bursting in little clouds of blood, feathers, and deadly electricity, my awe turns to disgust. The shield sparks again, burning up what's left of the birds until it shines like new. I almost retch at the sound of applause when the cold-blooded animos sinks back into the floor.

Another girl, hopefully the last, rises into an arena now reduced to dust.

"Evangeline, of House Samos," yells the patriarch of the silver-haired family. He speaks alone, and his voice echoes across the Spiral Garden.

From my vantage point, I notice the king and queen sit up a bit straighter. Evangeline already has their attention. In stark contrast, Cal looks down at his hands.

While the other girls wore silk dresses and a few had strange, gilded armor, Evangeline rises in an outfit of black leather. Jacket, pants, boots, all studded with hard silver. No, not silver. Iron. Silver is not so dull or hard. Her house cheers for her, all of them on their feet. She belongs to Ptolemus and the patriarch, but others cheer too, other families. They want her to be queen. *She is the favorite.* She salutes, two fingers to her brow, first to her family and then to the king's box. They return the gesture, blatantly favoring this Evangeline.

Maybe this is more like the Feats than I realized. Except instead of showing the Reds where we stand, this is the king showing his subjects, powerful as they are, where *they* stand. *A hierarchy within the hierarchy.*

I've been so preoccupied with the trials that I almost don't notice when it's my turn to serve again. Before anyone can nudge me in the right direction, I set off to the right box, barely hearing the Samos patriarch speak. "Magnetron," I think he says, but I have no idea what it means.

I move through the narrow corridors that were once open

walkways, down to the Silvers requiring service. The box is at the bottom, but I'm quick and take almost no time getting down to them. I find a particularly fat clan dressed in garish yellow silk and awful feathers, all enjoying a massive cake. Plates and empty cups litter the box, and I get to work cleaning them up, my hands quick and practiced. A video screen blares inside the box, displaying Evangeline, who seems to be standing still down on the floor.

"What a farce this is," one of the fat yellow birds grumbles as he stuffs his face. "The Samos girl has already won."

Strange. She seems to be the weakest of all.

I pile the plates but keep my eyes on the screen, watching her prowl across the wasted floor. It doesn't seem like there's anything for her to work with, to show what she can do, but she doesn't seem to mind. Her smirk is terrible, like she's totally convinced of her own magnificence. *She doesn't look magnificent to me.*

Then the iron studs on her jacket move. They float in the air, each one a hard round bullet of metal. Then, like shots from a gun, they rocket away from Evangeline, digging into the dust and the walls and even the lightning shield.

She can control metal.

Several boxes applaud for her, but she's far from finished. Groans and clanks echo up to us from somewhere deep down in the structure of the Spiral Garden. Even the fat family stops eating to look around, perplexed. They are confused and intrigued, but I can feel the vibrations deep beneath my feet. I know to be afraid.

With an earth-shattering noise, metal pipes splinter the floor of the arena, rising up from far below. They burst through the walls, surrounding Evangeline in a twisted crown of gray and silver metal. She looks like she's laughing, but the deafening crunch of metal drowns her out. Sparks fall from the lightning shield, and she protects herself with scrap, not even breaking a sweat. Finally she lets the metal drop with a horrible smash. She turns her eyes skyward, to the boxes above. Her mouth is open wide, showing sharp little teeth. *She looks hungry.*

It starts slowly, a slight change in balance, until the whole box lurches. Plates crash to the floor and glass cups roll forward, tumbling over the rail to shatter on the lightning shield. Evangeline is pulling our box out, bending it forward, making us tip. The Silvers around me squawk and scrabble, their applause turning to panic. They're not the only ones—every box in our row moves with us. Far below, Evangeline directs with a hand, her brow furrowed in focus. Like Silver fighters in the ring, she wants to show the world what she's made of.

That is the thought in my head as a yellow ball of skin and feathered clothing knocks into me, pitching me over the rail with the rest of the silverware.

All I see is purple as I fall, the lightning shield rising up to meet me. It hisses with electricity, singeing the air. I barely have time to understand, but I know the veined purple glass will cook me alive, electrocuting me in my red uniform. I bet the Silvers will only care about waiting for someone to clean me off.

My head bangs against the shield, and I see stars. No, not stars. *Sparks.* The shield does its job, lighting me up with bolts of electricity. My uniform burns, scorched and smoking, and I expect to see my skin do the same. *My corpse will smell wonderful.* But, somehow, I don't feel a thing. *I must be in so much pain that I cannot feel it.*

But—I *can* feel it. I feel the heat of the sparks, running up and down my body, setting every nerve on fire. It isn't a bad feeling though. In fact I feel, well, *alive.* Like I've been living my whole life blind and now I've opened my eyes. Something moves beneath my skin, but it's not the sparks. I look at my hands, my arms, marveling at the lightning as it glides over me. Cloth burns away, charred black by the heat, but my skin doesn't change. The shield keeps trying to kill me, but it can't.

Everything is wrong.

I am alive.

The shield gives off a black smoke, starting to splinter and crack. The sparks are brighter, angrier, but weakening. I try to push myself up, to get to my feet, but the shield shatters beneath me and I fall again, tumbling over myself.

Somehow I manage to land in a pile of dust not covered by jagged metal. Definitely bruised and weak in the muscles, but still in one piece. My uniform is not so lucky, barely holding together in a charred mess.

I struggle to my feet, feeling more of my uniform flake off. Above us, murmurs and gasps echo through the Spiral Garden. I can feel all eyes on me, the burned Red girl. The human lightning rod.

Evangeline stares at me, her eyes wide. She looks angry, confused—and scared.

Of me. Somehow, she is scared of me.

"Hi," I say stupidly.

Evangeline answers with a flurry of metal shards, all of them sharp and deadly, pointed at my heart as they rip through the air.

Without thinking, I throw up my hands, hoping to save myself from the worst of it. Instead of catching a dozen jagged blades in my palms, I feel something quite different. Like with the sparks before, my nerves sing, alive with some inner fire. It moves in me, behind my eyes, beneath my skin, until I feel more than myself. Then it bursts from me, pure power and energy.

A jet of light—no, *lightning*—erupts from my hands, blazing through the metal. The pieces shriek and smoke, bursting apart in the heat. They fall harmlessly to the ground as the lightning blasts into the far wall. It leaves a smoking hole four feet wide, barely missing Evangeline.

Her mouth falls open in shock. I'm sure I look the same as I stare at my hands, wondering what on earth just happened to me. High above, a hundred of the most powerful Silvers wonder the same thing. I look up to see them all peering at me.

Even the king leans over the edge of his box, his flaming crown silhouetted against the sky. Cal is right next to him, staring down at me with wide eyes.

"Sentinels."

The king's voice is sharp as a razor, full of menace. Suddenly, the red-orange uniforms of Sentinels blaze from almost every box. The elite guards wait for another word, another order.

I'm a good thief because I know when to run. Now is one of those times.

Before the king can speak, I bolt, pushing past the stunned Evangeline to slide feetfirst into the still-open hatch in the floor.

"Seize her!" echoes behind me as I drop into the semidarkness of the chamber below. Evangeline's flying metal show punched holes in the ceiling, and I can still see up into the Spiral Garden. To my dismay, it looks like the structure is bleeding, as uniformed Sentinels drop down from their boxes, all of them racing after me.

With no time to think, all I can do is run.

The antechamber below the arena connects to a dark and empty hallway. Boxy black cameras watch me as I run at full speed, turning down another corridor and another. I can feel them, hunting like the Sentinels not so far behind me. *Run*, repeats in my head. *Run, run, run.*

I have to find a door, a window, something to help me get my bearings. If I can get outside, into the market maybe, I might have a chance. I *might*.

The first set of stairs I find leads up to a long mirrored hall. But the cameras are there as well, sitting in the corners of the ceiling like great black bugs.

A blast of gunfire explodes over my head, forcing me to drop to the floor. Two Sentinels, their uniforms the color of fire, crash through a mirror and charge at me. *They're just like Security*, I tell myself. *Just bumbling officers who don't know you. They don't know what you can do.*

I don't know what I can do.

They expect me to run so I do the opposite, storming the pair of them. Their guns are big and powerful, but bulky. Before they can get them up to shoot, stab, or both, I drop to my knees on the smooth marble floor, sliding between the two giants. One of them shouts after me, his voice exploding another mirror in a storm of glass. By the time they manage to change directions, I'm already off and running again.

When I finally find a window, it's a blessing and a curse. I skid to a stop in front of a giant pane of diamondglass, looking out to the vast forest. It's right there, just on the other side, just beyond an impenetrable wall.

All right, hands, now might be a good time to do your thing. Nothing happens, of course. Nothing happens when I need it to.

A blaze of heat takes me by surprise. I turn to see an approaching wall of red and orange and I know—the Sentinels have found me. But the wall is hot, flickering, almost solid. *Fire.* And coming right at me.

My voice is faint, weak, defeated, as I laugh at my predicament. "Oh, great."

I turn to run but instead collide with a broad wall of black fabric. Strong arms wrap around me, holding me still when I try to squirm away. *Shock him, light him up,* I scream in my head. But nothing happens. The miracle isn't going to save me again.

The heat grows, threatening to crush the air from my lungs. I survived lightning today; I don't want to press my luck with fire.

But it's the smoke that's going to kill me. Thick and black and much too strong, choking me. My vision swirls, and my eyelids grow heavy. I hear footsteps, shouting, the roar of fire as the world darkens.

"I'm sorry," Cal's voice says. I think I'm dreaming.

EIGHT

I'm on the porch, watching as Mom says good-bye to my brother Bree. She weeps, holding on to him tightly, smoothing his freshly cut hair. Shade and Tramy wait to catch her if her legs fail. I know they want to cry too, watching their oldest brother go, but for Mom's sake, they don't. Next to me, Dad says nothing, content to stare at the legionnaire. Even in his armor of steel plate and bulletproof fabric, the soldier looks small next to my brother. Bree could eat him alive, but he doesn't. He doesn't do anything at all when the legionnaire grabs his arm, pulling him away from us. A shadow follows, haunting after him on terrible dark wings. The world spins around me, and then I'm falling.

I land a year later, my feet stuck in the squelching mud beneath our house. Now Mom holds on to Tramy, begging with the legionnaire. Shade has to pull her off. Somewhere, Gisa cries for her favorite brother. Dad and I keep silent, saving our tears. The shadow returns, this time swirling around me, blotting out the sky and the sun. I squeeze my eyes shut, hoping it will leave me alone.

When I open them again, I'm in Shade's arms, hugging him as

tightly as I can. He hasn't cut his hair yet, and his chin-length brown hair tickles the top of my head. As I press myself to his chest, I wince. My ear stings sharply, and I pull back, seeing drops of red blood on my brother's shirt. Gisa and I had pierced our ears again, with the tiny gift Shade left us. I guess I did it wrong, as I do everything wrong. This time, I feel the shadow before I see it. And it feels angry.

It drags me through a parade of memories, all raw wounds still healing. Some of them are even dreams. No, they are nightmares. My worst nightmares.

A new world materializes around me, forming a shadowed landscape of smoke and ash. *The Choke.* I've never been there, but I've heard enough to imagine it. The land is flat, pocked with craters from a thousand falling bombs. Soldiers in stained red uniforms cower in each of them, like blood filling a wound. I float through them all, searching the faces, looking for the brothers I lost to smoke and shrapnel.

Bree appears first, wrestling with a blue-clad Lakelander in a puddle of mud. I want to help him, but I keep floating until he's out of sight. Tramy comes next, bending over a wounded soldier, trying to keep him from bleeding to death. His gentle features, so like Gisa's, are twisted in agony. I will never forget the screams of pain and frustration. As with Bree, I can't help him.

Shade waits at the front of the line, beyond even the bravest of warriors. He stands on top of a ridge without regard for the bombs or the guns or the Lakelander army waiting on the other side. He even has the gall to smile at me. I can only watch when the ground beneath his feet explodes, destroying him in a plume of fire and ash.

"Stop!" I manage to scream, reaching for the smoke that was once my brother.

The ash takes shape, re-forming into the shadow. It engulfs me in darkness, until a wave of memories overtakes me again. Gisa's hand. Kilorn's conscription. Dad coming home half-dead. They blur together, a swirl of too-bright color that hurts my eyes. *Something is not right.* The memories move backward through the years, like I'm watching my life in reverse. And then there are events I can't possibly remember: learning to speak, to walk, my child brothers passing me between them while Mom scolds. *This is impossible.*

"Impossible," the shadow says to me. The voice is so sharp, I fear it might crack my skull. I fall to my knees, colliding with what feels like concrete.

And then they're gone. My brothers, my parents, my sister, my memories, my nightmares, gone. Concrete and steel bars rise around me. *A cage.*

I struggle to my feet, one hand on my aching head as things come into focus. A figure stares at me from beyond the bars. A crown glitters on her head.

"I'd bow, but I might fall over," I say to Queen Elara, and immediately I wish I could call back the words. She's a *Silver*, I can't talk to her that way. She could put me in the stocks, take away my rations, punish me, punish my family. *No*, I realize in my growing horror. *She's the queen. She could just kill me. She could kill us all.*

But she doesn't look offended. Instead, she smirks. A wave of nausea washes over me when I meet her eyes, and I double over again.

"That looks like a bow to me," she purrs, enjoying my pain.

I fight the urge to vomit and reach out to grab the bars. My fist clenches around cold steel. "What are you doing to me?"

"Not much of anything anymore. But this—" She reaches through the bars to touch my temple. The pain triples beneath her finger, and I fall against the bars, barely conscious enough to hold on. "This is to keep you from doing anything silly."

Tears sting my eyes, but I shake them away. "Like stand on my own two feet?" I manage to spit out. I can hardly think through the pain, let alone be polite, but still I manage to hold back a stream of curses. *For heaven's sake, Mare Barrow, hold your tongue.*

"Like electrocute something," she snaps.

The pain ebbs, giving me enough strength to make it to the metal bench. When I rest my head against the cool stone wall, her words sink in. *Electrocute.*

The memory flashes across my mind, coming back in jagged pieces. Evangeline, the lightning shield, the sparks, and me. *It's not possible.*

"You are not Silver. Your parents are Red, you are Red, and your blood is red," the queen murmurs, prowling before the bars of my cage. "You are a miracle, Mare Barrow, an impossibility. Something even I can't understand, and I have seen all of you."

"That was you?" I almost screech, reaching up to cradle my head again. "You were in my mind? My memories? My *nightmares*?"

"If you know someone's fear, you know them." She blinks at me like I'm some stupid creature. "And I had to know what it is we're dealing with."

"I am not an *it*."

"What you are remains to be seen. But be thankful for one thing, little lightning girl," she sneers, putting her face against the bars. Suddenly my legs seize up, losing all feeling like I sat on them wrong. *Like I'm paralyzed.* Panic rises in my chest as I realize I can't even wiggle my toes. This must be how Dad feels, broken and useless. But somehow I get to my feet, my legs moving on their own, marching me toward the bars. On the other side, the queen watches me. Her blinks match my steps.

She's a whisper, and she's playing with me. When I'm close enough, she grabs my face in her hands. I cry out as the pain in my head multiplies. What I would give now for the simple doom of conscription.

"You did that in front of hundreds of Silvers, people who will ask questions, people with power," she hisses in my ear, her sickly sweet breath washing over my face. "That is the only reason you are still alive."

My hands clench, and I wish for the lightning again, but it doesn't come. She knows what I'm doing and laughs openly. Stars explode behind my eyes, clouding my vision, but I hear her go in a swirl of rustling silk. My sight returns just in time to see her dress disappear around a corner, leaving me well and truly alone in the cell. I barely make it back to the bench, fighting the urge to throw up.

Exhaustion comes over me in waves, starting in my muscles and sinking into my bones. I am only human, and humans are not supposed to deal with days like today. With a jolt, I realize my wrist is bare. The red band is gone, taken away. What could that mean? Tears sting my eyes, threatening to fall, but I will not cry. I have that much pride left.

I can fight the tears but not the questions. Not the doubt growing in my heart.

What's happening to me?
What am I?

I open my eyes to see a Security officer staring at me from the other side of the bars. His silver buttons shine in the low light, but they're nothing compared to the glare bouncing off his bald head.

"You have to tell my family where I am," I blurt out, sitting straight up. *At least I said I loved them,* I remember, thinking back to our last moments.

"I don't have to do anything but take you upstairs," he replies, but without much bite. The officer is a pillar of calm. "Change your clothes."

Suddenly, I realize I still have a half-burned uniform hanging off me. The officer points at a neat pile of clothes near the bars. He turns his back, allowing me some semblance of privacy.

The clothes are plain but fine, softer than anything I've ever worn before. A long-sleeved white shirt and black pants, both of them decorated with a single silver stripe down each side. There are shoes as well, black oiled boots that rise to my knees. To my surprise, there isn't a stitch of red on the clothes. But why, I do not know. *My ignorance is becoming a theme.*

"All right," I grumble, fighting the last boot up my leg. As it slides into place, the officer turns around. I don't hear the jingle of keys, but then, I don't see a lock. How he plans to let me out of my doorless cage, I'm not sure.

But instead of opening some hidden gate, his hand twitches, and the metal bars bow open. Of course. The jailor would be a—

"Magnetron, yes," he says with a waggle of his fingers. "And in case you were wondering, the girl you nearly fried is a cousin."

I almost choke on the air in my lungs, not knowing how to respond. "I'm sorry." It sounds like a question.

"Be sorry you missed her," he replies without a hint of jest. "Evangeline is a bitch."

"Family trait?" My mouth moves faster than my brain, and I gasp, realizing what I've just said.

He doesn't strike me for speaking out of turn, though he has every right to. Instead, the officer's face twitches into the shadow of a smile. "I guess you'll find out," he says, black eyes soft. "I'm Lucas Samos. Follow me."

I don't have to ask to know I have no other choice in the matter.

He leads me out of my cell and up a winding stair, to no less than twelve Security officers. Without a word, they surround me in a well-practiced formation and force me along with them. Lucas stays by me, marching in time with the others. They keep their guns in hand, as if ready for battle. Something tells me the men aren't here to defend me but to protect everyone else.

When we reach the more beautiful upper levels, the glass walls are strangely black. *Tinted*, I tell myself, remembering what Gisa said about the Hall of the Sun. The diamondglass can darken on command to hide what shouldn't be seen. Obviously, I must fall into that category.

With a jolt I realize that the windows change not because of some mechanism but a red-haired officer. She waves a hand at every wall we pass, and some power within her blocks out the light, clouding the glass with thin shade.

"She's a shadow, a bender of light," Lucas whispers, noting my awe.

The cameras are here as well. My skin crawls, feeling their electric gaze running over my bones. Normally my head would ache under the weight of so much electricity, but the pain never comes. Something in the shield has changed me. Or maybe it released something, revealing a part of myself locked away for so long. *What am I?* echoes in my head again, more threatening than before.

Only when we pass through a monstrous set of doors does the electric sensation pass. *The eyes cannot see me here.* The chamber inside could encompass my house ten times, stilts and all. And directly across from me, his fiery gaze burning into mine, is the king, sitting on a diamondglass throne carved into an inferno. Behind him, a window full of daylight quickly fades to black. It might be the last glimpse of the sun I'll ever see.

Lucas and the other officers march me forward, but they don't stay long. With nothing but a backward glance, Lucas leads the others out.

The king sits before me, the queen standing on his left, the princes on his right. I refuse to look at Cal, but I know he must be gawking at me. I keep my gaze on my new boots, focusing on my toes so I don't give over to the fear turning my body to lead.

"You will kneel," the queen murmurs, her voice soft as velvet.

I *should* kneel, but my pride won't let me. Even here, in front of Silvers, in front of the *king*, my knees do not bend. "I will not," I say, finding the strength to look up.

"Do you enjoy your cell, girl?" Tiberias says, his kingly voice filling the room. The threat in his words is plain as day, but still I stand. He cocks his head, staring at me like I'm an experiment to puzzle over.

"What do you want with me?" I manage to force out.

The queen leans down next to him. "I told you, she's Red through and through—" But the king waves her off like he would a fly. She purses her lips and draws back, hands clasped tightly together. *Serves her right*.

"What I want concerning you is impossible," Tiberias snaps. His glare smolders, like he's trying to burn me up.

I remember the queen's words. "Well, I'm not sorry you can't kill me."

The king chuckles. "They didn't say you were quick."

Relief floods through me. Death does not wait for me here. Not yet.

The king throws down a stack of papers, all of them covered in writing. The top sheet has the usual information, including my name, birth date, parents, and the little brown smear that is my blood. My picture is there too, the one on my identification card. I stare down at myself, into bored eyes sick of waiting in line to have my picture taken.

How I wish I could jump into the photo, into the girl whose only problems were conscription and a hungry belly.

"Mare Molly Barrow, born November seventeenth, 302 of the New Era, to Daniel and Ruth Barrow," Tiberias recites from memory, laying my life bare. "You have no occupation and are scheduled for conscription on your next birthday. You attend school sparingly, your academic test scores are low, and you have a list of offenses that would land you in prison in most cities. Thievery, smuggling, resisting arrest, to name but a few. All together you are poor, rude, immoral, unintelligent, impoverished, bitter, stubborn, and a blight upon your village and my kingdom."

The shock of his blunt words takes a moment to sink in, but when it does, I don't argue. He's entirely right.

"And yet," he continues, rising to his feet. This close, I can see his crown is deathly sharp. The points can kill. "You are also something else. Something I cannot fathom. You are Red and Silver both, a peculiarity with deadly consequences you cannot understand. So what am I to do with you?"

Is he asking me? "You could let me go. I wouldn't say a word."

The queen's sharp laughter cuts me off. "And what about the High Houses? Will they keep silent as well? Will they forget the little lightning girl in a red uniform?"

No. No one will.

"You know my advice, Tiberias," the queen adds, her eyes on the king. "And it will solve both our problems."

It must be bad advice, bad for me, because Cal clenches a fist. The movement draws my eye, and I finally look at him fully. He remains still, stoic and quiet, as I'm sure he's been trained to do, but fire burns behind his eyes. For a moment, he meets my gaze, but I look away before I can call out and ask him to save me.

"Yes, Elara," the king says, nodding at his wife. "We cannot kill you, Mare Barrow." *Not yet* hangs in the air. "So we are going to hide you in plain sight where we can watch you, *protect* you, and attempt to understand you."

The way his eyes gleam makes me feel like a meal about to be devoured.

"Father!" The word bursts from Cal, but his brother—the paler, leaner prince—grabs him by the arm, holding him back from protesting further. He has a calming effect, and Cal steps back in line.

Tiberias goes on, ignoring his son. "You are no longer Mare Barrow, a Red daughter of the Stilts."

"Then who am I?" I ask, my voice shaking with dread, thinking of all the awful things they can do to me.

"Your father was Ethan Titanos, general of the Iron Legion, killed when you were an infant. A soldier, a Red man, took you for his own and raised you in the dirt, never telling you your true parentage. You grew up believing you were nothing, and now, thanks to chance, you are made whole again. You are Silver, a lady of a lost High House, a noble with great power, and one day, a princess of Norta."

Try as I might, I can't hold back a surprised yelp. "A Silver—a princess?"

My eyes betray me, flying to Cal. *A princess must marry a prince.*

"You will marry my son Maven, and you'll do it without putting a toe out of line."

I swear I hear my jaw hit the floor. A wretched, embarrassing sound escapes my mouth as I search for something to say, but I'm honestly speechless. In front of me, the younger prince looks equally confused, sputtering just as loudly as I want to. This time, it's Cal's turn to restrain him, though his eyes are on me.

The young prince manages to find his voice. "I don't understand," he blurts out, shrugging off Cal. He takes quick steps toward his father. "She's—why—?" Usually I'd be offended, but I have to agree with the prince's reservations.

"Quiet," his mother snaps. "You will obey."

He glares at her, every inch the young son rebelling against his parents. But his mother hardens, and the prince backs down, knowing her wrath and power as well as I do.

My voice is faint, barely audible. "This seems a bit . . . much." There's simply no other way to describe it. "You don't want to make me a lady, much less a princess."

Tiberias's face cracks into a grim smile. Like the queen, his teeth are blindingly white. "Oh, but I do, my dear. For the first time in your rudimentary little life, you have a purpose." The jab feels like a slap across the face. "Here we are, in the early stages of a badly timed rebellion, with terrorist groups or freedom fighters, or whatever the hell these idiotic Red fools call themselves, blowing things up in the name of equality."

"The Scarlet Guard." *Farley. Shade.* As soon as the name crosses my mind, I pray Queen Elara stays out of my head. "They bombed—"

"The capital, yes." The king shrugs, scratching his neck.

My years in the shadows have taught me many things. Who carries the most money, who won't notice you, and what liars look like. *The king is a liar*, I realize, watching as he forces another shrug. He's trying to be dismissive, and it's just not working. Something has him scared of Farley, of the Scarlet Guard. Something much bigger than a few explosions.

"And you," he continues, leaning forward. "You might be able to help us stop there from being any more."

I'd laugh out loud if I wasn't so scared. "By marrying—sorry, what's your name again?"

His cheeks go white in what I assume is the Silver version of a blush. After all, their blood is silver. "My name is Maven," he says, his voice soft and quiet. Like Cal and his father, his hair is glossy black, but the similarities end there. While they are broad and muscled, Maven is lean, with eyes like clear water. "And I still don't understand."

"What Father is trying to say is that she represents an opportunity for us," Cal says, cutting in to explain. Unlike his brother, Cal's voice is strong and authoritative. It's the voice of a king. "If the Reds see her, a Silver by blood but Red by nature, raised up with us, they can be placated. It's like an old fairy tale, a commoner becoming the princess. She's their champion. They can look to her instead of terrorists." And then, softer, but more important than anything else: "She's a distraction."

But this isn't a fairy tale, or even a dream. *This is a nightmare.* I'm being locked away for the rest of my life, forced into being someone else. *Into being one of them. A puppet. A show to keep people happy, quiet, and trampled.*

"And if we get the story right, the High Houses will be satisfied too. You're the lost daughter of a war hero. What better honor can we give you?"

I meet his eyes, silently pleading. He helped me once, maybe he can do it again. But Cal tips his head from side to side, shaking his head slowly. *He can't help me here.*

"This isn't a request, Lady Titanos," Tiberias says. He uses my new name, my new *title*. "You will go through with this, and you will do it *properly*."

Queen Elara turns her pale eyes on me. "You will live here, as is the custom for royal brides. Every day will be scheduled at my discretion, and you will be tutored in everything and anything possible to make you"—she searches for the word, chewing on her lip—"*suitable*." I don't want to know what that means. "You will be scrutinized. From now on you live on the edge of a knife. One false step, one wrong word, and you will suffer for it."

My throat tightens, like I can feel the chains the king and queen are wrapping around me. "What about my life—?"

"What life?" Elara crows. "Girl, you have fallen head over heels into a miracle."

Cal squeezes his eyes shut for a moment, as if the sound of the queen's laughter pains him. "She means her family. Mare—the girl—has a family."

Gisa, Mom, Dad, the boys, Kilorn—a life taken away.

"Oh, that," the king huffs, plopping back down into his chair. "I suppose we'll give them an allowance, keep them *quiet*."

"I want my brothers brought home from the war." For once, I feel like I've said something right. "And my friend, Kilorn Warren. Don't let the legions take him either."

Tiberias responds in half a heartbeat. A few Red soldiers mean nothing to him. "Done."

It sounds less like a pardon and more like a death sentence.

NINE

Lady Mareena Titanos, born *to Lady Nora Nolle Titanos and Lord Ethan Titanos, general of the Iron Legion. Heiress to House Titanos. Mareena Titanos. Titanos.*

My new name echoes in my head as the Red maids prepare me for the coming onslaught. The three girls work quickly and efficiently, never speaking to one another. They don't ask me questions either, even though they must want to. *Say nothing,* I remember. They're not allowed to speak to me, and they certainly aren't allowed to talk about me to anyone else. Even the strange things, the *Red* things, I'm sure they see.

Over many agonizing minutes, they try to make me *suitable*, bathing me, styling me, *painting* me into the silly thing I'm supposed to be. The makeup is the worst, especially the thick white paste applied to my skin. They go through three pots of it, covering my face, neck, collarbone, and arms with the glittery wet powder. In the mirror, it looks like the warmth is leeched from me, as if the powder has covered the heat in my skin. With a gasp, I realize it's supposed to hide my natural flush, the red bloom in my skin, the red *blood.* I'm pretending to be

Silver, and when they finish painting my face, I actually look the part. With my newly pale skin and darkened eyes and lips, I look cold, cruel, a living razor. I look Silver. I look beautiful. And I hate it.

How long will this last? Betrothed to a prince. Even in my head, it sounds crazy. *Because it is. No Silver in their right mind would marry you, let alone a prince of Norta. Not to calm rebellion, not to hide your identity, not for anything.*

Then why do this?

When the maids pinch and pull me into a gown, I feel like a corpse being dressed for her funeral. I know it's not far from the truth. Red girls do not marry Silver princes. I will never wear a crown or sit on a throne. Something will happen, an *accident* maybe. A lie will raise me up, and one day another lie will bring me down.

The dress is a dark shade of purple spattered with silver, made of silk and sheer lace. *All houses have a color,* I remember, thinking back to the rainbow of families. The colors of Titanos, *my name,* must be purple and silver.

When one of the maids reaches for my earrings, trying to take away the last bit of my old life, a surge of fear pulses through me. "Don't touch them!"

The girl jumps back, blinking quickly, and the others freeze at my outburst.

"Sorry, I—" *A Silver wouldn't apologize.* I clear my throat, collecting myself. "Leave the earrings." My voice sounds strong, hard—*regal.* "You can change everything else, but leave the earrings."

The three cheap pieces of metal, each one a brother, aren't going anywhere.

"The color suits you."

I whirl around to see the maids stooped in identical bows. And standing over them: Cal. Suddenly, I'm very glad the makeup covers the blush spreading over me.

He gestures quickly, his hand moving in a brushing motion, and the maids scurry from the room like mice fleeing from a cat.

"I'm sort of new to this royal thing, but I'm not sure you're supposed to be here. In my room," I say, forcing as much disdain into my voice as I can muster. After all, it's his fault I'm in this forsaken mess.

He takes a few steps toward me, and on instinct, I take a step back. My feet catch on the hem of my dress, making me choose between not moving or falling over. I don't know which is less desirable.

"I came to apologize, something I can't really do with an audience." He stops short, noting my discomfort. A muscle twitches in his cheek as he looks me over, probably remembering the hopeless girl who tried to pickpocket him only last night. I look nothing like her now. "I'm sorry for getting you into this, Mare."

"*Mareena.*" The name even *tastes* wrong. "That's my name, remember?"

"Then it's a good thing Mare's a suitable nickname."

"I don't think anything about me is *suitable*."

Cal's eyes rake over me, and my skin burns under his gaze. "How do you like Lucas?" he finally says, taking an obliging step back.

The Samos guard, the first decent Silver I've met here. "He's all right, I suppose." Perhaps the queen will take him away if I reveal how gentle the officer was to me.

"Lucas is a good man. His family thinks him weak for his kindness," he adds, eyes darkening a little. As if he knows the feeling. "But he'll serve you well, and fairly. I'll make sure of it."

How thoughtful. He's given me a kind jailer. But I bite my tongue. It won't do any good to snap at his mercy. "Thank you, Your Highness."

The spark returns to his eyes, and a smirk to his lips. "You know my name is Cal."

"And you know my name, don't you?" I tell him bitterly. "You know what I come from."

He barely nods, as if ashamed.

"You have to take care of them." *My family.* Their faces swim before my eyes, already so far away. "All of them, for as long as you can."

"Of course I will." He takes a step toward me, closing the gap between us. "I'm sorry," he says again. The words resound in my head, echoing off a memory.

The wall of fire. The choking smoke. I'm sorry, I'm sorry, I'm sorry.

It was Cal who caught me earlier, who kept me from escaping this awful place.

"Are you sorry for stopping my one chance of escape?"

"You mean if you got past the Sentinels, Security, the walls, the woods, back to your village to wait until the queen herself hunted you down?" he replies, taking my accusations in stride. "Stopping you was the best thing for you *and* your family."

"I could've gotten away. You don't know me."

"I know the queen would tear the world apart looking for the little lightning girl."

"Don't call me that." The nickname stings more than the fake name I'm still getting used to. *Little lightning girl.* "That's what your mother calls me."

He laughs bitterly. "She's not my mother. She's Maven's, not mine." Just by the set of his jaw, I know not to press the issue.

"Oh," is all I can say, my voice very small. It fades quickly, a faint echo against the vaulted ceiling. I crane my neck, looking around at my new room for the first time since I came in. It's finer than anything I've ever seen—marble and glass, silk and feathers. The light has changed, shifting to the orange color of dusk. Night is coming. And with it, the rest of my life.

"I woke up this morning as one person," I mutter, more to myself than to him, "and now I'm supposed to be someone else entirely."

"You can do this." I feel him take a step toward me, his heat filling the room in a way that makes my skin prickle. But I don't look up. I won't.

"How do you know?"

"Because you *must*." He bites his lip, eyes shifting over me. "As beautiful as this world is, it's just as dangerous. People who are not useful, people who make mistakes, they can be removed. *You* can be removed."

And I will be. Someday. But that is not the only threat I face. "So the moment I mess up could be my last?"

He doesn't speak, but I can see the answer in his eyes. *Yes.*

My fingers fiddle with the silver belt at my waist, pulling it tight. If this was a dream, I would wake up, but I don't. *This is really happening.* "What about me? About"—I hold out my hands, glaring at the infernal things—"this?"

In response, Cal smiles. "I think you'll get the hang of it."

Then he holds up his own bare hand. A strange contraption at his wrist, something like a bracelet with two metal ends, clicks, producing sparks. Instead of disappearing in a flash, the sparks glow and burst into red flame, giving off a blast of heat. *He's a burner, he controls heat and fire,* I remember. *He's a prince, and a dangerous one at that.* But the flame disappears as quickly as it came, leaving only Cal's encouraging smile and the humming of cameras hidden somewhere, watching over everything.

The masked Sentinels on the edge of my vision are a constant reminder of my new position. I'm nearly a princess, engaged to the second most eligible bachelor in the country. And I'm a lie. Cal is long gone, leaving me with my guards. Lucas isn't so bad, but the others are stern and quiet, never looking me in the eye. The guards and even Lucas are wardens to keep me imprisoned in my own skin, red behind a silver curtain that can never be pulled away. If I fall, if I even slip, I will die. *And others will die for my failure.*

As they escort me toward the feast, I go over the story the queen drilled into me, the pretty tale she was going to tell the court. It's simple, easy to remember, but it still makes me cringe.

I was born at the war front. My parents were killed in an attack on the camp. A Red soldier saved me from the rubble and brought me home to a wife who always wanted a daughter. They raised me in the village called the Stilts, and I was ignorant of my birthright or my ability until this morning. And now I am returned to my rightful place.

The thought makes me sick. My rightful place is at home, with my parents and Gisa and Kilorn. *Not here.*

The Sentinels lead the way through the maze of passages in the upper levels of the palace. Like the Spiral Garden, the architecture is all curves of stone, glass, and metal, slowly turning downward. Diamondglass is around every corner, showing breathtaking views of the marketplace, the river valley, and the woods beyond. From this height, I can see hills I didn't know existed rising in the distance, silhouetted against the setting sun.

"The last two floors are royal apartments," Lucas says, pointing up the sloping, spiraling hallway. Sunlight glitters like a firestorm, throwing speckles of light down on us. "The lift will take us down to the ballroom. Just here." Lucas reaches out, stopping next to a metal wall. It reflects us dully, then slides away when he waves a hand.

The Sentinels usher us into a box with no windows and harsh lighting. I force myself to breathe, even though I'd rather push out of what feels like a giant metal coffin.

I jump a mile when the lift suddenly *moves*, making my pulse race. My breath comes in short gasps as I look around in wide-eyed fright, expecting to see the others reacting in the same way. But no one else seems to mind the fact that the box we're in is *dropping*. Only Lucas notices my discomfort, and he slows our descent a little.

"The lift moves up and down, so we don't have to walk. This place is very big, Lady Titanos," he murmurs with the ghost of a smile.

I'm torn between wonder and fear as we drop, and I breathe a sigh of relief when Lucas opens the lift doors. We march out into the mirrored hall I ran through this morning. The broken mirrors are already fixed—it looks like nothing ever happened.

When Queen Elara appears around the corner, her own Sentinels in tow, Lucas sweeps into a bow. Now she wears black and red and silver, her husband's colors. With her blond hair and pale skin, she looks downright ghoulish.

She grabs me by the arm, pulling me to her as we walk. Her lips don't move, but I hear her voice all the same, echoing in my head. This time it doesn't hurt or make me nauseous, but the sensation still feels sick and wrong. I want to scream, to claw her out of my head. But there's nothing I can do except hate her.

The Titanos family were oblivions, she says, her voice all around. *They could explode things with a touch, like the Lerolan girl did at Queenstrial.* When I try to remember the girl, Elara projects an image of her directly into my brain. It flashes, barely there, but still I see a young girl in orange blow up rock and sand like military bombs. *Your mother, Nora Nolle, was a storm like the rest of House Nolle. Storms control the weather, to an extent. It's not common, but their union resulted in your unique abilities to control electricity. Say no more, if anyone asks.*

What do you really want with me? Even in my head, my voice quivers. Her laughter bounces inside my skull, the only answer I'll get.

Remember the person you're supposed to be, and remember well, she continues, ignoring my question. *You are pretending to be raised Red, but you're Silver by blood. You are now Red in the head, Silver in the heart.*

A shiver of fear shoots through me.

From now until the end of your days, you must lie. Your life depends on it, little lightning girl.

TEN

Elara leaves me standing in the hallway, mulling over her words.

I used to think there was only the divide, Silver and Red, rich and poor, kings and slaves. But there's much more in between, things I don't understand, and I'm right in the middle of it. I grew up wondering if I'd have food for supper; now I'm standing in a palace about to be eaten alive.

Red in the head, Silver in the heart sticks with me, guiding my motions. My eyes stay wide, taking in the grand palace both Mare and Mareena had never dreamed of, but my mouth presses into a firm line. Mareena is impressed, but she keeps her emotions in check. She is cold and unfeeling.

The doors at the end of the hall open, revealing the biggest room I've ever seen, bigger even than the throne room. I don't think I'll ever get used to the sheer size of this place. I step through the doors onto a landing. Stairs lead down to the floor, where every house sits in cool expectation, their eyes forward. Again, they keep to their colors. A few mutter among themselves, probably talking about me and my little show. King Tiberias and Elara stand on a raised surface a few feet higher than the floor, facing the crowd of their subjects. *They never miss an opportunity to lord over the others.* Either they're very vain or very aware. To look powerful is to be powerful.

The princes match their parents in different outfits of red and black, both decorated with military medals. Cal stands to his father's right, his face still and impassive. If he knows who he's going to marry, he doesn't look happy about it. Maven's there too, on his mother's left, his face a storm cloud of emotions. The younger brother is not as good as Cal at hiding his feelings.

At least I won't have to deal with a good liar.

"The right of Queenstrial is always a joyous event, representing the future of our great kingdom and the bonds that keep us strongly united in the face of our enemies," the king says, addressing the crowd. They don't see me yet, standing on the edge of the room, looking down on them all. "But as you saw today, Queenstrial has brought forth more than just the future queen."

He turns to Elara, who clasps the king's hand in her own with a dutiful smile. Her shift from devilish villain to blushing queen is astounding. "We all remember our bright hope against the darkness of war, our captain, our *friend*, the General Ethan Titanos," Elara says.

People murmur over the room, in fondness or sadness. Even the Samos patriarch, Evangeline's cruel father, bows his head. "He led the Iron Legion to victory, pushing back the lines of war that had stood for nearly a hundred years. The Lakelanders feared him; our soldiers loved him." I strongly doubt a single Red soldier loved their Silver general. "Lakelander spies killed our beloved friend Ethan, sneaking across the lines to destroy our one hope for peace. His wife, the Lady Nora, a good and just woman, died with him. On that fateful day sixteen years ago, House Titanos was lost. Friends were taken from us. Our blood was spilled."

Silence settles on the room as the queen pauses to dab at her eyes, wiping away what I know are fake, forced tears. A few of the girls, participants in Queenstrial, fidget in their seats. They don't care about a dead general, and neither does the queen, not really. This is about me, about somehow slipping a Red girl into a crown without anyone noticing. It's a magic trick, and the queen is a skilled magician.

Her eyes find me, blazing up to my spot at the top of the stairs, and everyone follows her gaze. Some look confused, while others recognize me from this morning. And a few stare at my dress. They know the colors of House Titanos better than I do and understand who I am. Or at least who I'm pretending to be.

"This morning we saw a miracle. We watched a Red girl fall into the arena like a bolt of lightning, wielding power she should not have." More murmurs rise, and a few Silvers even stand. The Samos girl looks furious, her black eyes fixed on me.

"The king and I interviewed the girl extensively, trying to discover how she came to be." Interview *is a funny way to describe scrambling my brain.* "She isn't Red, but she is still a miracle. My friends, please welcome back to us Lady Mareena Titanos, daughter of Ethan Titanos. Lost and now found."

With a twitch of her hand, she beckons me closer. I obey.

I descend the stairs to stilted applause, more focused on not tripping. But my feet are sure, my face still, as I plunge toward hundreds of faces wondering, staring, suspecting. Lucas and my guards don't follow, staying on the landing. I'm alone in front of these people once again, and I've never felt so bare, even with the layers of silk and powder. Again, I'm grateful for all the makeup. It's my shield, between them and the truth of who I am. A truth I don't even understand.

The queen gestures to an open seat in the front row of the crowd, and I make my way to it. The Queenstrial girls watch me, wondering why I'm here and why I'm so important all of a sudden. But they're only curious, not angry. They look at me with pity, empathizing as best they can with my sad story. Except Evangeline Samos. When I finally get to my seat, she's sitting right next to it, her eyes glaring into mine. Gone are her leather clothes and iron studs; now she wears a dress of interlocked metal rings. From the way her fingers tighten, I can tell she wants nothing more than to wrap her hands around my throat.

"Saved from her parents' fate, Lady Mareena was taken from the front and brought to a Red village not ten miles from here," the king continues, taking over so he can tell the grand twist in my tale. "Raised by Red parents, she worked as a Red servant. And until this morning, she believed she was one of them." The accompanying gasp makes my teeth grind. "Mareena was a diamond in the rough, working in my own palace, the daughter of my late friend under my nose. But no more. To atone for my ignorance, and to repay her father and her house for their great contributions to the kingdom, I would like to take this moment to announce the joining of House Calore and the resurrected House Titanos."

Another gasp, this one from the girls of Queenstrial. *They think I'm taking Cal away from them. They think I'm their competition.* I raise my eyes to the king, quietly pleading for him to continue before one of the girls murders me.

I can almost feel Evangeline's cold metal cutting into me. Her fingers lace together tightly, knuckles white as she resists the urge to skin me in front of everyone. On her other side, her brooding father puts a hand on her arm to still her.

When Maven steps forward, the tension in the room deflates. He stutters briefly, tripping over the words he's been taught, but he finds his voice. "Lady Mareena."

Trying my best not to shake, I rise to my feet and face him.

"In the eyes of my royal father and the noble court, I would ask for your hand in marriage. I pledge myself to you, Mareena Titanos. Will you accept?"

My heart pounds as he speaks. Though his words sound like a question, I know I have no choice in my answer. No matter how much I want to look away, my eyes stay on Maven. He gives me the smallest of encouraging smiles. I wonder to myself which girl would've been chosen for him.

Who would I have chosen? If none of this had happened, if Kilorn's master never died, if Gisa's hand was never broken, if nothing ever changed. *If.* It's the worst word in the world.

Conscription. Survival. Green-eyed children with my quick feet and Kilorn's last name. That future was almost impossible before; now it's nonexistent.

"I pledge myself to you, Maven Calore," I say, hammering the last nails into my coffin. My voice quivers, but I don't stop. "I accept."

It carries such finality, slamming a door on the rest of my life. I feel like collapsing but somehow manage to sit back down gracefully.

Maven slinks back to his seat, grateful to be out of the spotlight. His mother pats him on the arm in reassurance. She smiles softly, just for him. Even Silvers love their children. But she turns cold again as Cal stands, her smile disappearing in a heartbeat.

The air seems to go out of the room as every girl inhales, waiting for his decision. I doubt Cal had any say in choosing a queen, but he plays his part well, just like Maven, just like I'm trying to do. He smiles brightly, flashing even white teeth that make a few girls sigh, but his warm eyes are terribly solemn.

"I am my father's heir, born to privilege and power and strength. You owe me your allegiance, just as I owe you my life. It is my duty to serve you and my kingdom as best I can—and beyond." He's rehearsed his speech, but the fervor Cal has can't be faked. He believes in himself, that he'll be a good king—or die trying. "I need a queen who will sacrifice just as much as I will, to maintain order, justice, and balance."

The Queenstrial girls lean forward, eager to hear his next words. But Evangeline doesn't move, an obscene smirk twisting her face. House Samos looks equally calm. Her brother, Ptolemus, even stifles a yawn. *They know who has been chosen.*

"Lady Evangeline."

There's no gasp of surprise, no shock or excitement from her. Even the other girls, heartbroken as they are, sit back with only dejected shrugs. Everyone saw this coming. I remember the fat family back in the Spiral Garden, complaining that Evangeline Samos had already won. *They were right.*

With a fluid, cold grace, Evangeline rises to her feet. She barely looks at Cal, instead turning over her shoulder to sneer at the crestfallen girls. She basks in her moment of glory. A smile ghosts over her face when her eyes fall on me. I don't miss the feral flash of teeth.

When she turns back around, Cal echoes his brother's proposal. "In the eyes of my royal father and the noble court, I would ask for your hand in marriage. I pledge myself to you, Evangeline Samos. Will you accept?"

"I pledge myself to you, Prince Tiberias," she says in a voice that is oddly high and breathy, contrasting with her hard appearance. "I accept."

With a triumphant smirk, Evangeline sits back down and Cal retreats to his own seat. He keeps a smile fixed in place like a piece of armor, but she doesn't seem to notice.

Then I feel a hand find my arm, nails biting into my skin. I fight the urge to jump out of my chair. Evangeline doesn't react, still staring straight ahead at the place that will one day be hers. If this were the Stilts, I'd knock a few of her teeth out. Her fingers dig into me, down to the flesh. If she draws blood, red blood, our little game will be over before it even has a chance to begin. But she stops short of breaking skin, leaving bruises the maids will have to hide.

"Get in my way and I'll kill you slowly, little lightning girl," she mutters through her smile. *Little lightning girl.* The nickname is really starting to get on my nerves.

To cement her point, the smooth metal bracelet on her wrist shifts, turning into a circle of sharp thorns. Each tip glistens, begging to spill blood. I swallow hard, trying not to move. But she lets go quickly, returning her hand to her lap. Once again, she's the picture of a demure Silver girl. If there was ever a person begging for an elbow to the face, it is Evangeline Samos.

A quick glance around the room tells me the court has turned sullen. Some girls have tears in their eyes and throw wolfish glares at Evangeline and even me. They probably waited for this day all their lives, only to fail. I want to hand my betrothal over, to give away what they so desperately want, but no. I must look happy. I must *pretend.*

"As wonderful and happy as today has been," King Tiberias says, ignoring the sentiment in the room, "I must remind you why this choice has been made. The might of House Samos joined with my son, and all his children to follow, will help guide our nation. You all know the precarious state of our kingdom, with war in the north and foolish extremists, enemies to our way of life, attempting to destroy us from within. The Scarlet Guard might seem small and insignificant to us, but they represent a dangerous turn for our Red brothers." More than a few people in the crowd scoff at the term *brothers*, myself included.

Small and insignificant. Then why do they need me? Why use me, if the Scarlet Guard is nothing to them? *The king is a liar.* But what he's trying to hide, I'm still not sure. It could be the Guard's strength. It could be me.

It's probably both.

"Should this rebellious streak take hold," he continues, "it will end in bloodshed and a divided nation, something I cannot bear. We must maintain the balance. Evangeline *and* Mareena will help do that, for the sake of us all."

Murmurs go through the crowd at the king's words. Some nod, others look cross at the Queenstrial choices, but no one voices their dissent. No one speaks up. No one would listen if they did.

Smiling, King Tiberias bows his head. He has won, and he knows it. "Strength and power," he repeats. The motto echoes out from him, as every person says the words.

The words trip over my tongue, feeling foreign in my mouth. Cal stares down at me, watching me chant along with all the others. In that moment, I hate myself.

"Strength and power."

I suffer through the feast, watching but not seeing, hearing but not listening. Even the food, more food than I've ever seen, tastes plain in my mouth. I should be stuffing my face, enjoying what's probably the best meal of my life, but I can't. I can't even speak when Maven murmurs to me, his voice calm and level in assurance.

"You're doing fine," he says, but I try to ignore him. Like his brother, he wears the same metal bracelet, the flamemaker. It's a firm reminder of exactly who and what Maven is—powerful, dangerous, a burner, a Silver.

Sitting at a table made of crystal, drinking bubbly gold liquid until my head spins, I feel like a traitor. *What are my parents eating for dinner tonight? Do they even know where I am? Or is Mom sitting on the porch, waiting for me to come home?*

Instead, I'm stuck in a room full of people who would kill me if they knew the truth. And the royals of course, who would kill me if they could, who probably *will* kill me one day. They've pulled me inside out, swapping Mare for Mareena, a thief for a crown, rags for silk, *Red for Silver*. This morning I was a servant, tonight I'm a princess. *How much more will change? What else will I lose?*

"That's enough of that," Maven says, his voice swimming through the din of the feast. He pulls away my fancy goblet, replacing it with a glass of water.

"I liked that drink." But I gulp down the water greedily, feeling my head clear.

Maven just shrugs. "You'll thank me later."

"Thank you," I snap as snidely as possible. I haven't forgotten the way he looked at me this morning, like I was something on the bottom of his shoe. But now his gaze is softer, calmer, more like Cal's.

"I'm sorry about earlier today, Mareena."

My name is Mare. "I'm sure you are," comes out instead.

"Really," he says, leaning toward me. We're seated side by side, with the rest of the royals, at the high table. "It's just—usually younger princes get to choose. One of the few perks of not being the heir," he adds with a terribly forced smile.

Oh. "I didn't know that," I reply, not really knowing what to say. I should feel sorry for him, but I can't bring myself to feel any kind of pity for a prince.

"Yeah, well, you wouldn't. It's not your fault."

He looks back to the feasting hall, casting his gaze out like a fishing line. I wonder what face he's looking for. "Is she here?" I murmur, trying to sound apologetic. "The girl you would have chosen?"

He hesitates, then shakes his head. "No, I didn't have anyone in mind. But it was nice to have the option of a choice, you know?"

No, I don't know. I don't have the luxury of choice. Not now, not ever.

"Not like my brother. He grew up knowing he'd never have a say in his future. I guess now I'm getting a taste of what he feels."

"You and your brother have everything, Prince Maven," I whisper in a voice so fervent it might be a prayer. "You live in a palace, you have strength, you have *power*. You wouldn't know hardship if it kicked you in the teeth, and believe me, it does that a lot. So excuse me if I don't feel sorry for either of you."

There I go, letting my mouth run away with my brain. As I recover, drinking down the rest of the water in an attempt to cool my temper, Maven just stares at me, his eyes cold. But the wall of ice recedes, melting as his gaze softens.

"You're right, Mare. No one should feel sorry for me." I can hear the bitterness in his voice. With a shiver, I watch him throw a glance at Cal. His older brother beams like the sun, laughing with their father. When Maven turns back around, he forces another smile, but there's a surprising sadness in his eyes.

As much as I try, I can't ignore the sudden jolt of pity I feel for the forgotten prince. But it passes when I remember who he is and who I am.

I'm a Red girl in a sea of Silvers, and I can't afford to feel sorry for anyone, least of all the son of a snake.

ELEVEN

The crowd toasts at the end of the feast, their glasses raised to the royal table. On they go, lords and ladies in a rainbow of color trying to wiggle their way into favor. I'll have to learn them all soon, matching color to house and house to people. Maven whispers their names to me in turn, even though I won't remember them tomorrow. At first it's annoying, but soon I find myself leaning in to hear the names.

Lord Samos is the last to stand, and when he does, a hush falls. This man commands respect, even among titans. Though his black robes are plain, trimmed with simple silk, and he has no great jewels or badges to speak of, he has the undeniable air of power. I don't need Maven to tell me he's the highest of the High Houses, a person to be feared above all others.

"Volo Samos," Maven murmurs. "Head of House Samos. He owns and operates the iron mines. Every gun in the war comes from his land."

So he's not just a noble. His importance comes from more than just titles.

Volo's toast is short and to the point. "To my daughter," he rumbles, his voice low, steady, and strong. "The future queen."

"To Evangeline!" Ptolemus shouts, jumping to his feet next to his father. His eyes blaze around the room, daring someone to oppose them. A few lords and ladies look annoyed, angry even, but they raise their cups with the rest, saluting the new princess. Their glasses reflect the light, each one a tiny star in the hand of a god.

When he finishes, Queen Elara and King Tiberias rise, both of them smiling at their many guests. Cal gets up as well, then Evangeline, then Maven, and after one dumb moment, I join them. The many houses do the same at their tables, and the scraping of chairs on marble sounds like nails on a stone. Thankfully, the king and queen simply bow and walk down the short set of steps leading away from our high table. *It's over.* I've made it through my first night.

Cal takes Evangeline's hand and leads her after them, with Maven and me bringing up the rear. When Maven takes my hand, his skin is shockingly cold.

The Silvers press in on both sides, watching us pass in heavy silence. Their faces are curious, cunning, cruel—and behind every false smile is a reminder; *they are watching.* Every eye scraping over me, looking for cracks and imperfections, makes me squirm, but I cannot break.

I cannot slip. Not now, not ever. I'm one of them. I'm special. *I'm an accident. I'm a lie. And my life depends on maintaining the illusion.*

Maven tightens his fingers in mine, willing me onward. "It's almost over," he whispers as we near the far end of the hall. "Almost there."

The feeling of being smothered passes as we leave the feast behind, but the cameras follow us with heavy, electric eyes. The more I think about it, the stronger their gaze becomes, until I can sense where the cameras are before I see them. Maybe this is a side effect of my "condition." Maybe I've just never been surrounded by this much electricity before, and this is how everyone feels. *Or maybe I'm just a freak.*

Back in the passageway, a group of Sentinels waits to escort us upstairs. But then, what threats could there possibly be to these people? Cal, Maven, and King Tiberias can control fire. Elara can control *minds*. What could they fear?

We will rise, Red as the dawn. Farley's voice, my brother's words, the creed of the Scarlet Guard, comes back to me. They attacked the capital already; this could even be their next target. *I* could be a target. Farley could hold me up in another hijacked broadcast, revealing me to the world in an attempt to undermine the Silvers. "*Look at their lies, look at this lie,*" she would say, pushing my face into the camera, bleeding me red for all the world to see.

Crazier and crazier thoughts come to mind, each one more frightening and outlandish than the last. *This place is making me insane after just one day.*

"That went well," Elara says, snatching her hand away from the king when we reach the residence floors. He doesn't seem to mind in the least. "Take the girls to their rooms."

She doesn't direct her command at anyone in particular, but four Sentinels break off from the group. Their eyes glitter behind their black masks.

"I can do it," Cal and Maven say in unison. They glance at each other, startled.

Elara raises one perfect eyebrow. "That would be inappropriate."

"I'll escort Mareena, Mavey can take Evangeline," Cal offers quickly, and Maven purses his lips at the nickname. *Mavey.* Probably what Cal called him as a boy and now it's stuck, the emblem of a younger brother, always in shadow, always second.

The king shrugs. "Let them, Elara. The girls need a good night of sleep, and Sentinels would give any lady bad dreams." He chuckles, tossing a playful nod at the guards. They don't respond, silent as stone. I don't know if they're allowed to talk at all.

After a moment of tense silence, the queen turns on her heel. "Very well." Like any wife, she hates her husband for challenging her, and like any queen, she hates the power the king holds over her. *A bad combination.*

"To bed," the king says, his voice a bit more forceful and authoritative. The Sentinels stay with him, following when he goes the opposite way from his wife. I guess they don't sleep in the same room, but that's not much of a shock.

"My room is where, exactly?" Evangeline asks, glaring at Maven. The blushing queen-to-be is gone, replaced by the sharp she-devil I recognize.

He gulps at the sight of her. "Uh, this way, miss—ma'am—my lady." He holds out an arm to her, but she breezes right by him. "Good night, Cal, Mareena," Maven sighs, making a point of looking at me.

I can only nod at the retreating prince. *My betrothed.* The thought makes me want to be sick. Even though he seemed polite, nice even, he's *Silver.* And he's Elara's son, which might be even worse. His smiles and kind words cannot hide that from me. Cal's just as bad, raised to rule, to perpetuate this world of division even further.

He watches Evangeline disappear, his eyes lingering on her retreating form in a way that makes me strangely annoyed.

"You picked a real winner," I mutter once she's out of earshot.

Cal's smile dies with a downward twitch, and he starts walking toward my room, ascending the sloping spiral. My little legs fight to keep up with his long strides, but he doesn't seem to notice, lost in thought.

Finally he turns, his eyes like hot coals. "I didn't pick anything. Everyone knows that."

"At least you knew this was coming. I woke up this morning and didn't even have a boyfriend." Cal winces at my words, but I don't care. I can't handle his self-pity. "And, you know, there's the 'you're going to be king' thing. That must be a boost."

He chuckles to himself, but he's not laughing. His eyes darken, and he takes a step forward, surveying me from head to toe. Instead of looking judgmental, he seems sad. Deeply sad in the red-gold pools of his eyes, a little boy lost, looking for someone to save him.

"You're a lot like Maven," he says after a long moment that makes my heart race.

"You mean engaged to a stranger? We do have that in common."

"You're both very smart." I can't help but snort. Cal obviously doesn't know I can't get through a fourteen-year-old's math test. "You know people, you understand them, you see through them."

"I did a great job of that last night. I definitely knew you were the crown prince the whole time." I still can't believe it was only last night. *What a difference a day makes.*

"You knew I didn't belong."

His sadness is contagious, sending an ache over me. "So we've switched places."

Suddenly the palace doesn't seem so beautiful or so magnificent. The hard metal and stone is too severe, too bright, too unnatural, trapping me in. And underneath it all, the electric buzz of cameras drones on. It's not even a sound but a feeling in my skin, in my bones, in my blood. My mind reaches out to the electricity, as if on instinct. *Stop*, I tell myself. *Stop.* The hair stands up on my arm as something sizzles beneath my skin, a crackling energy I can't control. Of course it returns now, when it's the last thing I want.

But the feeling passes as quickly as it came, and the electricity shifts to a low hum again, letting the world return to normal.

"Are you okay?"

Cal stares down at me, confused.

"Sorry," I mumble, shaking my head. "Just thinking."

He nods, looking almost apologetic. "About your family?"

The words hit me like a slap. They hadn't even crossed my mind in the last few hours, and it sickens me. *A few hours of silk and royalty have already changed me.*

"I've sent a conscript release for your brothers and your friend, and an officer to your house, to tell your parents where you are," Cal continues, thinking this might calm me. "We can't tell them everything though."

I can only imagine how that went. *Oh, hello. Your daughter is a Silver now, and she's going to marry a prince. You'll never see her again, but we'll send you some money to help out. Even trade, don't you think?*

"They know you work for us and have to live here, but they still think you're a servant. For now, at least. When your life becomes more public, we'll figure out how to deal with them."

"Can I write to them at least?" Shade's letters were always a bright spot in our dark days. Maybe mine will be the same.

But Cal shakes his head. "I'm sorry, that's just not possible."

"I didn't think so."

He ushers me into my room, which quickly sparkles to life. Motion-activated lights, I think. Like back in the hallway, my senses sharpen and everything electrical becomes a burning feeling in my mind. Immediately I know there are no less than four cameras in my room and that makes me squirm.

"It's for your own protection. If anyone were to intercept the letters, to find out about you—"

"Are the cameras in here *for my own protection*?" I ask, gesturing to the walls. The cameras stab into my skin, watching every inch of me. It's maddening, and after a day like today, I don't know how much more I can take. "I'm locked in this nightmare palace, surrounded by walls and guards and people who will tear me to shreds, and I can't even get a moment's peace in my own room."

Instead of snapping back at me, Cal looks bewildered. His eyes blaze around. The walls are bare, but he must be able to sense them too. How can anyone not feel the eyes pressing down?

"Mare, there aren't any cameras in here."

I wave a hand at him, dismissive. The electrical hum still breaks against my skin. "Don't be stupid. I can feel them."

Now he truly looks lost. "Feel them? What do you mean?"

"I—" But the words die in my throat as I realize: he doesn't feel anything. He doesn't even *know* what I'm saying. How can I explain this to him, if he doesn't already know? How can I tell him I feel the energy in the air like a pulse, like another part of me? Like another sense? Would he even understand?

Would anyone?

"Is that—not normal?"

Something flickers in his eyes as he hesitates, trying to find the words to tell me I'm different. Even among the Silvers, I'm something else.

"Not to my knowledge," he finally says.

My voice sounds small, even to me. "I don't think anything about me is normal anymore."

He opens his mouth to speak but thinks better of it. There's nothing he can say to make me feel better. There's nothing he can do for me at all.

In the fairy tales, the poor girl smiles when she becomes a princess. Right now, I don't know if I'll ever smile again.

TWELVE

Your schedule is as follows:

0730—Breakfast / 0800—Protocol / 1130 Luncheon
1300—Lessons / 1800—Dinner.
Lucas will escort you to all. Schedule is not negotiable.

Her Royal Highness Queen Elara of House Merandus.

The note is short and to the point, not to mention rude. My mind swims at the thought of *five hours* of Lessons, remembering how terrible I was at school. With a groan, I throw the note back down on the nightstand. It lands in a pool of golden morning light, just to tease me.

Like yesterday, the three maids flutter in, quiet as a whisper. Fifteen minutes later, after suffering through tight leather leggings, a draping gown, and other strange, impractical clothes, we settle on the plainest thing I can find in the closet of wonders. Stretchy but sturdy black pants, a purple jacket with silver buttons, and polished gray boots.

Besides the glossy hair and the war paint, I almost look like myself again.

Lucas waits on the other side of the door, one foot tapping against the stone floor. "One minute behind schedule," he says the second I step into the hall.

"Are you going to babysit me every day or just until I learn my way around?"

He falls into step beside me, gently guiding me in the right direction. "What do you think?"

"Here's to a long and happy friendship, Officer Samos."

"Likewise, my lady."

"Don't call me that."

"Whatever you say, my lady."

Next to last night's feast, breakfast looks dull in comparison. The "smaller" dining room is still large, with a high ceiling and a view of the river, but the long table is only set for three. Unfortunately for me, the other two happen to be Elara and Evangeline. They're already halfway through their bowls of fruit by the time I shuffle in. Elara barely glances at me, but Evangeline's sharp-eyed stare is enough for both of them. With the sun bouncing off her metal getup, she looks like a blinding star.

"You should eat quickly," the queen says without looking up. "Lady Blonos does not tolerate tardiness."

Across from me, Evangeline laughs into her hand. "You're still taking Protocol?"

"You mean you aren't?" My heart leaps at the prospect of not having to sit through classes with her. "Excellent."

Evangeline scoffs at me, brushing off the insult. "Only children take Protocol."

To my surprise, the queen takes my side. "Lady Mareena has grown up under terrible circumstances. She knows nothing of our ways, of the expectations she must fulfill now. Surely you understand her needs, Evangeline?"

The reprimand is calm, quiet, and threatening. Evangeline's smile drops, and she nods, not daring to meet the queen's eye.

"Luncheon today will be on the Glass Terrace, with the ladies of Queenstrial and their mothers. Try not to gloat," Elara adds, though I never would. Evangeline, on the other hand, blushes white.

"They're still here?" I hear myself ask. "Even after—not being chosen?"

Elara nods. "Our guests will be here for the coming weeks, to properly honor the prince and his betrothed. They won't leave until after the Parting Ball."

My heart plummets in my chest until it bounces around my toes. So more nights like last night, with the pressing crowd and a thousand eyes. They'll ask questions too, questions I'll have to answer. "Lovely."

"And after the ball, we leave with them," Elara continues, twisting the knife. "To return to the capital."

The capital. *Archeon*. I know the royal family goes back to Whitefire Palace at the end of every summer, and now I'm going too. I'll have to leave, and this world I can't understand will become my only reality. I'll never be able to go home. *You knew this*, I tell myself, *you agreed to this*. But it doesn't hurt any less.

When I escape back into the hallway, Lucas ushers me down the passage. As we walk, he smirks at me. "You have watermelon on your face."

"Of course I do," I snap, wiping at my mouth with my sleeve.

"Lady Blonos is just through here," he says, gesturing to the end of the hall.

"What's the story about her? Can she fly or make flowers grow out of her ears?"

Lucas cracks a smile, humoring me. "Not quite. She's a healer. Now, there's two kinds of healers: skin healers and blood healers. All of House Blonos are blood healers, meaning they can heal themselves. I could throw her off the top of the Hall and she'd walk away without a scratch."

I'd like to see that tested, but I don't say so out loud. "I've never heard of a blood healer before."

"You wouldn't have, since they're not allowed to fight in the arenas. There's simply no point in them doing it."

Wow. Yet another Silver of epic proportions. "So if I have, um, an episode—"

Lucas softens, understanding what I'm trying to say. "She'll be just fine. The curtains, on the other hand . . ."

"That's why they gave her to me. Because I'm dangerous."

But Lucas shakes his head. "Lady Titanos, they gave her to you because your posture is terrible and you eat like a dog. Bess Blonos is going to teach you how to be a *lady* and if you light her up a couple of times, no one will blame you."

How to be a lady . . . this will be awful.

He raps his knuckles on the door, making me jump. It swings open on silent, smooth hinges, revealing a sunlit room.

"I'll be back to bring you to lunch," he says. I don't move, my feet planted, but Lucas nudges me into the dreaded room.

The door swings behind me, this time shutting out the hall and anything that might calm me down. The room is fine but plain with a wall of windows, and totally empty. The buzzing of cameras, lights, *electricity*, is vibrantly strong in here, almost burning the air around me with its energy. I'm sure the queen is watching, ready to laugh at my attempts to be proper.

"Hello?" I say, expecting a response, but nothing comes

I cross to the windows, looking out on the courtyard. Instead of another pretty garden, I'm surprised to find this window doesn't face outside at all but down into a gigantic white room.

The floor is several stories below me, and a track rings the outer edge. In the center, a strange contraption moves and turns, spinning round and round with outstretched metal arms. Men and women, all in uniform, dodge the spinning machine. It picks up speed, twirling faster, until only two remain. They're quick, dipping and dodging with grace and speed. At every turn the machine accelerates, until it finally slows, shutting down. *They've beaten it.*

This must be some kind of training, for Security or Sentinels.

But when the two trainees move on to target practice, I realize they aren't Security at all. The pair of them shoot bright red fireballs into the air, exploding targets as they rise and fall. Each one is a perfect shot, and even from up here, I recognize their smiling faces. *Cal and Maven.*

So this is what they do during the day. Not learning to rule, to be a king, or even a proper lord, but to train for war. Cal and Maven are deadly creatures, soldiers. But their battle isn't just on the lines. It's here, in a palace, on the broadcasts, in the heart of every person they rule. They will rule, not just by right of a crown but by might. *Strength and power.* It's all the Silvers respect, and it's all it takes to keep the rest of us slaves.

Evangeline steps up next. When the targets fly, she throws out a fan of sharp silver metal darts to take down each one in turn. No wonder she laughed at me for Protocol. While I'm in here learning how to eat properly, she's training to kill.

"Enjoying the show, Lady Mareena?" a voice crows behind me. I turn around, my nerves tingling a bit. What I see doesn't do anything to calm me.

Lady Blonos is a horrifying sight, and it takes all of my manners to keep my jaw from dropping. *Blood healer, able to heal herself.* I understand now what that means.

She must be over fifty, older than my mother, but her skin is smooth and shockingly tight over her bones. Her hair is perfectly white, slicked back, and her eyebrows seem fixed in a constant state of shock, arched on her unwrinkled forehead. Everything about her is wrong, from her too-full lips to the sharp, unnatural slope of her nose. Only her deep gray eyes look alive. The rest, I realize, is *fake*. Somehow she was able to heal or change herself into this monstrous thing in an attempt to look younger, prettier, *better*.

"Sorry," I finally manage, "I came in, and you weren't—"

"I observed," she clips, already hating me. "You stand like a tree in a storm."

She seizes my shoulders and pulls them back, forcing me to stand up straight. "My name is Bess Blonos, and I'm going to attempt to make you a lady. You're going to be a princess one day, and we can't have you acting like a savage, can we?"

Savage. For a brief, shining moment, I think about spitting in silly Lady Blonos's face. *But what would that cost me? What would that accomplish? And it would only prove her right.* Worst of all, I realize I need her. Her training will keep me from slipping and, most important, keep me *alive*.

"No," a hollow shell of my voice answers. "We can't have that."

★ ★ ★

Exactly three and a half hours later, Blonos releases me from her clutches and back into Lucas's care. My back aches from the posture lessons about how to sit, stand, walk, and even sleep (*on your back, arms at your sides, always still*), but it's nothing compared to the mental exercise she put me through. She drilled the rules of court into my head, filling me with names, protocols, and etiquette. In the last few hours I received a crash course in anything and everything I'm supposed to know. The hierarchy among the High Houses is slowly coming into focus, but I'm sure I'll mess up something anyway. We only scratched the surface of Protocol, but now I can go to the queen's stupid function with at least some idea of how to act.

The Glass Terrace is relatively close by, only a floor down and a hallway over, so I don't get much time to collect myself before facing Elara and Evangeline again. This time, when I step through the doorway, I'm greeted by invigorating fresh air. I'm outside for the first time since I became Mareena, but now, with the wind in my lungs and the sun on my face, I feel more like Mare again. If I close my eyes, I can pretend none of this ever happened. *But it did.*

The Glass Terrace is as ornate as Blonos's classroom was bare and lives up to its name. A glass canopy, supported by clear, artfully cut columns, stretches over us, refracting the sun into a million dancing colors to match the women milling about. It's beautiful in an artificial way, like everything else in this Silver world.

Before I have a chance to take a breath, a pair of girls steps in front of me. Their smiles are fake and cold, just like their eyes. Judging by the colors of their gowns (dark blue and red on one, solid black on the other), they belong to House Iral and House Haven. *Silks and shadows*, I remember, thinking back to Blonos's lessons on abilities.

"Lady Mareena," they say in unison, bowing stiffly. I do the same, inclining my head the way Lady Blonos showed me.

"I'm Sonya of House Iral," the first says, tossing her head proudly. Her movements are lithe and catlike. *Silks are quick and quiet, perfectly balanced and agile.*

"And I'm Elane of House Haven," the other adds, her voice barely a whisper. While the Iral girl is dark, with deeply tanned skin and black hair, Elane is pale, with glossy red locks. The dancing sunlight speckles her skin in a perfect halo, making her look flawless. *Shadow, bender of light.* "We wanted to welcome you."

But their pointed smiles and narrowed eyes don't look welcoming at all.

"Thank you. That's very kind." I clear my throat, trying to sound normal, and the girls don't miss the action, exchanging glances. "You also participated in Queenstrial?" I say quickly, hoping to distract them from my terrible social graces.

This only seems to incense them. Sonya crosses her arms, showing sharp nails the color of iron. "We did. Obviously we were not so lucky as you or Evangeline."

"Sorry—," comes out before I can stop it. *Mareena would not apologize.* "I mean, you know I had no intention of—"

"Your intentions remain to be seen," Sonya purrs, looking more like a cat with every passing second. When she turns, snapping her fingers in a way that makes her nails slice along each other, I flinch. "Grandmother, come meet Lady Mareena."

Grandmother. I almost breathe a sigh of relief, expecting a kindly old woman to come waddling over and save me from these biting girls. But I'm sorely mistaken.

Instead of a wizened crone, I'm met with a formidable woman

made of steel and shadow. Like Sonya, she has coffee-colored skin and black hair, though hers is shot with streaks of white. Despite her age, her brown eyes spark with life.

"Lady Mareena, this is my grandmother Lady Ara, the head of House Iral." Sonya explains with a pointed smirk. The older woman eyes me, and her gaze is worse than any camera, piercing straight through me. "Perhaps you know her as the Panther?"

"The Panther? I don't—"

But Sonya keeps talking, enjoying watching me squirm. "Many years ago, when the war slowed, intelligence agents became more important than soldiers. The Panther was the greatest of them all."

A spy. I'm standing in front of a spy.

I force myself to smile, if only to try and hide my fear. Sweat breaks out on my palms, and I hope I don't have to shake any hands. "A pleasure to meet you, my lady."

Ara simply nods. "I knew your father, Mareena. And your mother."

"I miss them terribly," I reply, saying the words to placate her.

But the Panther looks perplexed, tipping her head to the side. For a second, I can see thousands of secrets, hard-won in the shadows of war, reflecting in her eyes. "You remember them?" she asks, prodding at my lie.

My voice catches, but I have to keep talking, keep lying. "I don't, but I miss having parents." Mom and Dad flash in my mind, but I push them away. My Red past is the last thing I should think about. "I wish they were here to help me understand all this."

"Hmm," she says, surveying me again. Her suspicion makes me want to leap off the balcony. "Your father had blue eyes, as did your mother."

And my eyes are brown. "I am different in many ways, most I don't even understand yet," is all I can manage to say, hoping that explanation will be enough.

For once, the queen's voice is my savior. "Shall we sit, ladies?" she says, echoing over the crowd. It's enough to pull me away from Ara, Sonya, and the quiet Elane, to a seat where I can breathe a little sigh to myself.

Halfway to Lessons, I begin to feel calm again. I addressed everyone properly and only spoke as much as I had to, as instructed. Evangeline talked enough for both of us, regaling the women with her "undying love" for Cal and the honor she felt at being chosen. I thought the Queenstrial girls would band together and kill her, but they didn't, to my annoyance. Only the Iral grandmother and Sonya seemed to even care that I was there, though they didn't push their interrogation any further. *But they certainly will.*

When Maven appears around the corner, I'm so proud of my survival at lunch that I'm not even annoyed by his presence. In fact, I feel strangely relieved and let a bit of my cold act drop. He grins, coming closer with a few long strides.

"Still alive?" he asks. Compared to the Irals, he's like a friendly puppy.

I can't help but smile. "You should send Lady Iral back to the Lakelanders. She'll make them surrender in a week."

He forces a hollow laugh. "She's a battle-ax that one. Can't seem to understand she's not in the war any longer. Did she question you at all?"

"More like interrogate. I think she's angry I beat out her granddaughter."

Fear flickers in his eyes, and I understand it. *If the Panther is sniffing around my trail . . .* "She shouldn't bother you like that," he mutters. "I'll let my mother know, and she'll take care of it."

As much as I don't want his help, I don't see any other way around it. A woman like Ara could easily find the cracks in my story, and then I'll be truly finished. "Thanks, that would—that would be very helpful."

Maven's dress uniform is gone, replaced by casual clothes built for form and function. It calms me a little, to see at least someone looking so informal. But I can't let anything about him soothe me. *He's one of them. I can't forget that.*

"Are you done for the day?" he says, his face clearing to reveal an eager smile. "I could show you around if you want."

"No." The word comes out quickly, and his smile fades. His frown unsettles me as much as his smile. "I have Lessons next," I add, hoping to soften the blow. Why I care about his feelings, I don't exactly know. "Your mother loves her schedules."

He nods, looking a little better. "She does indeed. Well, I won't keep you."

He takes my hand gently. The cold I felt on his skin before is gone, replaced with a delightful heat. Before I get a chance to pull away, he leaves me standing there alone.

Lucas gives me a moment to collect myself before noting, "You know, we'd get there much faster if you actually *moved*."

"Shut up, Lucas."

THIRTEEN

My next instructor waits for me in a room cluttered from floor to ceiling with more books than I've ever seen, more books than I ever thought *existed*. They look old and completely priceless. Despite my aversion to school and books of any kind, I feel a pull to them. But the titles and pages are written in a language I don't understand, a jumble of symbols I could never hope to decipher.

Just as intriguing as the books are the maps along the wall, of the kingdom and other lands, old and new. Framed against the far wall, behind a pane of glass, is a vast, colorful map pieced together from separate sheets of paper. It's at least twice as tall as me and dominates the room. Faded and ripped, it's a tangled knot of red lines and blue coasts, green forests and yellow cities. This is the old world, the before world, with old names and old borders we no longer have any use for.

"It's strange to look at the world as it once was," the instructor says, appearing out of the book stacks. His yellow robes, stained and faded by age, make him look like a human piece of paper. "Can you find where we are?"

The sheer size of the map makes me gulp, but, like everything else, I'm sure this is a test. "I can try."

Norta is the northeast. The Stilts is on the Capital River, and the river goes to the sea. After a minute of pained searching, I finally find the river and the inlet near my village. "There," I say, pointing just north, where I suppose Summerton might be.

He nods, happy to know I'm not a total fool. "Do you recognize anything else?"

But like the books, the map is written in the unknown language. "I can't read it."

"I didn't ask if you could read it," he replies, still pleasant. "Besides, words can lie. See beyond them."

With a shrug, I force myself to look again. I was never a good student in school, and this man is going to find that out soon enough. But to my surprise, I like this game. Searching the map, looking for features I recognize. "That might be Harbor Bay," I finally murmur, circling the area around a hooked cape.

"Correct," he says, his face folding into a smile. The wrinkles around his eyes deepen with the action, showing his age. "This is Delphie now," he adds, pointing to a city farther south. "And Archeon is here."

He puts his finger over the Capital River, a few miles north of what looks like the largest city on the map, in the entire country of the before world. *The Ruins.* I've heard the name, in whispers between the older kids, and from my brother Shade. *The Ash City, the Wreckage,* he called it. A tremor runs down my spine at the thought of such a place, still covered in smoke and shadow from a war more than a thousand years ago. *Will this world ever be like that, if our war doesn't end?*

The instructor stands back to let me think. He has a very strange idea of teaching; it'll probably end with a four-hour game of me staring at a wall.

But suddenly, I'm very aware of the buzz in this room. Or lack thereof. This entire day I've felt the electrical weight of cameras, so much that I've stopped noticing. Until now, when I don't feel it at all. *It's gone.* I can feel the lights still pulsing with electricity, but no cameras. No eyes. Elara cannot see me here.

"Why isn't anyone watching us?"

He only blinks at me. "So there is a difference," he mutters. What that means I don't know, and it infuriates me.

"*Why?*"

"Mare, I'm here to teach you your histories, to teach you how to be Silver and how to be, ah, *useful*," he says, his expression souring.

I stare at him, confused. Cold fear bleeds through me. "My name is Mareena."

But he only waves a hand, brushing aside my feeble declaration. "I'm also going to try to understand exactly how *you* came to be and how your abilities work."

"My abilities came to be because—because I'm a Silver. My parents' abilities mixed—my father was an oblivion and my mother a storm." I stutter through the explanation Elara fed me, trying to make him understand. "I'm a Silver, sir."

To my horror, he shakes his head. "No you are not, Mare Barrow, and you must never forget it."

He knows. I'm finished. It's all over. I should beg, plead for him to keep my secret, but the words stick in my throat. The end is coming, and I can't even open my mouth to stop it.

"There's no need for that," he continues, noting my fear. "I have no plans of alerting anyone to your *heritage*."

The relief I feel is short-lived, shifting into another kind of fear. "Why? What do you want from me?"

"I am, above all things, a curious man. And when you entered Queenstrial a Red servant and ran out some long-lost Silver lady, I have to say I was quite curious."

"Is that why there aren't any cameras in here?" I bristle, backing away from him. My fists clench, and I wish the lightning would come to protect me from this man. "So there's no record of you *examining* me?"

"There are no cameras in here because I have the power to turn them off."

Hope sparks in me, like light in absolute darkness. "What is your power?" I ask shakily. *Maybe he's like me.*

"Mare, when a Silver says 'power,' they mean *might, strength*. 'Ability,' on the other hand, refers to all the silly little things we can do." *Silly little things*. Like break a man in two or drown him in the town square. "I mean that my sister was queen once, and that still counts for something around here."

"Lady Blonos didn't teach me that."

He chuckles to himself. "That's because Lady Blonos is teaching you nonsense. I will never do that."

"So, if the queen *was* your sister, then you're—"

"Julian Jacos, at your service." He sweeps into a comically low bow. "Head of House Jacos, heir to nothing more than a few old books. My sister was the late queen Coriane, and Prince Tiberias the Seventh, Cal as we all call him, is my nephew."

Now that he says it, I can see the resemblance. Cal's coloring is his father's, but the easy expression, the warmth behind his eyes—those must come from his mother.

"So, you're not going to turn me into some science experiment for the queen?" I ask, still wary.

Instead of looking offended, Julian laughs aloud. "My dear, the queen would like nothing more than for you to disappear. Discovering what you are, helping you understand it, is the *last* thing she wants."

"But you're going to do it anyway?"

Something flashes in his eyes, something like anger. "The queen's reach is not so long as she wants you to think. I want to know what you are, and I'm sure you do too."

As afraid as I was a moment ago, that's how intrigued I am now. "I do."

"That's what I thought," he says, smiling at me over a stack of books. "I'm sorry to say I must also do what was asked, to prepare you for the day you step forward."

My face falls, remembering what Cal explained in the throne room. *You are their champion. A Silver raised Red.* "They want to use me to stop a rebellion. Somehow."

"Yes, my dear brother-in-law and his queen believe you can do so, if used appropriately." Bitterness drips from his every word.

"It's a stupid idea and impossible. I won't be able to do anything, and then . . ." My voice trails away. *Then they'll kill me.*

Julian follows my train of thought. "You're wrong, Mare. You don't understand the power you have now, how much you could control." He clasps his hands behind his back, oddly tight. "The Scarlet Guard are too drastic for most, too much too fast. But you are the controlled change, the kind people can trust. You are the slow burn that will quench a revolution with a few speeches and smiles. You can speak to the Reds, tell them how noble, how benevolent, how *right* the king and his Silvers are. You can talk your people back into their chains.

Even the Silvers who question the king, the ones who have doubts, can be convinced by *you*. And the world will stay the same."

To my surprise, Julian seems disheartened by this. Without the buzzing cameras, I forget myself and my face curls into a sneer. "And you don't want that? You're a Silver, you should *hate* the Scarlet Guard—and me."

"Thinking all Silvers are evil is just as wrong as thinking all Reds are inferior," he says, his voice grave. "What my people are doing to you and yours is wrong to the deepest levels of humanity. Oppressing you, trapping you in an endless cycle of poverty and death, just because we think you are *different* from us? That is not *right*. And as any student of history can tell you, it will end poorly."

"But we are different." One day in this world taught me that. "We're not equal."

Julian stoops, his eyes boring into mine. "I'm looking at proof you are wrong."

You're looking at a freak, Julian.

"Will you let me prove you wrong, Mare?"

"What good will it do? Nothing will change."

Julian sighs, exasperated. He runs a hand through his thinning chestnut hair. "For hundreds of years the Silvers have walked the earth as living gods and the Reds have been slaves at their feet, *until you*. If that isn't change, I don't know what is."

He can help me survive. Better yet, he might even help me live.

"So what do we do?"

My days take on a rhythm, always the same schedule. Protocol in the morning, Lessons in the afternoon, while Elara parades me at lunches and dinners in between. The Panther and Sonya still seem wary of me but haven't said anything since the luncheon. Maven's help seems to have worked, as much as I hate to admit it.

At the next large gathering, this time in the queen's personal dining hall, the Irals ignore me completely. Despite my Protocol lessons, luncheon is still overwhelming as I try to remember what I've been taught. *Osanos, nymphs, blue and green. Welle, greenwardens, green and gold. Lerolan, oblivions, orange and red. Rhambos and Tyros and Nornus and Iral and many more.* How anyone keeps track of this, I'll never know.

As usual, I'm seated next to Evangeline. I'm painfully aware of the many metal utensils on the table, all lethal weapons in Evangeline's cruel hand. Every time she lifts her knife to cut her food, my body tenses, waiting for the blow. Elara knows what I'm thinking, as usual, but carries on through her meal with a smile. That might be worse than Evangeline's torture, to know she takes pleasure in watching our silent war.

"And how do you like the Hall of the Sun, Lady Titanos?" the girl across from me asks—*Atara, House Viper, green and black. The animos who killed the doves.* "I assume it's no comparison to the—the *village* you lived in before." She says the word *village* like a curse, and I don't miss her smirk.

The other women laugh with her, a few whispering in scandalized voices.

It takes me a minute to respond as I try to keep my blood from boiling. "The Hall and Summerton are very different from what I'm used to," I force out.

"Obviously," another woman says, leaning forward to join the conversation. A Welle, judging by her green-and-gold tunic. "I took a tour of the Capital Valley once, and I must say, the Red villages are simply deplorable. They don't even have proper roads."

We can barely feed ourselves, let alone pave streets. My jaw tightens until I think my teeth might shatter. I try to smile but instead end up grimacing as the other women voice their agreement.

"And the Reds, well, I suppose it's the best they can do with what they have," the Welle continues, wrinkling her nose at the thought. "They're suited to such lives."

"It's not our fault they were born to serve," a brown-robed Rhambos says airily, as if she's talking about the weather or the food. "It's simply nature."

Anger curls through me, but one glance from the queen tells me I cannot act on it. Instead, I must do my duty. I must lie. "It is indeed," I hear myself say. Under the table, my hands clench, and I think my heart might be breaking.

All over the table, the women listen attentively. Many smile, more nod as I reassert their terrible beliefs about my people. Their faces make me want to scream.

"Of course," I continue, unable to stop myself. "Being forced to live such lives, with no respite, no reprieve, and no escape, would make servants of anyone."

The few smiles fade, twitching into bewilderment.

"Lady Titanos is to have the best tutors and best help to make sure she adjusts properly," Elara says quickly, cutting me off. "She's already begun with Lady Blonos."

The women mutter appreciatively while the girls exchange eye rolls. It's enough time to recover, to reclaim the self-control I need to survive the meal.

"What does His Royal Highness intend to do about the rebels?" a woman asks, her gruff voice sending a shock of silence over lunch, drawing focus away from me.

Every eye at the table turns to the speaker, a woman in military uniform. A few other ladies wear uniforms as well, but hers shines with the most medals and ribbons. The ugly scar down her freckled face says she may actually have earned them. Here in a palace, it's easy to forget there's a war going on, but the haunted look in her eye says she will not, she *cannot*, forget.

Queen Elara puts down her spoon with practiced grace and an equally practiced smile. "Colonel Macanthos, I would hardly call them rebels—"

"And that's only the attack they've claimed," the colonel fires back, cutting off the queen. "What about the explosion in Harbor Bay, or the airfield in Delphie for that matter? Three airjets destroyed, and two more *stolen* from one of our own bases!"

My eyes widen, and I can't help but gasp with a few ladies. *More attacks?* But while the others look frightened, hands pressed to their mouths, I have to fight the urge to smile. *Farley has been busy.*

"Are you an engineer, Colonel?" Elara's voice is sharp, cold, and final. She doesn't give Macanthos a chance to shake her head. "Then you wouldn't understand how a gas leak in the Bay was at fault for the explosion. And remind me, do you command aerial troops? Oh no, I'm so sorry, your specialty lies with ground forces. The airfield incident was a training exercise overseen by Lord General Laris himself. He has personally assured His Highness of the utmost safety of the Delphie base."

In a fair fight, Macanthos could probably tear Elara apart with her bare hands. But instead, Elara tore the colonel apart with nothing but words. And she's not even finished. Julian's words echo in my head—*words can lie.*

"Their goal is to harm innocent civilians, Silver and Red, to incite fear and hysteria. They are small, contained, and cowardly, hiding from my husband's justice. To call every mishap and misunderstanding in this kingdom the work of such evil only furthers their efforts to terrorize the rest of us. Do not give these monsters the satisfaction of that."

A few women at the table clap and nod, agreeing with the queen's sweeping lie. Evangeline joins in, and the action quickly spreads, until only the colonel and I remain silent. I can tell she doesn't believe anything the queen says, but there's no way to call the queen a liar. Not here, not in her arena.

As much as I want to stay still, I know I can't. I'm Mareena, not Mare, and I have to support my queen and her wretched words. My hands come together, clapping for Elara's lie, as the scolded colonel bows her head.

Even though I'm constantly surrounded by servants and Silvers, loneliness sets in. I don't see Cal much, what with his busy schedule of training, training, and more training. He even gets to leave the Hall, going to address troops at a nearby base or accompanying his father on state business. I suppose I could talk to Maven, with his blue eyes and half smirk, but I'm still wary of him. Luckily we're never truly left alone. It's a silly court tradition, to keep noble boys and girls from being *tempted*, as Lady Blonos put it, but I doubt it'll ever apply to me.

Truthfully, half the time I forget I'm supposed to marry him one day. The idea of Maven being my husband doesn't seem real. We're not even friends, let alone partners. As nice as he is, my instincts tell me not to turn my back on Elara's son, that he's hiding something. What that might be, I don't know.

Julian's teachings make it all bearable; the education I once dreaded is now a bright spot in my sea of darkness. Without the cameras and Elara's eyes, we can spend our time discovering what I really am. But the going is slow, frustrating us both.

"I think I know what your problem is," Julian says at the end of my first week. I'm standing a few yards away, arms outstretched, looking like the usual fool. There's a strange electrical contraption at my feet, occasionally spitting sparks. Julian wants me to harness it, to use it, but once again, I've failed to produce the lightning that got me into this mess in the first place.

"Maybe I have to be in mortal danger," I huff. "Should we ask for Lucas's gun?"

Usually Julian laughs at my jokes, but right now he's too busy thinking.

"You're like a child," he finally says. I wrinkle my nose at the insult, but he continues anyway. "This is how children are at first, when they can't control themselves. Their abilities present in times of stress or fear, until they learn to harness those emotions and use them to their advantage. There's a trigger, and you need to find yours."

I remember how I felt in the Spiral Garden, falling to what I thought was my doom. But it wasn't fear running through my veins as I collided with the lightning shield—it was peace. It was *knowing* that my end had come and accepting there was nothing I could do to stop it—it was letting go.

"It's worth a try, at least," Julian prods.

With a groan, I face the wall again. Julian lined it with some stone bookshelves, all empty of course, so I have something to aim at. Out of the corner of my eye, I see him back away, watching me all the time.

Let go. Let yourself go, the voice in my head whispers. My eyes slide closed as I focus, letting my thoughts fall away so that my mind can reach out, feeling for the electricity it craves to touch. The ripple of energy, alive beneath my skin, moves over me again until it sings in every muscle and nerve. That's usually where it stops, just on the edge of feeling, but not this time. Instead of trying to hold on, to push myself into this force, I let go. And I fall into what I can't explain, into a sensation that is everything and nothing, light and dark, hot and cold, alive and dead. Soon the power is the only thing in my head, blotting out all my ghosts and memories. Even Julian and the books cease to exist. My mind is clear, a black void humming with force. Now when I push at the sensation, it doesn't disappear and it moves within me, from my eyes to the tips of my fingers. To my left, Julian gasps aloud.

My eyes open to see purple-white sparks jumping from the contraption to my fingers, like electricity between wires.

For once, Julian has nothing to say. And neither do I.

I don't want to move, afraid that any small change might make the lightning disappear. But it doesn't fade. It remains, jumping and twisting in my hand like a kitten with a ball of yarn. It seems just as harmless, but I remember what I almost did to Evangeline. *This power can destroy if I let it.*

"Try to move it," Julian breathes, watching me with wide, excited eyes.

Something tells me this lightning will obey my wishes. It's part of me, a piece of my soul alive in the world.

My fist clenches into a tight ball, and the sparks react to my straining muscles, becoming larger and brighter and faster. They eat away at the sleeve of my shirt, burning through the fabric in seconds. Like a child throwing a ball, I whip my arm toward the stone shelves, releasing my fist at the last moment. The lightning flies through the air in a circle of bright sparks, colliding with the bookshelves.

The resulting *boom* makes me scream and fall back into a stack of books. As I tumble to the ground, heart racing in my chest, the solid stone bookshelf collapses on itself in a cloud of thick dust. Sparks flash over the rubble for a moment before disappearing, leaving nothing but ruins behind.

"Sorry about the shelf," I say from beneath a pile of fallen books. My sleeve still smokes in a ruin of thread, but it's nothing compared to the buzz in my hand. My nerves sing, tingling with power—that felt *good*.

Julian's shadow moves through the cloudy air, a laugh resounding deep in his chest as he examines my handiwork. His white grin glows through the dust.

"We're going to need a bigger classroom."

He's not wrong. We're forced to find newer and bigger rooms to practice in each day, until we finally find a spot in the underground levels a week later. Here the walls are metal and concrete, stronger than the decorative stone and wood of the upper floors. My aim is dismal to say the least, and Julian is very careful to steer clear of my practicing, but it becomes easier and easier for me to call up the lightning.

Julian takes notes the whole time, jotting down everything from my heartbeat to the heat of a recently electrified cup. Each new note brings another puzzled but happy smile to his face, though he doesn't tell me why. I doubt I'd understand even if he did.

"Fascinating," he murmurs, reading something off another metal contraption I can't name. He says it measures electrical energy, but how I don't know.

I brush my hands together, watching them "power down," as Julian calls it. My sleeves remain intact this time, thanks to my new clothing.

It's fireproof fabric, like what Cal and Maven wear, though I suppose mine should be called shockproof. "What's fascinating?"

He hesitates, like he doesn't want to tell me, like he *shouldn't* tell me, but finally shrugs. "Before you powered up and fried that poor statue"—he gestures to the smoking pile of rubble that was once a bust of some king—"I measured the amount of electricity in this room. From the lights, the wiring, that sort of thing. And now I just measured you."

"And?"

"You gave off *twice* what I recorded before," he says proudly, but I don't see why it matters at all. With a quick dip, he switches off the spark box, as I've taken to calling it. I can feel the electricity in it die away. "Try again."

Huffing, I focus again. After a moment of concentration, my sparks return, just as strong as before. But this time they come from within me.

Julian's grin splits his face from ear to ear.

"So . . . ?"

"So this confirms my suspicions." Sometimes I forget Julian is a scholar and a scientist. But he's always quick to remind me. "You produced electrical energy."

Now I'm really confused. "Right. That's my *ability*, Julian."

"No, I thought your ability was the power to manipulate, not create," he says, his voice dropping gravely. "No one can *create*, Mare."

"But that doesn't make sense. The nymphs—"

"Manipulate water that already exists. They can't use what isn't there."

"Well, what about Cal? Maven? I don't see many raging infernos around for them to play with."

Julian smiles, shaking his head. "You've seen their bracelets, yes?"

"They always wear them."

"The bracelets make sparks, little tiny flames for the boys to control. Without something to start the fire, they are powerless. All elementals are the same, manipulating metal or water or plant life that already exists. They're only as strong as their surroundings. Not like you, Mare."

Not like me. I'm not like anyone. "So what does this mean?"

"I'm not quite sure. You are something else entirely. Not Red, not Silver. Something else. Something *more*."

"Something different." I expected Julian's tests to bring me closer to some kind of answer, but instead they only raise more questions. "What am I, Julian? What's wrong with me?"

Suddenly it's very difficult to breathe, and my eyes swim. I have to blink back hot tears, trying to hide them from Julian. It's all catching up to me, I think. Lessons, Protocol, this place where I can't trust anyone, where I'm not even myself. It's suffocating. I want to scream, but I know I can't.

"There's nothing *wrong* with being different," I hear Julian say, but the words are just an echo. My own thoughts, memories of home, of Gisa and Kilorn, drown him out.

"Mare?" He takes a step toward me, his face a picture of kindness—but he keeps me at an arm's length. Not for my sake—his own. To protect himself from me. With a gasp, I realize the sparks have returned, running up my forearms now, threatening to engulf me in a raging bright storm. "Mare, focus on me. Mare, control it."

He speaks softly, calmly, but with steady force. He even looks *frightened* of me.

"*Control*, Mare."

But I can't control anything. Not my future, not my thoughts, not even this *ability* that is the root of all my troubles.

There is one thing I can still control though, for now, at least. My feet.

Like the wretched coward that I am, I run.

The halls are empty as I tear through them, but the invisible weight of a thousand cameras presses down on me. I don't have much time until Lucas or, worse, the Sentinels, find me. I just need to breathe. I just need to see the sky above me, not glass.

I'm standing on the balcony a full ten seconds before I realize it's raining, washing me clean of my boiling anger. The sparks are gone, replaced by fierce, ugly tears that track down my face. Thunder rumbles somewhere far off, and the air is warm. But the humid temperature is gone. The heat has broken, and summer will soon be over. Time is passing. My life is moving on, no matter how much I want it to stay the same.

When a strong hand closes around my arm, I almost scream. Two Sentinels stand over me, their eyes dark behind their masks. Both are twice my size and heartless, trying to drag me back into my prison.

"My lady," one of them growls, but it doesn't sound respectful at all.

"Let me go." The command is weak, almost a whisper. I gulp down air like I'm drowning. "Just give me a few minutes, please—"

But I'm not their master. They don't answer to me. No one does.

"You heard my bride," another voice says. His words are firm and hard, the voice of royalty. *Maven.* "Let her go."

When the prince steps out onto the balcony, I can't help but feel a rush of relief. The Sentinels straighten at his presence, both inclining their heads in his direction. The one holding me speaks up. "We must keep the Lady Titanos to her schedule," he says, but he loosens his grip. "It's orders, sir."

"Then you have new orders," Maven replies, his voice like ice. "I will accompany Mareena back to her lessons."

"Very well, sir," the Sentinels say in unison, unable to refuse a prince.

When they stomp away, their flaming cloaks dripping rain, I sigh out loud. I didn't realize it before, but my hands are shaking, and I have to clench my fists to hide the tremors. But Maven is nothing if not polite and pretends not to notice.

"We have working showers *inside*, you know."

My hands wipe at my eyes, though my tears are long lost in the rain, leaving behind only an embarrassingly runny nose and some black makeup. Thankfully, my silver powder holds. It's made of stronger stuff than I am.

"First rain of the season," I manage, forcing myself to sound normal. "Had to see it for myself."

"Right," he says, moving to stand next to me. I turn my head, hoping to hide my face for just a little bit longer. "I understand, you know."

Do you, Prince? Do you understand what it's like to be taken away from everything you love, forced to be something else? To lie every minute of every day for the rest of your life? To know there's something wrong with you?

I don't have the strength to deal with his knowing smiles. "You can stop pretending to know anything about me or my feelings."

His expression sours at my tone, his mouth twisting into a grimace. "You think I don't know how difficult it is to be here? With these *people*?" He casts a glance over his shoulder like he's worried someone might hear. But there's no one listening except the rain and thunder. "I can't say what I want, do what I want—with my mother around I can barely even *think* what I want. And my brother—!"

"What about your brother?"

The words stick in his mouth. He doesn't want to say them, but he feels them all the same. "He's strong, he's talented, he's powerful—and I'm his shadow. The shadow of the flame."

Slowly, he exhales, and I realize the air around us is strangely hot. "Sorry," he adds, taking a step away, letting the air cool. Before my eyes, he melts back into the Silver prince more suited to banquets and dress uniforms. "I shouldn't have said that."

"It's fine," I murmur. "It's nice to hear that I'm not completely alone in feeling out of place."

"That's something you should know about us Silvers. We're always alone. In here, and here," he says, pointing between his head and his heart. "It keeps you strong."

Lightning cracks overhead, illuminating his blue eyes until they seem to glow. "That's just stupid," I tell him, and he chuckles darkly.

"You better hide that heart of yours, Lady Titanos. It won't lead you anywhere you want to go."

The words make me shiver. Finally I remember the rain and the mess I must look like. "I should get back to my lessons," I mutter, fully intending to leave him on the balcony. Instead, he catches my arm.

"I think I can help you with your problem."

I quirk an eyebrow at him. "What problem?"

"You don't seem like the type of girl to weep at the drop of a hat. You're homesick." He holds up a hand before I can protest. "I can fix that."

FOURTEEN

Security patrols my hallway in roving pairs, but with Maven on my arm, they don't stop me. Even though it's night, long past when I should be in bed, no one says a word. No one crosses a prince. Where he's leading now, I don't know, but he promised to get me there. *Home.*

He's quiet but determined, fighting a small smile. I can't help but beam at him. *Maybe he isn't so bad.* But he stops us long before I assume he should—we never even leave the residence floors.

"Here we are," he says, and raps on the door.

It swings open after a moment, revealing Cal. His appearance takes me back a step. His chest is bare, while the rest of his strange armor hangs off him. Metal plates woven into fabric, some of it dented. I don't miss the purple bruise above his heart, or the faint stubble on his cheeks. It's the first time I've seen him in over a week, and I've caught him at a bad moment, obviously. He doesn't notice me at first; he's focused on removing more of his armor. It makes me gulp.

"Got the board set, Mavey—," he begins, but stops when he looks up to see me standing with his brother. "Mare, how can I, uh, what can

I do for you?" He stumbles over his words, at a loss for once.

"I'm not exactly sure," I reply, looking from him to Maven. My betrothed only smirks, raising an eyebrow a little.

"For being the good son, my brother has his own discretions," he says, and his air is surprisingly playful. Even Cal grins a little, rolling his eyes. "You wanted to go home, Mare, and I've found you someone who's been there before."

After a second of confusion, I realize what Maven is saying and how stupid I am for not realizing it before. *Cal can get me out of the palace. Cal was at the tavern. . . . He got himself out of here, so he can do the same for me.*

"Maven," Cal says through gritted teeth, his grin gone. "You know she can't. It's not a good idea—"

It's my turn to speak up, to take what I want. "Liar."

He looks at me with his burning eyes, his stare going right through me. I hope he can see my determination, my desperation, my *need*.

"We've taken everything from her, brother," Maven murmurs, drawing close. "Surely we can give her this?"

And then slowly, reluctantly, Cal nods and waves me into his room. Dizzy with excitement, I hurry inside, almost hopping from foot to foot.

I'm going home.

Maven lingers at the door, his smile fading a little when I leave his side. "You're not coming." It isn't a question.

He shakes his head. "You'll have enough to worry about without me tagging along."

I don't have to be a genius to see the truth in his words. But just because he isn't coming doesn't mean I will forget what he's done for me already. Without thinking, I throw my arms around Maven. He doesn't respond for a second but slowly lets an arm drop around my shoulders. When I pull back, a silver blush paints his cheeks. I can feel my own blood run hot beneath my skin, pounding in my ears.

"Don't be too long," he says, tearing his eyes away from me to look at Cal.

Cal barely smirks. "You act like I've never done this before."

The brothers share a chuckle, laughing just for each other like I've seen my brothers do a thousand times before. When the door shuts behind Maven, leaving me with Cal, I can't help but feel a little less animosity toward the princes.

Cal's room is twice the size of mine but so cluttered it seems smaller. Armor and uniforms and combat suits fill the alcoves along the walls, all hanging from what I assume are models of Cal's body. They tower over me like faceless ghosts, staring with invisible eyes. Most of the armor is light, steel plate and thick fabric, but a few are heavy-duty, meant for battle, not training. One even has a helmet of shining metal, with a tinted glass faceplate. An insignia glitters on the sleeve, sewn into the dark gray material. The flaming black crown and silver wings. What it means, what the uniforms are for, what Cal has *done* in them, I don't want to think about.

Like Julian, Cal has stacks of books piled all over, spilling out in little rivers of ink and paper. They aren't as old as Julian's though—most look newly bound, typed out and reprinted on plastic-lined sheets to preserve the words. And all are written in Common, the language of Norta, the Lakelands, and Piedmont. While Cal disappears into his closet, stripping off the rest of his armor as he goes, I sneak a glance at his books. These are strange, full of maps, diagrams, and charts—guides to the terrible art of warfare. Each one is more violent than the last, detailing military movements from recent years and even before. Great victories, bloody defeats, weapons, and maneuvers, it's enough to make my head spin. Cal's notes inside them are worse, outlining the tactics he favors, which ones are worth the cost of life. In the pictures, tiny squares represent soldiers, but I see my brothers and Kilorn and everyone like them.

Beyond the books, by the window, there's a little table and two chairs. On the tabletop, a game board lies ready, pieces already in place. I don't recognize it, but I know it was meant for Maven. They must meet nightly, to play and laugh as brothers do.

"We won't have very long to visit," Cal calls out, making me jump. I glance at the closet, catching sight of his tall, muscled back as he pulls a shirt on. There are more bruises, and scars as well, even though I'm sure he has access to an army of healers if he wants them. For some reason, he's chosen to keep the scars.

"As long as I get to see my family," I answer back, maneuvering myself away so I don't keep staring at him.

Cal emerges, this time fully dressed in plain clothes. After a moment, I realize it's the same thing he wore the night I met him. I can't believe I didn't see him for what he was from the beginning: a wolf in sheep's clothing. And now I'm the sheep pretending to be a wolf.

We leave the residence floors quickly, moving downward. Eventually, Cal turns a corner, directing us into a wide concrete room. "Just in here."

It looks like some kind of storage facility, filled with rows of strange shapes covered in canvas sheets. Some are big, some are small, but all are hidden.

"It's a dead end," I protest. There's no way out but to go the way we came in.

"Yes, Mare, I brought you to a dead end," he sighs, walking down a particular row. The sheets ripple as he passes, and I glimpse shining metal underneath.

"More armor?" I poke at one of the shapes. "I was going to say, you should probably get some more. Didn't seem like you had enough upstairs. Actually, you might want to put some on. My brothers are pretty huge and like to beat on people." Though, judging by Cal's book collection and muscles, he can hold his own. *Not to mention the whole controlling-fire thing.*

He just shakes his head. "I think I'll be fine without it. Besides, I look like a Security officer in that stuff. We don't want your family getting the wrong idea, do we?"

"What idea do we want them to get? I don't think I'm exactly allowed to introduce you properly."

"I work with you, we got a leave pass for the night. Simple," he says, shrugging. *Lying comes so easily to these people.*

"So why would you come with me? What's the story there?"

With a sly grin, Cal gestures to the canvas shape next to him. "I'm your ride."

He throws back the sheet, revealing a gleaming contraption of metal and black paint. Two treaded wheels, mirrored chrome, lights, a long leather seat—it's a transport like I've never seen.

"It's a cycle," Cal says, running a hand over the silver handlebars like a proud father. He knows and loves every inch of the metal beast. "Fast, agile, and it can go where transports can't."

"It looks—like a death trap," I finally say, unable to mask my trepidation.

Laughing, he pulls a helmet from the back of the seat. I sure hope he doesn't expect me to wear it, much less ride this thing. "That's what Father said, and Colonel Macanthos. They won't mass-produce for the armies yet, but I'll win them over. Haven't crashed once since I perfected the wheels."

"*You* built it?" I say, incredulous, but he shrugs like it's nothing. "Wow."

"Just wait until you ride it," he says, holding out the helmet to me. As if on cue, the far wall jolts, its metal mechanisms groaning somewhere, and begins to slide away, revealing the dark night beyond.

Laughing, I take a step back from the death machine. "That's not happening."

But Cal just smirks and swings one leg over the cycle, sinking down into the seat. The engine rumbles to life beneath him, purring and growling with energy. I can sense the battery deep in the machine, powering it on. It begs to be let loose, to consume the long road between here and home. *Home.*

"It's perfectly safe, I promise," he shouts over the engine. The headlight blazes on, illuminating the dark night beyond. Cal's red-gold eyes meet mine and he stretches out a hand. "Mare?"

Despite the horrible sinking in my stomach, I slide the helmet onto my head.

I've never ridden in an airship, but I know this must feel like flying. Like freedom. Cal's cycle eats up the familiar road in elegant, arcing curves. He's a good driver, I'll give him that. The old road is full of bumps and holes, but he dodges each one with ease, even as my heart rises in my throat. Only when we coast to a stop half a mile from town do I realize I'm holding on to him so tightly he has to pry me off. I feel suddenly cold without his warmth, but I push the thought away.

"Fun, right?" he says, powering down the cycle. My legs and back are already sore from the strange, small seat, but he hops off with an extra spring in his step.

With some difficulty, I slide off as well. My knees wobble a bit, more from the pounding heartbeat still thrumming in my ears, but I think I'm okay.

"It won't be my first choice in transportation."

"Remind me to take you up in an airjet sometime. You'll stick to cycles after that," he replies as he rolls the cycle off the road, into the cover of the woods. After throwing a few leafy branches over it, he stands back to admire his handiwork. If I didn't know exactly where to look, I wouldn't notice the cycle was there at all.

"You do this a lot, I see."

Cal turns back to me, one hand in his pocket. "Palaces can get . . . stuffy."

"And crowded bars, Red bars, aren't?" I ask, pushing the topic. But he starts walking toward the village, setting a fast pace like he can outrun the question.

"I don't go out to drink, Mare."

"So, what, you just catch pickpockets and hand out jobs willy-nilly?"

When he stops short and whirls around, I knock into his chest, feeling for a moment the solid weight behind his frame. Then I realize he's laughing deeply.

"Did you just say willy-nilly?" he says between chuckles.

My face blushes red beneath my makeup, and I give him a little shove. *Very inappropriate*, my mind chides. "Just answer the question."

His smile remains, though the laughter fades away. "I don't do this for myself," he says. "You have to understand, Mare. I don't—I'm going to be king one day. I don't have the luxury of being selfish."

"I'd think the king would be the only person *with* that luxury."

He shakes his head, his eyes forlorn as they run over me. "I wish that were true."

Cal's fist clenches open and closed, and I can almost see the flames on his skin, hot and rising with his anger. But it passes, leaving only an ember of regret in his eyes. When he finally starts walking again, it's at a more forgiving pace.

"A king should know his people. That's why I sneak out," he murmurs. "I do it in the capital too, and at the war front. I like to see how things really are in the kingdom, instead of being told by advisers and diplomats. That's what a good king would do."

He acts like he should be ashamed for wanting to be a good leader. Maybe, in the eyes of his father and all those other fools, that's the way it should be. *Strength* and *power* are the words Cal has been raised to know. Not goodness. Not kindness. Not empathy or bravery or equality or anything else that a ruler should strive for.

"And what do you see, Cal?" I ask, gesturing toward the village coming into view between the trees. My heart jumps in my chest, knowing I'm so close.

"I see a world on the edge of a blade. Without balance, it will fall," he sighs, knowing it's not the answer I want to hear. "You don't know how precarious things are, how close this world is to falling back into ruin. My father does everything he can to keep us all safe, and so will I."

"My world is already in ruin," I say, kicking at the dirt road beneath us. All around us, the trees seem to open, revealing the muddy place I call home. Compared to the Hall, it must look like a slum, like a hell. *Why can't he see that?* "Your father keeps *your* people safe, not mine."

"Changing the world has costs, Mare," he says. "Many would die, Reds most of all. And in the end, there wouldn't be victory, not for you. You don't know the bigger picture."

"So tell me." I bristle, hating his words. "Show me the bigger picture."

"The Lakelands, they're like us, a monarchy, nobles, a Silver elite to rule the rest. And the Piedmont princes, our own allies, would never back a nation where Reds are equal. Prairie and Tiraxes are the same. Even *if* Norta changed, the rest of the continent would not let it last. We would be invaded, divided, torn apart. More war, more death."

I remember Julian's map, the breadth of the greater world beyond our country. All controlled by Silvers with nowhere for us to turn. "What if you're wrong? What if Norta is the beginning? The change the others need? You don't know where freedom leads."

Cal has no answer for that, and we fall into bitter silence. "This is it," I mutter, stopping under the familiar outline of my house.

My feet are silent on the porch, a far cry from Cal's heavy, stomping steps that make the wood beams creak. His familiar heat rolls off him, and for a split second I imagine him sending the house up in flames. He senses my unease and puts a warm hand on my shoulder, but that does nothing to settle me.

"I can wait below if you want," he whispers, taking me by surprise. "We don't want to chance them recognizing me."

"They won't. Even though my brothers served, they probably wouldn't know you from a bedpost." *Shade would*, I thought, *but Shade is smart enough to keep his mouth shut.* "Besides, you said you want to know what's not worth fighting for."

With that I pull open the door, stepping through to the home that is no longer my own. It feels like taking a step back in time.

The house ripples with a chorus of snores, not just from my father but from the lumpy shape in the sitting area as well. Bree slumps in the overstuffed chair, a pile of muscle and thin blankets. His dark hair is still closely shaved in the army style, and there are scars on his arms and face, testaments to his time fighting. He must've lost a bet with Tramy, who tosses and turns up in my cot. Shade is nowhere to be seen, but he's never been one for sleep. Probably out prowling the village, looking up old girlfriends.

"Rise and shine." I laugh, ripping the blanket off Bree in a smooth motion.

He crashes to the floor, probably hurting the floor more than himself, and rolls to a stop at my feet. For half a second, it looks like he might fall back asleep.

Then he blinks at me, bleary-eyed and confused. In short, his usual self. "Mare?"

"Shut your face, Bree, people are trying to sleep!" Tramy groans in the dark.

"ALL OF YOU, QUIET!" Dad roars from his bedroom, making us all jump.

I never realized how much I missed this. Bree blinks the sleep from his eyes and hugs me to him, laughing deep in his chest. A nearby thunk announces Tramy as he jumps from the upper loft, landing beside us on nimble feet.

"It's Mare!" he shouts, pulling me up from the floor and into his arms. He's thinner than Bree but not the weedy string bean I remember. There are hard knots of muscle under my hands; the last few years have not been easy for him.

"Good to see you, Tramy," I breathe against him, feeling like I might burst.

The bedroom door bangs open, revealing Mom in a tattered bathrobe. She opens her mouth to scold the boys, but the sight of me kills her words. Instead, she smiles and claps her hands together. "Oh, you've finally come to visit!"

Dad follows her, wheezing and wheeling his chair into the main room. Gisa is the last to wake up, but she only pokes her head out over the loft ledge, looking down.

Tramy finally lets me go, putting me back down next to Cal, who's doing a wonderful job looking awkward and out of place.

"Heard you caved and got a job," Tramy teases, poking me in the ribs.

Bree chuckles, ruffling my hair. "The army wouldn't want her anyway, she'd rob her legion blind."

I shove him with a smile. "Seems the army doesn't want you either. Discharged, eh?"

Dad answers for them, wheeling forward. "Some lottery, the letter said. Won an honorable discharge for the Barrow boys. Full pension too." I can tell he doesn't believe a word of it, but Dad doesn't press the subject. Mom, on the other hand, eats it right up.

"Brilliant, isn't it? The government finally doing something for us," she says, kissing Bree on the cheek. "And now you, with a job." The pride radiates off her like I've never seen—usually she saves all of it for Gisa. *She's proud of a lie.* "It's about time this family came into some luck."

Up above us, Gisa scoffs. I don't blame her. My luck broke her hand and her future. "Yes, we're very lucky," she huffs, finally moving to join us.

Her going is slow, moving down the ladder with one hand. When she reaches the floor, I can see her splint is wrapped in colored cloth. With a pang of sadness, I realize it's a piece of her beautiful embroidery that will never be finished.

I reach out to hug her, but she pulls away, her eyes on Cal. She seems to be the only one to notice him. "Who's that?"

Flushing, I realize I've almost forgotten him completely. "Oh, this is Cal. He's another servant up at the Hall with me."

"Hi," he manages, giving a stupid, little wave.

Mom giggles like a schoolgirl and waves back, her gaze lingering on his muscled arms. But Dad and my brothers aren't so charmed.

"You're not from these parts," Dad growls, staring at Cal like he's some kind of bug. "I can smell it on you."

"That's just the Hall, Dad—," I protest, but Cal cuts me off.

"I'm from Harbor Bay," he says, making sure to drop his *r*'s in the usual Harbor accent. "I started serving at Ocean Hill, the royal residence out there, and now I travel with the pack when they move." He glances at me sideways, a knowing look in his eye. "A lot of the servants do that."

Mom draws a rattled breath and reaches for my arm. "Will you? Do you have to go with those *people* when they leave?"

I want to tell them that I didn't choose this, that I'm not walking away willingly. But I have to lie, for their sake. "It was the only position they had. Besides, it's good money."

"I think I've got a pretty good idea what's going on," Bree growls, face-to-face with Cal. To his credit, Cal barely bats an eye at him.

"Nothing's going on," he says coolly, meeting Bree's glare with equal fire in his eyes. "Mare chose to work for the palace. She signed a contract for a year of service, and that's it."

With a grunt, Bree backs away. "I liked the Warren boy better," he grumbles.

"Stop being a child, Bree," I snap. My mom flinches at my harsh voice, like she's forgotten what I sound like after only three weeks.

Strangely, her eyes swim with tears. *She's forgetting you. That's why she wants you to stay. So she doesn't forget.*

"Mom, don't cry," I say, stepping forward to hug her. She feels so thin in my arms, thinner than I remember. Or maybe I just never noticed how frail she's become.

"It's not just you, dear, it's—" She looks away from me, to Dad. There's a pain in her eyes, a pain I don't understand. The others can't bear to look at her. Even Dad stares at his useless feet. A grim weight settles on the house.

And then I realize what's going on, what they're trying to protect me from.

My voice shakes when I speak, asking a question I don't want to know the answer to. "Where's Shade?"

Mom crumples in on herself, barely making it to a chair at the kitchen table before she devolves into sobs. Bree and Tramy can't bear to watch, both turning away. Gisa doesn't move, staring at the floor like she wants to drown in it. No one speaks, leaving only the sound of my mother's tears and my father's labored breathing to fill the hole my brother once occupied. *My brother, my closest brother.*

I fall backward, almost missing a step in my anguish, but Cal steadies me. I wish he wouldn't. I want to fall down, to feel something hard and real so the pain in my head won't hurt so badly. My hand strays to my ear, grazing over the three stones I hold so dearly. The third, Shade's stone, feels cold against my skin.

"We didn't want to tell you in a letter," Gisa whispers, picking at her splint. "He died before the discharge came."

The urge to electrify something, to pour my rage and sorrow into a single bolt of biting power, has never felt so strong. *Control it,* I tell myself. I can't believe I was worried about Cal burning the house down; *lightning can destroy as easily as flame.*

Gisa fights tears, forcing herself to say the words. "He tried to run away. He was executed. Beheaded."

My legs give way so quickly even Cal doesn't have a chance to catch me. I can't hear, I can't see, I can only *feel*. Sorrow, shock, pain, the whole world spinning around me. The lightbulbs buzz with electricity, screaming at me so loudly I think my head might split. The fridge crackles in the corner, its old, bleeding battery pulsing like a dying heart. They taunt me, tease me, trying to make me crack. But I won't. *I won't.*

"Mare," Cal breathes in my ear, his arms warm around me, but he might as well be talking to me from across an ocean. "Mare!"

I heave a painful gasp, trying to catch my breath. My cheeks feel wet, though I don't remember crying. *Executed.* My blood boils under my skin. *It's a lie. He didn't run. He was in the Guard. And they found out. They killed him for it. They murdered him.*

I have never known anger like this. Not when the boys left, not when Kilorn came to me. Not even when they broke Gisa's hand.

An earsplitting whine screeches through the house, as the fridge, the lightbulbs, and the wiring in the walls kick into high gear. Electricity hums, making me feel alive and angry and dangerous. Now I'm creating the energy, pushing my own strength through the house just like Julian taught me.

Cal yells, shaking me, trying to get through somehow. But he can't. The power is in me and I don't want to let go. It feels better than pain.

Glass rains down on us as the lightbulbs explode, popping like corn in a skillet. *Pop pop pop.* It almost drowns out Mom's scream.

Someone pulls me to my feet with rough strength. Their hands go to my face, holding me still as they speak. Not to comfort me, not to empathize, but to snap me out of it. *I would know that voice anywhere.*

"Mare, pull yourself together!"

I look up to see clear green eyes and a face full of worry.

"Kilorn."

"Knew you'd stumble back eventually," he mumbles. "Kept an eye out."

His hands are rough against my skin, but calming. He brings me back to reality, to a world where my brother is dead. The last surviving lightbulb swings above us, barely illuminating the room and my stunned family.

But that's not the only thing lighting up the darkness.

Purple-white sparks dance around my hands, growing weaker by the moment, but plain as day. My lightning. *I won't be able to lie my way out of this one.*

Kilorn pulls me to a chair, his face a storm cloud of confusion. The others only stare, and with a pang of sadness, I realize they're afraid. But Kilorn isn't afraid at all—he's angry.

"What did they do to you?" he rumbles, his hands inches from mine. The sparks fade away entirely, leaving just skin and shaking fingers.

"They didn't do anything." *I wish this was their fault. I wish I could blame this on someone else.* I look over Kilorn's head, meeting Cal's eyes. Something releases in him, and he nods, communicating without words. *I don't have to lie about this.*

"This is what I am."

Kilorn's frown deepens. "Are you one of *them*?" I've never heard so much anger, so much *disgust*, forced into a single sentence. It makes me feel like dying. *"Are you?"*

Mom recovers first and, without a glimmer of fear, takes my hand. "Mare is my daughter, Kilorn," she says, fixing him with a frightening stare I didn't know she could muster. "We all know that."

My family murmurs in agreement, rallying to my side, but Kilorn remains unconvinced. He stares at me like I'm a stranger, like we haven't known each other all our lives.

"Give me a knife and I'll settle this right now," I say, glaring back at him. "I'll show you what color I bleed."

This calms him a bit and he pulls back. "I just—I don't understand."

That makes two of us.

"I think I'm with Kilorn on this one. We know who you are, Mare, but—" Bree stumbles, searching for the right thing to say. He's never been one for words. *"How?"*

I barely know what to say, but I do my best to explain. Again, I'm painfully aware of Cal's presence, always listening, so I leave out the Guard and Julian's findings, to lay out the last three weeks as plainly as possible. Pretending to be Silver, being betrothed to a prince, learning to control myself—it sounds preposterous, but they listen intently.

"We don't know how or why, just that this *is*," I finish, holding out my other hand. I don't miss Tramy flinch away. "We might never know what this means."

Mom's hand tightens on mine in a display of support. The small comfort does wonders for me. I'm still angry, still devastatingly sad, but the need to destroy something fades. I'm gaining back some semblance of control, enough to keep myself in check.

"I think it's a miracle," she murmurs, forcing a smile for my sake. "We've always wanted better for you, and now, we're getting it. Bree and Tramy are safe, Gisa won't have to worry, we can *live* happy, and you"—her watery eyes meet mine—"you, my dear, will be someone special. What more can a mother ask?"

I wish her words were true, but I nod anyway, smiling for my mother and my family. I'm getting better at lying, and they seem to believe me. But not Kilorn. He still seethes, trying to hold back another outburst.

"What's he like, the prince?" Mom prods. "Maven?"

Dangerous ground. I can feel Cal listening, waiting to hear what I have to say about his younger brother. *What can I say? That he's kind? That I'm beginning to like him? That I still don't know if I can trust him? Or worse, that I can never trust anyone again?* "He's not what I expected."

Gisa notes my discomfort and turns toward Cal. "So who's this, your bodyguard?" she says, changing the subject with the slightest wink.

"I am," Cal says, answering for me. He knows I don't want to lie to my family, not more than I have to. "And I'm sorry, but we have to be going soon."

His words are like a twisting knife, but I must obey them. "Yes."

Mom stands with me, holding on to my hand so tightly I'm afraid it might break. "We won't say anything, of course."

"Not a word," Dad agrees. My siblings nod as well, swearing to be silent.

But Kilorn's face falls into a dark scowl. For some reason, he's become so angry and I can't for the life of me say why. *But I'm angry too.* Shade's death still weighs on me like a terrible stone. "Kilorn?"

"Yeah, I won't talk," he spits. Before I can stop him, he gets up from his chair and sweeps out in a whirlwind that spins the air. The door slams behind him, shaking the walls. I'm used to Kilorn's emotions, his rare moments of despair, but this rage is something new from him. I don't know how to deal with it.

My sister's touch brings me back, reminding me that this is goodbye. "This is a gift," she whispers in my ear. "Don't waste it."

"You'll come back, won't you?" Bree says, and Gisa pulls away. For the first time since he left for war, I see fear in his eyes. "You're a princess now, you get to make the rules."

I wish.

Cal and I exchange glances. I can tell by the tight set of his mouth and the darkness in his eyes what my answer should be.

"I'll try," I whisper, my voice breaking. One more lie can't hurt.

When we reach the edge of the Stilts, Gisa's good-bye still haunts me. There was no blame in her eyes, even though I've taken everything from her. Her last words echo on the wind, drowning out everything else. *Don't waste it.*

"I'm sorry about your brother," Cal blurts out. "I didn't know he—"

"—was already dead?" *Executed for desertion. Another lie.* The rage rises again, and I don't even *want* to control it. But what can I do about it? What can I do to avenge my brother, or even try to save the others?

Don't waste it.

"I need to make one more stop." Before Cal can protest, I put on my best smile. "It won't take long at all, I promise."

To my surprise, he nods slowly in the dark.

"A job at the Hall, that's very prestigious." Will chortles as I take a seat inside his wagon. The old blue candle still burns, casting shifting light around us. As I suspected, Farley is long gone.

When I'm sure the door and windows are shut, I drop my voice. "I'm not working there, Will. They—"

To my surprise, Will waves a hand at me. "Oh, I know all that. Tea?"

"Uh, no." My words shake with shock. "How did you—?"

"The royal monkeys chose a queen this past week, of course they had to broadcast it in the Silver cities," a voice says from behind a curtain. The figure steps out, revealing not Farley but what looks like a beanpole in human form. His head scrapes the ceiling, making him duck awkwardly. His crimson hair is long, matching the red sash draped across his body from shoulder to hip. It's clasped with the same sun badge Farley wore in her broadcast. And I don't miss the gun belt around his waist, full of shiny bullets and a pair of pistols. He's Scarlet Guard too.

"You've been all over the Silver screens, *Lady Titanos*." He says my title like a curse. "You and that Samos girl. Tell me, is she as unpleasant as she looks?"

"This is Tristan, one of Farley's lieutenants," Will pipes in. He turns a chiding eye on him. "Tristan, be gentle."

"Why?" I scoff. "Evangeline Samos is a bloodthirsty jerk."

Smiling, Tristan throws a smug look at Will.

"They aren't all monkeys," I add quietly, remembering Maven's kind words earlier today.

"Are you talking about the prince you're engaged to or the one waiting in the woods?" Will asks calmly, like he's asking about the price of flour.

In stark contrast, Tristan erupts, vaulting out of his seat. I beat him to the door, two hands outstretched. Thankfully I keep myself in check. The last thing I need is to electrify a member of the Scarlet Guard.

"You brought a Silver here?" he hisses down at me. "The *prince*? Do you know what we could do if we took him in? What we could bargain for?"

Though he towers over me, I don't back down. "You leave him alone."

"A few weeks in the lap of luxury and your blood is as silver as theirs," he spits, looking like he wants to kill me. "You going to electrocute me too?"

That stings, and he knows it. I drop my hands, afraid they might betray me. "I'm not protecting him, I'm protecting *you*, you stupid fool. Cal is a soldier born and bred, and he could burn this whole village down if he really wanted to." Not that he would. *I hope.*

Tristan's hand strays to his gun. "I'd like to see him try."

But Will lays a wrinkled hand on his arm. The touch is enough to make the rebel deflate. "That's enough," he whispers. "What did you come here for, Mare? Kilorn is safe, and so are your siblings."

I heave a breath, still staring down Tristan. He just threatened to kidnap Cal and hold him for ransom. And for whatever reason, the thought of such a thing unsettles me to my core.

"My—" One word out and I'm already struggling. "Shade was part of the Guard." It's not a question anymore, but a truth. Will lowers his gaze, apologetic, and Tristan even hangs his head. "They killed him for it. They killed my brother, and I have to act like it doesn't bother me."

"You're dead if you don't."

"I know that. I'll say whatever they want when the time comes. But—" My voice catches a little, on the edge of this new path. "I'm in the palace, the center of their world. I'm quick, I'm quiet, and I can help the cause."

Tristan sucks in a ragged breath, pulling back to his full height. Despite his anger earlier, there's now something like pride shining in his eyes. "You want to join up."

"I do."

Will clenches his jaw, his stare piercing through me. "I hope you know what you're committing to. This isn't just my war or Farley's or the Scarlet Guard's—it's yours. Until the very end. And not to avenge your brother but to avenge us all. To fight for the ones before, and to save the ones yet to come."

His gnarled hand reaches for mine and for the first time, I notice a tattoo around his wrist: a red band. Like the ones they make us wear. Except now he's wearing his forever. It's part of him, like the blood in our veins.

"Are you with us, Mare Barrow?" he says, his hand closing over mine. *More war, more death*, Cal said. *But there's a chance he's wrong. There's a chance we can change it.*

My fingers tighten, holding on to Will. I can feel the weight of my action, the importance behind it.

"I'm with you."

"We will rise," he breathes, in unison with Tristan. I remember the words and speak with them. "Red as the dawn."

In the flickering candlelight, our shadows look like monsters on the walls.

When I join back up with Cal at the edge of town, I feel lighter somehow, emboldened by my decision and the prospect of what's to come. Cal walks alongside me, glancing over occasionally, but says nothing. Where I would poke and prod and forcibly pull an answer out of someone, Cal is the complete opposite. Maybe it's a military tactic he picked up in one of his books: *let the enemy come to you.*

Because that's what I am now. His enemy.

He perplexes me, just like his brother. Both of them are kind, even though they know I'm Red, even though they shouldn't even see me at all. But Cal took me home, and Maven was good to me, wanting to help. *They are strange boys.*

When we enter the woods again, Cal's demeanor changes, hardening to something serious. "I'll have to talk with the queen about changing your schedule."

"Why?"

"You almost exploded in there," he says gently. "You'll have to go into Training with us, to make sure something like that doesn't happen again."

Julian is training me. But even the little voice in my head knows Julian is no substitute for what Cal, Maven, and Evangeline go through. If I learned even *half* of what they know, who knows what help I could be to the Guard? To Shade's memory?

"Well, if it gets me out of Protocol, I won't say no."

Suddenly, Cal jumps back from his cycle. His hands are on fire and an equal, blazing light burns in his eyes.

"Someone's watching us."

I don't bother questioning him. Cal's soldier's sense is sharp, but what could threaten him here? What could he possibly be afraid of in the woods of a sleepy, poor village? *A village crawling with rebels,* I remind myself.

But instead of Farley or armed revolutionaries, Kilorn steps out of the leaves. I forgot how sly he is, how easily he can move through darkness.

Cal's hands extinguish in a puff of smoke. "Oh, you."

Kilorn tears his eyes away from me, glaring at Cal. He inclines his head in a condescending bow. "Excuse me, Your Highness."

Instead of trying to deny it, Cal stands a little straighter, looking like the king he was born to be. He doesn't reply and goes back to freeing his cycle from the leaves. But I feel his eyes on me, watching every second that passes between Kilorn and me.

"You're really doing this?" Kilorn says, looking like a wounded animal. "You're really leaving? To be one of them?"

The words sting more than a slap. *This is not a choice*, I want to tell him.

"You saw what happened in there, what I can do. They can *help* me." Even I'm surprised at how easily the lie comes. One day I might even be able to lie to myself, to trick my mind into thinking I'm happy. "I'm where I'm supposed to be."

He shakes his head, one hand grabbing my arm like he can pull me back into the past, where our worries were simple. "You're supposed to be here."

"Mare." Cal waits patiently, leaning against the seat of the cycle, but his voice is firm, a warning.

"I have to go." I try to push past Kilorn, to leave him behind, but he won't let me. He's always been stronger than me. And as much as I want to let him hold on to me, it just can't be.

"Mare, please—"

A wave of heat pulses against us, like a strong beam of sunlight.

"Let her go," Cal rumbles, standing over me. The heat rolls off him, almost rippling the air. The calm he fights to maintain thins, threatening to come undone.

Kilorn scoffs in his face, itching for a fight. But he's like me; we're thieves, we're *rats*. We know when to fight and when to run. Reluctantly, he pulls back, letting his fingers trail along my arm. This might be the last time we see each other.

The air cools, but Cal doesn't step back. I'm his brother's betrothed—he has to be protective of me.

"You bargained for me too, to save me from conscription," Kilorn says softly, finally understanding the price I've paid. "You have a bad habit of trying to save me."

I can barely nod, and I have to pull the helmet onto my head to hide the tears welling in my eyes. Numbly, I follow Cal to the cycle and slide onto the seat behind him.

Kilorn backs away, flinching when the cycle revs up. Then he smirks at me, his features curling into an expression that used to make me want to punch him.

"I'll tell Farley you said hello."

The cycle growls like a beast, tearing me away from Kilorn and the Stilts and my old life. Fear curls through me like a poison, until I'm scared from head to toe. But not for myself. Not anymore. I'm scared for Kilorn, for the idiotic thing he's going to do.

He's going to find Farley. *And he's going to join her.*

FIFTEEN

The next morning, I open my eyes to see a shaded figure standing by my bedside. *This is it. I left, I broke the rules, and they're going to kill me for it.*

But not without a fight.

Before the figure gets a chance, I fly out of bed, ready to defend myself. My muscles tense while the delightful buzzing comes to life inside me. But instead of an assassin, I'm staring at a red uniform. And I recognize the woman wearing it.

Walsh looks the same as she did before, though I certainly don't. She stands next to a metal cart filled with tea and bread and anything else I might want for breakfast. Ever the dutiful servant, she keeps her mouth clamped shut, but her eyes scream at me. She stares at my hand, at the now too-familiar sparks creeping around my fingers. I shake them away, brushing off the veins of light until they disappear back into my skin.

"I'm so sorry," I exclaim, jumping away from her. Still, she doesn't speak. "Walsh—"

But she busies herself with the food. Then, to my great surprise, she mouths five words to me. They are words I'm beginning to know like a prayer—or a curse. *Rise, Red as the dawn.*

Before I can respond, before my shock can register, Walsh presses a cup of tea into my hand.

"Wait—" I reach out for her, but she dodges my hand, sweeping into a low bow.

"My lady," she says, sharply ending our conversation.

I let her go, watching her back out of the room until there's nothing left but the echo of her unspoken words.

Walsh is in the Guard too.

The teacup feels cold in my hand. Strangely cold.

I look down to find it's not full of tea but water. And at the bottom of the cup, a piece of paper bleeds ink. The ink swirls as I read the message, the water leeching it away, erasing any trace, until there's nothing left but cloudy, gray liquid and a blank curl of paper. No evidence of my first act of rebellion.

The message isn't hard to remember. It's only one word.

Midnight.

This knowledge that I have a connection to the group so close by should comfort me, but for some reason, I find myself shivering. *Maybe cameras aren't the only things watching me here.*

And it's not the only note waiting for me. My new schedule sits on the nightstand, written in the queen's maddeningly perfect handwriting.

Your schedule has changed.

0630—Breakfast / 0700—Training / 1000—Protocol
1130—Luncheon / 1300—Protocol / 1400—Lessons
1800—Dinner.

Lucas will escort you to all. Schedule is not negotiable.

HRH Queen Elara.

"So, they've finally bumped you up to Training?" Lucas grins at me, a rare bit of pride shining through as he leads me to my first session. "Either you've been very good or very bad."

"A little bit of both."

More bad, I think, remembering my episode last night at home. I know the new schedule is Cal's doing, but I didn't expect him to work so fast. Truthfully, I'm excited for Training. If it's anything like what I saw Cal and Maven go through, the ability practice in particular, I'll be hopelessly far behind, but at least I'll have someone to talk to. And if I'm really lucky, Evangeline will be deathly ill and stuck in bed for the rest of her miserable life.

Lucas shakes his head, chuckling. "Be prepared. The instructors are famous for being able to break even the strongest soldiers. They won't take well to your sass."

"I don't take well to being broken," I retort. "What was your Training like?"

"Well, I went straight to the army when I was nine, so my experience was a bit different," he says, eyes darkening at the memory.

"Nine?" The thought seems impossible to me. Abilities or not, this can't be true.

But Lucas shrugs like it's nothing. "The front is the best place for training. Even the princes were trained at the front, for a time."

"But you're here now," I say. My eyes linger on Lucas's uniform, on the black and silver of Security. "You're not a soldier anymore."

For the first time, Lucas's dry smile disappears completely. "It wears on you," he admits, more to himself than to me. "Men are not meant to be at war for long."

"And what about Reds?" I hear myself ask. *Bree, Tramy, Shade, Dad, Kilorn's father. And a thousand others. A million others.* "Can they stand war better than Silvers?"

We reach the door to the training hall before Lucas finally answers, looking a little uncomfortable. "That's the way the world works. Reds serve, Reds work, Reds fight. It's what they're good at. It's what they're *meant* to do." I have to bite my tongue to keep myself from shouting at him. "Not everyone is special."

Anger boils in me, but I don't say a word against Lucas. Losing my temper, even with him, won't be smiled upon. "I can take it from here," I say stiffly.

He notes my discomfort, frowning a little. When he speaks, his voice is low and fast, as if he doesn't want to be overheard. "I don't have the luxury of questions," he mutters. His black eyes bore into mine, full of meaning. "And neither do you."

My heart clenches, terrified by his words and their veiled meaning. *Lucas knows there's more to me than what he's been told.* "Lucas—"

"It's not my place to ask questions." He furrows his brow, trying to make me understand, trying to put me at ease. "Lady Titanos." The title sounds firmer than ever, becoming my shield as well as the queen's weapon.

Lucas will not ask questions. Despite his black eyes, his Silver blood, his Samos family, he will not pull at the thread that could unravel my existence.

"Keep to your schedule, my lady." He pulls back, more formal than I've ever seen him. With a flick of his head, he gestures to the door where a Red attendant waits. "I'll collect you after Training."

"Thank you, Lucas," is all I can manage. He's given me so much more than he knows.

The attendant hands me a stretchy black suit with purple and silver stripes. He points me to a tiny room, where I change quickly, slipping out of my usual clothes and into the jumpsuit. It reminds me of my old clothes, the ones I used back in the Stilts. Worn by time and movement, but trim and tight enough not to slow me down.

When I enter the training hall, I'm painfully aware of everyone staring at me, not to mention the dozens of cameras. The floor feels soft and springy beneath my feet, cushioning each step. An immense skylight rises above us, showing a blue summer sky full of clouds to taunt me. Winding stairs connect the several levels cut into the walls, each at varying heights with different equipment. There are many windows as well, one of which I know opens to Lady Blonos's classroom. Where the others go or who might be watching from them, I have no idea.

I should be nervous about walking into a room full of teen warriors, all of them better trained than me. Instead, I'm thinking about the insufferable icicle of bone and metal known as Evangeline Samos. I barely make it halfway across the floor before her mouth opens, dripping venom.

"Graduated from Protocol already? Did you finally master the art of sitting with your legs crossed?" she sneers, jumping up from a weight-lifting machine. Her silver hair is tied back into a complicated braid I'd very much like to cut off, but the deathly sharp metal blades at her waist give me pause. Like me, like everyone else, she wears a jumpsuit emblazoned with the colors of her house. In black and silver, she looks deadly.

Sonya and Elane flank her with matching smirks. Now that they're not intimidating me, they seem to be sucking up to the future queen herself.

I do my best to ignore them all and find myself looking for Maven. He sits in a corner, separated from the others. *At least we can be alone together.* Whispers follow me, as more than a dozen noble teenagers watch me walk toward him. A few bow their heads, trying to be courteous, but most look cautious. The girls are especially on edge; after all, I did take one of their princes away.

"Took you long enough." Maven chuckles once I sit down next to him. He doesn't seem to be part of the crowd, nor does he want to be. "If I didn't know any better, I'd say you were trying to stay away from us."

"Just one person in particular," I reply, casting a glance back to Evangeline. She holds court near the target wall, where she shows off for her cronies in a dazzling display. Her metal knives sing through the air, digging into the dead center of their targets.

Maven watches me watch her, his eyes thoughtful. "When we go back to the capital, you won't have to see her so much," he murmurs. "She and Cal will have their hands full touring the country, fulfilling their duties. And we'll have ours."

The prospect of getting far away from Evangeline is exciting, but also reminds me of the steadily ticking clock moving against me. Soon I'll be forced to leave the Hall, the river valley, and my family far behind.

"Do you know when you—" I stumble, correcting myself. "I mean, when we go back to the capital?"

"After the Parting Ball. You were told about that?"

"Yes, your mother mentioned it—and Lady Blonos is trying to teach me how to dance. . . ." I trail off, feeling embarrassed. She tried to teach me a few steps yesterday, but I just ended up falling all over myself. Thieving I can do just fine, but dancing is apparently out of my reach. "Key word, *trying*."

"Don't worry, we won't have to deal with the worst of it."

The thought of dancing terrifies me, but I swallow the fear. "Who will?"

"Cal," he says without hesitation. "Big brother has to tolerate too many silly conversations and dance with a lot of annoying girls. I remember last year . . ." He stops to laugh at the memory. "Sonya Iral spent the entire time following him around, cutting into dances, trying to drag him away for some *fun*. I had to interfere and suffer through two songs with her to give Cal some respite."

The thought of the two brothers united against a legion of desperate girls makes me laugh, thinking about the lengths they must've gone to, to save each other. But as my smirk spreads, Maven's smile fades.

"At least this time, he'll have Samos hanging off his arm. The girls wouldn't dare cross her."

I snort, remembering her sharp, biting grip on my arm. "Poor Cal."

"And how was your visit yesterday?" he says, referring to my jaunt home. *So Cal didn't fill him in.*

"Difficult." It's the only way I know how to describe it. Now my family knows what I am, and Kilorn has thrown himself to the wolves. And of course, Shade is dead. "One of my brothers was executed, just before the release came."

He shifts next to me, and I expect him to be uncomfortable. After all, it was his own people who did it. Instead, he puts a hand over mine. "I'm so sorry, Mare. I'm sure he didn't deserve it."

"No, he didn't," I whisper, remembering why my brother died. Now I'm on the same path.

Maven stares at me intently, like he's trying to read the secret in my eyes. For once I'm glad for Blonos's lessons, or else I would assume Maven could read minds as well as the queen. But no, he's a burner and a burner alone. Few Silvers inherit abilities from their mothers, and no one has ever had more than one ability. So my secret, my new allegiance to the Scarlet Guard, is mine.

When he extends a hand to help me up, I take it. All around us, the others warm up, mostly stretching or jogging around the room, but a few are more impressive. Elane slips in and out of my vision as she bends the light around herself until she disappears altogether. A windweaver boy, Oliver of House Laris, creates a miniature whirlwind between his hands, stirring up tiny bits of dust. Sonya lazily trades blows with Andros Eagrie, a short but muscular eighteen-year-old. As a silk, Sonya is brutally skilled and fast and should be able to best him, but Andros matches her blow for blow in a violent dance. The Silvers of House Eagrie are eyes, meaning they can see the immediate future, and Andros is using his abilities to their full extent. Neither one seems to gain the upper hand, playing a game of balance rather than strength.

Just imagine what they can really do. So strong, so *powerful*. And these are only the kids. And just like that, my hope evaporates, shifting into fear.

"Lines," a voice says, barely a whisper.

My new instructor enters without a sound, Cal at his side, with a telky from House Provos behind them both. Like a good soldier, Cal walks in step with the instructor, who seems tiny and unassuming next to Cal's bulk. There are wrinkles in his pale skin, and his hair is as white as his clothing, a testament to his true age and his house. *House Arven, the silent house*, I remember, thinking back to my lessons. A major house, full of power and strength and all the things the Silvers put their faith in. I even remember him from before I became Mareena Titanos, from when I was a little girl. He would oversee the broadcasted executions in the capital, lording over the Reds and even the Silvers sentenced to die. And now I know why they chose him to do it.

The Haven girl blinks back into existence, suddenly visible again, while the churning wind dies in Oliver's hands. Evangeline's knives drop out of the air, and even I feel a calm blanket of nothing fall over me, blotting out my electrical sense.

He is Rane Arven, the instructor, the executioner, the *silence*. He can reduce a Silver to what they hate most: a Red. He can turn their abilities *off*. He can make them *normal*.

While I gawk, Maven pulls me into place behind him, with Cal at the head of our line. Evangeline leads the line next to us, and for once she doesn't seem concerned with me. Her eyes stay on Cal as he settles in, looking quite at home in his place of authority.

Arven doesn't waste time introducing me. In fact, he barely seems to notice I've joined his session.

"Laps," he says, his voice rough and low.

Good. Something I can actually do.

We set off in our lines, circling the room at an easy pace in blissful quiet. I push myself faster, enjoying the exercise I missed so much, until I'm speeding right past Evangeline. Then it's just Cal next to me, setting the pace for the rest of them. He quirks a smile at me, watching me run. This is something I can do, something I even enjoy.

My feet feel strange on the cushioned floor, bouncing with every step, but the blood pounding in my ears, the sweat, the pace are all familiar. If I close my eyes, I can pretend I'm back in the village, with Kilorn or my brothers or just by myself. Just free.

That is until a section of the wall swings out, catching me in the stomach.

It knocks me to the floor, sending me sprawling, but it's my pride that really hurts. The pack of runners pulls away, and Evangeline smirks over her shoulder, watching me fall behind. Only Maven slows his pace, waiting for me to catch up.

"Welcome to training." He chuckles, watching me pry myself off the obstacle.

All over the room, other parts of the wall shift, forming barriers for the runners. Everyone else takes it in stride; they're used to this. Cal and Evangeline lead the pack, moving over and under each obstacle as it appears before them. Out of the corner of my eye, I notice the Provos telky directing the pieces of wall, making them move. He even seems to be smirking at me.

I fight back the urge to snap at the telky and push myself back into a jog. Maven runs next to me, never more than a step away, and it's strangely infuriating. My pace quickens, until I'm sprinting and hurdling to the best of my ability. But Maven isn't like the Security at home—it's hard to leave him in the dust.

By the time we finish laps, Cal is the only one who hasn't broken a sweat. Even Evangeline looks ragged, though she tries her best to hide it. My breath comes in heavy pants, but I'm proud of myself. Despite the rough start, I managed to keep up.

Instructor Arven surveys us for a moment, his eyes lingering on me, before turning to the telky. "Targets please, Theo," he says, again barely a whisper. Like drawing away a curtain to reveal the sun, I feel my abilities rushing back.

The telky assistant waves a hand, sliding away a section of the floor, revealing the strange gun I saw from the window of Blonos's classroom. I realize it's not a gun at all but a cylinder. Only the telky's power makes it move, not some greater, strange technology. *The abilities are all they have.*

"Lady Titanos," Arven murmurs, making me shudder. "I understand you have an interesting ability."

He's thinking of the lightning, the purple-white bolts of destruction, but my mind strays to what Julian said yesterday. *I don't just control, I can create. I am special.*

Every eye turns to me, but I set my jaw, trying to will myself into being strong. "Interesting but not unheard of, Instructor," I say. "I'm very eager to learn about it, sir."

"You may start now," the instructor says, and the telky behind him tenses.

On cue, one of the ball targets flies into the air, faster than I thought possible.

Control, I tell myself, repeating Julian's words. *Focus.*

This time, I can feel the pull as I suck the electricity from the air—and from somewhere inside myself. It manifests in my hands, shining to life in little sparks. But the ball smacks the floor before I can throw it, its sparks bleeding into the floor and disappearing. Evangeline snickers behind me, but when I turn to glare at her, my eyes find Maven instead. He barely nods, urging me to try again. And next to him, Cal crosses his arms, his face dark with an emotion I can't place.

Another target rockets up, turning over in the air. The sparks come sooner now, alive and bright as the target reaches its zenith. Like before in Julian's classroom, I ball my fist and, feeling the power rage through me, I throw.

It arcs in a beautiful display of destructive light, clipping the side of the falling target. It shatters under my power, smoking and sparking as it hits the floor with a crash.

I can't help but grin, pleased with myself. Behind me, Maven and Cal clap, as do a few of the other kids. Evangeline and her friends certainly do not—they look almost insulted by my victory.

But Instructor Arven doesn't say anything, not bothering to

congratulate me. He simply looks over me, to the rest of the unit. "Next."

The instructor runs the class ragged, forcing us through round after round of exercises meant to fine-tune our abilities. Of course, I fall behind in all of them, but I can also feel myself improving. By the time the session ends, I'm dripping sweat and sore all over. Julian's lesson is a blessing, allowing me to sit and recover my strength. But even the session that morning cannot entirely drain me—*midnight is coming*. The faster time passes, the closer to midnight I get. The closer to taking the next step, to taking control of my fate.

Julian doesn't notice my unease, probably because he's elbow-deep in a pile of newly bound books. Each one is about an inch thick and neatly labeled with a year but nothing else. What they could possibly be, I don't know.

"What are these?" I ask, picking up one. Inside it's a mess of lists: names, dates, locations—and causes of death. Most just say blood loss, but there's also disease, suffocation, drowning, and some more specific and gruesome details. My blood runs cold in my veins as I realize exactly what I'm reading. "A death list."

Julian nods. "Every person who ever died fighting in the Lakelander War."

Shade, I think, feeling my meal churn in my stomach. Something tells me he won't get his name in one of these. Deserters don't get the honor of a line of ink. Angry, I let my mind reach out to the desk lamp illuminating my reading. The electricity in it calls to me, as familiar as my own pulse. With nothing more than my brain, I turn it on and off, blinking in time with my ragged heartbeat.

Julian notes the flashing light, lips pursed. "Something wrong,

Mare?" he asks dryly.

Everything is wrong.

"I'm not a fan of the schedule change," I say instead, letting the lamp be. It's not a lie, but it's not the truth either. "We won't be able to train."

He only shrugs, his parchment-colored clothes shifting with the motion. They look dirtier somehow, like he's turning into the pages of his books. "From what I hear, you need more guidance than I can give you."

My teeth grind together, chewing on the words before I can spit them out. "Did Cal tell you what happened?"

"He did," Julian replies evenly. "And he's right. Don't fault him for it."

"I can fault him for whatever I want," I snort, remembering the war books and death guides all over his room. "He's just like all the others."

Julian opens his mouth to say something but thinks better of it at the last moment and turns back to his books. "Mare, I wouldn't exactly call what we do training. Besides, you looked very good in your session today."

"You saw that? How?"

"I asked to watch."

"Wha—?"

"It doesn't matter," he says, looking straight through me. His voice is suddenly melodic, humming with deep, soothing vibrations. Exhaling, I realize he's right.

"It doesn't matter," I repeat. Even though he isn't speaking, the echo of Julian's voice still hangs in the air like a calming breeze. "So, what are we working on today?"

Julian smirks, amused with himself. "Mare."

His voice is normal again, simple and familiar. It breaks apart the echoes, wiping them away from me in a lifting cloud. "What—what the hell was that?"

"I take it Lady Blonos hasn't spoken much about House Jacos in Lessons?" he says, still smirking. "I'm surprised you never asked."

Truly, I've never wondered about Julian's ability. I always thought it would be something weak, because he doesn't seem as pompous as the others—but it looks like that isn't true at all. He's much stronger and more dangerous than I ever realized.

"You can control people. You're like *her*." The thought of Julian, a sympathizer, a good person, being at all like the queen makes me shake.

He takes the accusation in stride, shifting his attention back to his book. "No, I'm not. I have nowhere near her strength. Or her brutality." He heaves a sigh, explaining. "We're called singers. Or at least we would be, if there were any more of us. I'm the last of my house, and the last of, well, my kind. I can't read minds, I can't control thoughts, I can't speak in your head. But I can sing—as long as someone hears me, as long as I can look into their eyes—I can make a person do as I wish."

Horror bleeds through me. *Even Julian.*

Slowly, I lean back, wanting to put some distance between him and myself. He notices, of course, but doesn't look angry.

"You're right not to trust me," he murmurs. "No one does. There's a reason my only friends are written words. But I don't do it unless I absolutely need to, and I've never done it with malice." Then he snorts, laughing darkly. "If I really wanted, I could talk my way to the throne."

"But you haven't."

"No. And neither did my sister, no matter what anyone else might say."

Cal's mother. "No one seems to say anything about her. Not to me, anyways."

"People don't like to talk about dead queens," he snaps, turning away from me in a smooth motion. "But they talked when she was alive. Coriane Jacos, the Singer Queen." I've never seen Julian this way, not once. Usually he's quiet, calm, a little obsessed maybe, but never angry. Never so hurt. "She wasn't chosen by Queenstrial, you know. Not like Elara, or Evangeline, or even you. No, Tibe married my sister because he loved her—and she loved him."

Tibe. Calling Tiberias Calore the Sixth, King of Norta, Flame of the North, anything with less than eight syllables seems preposterous. But he was young once too. He was like Cal, a boy born to become a king.

"They hated her because we were from a low house, because we didn't have strength or power or any other silly thing those people uphold," Julian rails on, still looking away. His shoulders heave with each breath. "And when my sister became queen, she threatened to change all that. She was kind, compassionate, a mother who could raise Cal to be the king this country needed to unite us all. A king who wouldn't be afraid of change. But that never came to be."

"I know what it's like to lose a sibling," I murmur, remembering Shade. It doesn't seem real, like maybe everyone is just lying and he's at home now, happy and safe. But I know that isn't true. And somewhere, my brother's decapitated body lies as proof of that. "I only found out last night. My brother died at the front."

Julian finally turns back around, his eyes glassy. "I'm sorry, Mare. I didn't realize."

"You wouldn't. The army doesn't report executions in their little books."

"Executed?"

"Desertion." The word tastes like blood, like a lie. "Even though he never would."

After a long moment of silence, Julian puts a hand on my shoulder. "It seems we have more in common than you think, Mare."

"What do you mean?"

"They killed my sister too. She stood in the way, and she was removed. And"—his voice drops—"they'll do it again, to anyone they have to. Even Cal, even Maven, and especially *you*."

Especially me. The little lightning girl.

"I thought you wanted to change things, Julian."

"I do indeed. But these things take time, planning, and too much luck to count on." He stares me up and down, like somehow he knows I've already taken the first step down a dark path. "I don't want you getting in over your head."

Too late.

SIXTEEN

After a week of staring at my clock, waiting for midnight, I begin to despair. Of course Farley can't reach us here. Even she is not so talented. But tonight, when the clock ticks, I feel nothing for the first time since Queenstrial. No cameras, no electricity, *nothing*. The power is completely out. I've been in blackouts before, too many to count, but this is different. This isn't an accident. This is for me.

Moving quickly, I slip into my boots, now broken in by weeks of wear, and head for the door. I'm barely out in the hallway before I hear Walsh in my ear, speaking softly and quickly as she pulls me through the forced darkness.

"We don't have much time," she murmurs, hustling me into a service stairwell. It's pitch-black, but she knows where we're going, and I trust her to get me there. "They'll have the power back on in fifteen minutes if we're lucky."

"And if we aren't?" I breathe in the darkness.

She hustles me down the stairs and shoulders open a door. "Then I hope you're not too attached to your head."

The smell of earth and dirt and water hits me first, churning up all my memories of life in the woods. But even though it looks like a forest, with gnarled old trees and hundreds of plants painted blue and black by the moon, a glass roof rises overhead. *The conservatory.* Twisting shadows sprawl across the ground, each one worse than the next. I see Security and Sentinels in every dark corner, waiting to capture and kill us like they did my brother. But instead of their horrific black or flame uniforms, there's nothing but flowers blooming beneath the glass ceiling of stars.

"Excuse me if I don't curtsy," a voice says, emerging from a grove of white-spangled magnolia trees. Her blue eyes reflect the moon, glowing in the dark with cold fire. *Farley has a real talent for theatrics.*

Like in her broadcast, she wears a red scarf across her face, hiding her features. But it doesn't hide a ruinous scar that marches down her neck, disappearing beneath the collar of her shirt. It looks new, barely beginning to heal. She's been busy since I last saw her. But then, so have I.

"Farley," I say, tipping my head in greeting.

She doesn't nod back, but then, I didn't expect her to. All business. "And the other one?" she murmurs. *Other one?*

"Holland's bringing him. Any second now." Walsh sounds breathless, excited even, about whoever we're waiting for. Even Farley's eyes shine.

"What is it? Who else joined up?" They don't answer me, exchanging glances instead. A few names run through my head, servants and kitchen boys who would support the cause.

But the person who joins us is no servant. He's not even Red.

"Maven."

I don't know whether to scream or run when I see my betrothed appear from the shadows. He's a prince, he's Silver, he's the enemy, and yet, here he is, standing with one of the leaders of the Scarlet Guard. His companion Holland, an aging Red servant with years of service behind him, seems to swell with pride.

"I told you, you're not alone, Mare," Maven says, but he doesn't smile. A hand twitches at his side—he's all nerves. Farley *scares* him.

And I can see why. She steps toward us, gun in hand, but she's just as nervous as he is. Still, her voice does not shake. "I want to hear it from your lips, little prince. Tell me what you told him," she says, tipping her head toward Holland.

Maven sneers at "little prince," his lips curving in distaste, but he doesn't snap at her. "I want to join the Guard," he says, his voice full of conviction.

She moves quickly, cocking the pistol and taking aim in the same motion. My heart seems to stop when she presses the barrel to his forehead, but Maven doesn't flinch. "Why?" she hisses.

"Because this world is wrong. What my father has done, what my brother will do, *is wrong*." Even with a gun to his head, he manages to speak calmly, but a bead of sweat trickles down his neck. Farley doesn't pull away, waiting for a better answer, and I find myself doing the same.

His eyes shift, moving to mine, and he swallows hard. "When I was twelve, my father sent me to the war front, to toughen me up, to make me more like my brother. Cal is perfect, you see, so why couldn't I be the same?"

I can't help but flinch at his words, recognizing the pain in them. *I lived in Gisa's shadow, and he lived in Cal's. I know what that life is like.*

Farley sniffs, almost laughing at him. "I have no use for jealous little boys."

"I wish it was jealousy that drove me here," Maven murmurs. "I spent three years in the barracks, following Cal and officers and generals, watching soldiers fight and die for a war no one believed in. Where Cal saw honor and loyalty, I saw foolishness. I saw waste. Blood on both sides of the dividing line, and your people gave so much more."

I remember the books in Cal's room, the tactics and maneuvers laid out like a game. The memory makes me cringe, but what Maven says next chills my blood.

"There was a boy, just seventeen, a Red from the frozen north. He didn't know me on sight, not like everyone else, but he treated me just fine. He treated me like a *person*. I think he was my first real friend." Maybe it's a trick of the moonlight, but something like tears glimmer in his eyes. "His name was Thomas, and I watched him die. I could've saved him, but my guards held me back. His life wasn't worth mine, they said." Then the tears are gone, replaced by clenched fists and an iron will. "Cal calls this the balance, Silver over Red. He's a good person, and he'll be a just ruler, but he doesn't think change is worth the cost," he says. "I'm trying to tell you that I'm not the same as the rest of them. I think my life is worth yours, and I'll give it gladly, if it means change."

He is a prince and, worst of all, the queen's son. I didn't want to trust him before for this very reason, for the secrets he kept hidden. *Or maybe this is what he was hiding all along . . . his own heart.*

Though he tries his best to look grim, to keep his spine straight and his lips from trembling, I can see the boy beneath the mask. Part of me wants to embrace him, to comfort him, but Farley would stop me before I could. When she lowers her gun, slowly but surely, I let go of a breath I didn't realize I was holding in.

"The boy speaks true," the manservant Holland says. He shifts to stand next to Maven, strangely protective of his prince. "He's felt this way for months now, since he returned from the front."

"And you told him of us after a few tear-filled nights?" Farley sneers, turning her fearsome gaze on Holland. But the man holds firm.

"I've known the prince since boyhood. Anyone close to him can see his heart has changed." Holland glances sidelong at Maven, as if remembering the boy he was. "Think what an ally he could be. What a difference he could make."

Maven is different. I know that firsthand, but something tells me my words won't sway Farley. Only Maven can do that now.

"Swear on your colors," she growls at him.

An ancient oath, according to Lady Blonos. Like swearing on your life, your family, and your children to come, all at once. And Maven doesn't hesitate to do it.

"I swear on my colors," he says, dipping his head. "I pledge myself to the Scarlet Guard." It sounds like his marriage proposal, but this is far more important, and more deadly.

"Welcome to the Scarlet Guard," she finally says, pulling away her scarf.

I move quietly over the tile floor until I feel his hand in mine. It blazes with now familiar heat. "Thank you, Maven," I whisper. "You don't know what this means to us." *To me.*

Any other would smile at the prospect of recruiting a Silver, and a *royal* at that, but Farley barely reacts at all. "What are you willing to do for us?"

"I can give you information, intelligence, whatever you might need to continue forward with your operation. I sit on tax councils with my father—"

"We don't care about taxes," Farley snaps. She casts an angry glance at me, as if it's my fault she doesn't like what he's offering. "What we need are names, locations, *targets*. What to hit and when to cause the most damage. Can you give me that?"

Maven shifts, uncomfortable. "I would prefer a less hostile path," he mutters. "Your violent methods aren't winning you any friends."

Farley scoffs, letting the sound echo over the conservatory. "Your people are a thousand times more violent and cruel than mine. We've spent the last few centuries under a Silver boot, and we're not going to get out by being *nice*."

"I suppose," Maven murmurs. I can tell he's thinking of Thomas, of everyone he watched die. His shoulder brushes mine as he pulls back, retreating into me for protection. Farley doesn't miss it and almost laughs out loud.

"The little prince and the little lightning girl." She laughs. "You two suit each other. One, a coward, and you"—she turns to me, her steel-blue eyes burning—"the last time we met, you were scrabbling in the mud for a miracle."

"I found it," I tell her. To cement my point, my hands spark up, casting dancing purple light over us.

The darkness seems to shift, and members of the Scarlet Guard reveal themselves in menacing order, stepping out from trees and bushes. Their faces are masked with scarves and bandannas, but they don't hide everything. The tallest one must be Tristan, with his long limbs. I can tell by the way they stand, tense and ready for action, that they're afraid. But Farley's face doesn't change. She knows the people meant to protect her won't do much against Maven, or even me, but she doesn't look at all intimidated. To my great surprise, she finally smiles. Her grin is fearsome, full of teeth and a wild hunger.

"We can bomb and burn every inch of this country down," she murmurs, looking between us with something like pride, "but that will never do the damage you two can do. A Silver prince turning against his crown, a Red girl with abilities. What will people say, when they see you standing with us?"

"I thought you wanted—," Maven starts, but Farley waves the words away.

"The bombings are just a way to get attention. Once we have it, once every Silver in this forsaken country is watching, we need something to show them." Her gaze turns calculating as she measures us up, weighing us against whatever she has in mind. "I think you'll do quite nicely."

My voice trembles, dreading what she might say. "As what?"

"The face of our glorious revolution," she says proudly, tossing her head back. Her golden hair catches the moonlight. For a second, she seems to wear a sparkling crown. "The drop of water to break the dam."

Maven nods with fervor.

"So, where do we start?"

"Well, I think it's time we took a page out of Mare's book of mischief."

"What's that supposed to mean?" I don't understand, but Maven follows Farley's line of thought easily.

"My father has been covering up other attacks by the Guard," he mutters, explaining her plan.

My mind flickers back to Colonel Macanthos and her outburst at luncheon. "The airfield, Delphie, Harbor Bay."

Maven nods. "He called them accidents, training exercises, *lies*. But when you sparked up at Queenstrial, even my mother couldn't talk you away. We need something like that, something no one can hide. To show the world the Scarlet Guard is very dangerous and very real."

"But won't that have consequences?" My thoughts flash back to the riot, to the innocent people tortured and killed by a mindless horde. "The Silvers will turn on us, things will get *worse*."

Farley looks away, unable to hold my gaze. "And more will join us. More will realize the lives we live are *wrong* and that something can be done to change it. We've stood still for far too long; it's time to make sacrifices and move forward."

"Was my brother your sacrifice?" I snap, feeling anger flare within me. "Was his death worth it to you?"

To her credit, she doesn't try to lie. "Shade knew what he was getting into."

"And what about everyone else? What about the kids and the elders and anyone who hasn't signed up for your 'glorious revolution'? What happens when Sentinels start rounding them up for punishment when they can't find you?"

Maven's voice is warm and soft in my ear. "Think of your histories, Mare. What has Julian taught you?"

He taught me about death. The before. The wars. But beyond that, in a time when things could still change, there were revolutions. The people rose, the empires fell, and things changed. Liberty moved in arcs, rising and falling with the tide of time.

"Revolution needs a spark," I murmur, repeating what Julian would say in our lessons. "And even sparks burn."

Farley smiles. "You should know that better than anyone."

But I'm still not convinced. The pain of losing Shade, of knowing my parents have lost a child, will only multiply if we do this. How many more Shades will die?

Strangely it's Maven, not Farley, who tries to sway me.

"Cal believes that change is not worth the cost," he says. His voice shakes, quivering with nerves and conviction. "And he's going to rule one day—do you want to let him be the future?"

For once, my answer is easy. "No."

Farley nods, pleased. "Walsh and Holland"—she jerks her head toward them—"tell me there's going to be a little party here."

"The ball," Maven offers.

"It's an impossible target," I snap. "Everyone will have guards; the queen will *know* if something goes wrong—"

"She will *not*," Maven breaks in, almost scoffing at the idea. "My mother is not all-powerful, as she would want you to believe. Even she has limits."

Limits? The queen? Just the thought makes my mind run wild. "How can you say that? You know what she can do—"

"I know that in the middle of a ball, with so many voices and thoughts swirling around her, she'll be *useless*. And so long as we stay out of her path, give her no reason to prod, she won't know a thing. The same goes for the Eagrie eyes. They won't be looking ahead for trouble, and so they won't see it." He turns back to Farley, his spine straight as an arrow. "Silvers might be strong, but we are not invincible. It can be done."

Farley nods smoothly, smiling with her teeth. "We'll be in contact again, once things are set in motion."

"Can I ask something in return?" I blurt, reaching out to grab her arm. "My friend, the one I came to you about before, wants to join the Guard. But you can't let him. Just make sure he doesn't get involved in any of this."

Gently, she peels my fingers from her arm as regret clouds her eyes. "I hope you don't mean me."

To my horror, one of her shadowy guards steps forward. The red rag around his face doesn't hide the set of his broad shoulders or the ratty shirt I've seen a thousand times. But the steely look in his eyes, the determination of a man twice his age, is something I don't recognize at all. Kilorn looks years away already. Scarlet Guard to the bone, willing to fight and die for the cause. *He's Red as the dawn.*

"No," I whisper, drawing back from Farley. Now I can only see Kilorn running full speed toward his doom. "You know what happened to Shade. You can't do this."

He pulls away the rag and reaches out to embrace me, but I step away. His touch feels like a betrayal. "Mare, you don't have to keep trying to save me."

"I will as long as you won't." How can he expect to be anything but a human shield? *How can he do this?* Far away, something hums at me, growing louder by the second, but I barely notice. I'm more focused on keeping the tears from falling in front of Farley and the Guard and Maven.

"Kilorn, please."

He darkens at my words, like they're an insult rather than a young girl's plea.

"You made your choice, and I'm making mine."

"I made the choice for *you*, to keep you safe," I snap. It's amazing how easily we fall back into our old rhythm, bickering like always. But there's much more on the line now. I can't just shove him into the mud and walk away. "I bargained for you."

"You're doing what you think will protect me, Mare," he mutters, his voice a low rumble. "So let me do what I can to save you."

My eyes squeeze shut, letting my heartache take over. I've been protecting Kilorn every day since his mother left, since he almost starved to death in my doorway. And now he won't let me, no matter how dangerous the future has become.

Slowly, I open my eyes again.

"Do what you want, Kilorn." My voice is cold and mechanical, like the wires and circuits trying to switch back on. "The power's coming back soon. We should be on the move."

The others spring into action, disappearing into the conservatory, and Walsh takes me by the arm. Kilorn backs away, following the others into the shadows, but his eyes stay on me.

"Mare," he calls after me. "At least say good-bye."

But I'm already walking, Maven by my side, Walsh leading us both. I won't look back, not now when he's betrayed all I've ever done for him.

Time moves slowly when you're waiting for something good, so naturally the days fly by as the dreaded ball approaches. A week passes without any contact, leaving Maven and me in the dark as the hours march on. More Training, more Protocol, more brainless lunches that almost leave me in tears. Every time I have to lie, to praise the Silvers and rip down my own. Only the Guard keeps me strong.

Lady Blonos scolds me for being distracted in Protocol. I don't have the heart to tell her that, distracted or not, I'll never be able to learn the dance steps she's trying to teach for the Parting Ball. As suited as I might be to sneaking, I'm horrible with rhythmic motion. Meanwhile, the once dreaded Training is an outlet for all my anger and stress, allowing me to run or spark off everything I'm trying to keep inside.

But just when I'm finally beginning to get the hang of things, the mood of Training shifts drastically. Evangeline and her lackeys don't snipe at me, instead focusing intently on their warm-ups. Even Maven goes through his stretches more carefully, like he's preparing for something.

"What's going on?" I ask him, nodding to the rest of the class. My eyes linger on Cal, currently doing push-ups in perfect form.

"You'll see in a minute," Maven replies, his voice oddly dull.

When Arven enters with Provos, even he has a strange spring in his step. He doesn't bark out an order to run and approaches the class instead.

"Tirana," Instructor Arven murmurs.

A girl in a blue-striped suit, the nymph from House Osanos, jumps to attention. She makes her way toward the center of the floor, waiting for something. She looks equal parts excited and terrified.

Arven turns, searching through us. For a second, his eyes linger on me but thankfully shift to Maven.

"Prince Maven, if you please." He gestures to where Tirana waits.

Maven nods and moves to stand beside her. Both of them tense, fingers twitching as they await whatever's coming.

Suddenly, the training floor moves around them, pushing clear walls up to form something. Again, Provos raises his arms, using his abilities to transform the training hall. As the structure takes shape, my heart hammers, realizing exactly what it is.

An arena.

Cal takes Maven's place at my side, his movements quick and silent. "They won't hurt each other," he explains. "Arven stops us before anyone can do real damage, and there are healers on hand."

"Comforting," I choke out.

In the center of the quickly forming arena, both Maven and Tirana prepare for their match. Maven's bracelet sparks, and fire blazes in his hands, streaking up his arms, while droplets of moisture leech from the air to swirl around Tirana in a ghostly display. Both of them look ready for battle.

Something about my unease sets Cal on edge. "Is Maven the only thing you're worried about?"

Not even close. "Protocol's not exactly easy right now." I'm not lying, but on my list of problems, learning to dance is at the very bottom. "It seems I'm even worse at dancing than memorizing court etiquette."

To my surprise, Cal laughs loudly. "You must be horrible."

"Well, it's difficult to learn without a partner," I snap, bristling at him.

"Indeed."

The last two pieces lock together, completing the training arena and fencing in Maven and his opponent. Now they're separated from the rest of us by thick glass, trapped together in a miniature version of a battle arena. *The last time I watched Silvers fight, someone almost died.*

"Who has the advantage?" Arven says, questioning the class. Every hand but mine shoots into the air. "Elane?"

The Haven girl juts her chin forward, speaking proudly. "Tirana has the advantage. She is older and more experienced." Elane says this like it's the most obvious thing in the world. Maven's cheeks flush white, though he tries to hide it. "And water defeats fire."

"Very good." Arven shifts his eyes back to Maven, daring him to argue. But Maven holds his tongue, letting the growing fire speak for him. "Impress me."

They collide, spitting fire and rain in a duel of the elements. Tirana uses her water like a shield, and to Maven's fiery attacks, it's impenetrable. Every time he gets close to her, swinging with flaming fists, he comes back with nothing but steam. The battle looks even, but somehow Maven seems to have the edge. He's on the offensive, backing her into a wall.

All around us, the class cheers, goading on the warriors. I used to be disgusted by displays like this, but now I'm having a hard time keeping quiet. Every time Maven attacks, closer to pinning down Tirana, it's all I can do not to cheer with the others.

"It's a trap, Mavey," Cal whispers, more to himself than anyone.

"What is it? What's she going to do?"

Cal shakes his head. "Just watch. She's got him."

But Tirana looks anything but victorious. She's flat against the wall, dueling hard behind her watery shield as she blocks blow after blow.

I don't miss the lightning-quick moment as Tirana literally turns the tide on Maven. She grabs his arm and pulls, spinning around so they trade places in a heartbeat. Now it's Maven behind her shield, pinned between the water and the wall. But he can't control the water, and it presses against him, holding him back even as he tries to burn it away. The water only boils, bubbling over his blazing skin.

Tirana stands back, watching him struggle with a smile on her face. "Yield?"

A stream of bubbles escapes Maven's lips. *Yield*.

The water drops from him, vaporizing back into the air to the sound of applause. Provos waves a hand again, and one of the arena walls slides back. Tirana gives a tiny bow while Maven trudges out of the circle, a soggy, pouting mess.

"I challenge Elane Haven," Sonya Iral says sharply, trying to get the words out before our instructor can pair her with someone else. Arven nods, allowing the challenge, before turning his gaze on Elane. To my surprise, she smiles and saunters toward the arena, her long red hair swaying with the movement.

"I accept your challenge," Elane replies, taking a spot in the center of the arena. "I hope you've learned some new tricks."

Sonya follows, eyes dancing. She even laughs. "You think I'd tell you if I did?"

Somehow they manage to giggle and smile right up until Elane Haven disappears entirely and grabs Sonya around the throat. She chokes, gasping for air, before twisting in the invisible girl's arms and slipping away. Their match devolves quickly into a deadly, violent game of cat and invisible mouse.

Maven doesn't bother to watch, angry with himself over his performance. "Yes?" he says to Cal, and his brother launches headfirst into a hushed lecture. I get the feeling this is normal.

"Don't corner someone better than you, it makes them more dangerous," he says, putting an arm around his brother's shoulder. "You can't beat her with ability, so beat her with your head."

"I'll keep that in mind," Maven mutters, begrudging the advice but taking it all the same.

"You're getting better though," Cal murmurs, patting Maven on the shoulder. He means well but comes off as patronizing. I'm surprised Maven doesn't snap at him—but he's used to this, like I was used to Gisa.

"Thanks, Cal. I think he gets it," I say, speaking for Maven.

His older brother isn't stupid and takes the hint with a frown. With nothing but a backward glance at me, Cal leaves us to stand with Evangeline. I wish he wouldn't, just so I don't have to watch her smirk and gloat. Not to mention I get this strange twist in my stomach every time he looks at her.

Once he's out of earshot, I nudge Maven with my shoulder. "He's right, you know. You have to outsmart people like that."

In front of us, Sonya grabs on to what seems like air and slams it against the wall. Silver liquid spatters, and Elane flutters back into visibility, a trail of blood streaming from her nose.

"He's always right when it comes to the arena," he rumbles, strangely upset. "Just wait and see."

Across the arena, Evangeline smiles at the murderous display between us. How she can watch her friends bleeding on the floor, I don't know. *Silvers are different*, I remind myself. *Their scars don't last. They don't remember pain.* With skin healers waiting in the wings, violence has taken on a new meaning for them. A broken spine, a split stomach, it doesn't matter. Someone will always come to fix you. They don't know the meaning of danger or fear or pain. It's only their pride that can be truly hurt.

You are Silver. You are Mareena Titanos. You enjoy this.

Cal's eyes dart between the girls, studying them like a book or a painting rather than a moving mass of blood and bone. Beneath the black cut of his training suit, his muscles tense, ready for his turn.

And when it comes, I understand what Maven means.

Instructor Arven pits Cal against two others, the windweaver Oliver and Cyrine Macanthos, a girl who turns her skin to stone. It's a match in name only. Despite being outnumbered, Cal toys with the other two. He incapacitates them one at a time, trapping Oliver in a swirl of fire while trading blows with Cyrine. She looks like a living statue, made of solid rock rather than flesh, but Cal's stronger. His blows splinter her rocky skin, sending spider cracks through her body with every punch. This is just practice to him; he almost looks bored. He ends the match when the arena explodes into a churning inferno that even Maven steps back from. By the time the smoke and fire clears, both Oliver and Cyrine have yielded. Their skin cracks in bits of burned flesh, but neither cries out.

Cal leaves them both behind, not bothering to watch as a skin healer appears to fix them up. He saved me, he brought me home, he broke the rules for me. And he's a merciless soldier, the heir to a bloody throne.

Cal's blood might be silver, but his heart is black as burned skin.

When his eyes trail to mine, I force myself to look away. Instead of letting his warmth, his strange kindness confuse me, I commit the inferno to memory. *Cal is more dangerous than all of them put together. I cannot forget that.*

"Evangeline, Andros," Arven clips, nodding at the pair of them. Andros deflates, almost annoyed at the prospect of fighting—and losing—to Evangeline, but dutifully trudges into the arena. To my surprise, Evangeline doesn't budge.

"No," she says boldly, planting her feet.

When Arven whirls to her, his voice rises above his usual whisper and it cuts like a razor. "I beg your pardon, Lady Samos?"

She turns her black eyes on me, and her gaze is sharp as any knife.

"I challenge Mareena Titanos."

SEVENTEEN

"Absolutely not," Maven rumbles. "She's been training for only two weeks; you'll cut her apart."

In response, Evangeline just shrugs, letting a lazy smirk rise to her features. Her fingers dance against her leg, and I can almost feel them like claws across my skin.

"So what if she does?" Sonya breaks in, and I think I see a gleam of her grandmother in her eye. "The healers are here. There'll be no harm done. Besides, if she's going to train with us, she might as well do it properly, right?"

No harm done, I scoff in my head. *No harm but my blood exposed for all to see.* My heartbeat thumps in my head, quickening with every passing second. Overhead, the lights shine brightly, illuminating the ring; my blood will be hard to hide, and they'll see me for what I am. The Red, the liar, the thief.

"I'd like some more time observing before I get in the ring, if you don't mind," I reply, trying my best to sound Silver. Instead, my voice quavers. Evangeline catches it.

"Too scared to fight?" she goads, lazily flicking a hand. One of her knives, a little thing like a tooth of silver, circles her wrist slowly in open threat. "Poor little lightning girl."

Yes, I want to scream. *Yes, I am scared*. But Silvers don't admit things like that. Silvers have their pride, their strength—and nothing else. "When I fight, I intend to win," I say instead, throwing her words back in her face. "I'm not a fool, Evangeline, and I cannot win yet."

"Training outside the ring can only get you so far, Mareena," Sonya purrs, latching on to my lie with glee. "Don't you agree, Instructor? How can she ever expect to win if she doesn't try?"

Arven knows there's something different about me, a reason for my ability and my strength. But what that is, he cannot fathom, and there's a glint of curiosity in his eye. He wants to see me in the ring as well. And my only allies, Cal and Maven, exchange worried glances, wondering how to proceed across such shaky ground. *Didn't they expect this? Didn't they think it would come to this?*

Or maybe this is what I've been headed for all along. An accidental death in Training, another lie for the queen to tell, a fitting death for the girl who doesn't belong. It's a trap I willingly stepped into.

The game will be over. And everyone I love will have lost.

"Lady Titanos is the daughter of a dead war hero and you can do nothing but tease her," Cal growls, throwing daggered glances at the girls. They barely seem to notice, almost laughing at his poor defense. He might be a born fighter, but he's at a loss when it comes to words.

Sonya is even more incensed, her sly nature taking hold. Whereas Cal is a warrior in the ring, she is a soldier of speech, and twists his words with frightening ease. "A general's daughter should do well in the ring. If anything, Evangeline should be afraid."

"She wasn't raised by a general, don't be foolish—," Maven sneers.

He's much better at this sort of thing, but I cannot let him win my battles. Not with these girls.

"I will not fight," I say again. "Challenge someone else."

When Evangeline smiles, her teeth white and sharp, my old instincts ring in my head like a bell. I barely have time to drop as her knife burns through the air, cutting through the spot where my neck was seconds before.

"I challenge you," she snaps, and another blade flies at my face. More rise from her belt, ready to cut me to ribbons.

"Evangeline, stop—," Maven shouts, and Cal pulls me to my feet, his eyes alive with worry. My blood sings, coursing with adrenaline, my pulse so loud I almost miss his whispered words.

"You're faster. Keep her on the run. *Don't be afraid.*" Another knife blazes by, this time digging into the ground at my feet. "Don't let her see you bleed."

Over his shoulder, Evangeline prowls like a predatory cat, a glittering storm of knives in her fist. In that instant, I know nothing and no one will stop her. Not even the princes. And I cannot give her the chance to win. *I cannot lose.*

A bolt of lightning escapes me, streaking through the air at my command. It hits her in the chest and she staggers back, colliding with the outer wall of the arena. But instead of looking angry, Evangeline regards me with glee.

"This will be quick, little lightning girl," she snarls, wiping away a trickle of silverblood.

All around, the other students draw back, glancing between the two of us. This could be the last time they see me alive. *No*, I think again. *I cannot lose.* My focus intensifies, deepening my sense of power until it's so strong I hardly notice the walls shifting around us. With a click, Provos re-forms the arena, locking us in together, a Red girl and a smiling Silver monster.

She grins across at me, and razor-thin pieces of metal peel off the floor, shaped to her will. They curl and shudder and scrape into a living nightmare. Her usual blades are gone, tossed aside for a new tactic. The metal things, creatures of her mind, skitter across the floor to stop at her feet. Each one has eight razored legs, sharp and cruel. They quiver as they wait to be released, to cut me apart. *Spiders*. A horrible crawling sensation prickles my skin, like they're already upon me.

Sparks come to life in my hands, dancing between my fingers. The lights flicker as the energy in the room bleeds into me like water soaking into a sponge. Power races through me, driven by my own strength—and by need. *I will not die here.*

On the other side of the wall, Maven smiles, but his face is pale, afraid. Next to him, Cal doesn't move. A soldier doesn't blink until the battle is won.

"Who has the advantage?" Instructor Arven asks. "Mareena or Evangeline?"

No one raises a hand. Not even Evangeline's friends. Instead, they stare between us, watching our abilities grow.

Evangeline's smile fades into a sneer. She's used to being favored, to being the one everyone's afraid of. And now she's angrier than ever.

Again, the lights flicker on and off, as my body hums like an overloaded wire. In the flashing darkness, her spiders scrabble over the floor, their metal legs clanging in terrible harmony.

And then all I know is fear and power and the surge of energy in my veins.

Darkness and light explode back and forth, plunging us both into a strange battle of flickering color. My lightning bursts through the darkness, streaking purple and white as it shatters through spiders at every turn. Cal's advice echoes in my head, and I keep moving, never sticking to one spot on the floor long enough for Evangeline to hurt me. She weaves through her spiders, dodging my sparks as best she can. Jagged metal tears at my arms, but the leather suit holds firm. She's fast, but I'm faster, even with spiders clawing around my legs. For a second, her infuriating silver braid passes through my fingertips, before she's out of reach again. But I've got her on the run. *I'm winning.*

I hear Maven through the shriek of metal and cheering classmates, roaring for me to finish her. The lights flash, making her hard to spot, but for a brief moment, I feel what it's like to be one of them. To feel strength and power absolutely, to know you can do what millions can't. Evangeline feels like this every day, and now it's my turn. *I'll teach you what it's like to know fear.*

A fist slams against the small of my back, shooting pain through the rest of my body. My knees buckle with the agony, sending me to the ground. Evangeline pauses above me, her smile surrounded by a messy curtain of silver hair.

"Like I said," she snarls. "Quick."

My legs move on their own, swinging out in a maneuver I've used in the back alleys of the Stilts a hundred times. Even on Kilorn once or twice. My foot connects with her leg, sweeping it out from under her, and she crashes to the floor next to me. I'm on her in a second, despite the exploding pain in my back. My hands crackle with hot energy, even as they collide against her face. Pain sears through my knucklebones but I keep going, wanting to see sweet silverblood.

"You'll wish it was quick," I roar, bearing down on her.

Somehow, through her bruising lips, Evangeline manages to laugh. The sound melts away, replaced by metallic screeching. And all around us, the fallen, electrified spiders twitch to life. Their metal bodies re-form, weaving together at the seams, into a ruinous, smoking beast.

It skitters with surprising speed, knocking me off her. I'm the one pinned now, looking up at the heaving, twisting shards of metal. The sparks die in my hands, driven away by fear and exhaustion. *Even the healers won't be able to save me after this.*

A razor leg drags across my face, drawing red, hot blood. I hear myself scream, not in pain, but defeat. *This is the end.*

And then a blazing arm of fire knocks the metal monster off me, burning it into nothing more than a charred black pile of ash. Strong hands pull me to my feet and then go to my hair, pulling it across my face to hide the red mark that could betray me. I turn in to Maven, letting him walk me from the training room. Every inch of me shakes, but he keeps me steady and moving. A healer comes my way, but Cal heads him off, blocking my face from his sight.

Before the door slams behind us, I hear Evangeline yelling and Cal's usually calm voice yelling right back, roaring over her like a storm.

My voice breaks when I finally speak again. "The cameras, the cameras can see."

"Sentinels sworn to my mother man the cameras, trust me, they aren't what we should be worrying about," Maven says, almost tripping over his words. He keeps a tight grip on my arm, like he's afraid I might be pulled away from him. His hand ghosts over my face, wiping away the blood with his sleeve. *If anyone sees* . . .

"Take me to Julian."

"Julian's a fool," he mutters.

Figures appear at the far end of the hall, a pair of roaming nobles, and he pushes us down a service passage to avoid them.

"Julian knows who I am," I whisper back, grabbing on to him. As his grip tightens, so does mine. "Julian will know what to do."

Maven looks down on me, conflicted, but finally nods. By the time we reach Julian's quarters, the bleeding has stopped, but my face is still a mess.

He opens the door on the first knock, looking his usual haphazard self. To my surprise, he frowns at Maven.

"Prince Maven," he says, bending into a stiff, almost insulting bow. Maven doesn't respond, only pushes me past Julian into the sitting room beyond.

Julian has a small set of rooms, made smaller by darkness and stale air. The curtains are drawn, blotting out the afternoon sun, and the floor is slippery with loose stacks of paper. A kettle simmers in the corner, on an electric piece of metal meant to replace a stove. No wonder I never see him outside of Lessons; he appears to have everything he needs right here.

"What's going on?" he asks, waving us to a pair of dusty chairs. Obviously he doesn't entertain much. I take a seat, but Maven refuses, still standing.

I draw aside my curtain of hair, revealing the shining red flag of my identity. "Evangeline got carried away."

Julian shifts, uncomfortable on his own two feet. But it's not me making him squirm; it's Maven. The two glare at each other, at odds over something I don't understand. Finally, he turns his gaze back on me. "I'm not a skin healer, Mare. The best I can do is clean you up."

"I told you," Maven says. "He can't do anything."

Julian's lip curls into a snarl. "Find Sara Skonos," he snaps, his jaw tightening as he waits for Maven to move. I've never seen Maven this angry, not even with Cal. But then, it's not anger spilling out from

Maven or Julian—it's *hate*. They absolutely despise each other.

"Do it, *my prince*." The title sounds like a curse coming from Julian's lips.

Maven finally concedes and slips out the door.

"What's that all about?" I whisper, gesturing between Julian and the door.

"Not now," he says, and tosses me a white cloth to clean myself with. It stains a dark red as my blood ruins the fabric.

"Who's Sara Skonos?"

Again, Julian hesitates. "A skin healer. She'll take care of you." He sighs. "And she's a friend. A discreet friend."

I didn't know Julian had friends beyond me and his books, but I don't question him.

When Maven slips back into the room a few moments later, I've managed to clean my face properly, though it still feels sticky and swollen. I'll have a few bruises to hide tomorrow, and I don't even want to know what my back looks like now. Gingerly, I touch the growing lump where Evangeline punched me.

"Sara's not . . ." Maven pauses, mulling over the words. "She's not who I would have chosen for this."

Before I can ask why, the door opens, revealing the woman I assume is Sara. She enters silently, barely raising her eyes. Unlike the others, the Blonos blood healers, her age is displayed proudly on her face, in every wrinkle and her sunken, hollow cheeks. She looks to be about Julian's age, but her shoulders droop in a way that tells me her life has felt far longer than his.

"Nice to meet you, Lady Skonos." My voice is calm, like I'm asking about the weather. It seems my Protocol lessons might be sinking in after all.

But Sara doesn't respond. Instead, she drops to her knees in front of my chair and takes my face in her rough hands. Her touch is cool, like water on a sunburn, and her fingers trail over the gash on my cheek with surprising gentleness. She works diligently, healing over the other bruises on my face. Before I can mention my back, she slips a hand down to the injury, and something like soothing ice bleeds through the pain. It's all over in a few moments, and I feel like I did when I first came here. Better, in fact. My old aches and bruises are completely gone.

"Thank you," I say, but again, I get no response.

"Thank you, Sara," Julian breathes, and her eyes dart to his in a flash of gray color. Her head bows slightly, in the tiniest nod. He reaches forward, a hand brushing her arm as he helps her to her feet. The two of them move like partners in a dance, listening to music no one else can hear.

Maven's voice shatters their silence. "That will be all, Skonos."

Sara's quiet calm melts into barely concealed anger as she spins out of Julian's grip, scrambling for the door like a wounded animal. The door shuts behind her with a slam, shaking the framed maps in their glass prisons. Even Julian's hands shake, trembling long after she's gone, like he can still feel her.

He tries to hide it, but not well: Julian was in love with her once, and maybe even still is. He looks at the door like a man haunted, waiting for her to come back.

"Julian?"

"The longer you're gone, the more people will start to talk," he mutters, gesturing for us to leave.

"I agree." Maven moves to the door, ready to open it and shove me back out.

"Are you sure no one saw?" My hand moves to my cheek, now smooth and clean.

Maven pauses, thinking. "No one who would say anything."

"Secrets don't stay secrets here," Julian mutters. His voice quivers with rare anger. "You know that, Your Highness."

"*You* should know the difference between secrets," Maven snaps, "and lies."

His hand closes around my wrist, pulling me back out into the hall before I can bother to ask what's going on. We don't make it far before a familiar figure stops us.

"Trouble, dear?"

Queen Elara, a vision in silk, addresses Maven. Strangely, she's alone, with no Sentinels to guard her. Her eyes linger on his hand still in mine. For once, I don't feel her try to push her way into my thoughts. *She's in Maven's head right now, not mine.*

"Nothing I can't handle," Maven says, tightening his grip on me like I'm some kind of anchor.

She raises an eyebrow, not believing a word he says, but doesn't question him. I doubt she really questions anyone; *she knows all the answers.*

"Best hurry up, Lady Mareena, or you'll be late for luncheon," she purrs, finally turning her ghostly eyes on me. And then it's my turn to hold on to Maven. "And take a little more care in your Training sessions. Red blood is just so hard to clean up."

"You would know," I snap, remembering Shade. "Because no matter how hard you try to hide it, I see it all over your hands."

Her eyes widen, surprised at my outburst. I don't think anyone's ever spoken to her this way, and it makes me feel like a conqueror. But it doesn't last long.

Suddenly my body twitches backward, throwing itself into the passage wall with a resounding smack. She makes me dance like a puppet on violent strings. Every bone rattles and my neck cracks, slamming my head back until I see icy blue stars.

No, not stars. Eyes. Her eyes.

"Mother!" Maven shouts, but his voice sounds far away. "Mother, stop!"

A hand closes around my throat, holding me in place as control of my own body ebbs away. Her breath is sweet on my face, too sweet to stand.

"You will not speak to me like that again," Elara says, too angry to bother whispering in my head. Her grip tightens, and I couldn't even agree with her if I wanted to.

Why doesn't she just kill me? I wonder as I gasp for breath. *If I'm such a burden, such a problem, why doesn't she just kill me?*

"That's enough!" Maven roars, the heat of his anger pulsing through the passage. Even through the hazy darkness eating at my vision, I see him pull her off me with surprising strength and boldness.

Her ability's hold on me breaks, letting me slump against the wall. Elara almost stumbles herself, reeling with shock. Now her glare turns on Maven, on her own son standing against her.

"Return to your schedule, Mare." He seethes, not breaking eye contact with his mother. I don't doubt she's screaming in his head, scolding him for protecting me. "Go!"

Heat crackles all around, radiating off his skin, and for a moment I'm reminded of Cal's guarded temper. It seems Maven hides a fire as well, an even stronger one, and I don't want to be around when it explodes.

As I scramble away, trying to put as much distance as I can between myself and the queen, I can't help but look back at them. They stare at each other, two pieces squaring off in a game I don't understand.

Back in my room, the maids wait silently, another gilded dress laid across their arms. While one slips me into the spectacle of silk and purple gemstones, the others fix my hair and makeup. As usual, they don't say a word, even though I look frantic and harried after such a morning.

Lunch is a mixed affair. Usually the women eat together to discuss the upcoming weddings and all the silly things rich ladies talk about, but today is different. We're back on the terrace overlooking the river, the red uniforms of servants floating through the crowd, but there are far more military uniforms than ever before. It seems like we're dining with a full legion.

Cal and Maven are there as well, both glittering in their medals, and they smile through pleasant conversation while the king himself shakes hands with the soldiers. All the soldiers are young, in gray uniforms cut with silver insignia. Nothing like the ratty red fatigues my brothers and any other Reds get when they're conscripted. These Silvers are going to war, yes, but not to the real fighting. They're the sons and daughters of important people, and to them, the war is just another place to visit. Another step in their training. To us, to me once, it is a dead end. It is doom.

But I still have to do my duty, to smile and shake their hands and thank them for their brave service. Each word tastes bitter, until I have to duck away from the crowd to an alcove half hidden by plants. The noise of the crowd still rises with the midday sun, but I can breathe again. For a second, at least.

"Everything okay?"

Cal stands over me, looking worried but strangely relaxed. He likes being around soldiers; I suppose it's his natural habitat.

Even though I want to disappear, my spine straightens. "I'm not a fan of beauty pageants."

He frowns. "Mare, they're going to the front. I'd think you of all people would want to give them a proper send-off."

The laugh escapes me like gunfire. "What part of my life makes you think I'd *care* about these brats going off to war like it's some kind of vacation?"

"Just because they've chosen to go doesn't make them any less brave."

"Well, I hope they enjoy their barracks and supplies and reprieves and all the things my brothers were never given." I doubt these willing soldiers will ever want for so much as a button.

Even though he looks like he wants to yell at me, Cal swallows the urge. Now that I know what his temper is capable of, I'm surprised he can keep himself in check at all.

"This is the first completely Silver legion going into the trenches," he says evenly. "They're going to fight with the Reds, dressed as Reds, serving with Reds. The Lakelanders won't know who they are when they get to the Choke. And when the bombs fall, when the enemy tries to break the line, they're going to get more than they bargained for. The Shadow Legion will take them all."

Suddenly I feel hot and cold at the same time. "Original."

But Cal doesn't gloat. Instead, he looks sad. "You gave me the idea."

"What?"

"When you fell into Queenstrial, no one knew what to do. I'm sure the Lakelanders will feel the same."

Though I try to speak, no sound comes out. I've never been a point of inspiration for anything, let alone combat maneuvers. Cal stares at me like he wants to say more, but he doesn't speak. Neither of us knows what to say.

A boy from our training, the windweaver Oliver, claps a hand on Cal's shoulder while the other clutches a sloshing drink. He wears a uniform too. *He's going to fight.*

"What's with the hiding, Cal?" He chuckles, gesturing to the crowd around us. "Next to the Lakelanders, this bunch will be easy!"

Cal meets my eyes, a silver blush tingeing his cheeks. "I'll take the Lakelanders any day," he replies, his eyes never leaving mine.

"You're going with them?"

Oliver answers for Cal, smiling much too wide for a boy going off to war. "Going?" he says. "Cal's leading us! His own legion, all the way to the front."

Slowly, Cal shifts out of Oliver's grip. The drunk windweaver doesn't seem to notice and keeps babbling. "He'll be the youngest general in history and the first prince to fight on the lines."

And the first to die, a morose voice in my head whispers. Against my better instincts, I reach out to Cal. He doesn't pull away from me, allowing me to hold his arm. Now he doesn't look like a prince or a general or even a Silver, but that boy at the bar, the one who wanted to save me.

My voice is small but strong. "When?"

"When you leave for the capital, after the ball. You'll go south," he murmurs, "and I'll go north."

A cold shock of fear ripples through me, like when Kilorn first told me he was going to fight. But Kilorn is a fisher boy, a thief, someone who knows how to survive, how to slip through the cracks; not like Cal. He's a soldier. He'll die if he has to. He'll bleed for his war. And why this frightens me, I don't know. Why I care, I can't say.

"With Cal on the lines, this war will finally be over. With Cal, we can win," Oliver says, grinning like a fool. Again, he takes Cal by the shoulder, but this time he steers him away, back toward the party—leaving me behind.

Someone presses a cold drink into my hand, and I down it in a single gulp.

"Easy there," Maven mutters. "Still thinking about this morning? No one saw your face, I checked with the Sentinels."

But that's the farthest thing from my mind as I watch Cal shake hands with his father. He pastes a magnificent smile on his face, donning a mask only I can see through.

Maven follows my gaze and my thoughts. "He wanted to do this. It was his choice."

"That doesn't mean we have to like it."

"My son the general!" King Tiberias booms, his proud voice cutting through the din of the party. For a second, when he pulls Cal close, putting an arm around his son, I forget he's a king. I almost understand Cal's need to please him.

What would I give to see my mother look at me like that, back when I was nothing but a thief? What would I give now?

This world is Silver, but it is also gray. There is no black-and-white.

When someone knocks at my door that night, long after dinner, I'm expecting Walsh and another cup of secret-message tea, but Cal stands there instead. Without his uniform or armor, he looks like the boy he is. *Barely nineteen, on the edge of doom or greatness or both.*

I shrink in my pajamas, wishing very much for a robe. "Cal? What do you need?"

He shrugs, smirking a little bit. "Evangeline almost killed you in the ring today."

"So?"

"So I don't want her to kill you on the dance floor."

"Did I miss something? Are we going to be fighting at the ball?"

He laughs, leaning against the doorframe. But his feet never enter my room, like he can't. Or he shouldn't. *You're going to be his brother's wife. And he's going to war.*

"If you know how to dance properly, you won't have to."

I remember mentioning how I can't dance for my life, let alone under Blonos's terrible direction, but how can Cal help me here? And why would he want to?

"I'm a surprisingly good teacher," he adds, smiling crookedly. When he stretches out a hand to me, my body shivers.

I know I shouldn't. I know I should shut the door and not go down this road.

But he's leaving to fight, maybe to die.

Shaking, I put my hand in his and let him pull me out of my room.

EIGHTEEN

Moonlight falls on the floor, bright enough for us to see by. In the silvery light, the red blush in my skin is barely visible—I look the same as a Silver. Chairs scrape along the wood floor as Cal rearranges the sitting room, clearing space for us to practice. The chamber is secluded, but the hum of cameras is never far away. Elara's men are watching, but no one comes to stop us. Or rather, to stop Cal.

He pulls a strange device, a little box, out of his jacket and sets it in the middle of the floor. He stares at it expectantly, waiting for something.

"Can that thing teach me how to dance?"

He shakes his head, still smiling. "No, but it'll help."

Suddenly, a pulsing beat explodes from the box, and I realize it's a speaker, like the ones in the arena back home. Only this is for music, not battle. Life, not death.

The melody is light and quick, like a heartbeat. Across from me, Cal smiles wider, and his foot taps in time. I can't resist, my own toes wiggling with the music. It's so bouncy and upbeat, not at all like the cold, metallic music of Blonos's classroom or the sorrowful songs of home. My feet slide along, trying to remember the steps Lady Blonos taught me.

"Don't worry about that, just keep moving." Cal laughs. A drumbeat trills over the music, and he spins, humming along. For the first time, he looks like he doesn't have the weight of a throne on his shoulders.

I feel it too as my fears and worries lift, if only for a few minutes. This is a different kind of freedom, like flying along on Cal's cycle.

Cal's much better at this than me, but he still looks like a fool; I can only imagine how idiotic I must appear. Still, I'm sad when the song ends. As the notes fade away into the air, it feels like I'm falling back to reality. Cold understanding creeps through me; *I shouldn't be here.*

"This probably isn't the best idea, Cal."

He cocks his head, pleasantly confused. "Why's that?"

He's really going to make me say it. "I'm not even supposed to be alone with Maven." I stumble over the words, feeling myself flush. "I don't know if dancing with you in a dark room is exactly okay."

Instead of arguing, Cal just laughs and shrugs. Another song, slower with a haunting tune, fills the room. "The way I see it, I'm doing my brother a favor." Then he grins crookedly. "Unless you want to step on his feet all night?"

"I have *excellent* footing, thank you very much," I say, crossing my arms.

Slowly, softly, he takes my hand. "Maybe in the ring," he says. "The dance floor, not so much." I look down to watch his feet, moving in time with the music. He pulls me along, forcing me to follow, and, despite my best efforts, I stumble against him.

He smiles, happy to prove me wrong. He's a soldier at heart, and soldiers like to win. "This is the same timing as most of the songs you'll hear at the ball. It's a simple dance, easy to learn."

"I'll find some way to mess it up," I grumble, allowing him to push me around the floor. Our feet trace a rough box, and I try not to think about his closeness, or the calluses of his hands. To my surprise, they feel like mine: rough with years of work.

"You might," he murmurs, all his laughter gone.

I'm used to Cal being taller than me, but he seems smaller tonight. Maybe it's the darkness, or maybe it's the dance. He seems like he did when I first met him; not a prince but a person.

His eyes linger on my face, tracing over where my wound was. "Maven fixed you up nicely." There's an odd bitterness to his voice.

"It was Julian. Julian and Sara Skonos." Though Cal doesn't react as strongly as Maven did, his jaw tightens all the same. "Why don't you two like her?"

"Maven has his reasons, good reasons," he mumbles. "But it's not my story to tell. And I don't *dislike* Sara. I just don't—I don't like thinking about her."

"Why? What's she done to you?"

"Not to me," he sighs. "She grew up with Julian, and my mother." His voice drops at the mention of his mom. "She was her best friend. And when she died, Sara didn't know how to grieve. Julian was a wreck, but Sara . . ." He trails off, wondering how to continue. Our steps slow until we stop, frozen as the music echoes around us.

"I don't remember my mother," he says sharply, trying to explain himself. "I wasn't even a year old when she died. I only know what my father tells me, and Julian. And neither of them like to talk about her at all."

"I'm sure Sara could tell you about her, if they were best friends."

"Sara Skonos can't speak, Mare."

"At all?"

Cal continues slowly, in the level, calm voice his father uses. "She said things she shouldn't have, terrible lies, and she was punished for it."

Horror bleeds through me. *Can't speak.* "What did she say?"

In a single heartbeat, Cal goes cold under my fingers. He draws back, stepping out of my arms as the music finally dies. With quick motions, he pockets the speaker, and there is nothing but our beating hearts to fill the silence.

"I don't want to talk about her anymore." He breathes heavily. His eyes seem oddly bright, flickering between me and the windows full of moonlight.

Something twists in my heart; the pain in his voice hurts me. "Okay."

With quick, deliberate steps, he moves toward the door like he's trying very hard not to run. But when he turns back around and faces me across the room, he looks the same as usual—calm, collected, detached.

"Practice your steps," he says, sounding very much like Lady Blonos. "Same time tomorrow." And then he's gone, leaving me alone in a room full of echoes.

"What the hell am I doing?" I mutter to no one but myself.

I'm halfway to my bed before I realize something is very wrong with my room: the cameras are off. Not a single one hums at me, seeing with electric eyes, recording everything I do. But unlike the outage before, everything else around me still buzzes along. Electricity still pulses through the walls, to every room but mine.

Farley.

But instead of the revolutionary, Maven steps out of the darkness.

He throws aside the curtains, letting in enough moonlight to see by.

"Late-night walk?" he says with a bitter smile.

My mouth falls open, struggling for words. "You know you're not supposed to be in here." I force a smile, hoping to calm myself. "Lady Blonos will be scandalized. She'll punish us both."

"Mother's men owe me a favor or two," he says, pointing to where the cameras are hidden. "Blonos won't have evidence to convict."

Somehow that doesn't comfort me. Instead, I feel shivers run over my skin. Not in fear though, but anticipation. The shivers deepen, electrifying my nerves like my lightning as Maven takes measured steps toward me.

He watches me blush with what looks like satisfaction. "Sometimes I forget," he murmurs, letting a hand touch my cheek. It lingers, like he can feel the color that pulses in my veins. "I wish they wouldn't have to paint you up every day."

My skin buzzes under his fingers, but I try to ignore it. "That makes two of us."

His lips twist, trying to form a smile, but it just won't come.

"What's wrong?"

"Farley made contact again." He draws back, shoving his hands into his pockets to hide trembling fingers. "You weren't here."

Just my luck. "What did she say?"

Maven shrugs. He walks to the window, staring out at the night sky. "She spent most of her time asking questions."

Targets. She must've pressed him again, asking for information Maven didn't want to give. I can tell by the droop of his shoulders, the tremor in his voice, that he said more than he wanted to. *A lot more.*

"Who?" My mind flies to the many Silvers I've met here, the ones who have been kind to me, in their own way. Would any of them be a sacrifice to her revolution? Who would be marked?

"Maven, who did you give up?"

He spins around, a ferocity I've never seen flashing in his eyes. For a second, I'm afraid he might burst into flames. "I didn't want to do it, but she's right. We can't sit still; we have to *act*. And if that means I'm going to give her people, I'm going to do it. I won't like it, but I will. And I have."

Like Cal, he draws a shaky breath in an attempt to calm himself. "I sit on councils with my father, for taxes and security and defense. I know who will be missed by my—by the Silvers. I gave her four names."

"Who?"

"Reynald Iral. Ptolemus Samos. Ellyn Macanthos. Belicos Lerolan."

A sigh escapes me, before I feel myself nod. These deaths will not be hidden. Evangeline's brother, the colonel—*they will be missed indeed*. "Colonel Macanthos knew your mother was lying. She knows about the other attacks—"

"She commands a half legion and heads the war council. Without her, the front will be a mess for months."

"The front?" *Cal. His legion.*

Maven nods. "My father will not send his heir to war after this. An attack so close to home, I doubt he'll even let him out of sight of the capital."

So her death will save Cal. And help the Guard.

Shade died for this. His cause is mine now.

"Two birds with one stone," I breathe, feeling hot tears threaten to fall. As difficult as this might be, I'll trade her life for Cal's. I'll do it a thousand times.

"Your friend's part of this too."

My knees shake, but I manage to keep myself upright. I alternate between anger and fear as Maven explains the plan with a heavy, hardened heart.

"And what if we fail?" I ask when he finishes, finally speaking aloud the words he's been skirting around.

He barely shakes his head. "That won't happen."

"But what if we do?" I'm not a prince, my life has not been charming. I know to expect the worst out of everything and everyone. "What happens if we *fail*, Maven?"

His breath rattles in his chest as he inhales, fighting to remain calm. "Then we'll be traitors, both of us. Tried for treason, convicted—and killed."

During my next lesson with Julian, I can't concentrate. I can't focus on anything but what's coming. So much can go wrong, and so much is at stake. My life, Kilorn's, Maven's—we're all putting our necks on the line for this.

"It's really not my business, but," Julian begins, his voice startling me, "you seem, well, very *attached* to Prince Maven."

I almost laugh in relief, but I can't help but feel stung at the same time. Maven's the last person I should be wary of in this pit of snakes. Just the suggestion makes me bristle. "I am engaged to him," I reply, trying my best not to snap.

But instead of letting it drop, Julian leans forward. His placid demeanor usually soothes me, but today it's nothing but frustrating. "I'm just trying to help you. Maven is his mother's son."

This time I really do snap. "You don't know a thing about him." *Maven's my friend. Maven's risking more than me.* "Judging him by his parents is like judging me for my blood. Just because you hate the king and queen doesn't mean you can hate him too."

Julian stares at me, his gaze level and full of fire. When he speaks, his voice sounds more like a growl. "I hate the king because he couldn't save my sister, because he replaced her with that viper. I hate the queen because she ruined Sara Skonos, because she took the girl I loved and broke her apart. Because she cut Sara's *tongue* out." And then lower, a lament, "She had such a beautiful voice."

A wave of nausea washes over me. Suddenly Sara's painful silence, her sunken cheeks make sense. No wonder Julian had her heal me; she couldn't tell anyone the truth.

"But"—my words are small and hoarse, like it's my voice being taken away—"she's a healer."

"Skin healers can't heal themselves. And no one would cross the queen's punishment. So Sara has to live like that, shamed, forever." His voice echoes with memories, each one worse than the last. "Silvers don't mind pain, but we are proud. Pride, dignity, honor—those are things no ability can replace."

As terrible as I feel for Sara, I can't help but fear for myself. *They cut her tongue out for something she said. What will they possibly do to me?*

"You forget yourself, little lightning girl."

The nickname feels like a slap in the face, shocking me back to reality.

"This world is not your own. Learning to curtsy has not changed that. You don't *understand* the game we're playing."

"Because this isn't a game, Julian." I push his book of records toward him, shoving the list of dead names into his lap. "This is life and death. I'm not playing for a throne or a crown or a prince. I'm not playing at all. I'm *different*."

"You are," he murmurs, running a finger over the pages. "And that's why you're in danger, from everyone. Even Maven. Even me. *Anyone can betray anyone.*"

His mind drifts, and his eyes cloud over. In this light he looks old and gray, a bitter man haunted by a dead sister, in love with a broken woman, doomed to teach a girl who can do nothing but lie. Over his shoulder, I glimpse the map of what was, of before. *This whole world is haunted.*

And then, the worst thought I've ever had comes. *Shade is already my ghost. Who else will join him?*

"Make no mistake, my girl," he finally breathes. "You are playing the game as someone's pawn."

I don't have the heart to argue. *Think what you want, Julian. I'm no one's fool.*

Ptolemus Samos. Colonel Macanthos. Their faces dance in my head as Cal and I spin across the floor of the sitting room. Tonight the moon is shrinking, fading away, but my hope has never been stronger. The ball is tomorrow, and afterward, well, I'm not sure where that path might go. But it will be a different path, a new road to lead us toward a better future. There will be collateral damage, injuries and deaths we can't avoid, as Maven put it. But we know the risks. If all goes to plan, the Scarlet Guard will have raised its flag where everyone can see. Farley will broadcast another video after the attack, detailing our demands. *Equality, liberty, freedom.* Next to all-out rebellion, it sounds like a good deal.

My body dips, moving toward the floor in a slow arc that makes me yelp. Cal's strong arms close around me, pulling me back up in an easy second.

"Sorry," he says, half embarrassed. "Thought you were ready for it."

I'm not ready. I'm scared. I force myself to laugh, to hide what I can't show him. "No, my fault. Mind wandered off again."

He isn't easy to chase off and dips his head a little, looking me in the eyes. "Still worried about the ball?"

"More than you know."

"One step at a time, that's the best you can do." Then he laughs at himself, moving us back into simpler steps. "I know it's hard to believe, but I wasn't always the best dancer either."

"How shocking," I answer, matching his smile. "I thought princes were born with the ability to dance and make idle conversation."

He chuckles again, quickening our pace with the movement. "Not me. If I had my way, I'd be in the garage or the barracks, building and training. Not like Maven. He's twice the prince I'll ever be."

I think of Maven, of his kind words, perfect manners, impeccable knowledge of court—all the things he pretends to be to hide his true heart. *Twice the prince indeed.* "But he'll only ever be a prince," I mutter, almost lamenting at the thought. "And you'll be king."

His voice drops to meet my own, and something dark shadows his gaze. There's a sadness in him, growing stronger every day. *Maybe he doesn't like war as much as I think.* "Sometimes I wish it didn't have to be that way."

He speaks softly, but his voice fills my head. Though the ball looms on tomorrow's horizon, I find myself thinking more about him and his hands and the faint smell of wood smoke that seems to follow Cal wherever he goes. It makes me think of warmth, of autumn, of home.

I blame my rapidly beating heart on the melody, the music that brims with so much life. Somehow this night reminds me of Julian's lessons, his histories of the world before our own. That was a world of empires, of corruption, of war—and more freedom than I've ever known. But the people of that time are gone, their dreams in ruin, existing only in smoke and ash.

It's our nature, Julian would say. *We destroy. It's the constant of our kind. No matter the color of blood, man will always fall.*

I didn't understand that lesson a few days ago, but now, with Cal's hands in mine, guiding me with the lightest touch, I'm beginning to see what he meant.

I can feel myself falling.

"Are you really going to go with the legion?" Even the words make me afraid.

He barely nods. "A general's place is with his men."

"A prince's place is with his princess. With Evangeline," I add hastily. *Good one, Mare*, my mind screams.

The air around us thickens with heat, though Cal doesn't move at all. "She'll be all right, I think. She's not exactly attached to me. I won't miss her either."

Unable to meet his gaze, I focus on what's right in front of me. Unfortunately, that happens to be his chest and a much-too-thin shirt. Above me, he takes a ragged breath.

Then his fingers are under my chin, tipping my head up to meet his gaze. Gold flame flickers in his eyes, reflecting the heat beneath. "I'll miss you, Mare."

As much as I want to stand still, to stop time and let this moment last forever, I know it's not possible. Whatever I might feel or think, Cal is not the prince I'm promised to. More important, he's on the wrong side. He's my enemy. Cal is forbidden.

So with hesitant, reluctant steps, I back away, out of his grasp and out of the circle of warmth I've gotten so used to.

"I can't," is all I can manage, though I know my eyes betray me. Even now I can feel tears of anger and regret, tears I swore not to cry.

But maybe the prospect of going off to war has made Cal bold and reckless, things he never was before. He takes me by the hand, pulling me to him. He's betraying his only brother. I'm betraying my cause, Maven, and myself, but I don't want to stop.

Anyone can betray anyone.

His lips are on mine, hard and warm and pressing. The touch is electrifying, but not like I'm used to. This isn't a spark of destruction but a spark of life.

As much as I want to pull away, I just can't do it. Cal is a cliff, and I throw myself over the edge, not bothering to think of what it could do to us both. One day he'll realize I'm his enemy, and all this will be a far-gone memory. But not yet.

NINETEEN

It takes hours to paint and polish me into the girl I'm supposed to be, but it seems like just a few minutes. When the maids stand me up in front of the mirror, silently asking for my approval, I can only nod at the girl staring back at me from the glass. She looks beautiful and terrified by what's to come, wrapped in shimmering silk chains. I have to hide her, the scared girl; I have to smile and dance and look like one of them. With great effort, I push my fear away. *Fear will get me killed.*

Maven waits for me at the end of the hall, a shadow in his dress uniform. The charcoal black makes his eyes stand out, vibrantly blue against pale white skin. He doesn't look scared at all, but then, he's a prince. He's Silver. He won't flinch.

He extends an arm toward me, and I gladly take it. I expect him to make me feel safe or strong or both, but his touch reminds me of Cal and our betrayal. Last night comes into sharper focus, until every breath stands out in my head. For once, Maven doesn't notice my unease. He's thinking about more important things.

"You look beautiful," he says quietly, nodding down at my dress.

I don't agree with him. It's a silly, overdone thing, a complication of purple jewels that sparkle whenever I turn, making me look like a glittery bug. Still, I'm supposed to be a lady tonight, a future princess, so I nod and smile gratefully. I can't help but remember that my lips, now smiling for Maven, were kissing his brother last night.

"I just want this to be over."

"It won't end tonight, Mare. This won't be over for a long time. You know that, right?" He speaks like someone much older, much wiser, not like a seventeen-year-old boy. When I hesitate, truly not knowing how to feel, his jaw tightens. "Mare?" he prods, and I can hear the tremors in his voice.

"Are you afraid, Maven?" My words are weak, a whisper. "I am."

His eyes harden, shifting into blue steel. "I'm afraid of failing. I'm afraid of letting this opportunity pass us by. And I'm afraid of what happens if nothing in this world ever changes." He turns hot under my touch, driven by an inner resolve. "That scares me more than dying."

It's hard not to be swept away by his words, and I nod along with him. How can I back out? *I will not flinch.*

"Rise," he murmurs, so low I barely hear him. *Red as the dawn.*

His grip tightens on me as we come to the hall in front of the lifts. A troop of Sentinels guards the king and queen, both waiting for us. Cal and Evangeline are nowhere to be found, and I hope they stay away. The longer I don't have to look at them together, the happier I'll be.

Queen Elara wears a sparkling monstrosity of red, black, white, and blue, displaying the colors of her house and her husband's. She forces a smile, staring right through me to her son.

"Here we go," Maven says, letting go of my hand to stand at his mother's side. My skin feels strangely cold without him.

"So how long do I have to be here?" He forces a whine into his voice, playing his part well. The more he can keep her distracted, the better our chances. One poke into the wrong head and everything will go up in smoke. *And get us all killed for good measure.*

"Maven, you can't just come and go as you please. You have duties, and you'll stay as long as you're needed." She fusses over him, adjusting his collar, his medals, his sleeves, and for a moment, it takes me off guard. This is a woman who invaded my thoughts, who took me away from my life, who I *hate*, and still there's something good. She loves her son. And for all her faults, Maven loves her.

King Tiberias, on the other hand, doesn't seem bothered by Maven at all. He barely glances his way. "The boy's just bored. Not enough excitement in his day, not like back at the front," he says, running a hand over his trimmed beard. "You need a cause, Mavey."

For a brief moment, Maven's annoyed mask drops. *I have one*, his eyes scream, but he keeps his mouth shut.

"Cal's got his legion, he knows what he's doing, what he *wants*. You need to figure out what you're going to do with yourself, eh?"

"Yes, Father," Maven says. Though he tries to hide it, a shadow crosses his face.

I know that look very well. I used to wear it myself, when my parents would hint at me to be more like Gisa, even though that was impossible. I went to sleep hating myself, wishing I could change, wishing I could be quiet and talented and pretty like her. There's nothing that hurts more than that feeling. But the king doesn't notice Maven's pain, just like my parents never noticed mine.

"I think helping me fit in here is cause enough for Maven," I say, hoping to draw the king's disapproving eye away. When Tiberias turns to me, Maven sighs and shoots me a grateful smile.

"And what a job he's done," the king replies, looking me over. I know he's remembering the poor Red girl who refused to bow to him. "From what I hear, you're close to a proper lady now."

But the smile he forces doesn't reach his eyes, and there's no mistaking the suspicion there. He wanted to kill me back in the throne room, to protect his crown and the balance of his country, and I don't think the urge will ever fade away. I'm a threat, but I'm also an investment. He'll use me when he wants and kill me when he must.

"I've had good help, my king." I bow, pretending to be flattered, even though I don't care what he thinks. His opinion isn't worth the rust on my father's wheelchair.

"Are we just about ready?" Cal's voice says, shattering my thoughts.

My body reacts, spinning around to see him enter the hall. My stomach churns, but not with excitement or nerves or any of the things silly girls talk about. I feel sick with myself, with what I let happen—with what I *wanted* to happen. Though he tries to hold my gaze, I tear my eyes away, to Evangeline hanging off his arm. She's wearing metal again, and she manages to smirk without moving her lips.

"Your Majesties," she murmurs, dipping into a maddeningly perfect curtsy.

Tiberias smiles at her, his son's bride, before clapping a hand down on Cal's shoulder. "Just waiting on you, son," he chortles.

When they stand next to each other, the family resemblance is undeniable—same hair, same red-gold eyes, even the same posture. Maven watches, his blue eyes soft and thoughtful, while his mother keeps her grip on his arm. With Evangeline on one side and his father on the other, Cal can't do much more than meet my eyes. He nods slightly, and I know it's the only greeting I deserve.

★ ★ ★

Despite the decorations, the ballroom looks the same as it did more than a month ago, when the queen first pulled me into this strange world, when my name and identity were officially stripped away. They struck a blow against me here, and now it's my turn to strike back.

Blood will spill tonight.

But I can't think of that now. I have to stand with the others, to speak with the hundred members of court lined up to trade words with royalty and one jumped-up Red liar. My eyes flit down the line, looking for the marked ones—Maven's targets given to the Guard, the sparks to light a fire. *Reynald, the colonel, Belicos—and Ptolemus.* The silver-haired, dark-eyed brother of Evangeline.

He is one of the first to greet us, standing just behind his severe father, who hurries along to his daughter. When Ptolemus approaches me, I fight the urge to be sick. Never have I done anything so difficult as looking into the eyes of a dead man walking.

"My congratulations," he says, his voice hard as rock. The hand he extends is just as firm. He doesn't wear a military uniform but a suit of black metal that fits together in smooth, gleaming scales. He's a warrior but not a soldier. Like his father before him, Ptolemus leads the Archeon city guard, protecting the capital with his own army of officers. *The head of a snake*, Maven called him before. *Cut him down and the rest will die.* His hawkish eyes are on his sister, even while he holds my hand. He lets me go in a hurry, quickly passing by Maven and Cal before embracing Evangeline in a rare display of affection. I'm surprised their stupid outfits don't get stuck together.

If all goes to plan, he'll never hug his sister again. Evangeline will have lost a brother, just like me. Even though I know that pain firsthand, I can't bring myself to feel sorry for her. Especially not with the way she holds on to Cal. They look like complete opposites, he in his simple uniform while she glitters like a star in a dress of razor spikes. I want to kill her, I want to *be* her. But there's nothing I can do about that. Evangeline and Cal are not my problem tonight.

As Ptolemus disappears and more people pass with cold smiles and sharp words, it gets easier to forget myself. House Iral greets us next, led by the lithe, languid movements of Ara, the Panther. To my surprise, she bows lowly to me, smiling as she does so. But there's something strange about it, something that tells me she knows more than she lets on. She passes without a word, sparing me from another interrogation.

Sonya follows her grandmother, arm in arm with another target: Reynald Iral, her cousin. Maven told me he's a financial adviser, a genius who keeps the army funded with taxes and trade schemes. If he dies, so does the money, and so will the war. I'm willing to trade one tax collector for that. When he takes my hand, I can't help but notice his eyes are frozen and his hands are soft. Those hands will never touch mine again.

It's not as easy to dismiss Colonel Macanthos when she approaches. The scar on her face stands out sharply, especially tonight when everyone seems so polished. She might not care for the Guard, but she didn't believe the queen either. She wasn't ready to swallow the lies being spoon-fed to the rest of us.

Her grip is strong as she shakes my hand; for once someone isn't afraid I'll break like glass. "Every happiness to you, Lady Mareena. I can see this one suits you." She jerks her head toward Maven. "Not like fancy Samos," she adds in a playful whisper. "She'll make a sad queen, and you a happy princess, mark my words."

"Marked," I breathe. I manage to smile, even though the colonel's life will soon be at an end. No matter how many kind words she says, her minutes are numbered.

When she moves on to Maven, shaking his hand and inviting him to inspect troops with her in a week or so, I can tell he's just as affected. After she's gone, his hand drops to mine, giving me a reassuring squeeze. I know he regrets naming her, but like Reynald, like Ptolemus, her death will serve a purpose. Her life will be worth it all, in the end.

The next target comes from much farther down the line, from a lower house. Belicos Lerolan has a jolly grin, chestnut hair, and sunset-colored clothes to match his house colors. Unlike the others I've greeted tonight, he seems warm and kind. The smile behind his eyes is as real as his handshake.

"A pleasure, Lady Mareena." He inclines his head in greeting, polite to a fault. "I look forward to many years in your service."

I smile for him, pretending that there will be many years to come, but the facade becomes harder to hold as the seconds drag on. When his wife appears, leading a pair of twin boys, I want to scream. Barely four years old and yowling like puppies, they clamber around their father's legs. He smiles softly, a private smile just for them.

A diplomat, Maven called him, an ambassador to our allies in Piedmont, far to the south. Without him, our ties to that country and their army would be cut off, forcing Norta to stand alone against our Red dawn. He's another sacrifice we must make, another name to throw away. And he's a father. *He's a father and we're going to kill him.*

"Thank you, Belicos," Maven says, holding out his hand for him to shake, trying to draw the Lerolans away before I break.

I try to speak, but I can only think about the father I'm about to steal from such young children. In the back of my mind, I remember Kilorn crying after his father died. *He was young too.*

"Excuse us a minute, wouldn't you?" Maven's voice sounds far away as he speaks. "Mareena's still getting used to the excitement of court."

Before I can glance back at the doomed father, Maven hurries me away. A few people gawk at us, and I can feel Cal's eyes following us out. I almost stumble, but Maven keeps me upright as he pushes me out onto a balcony. Normally the fresh air would cheer me up, but I doubt anything can help now.

"Children." The words rip out of me. "He's a *father*."

Maven lets me go, and I slump against the balcony rail, but he doesn't step away. In the moonlight his eyes look like ice, glowing and glaring into me. He puts one hand on either side of my shoulders, trapping me in, forcing me to listen.

"Reynald is a father, too. The Colonel has children of her own. Ptolemus is now engaged to the Haven girl. They all have people; they *all* have someone who will mourn them." He forces out the words; he's just as torn as I. "We can't pick and choose how to help the cause, Mare. We must do what we can, whatever the cost."

"I can't do this to them."

"You think I want to do this?" he breathes, his face inches from mine. "I know them all, and it hurts me to betray them, but *it must be done*. Think what their lives will buy, what their deaths will accomplish. How many of your people could be saved? I thought you understood this!"

He stops himself, squeezing his eyes shut for a moment. When he collects himself, he raises a hand to my face, tracing the outline of my cheek with shaking fingers. "I'm sorry, I just—" His voice falters. "You might not be able to see where tonight will lead, but I can. And I know this will change things."

"I believe you," I whisper, reaching up to hold his hand in my own. "I just wish it didn't have to be this way."

Over his shoulder, back in the ballroom, the receiving line dwindles. The handshakes and pleasantries are over. The night has truly begun.

"But it does, Mare. I promise you, this is what we *must* do."

As much as it hurts, as much as my heart twists and bleeds, I nod. "Okay."

"You two all right out here?"

For a second, Cal's voice sounds strange and high, but he clears his throat as he pokes out onto the balcony. His eyes linger on my face. "You ready for this, Mare?"

Maven answers for me. "She's ready."

Together, we walk away from the railing and the night and the last bit of quiet we might ever have. As we pass through the archway, I feel the ghost of a touch on my arm: *Cal.* I look back to see him still staring, fingers outstretched. His eyes are darker than ever, boiling with some emotion I can't place. But before he can speak, Evangeline appears at his side. When he takes her by the hand, I have to tear my eyes away.

Maven leads us to the cleared spot in the center of the ballroom. "This is the hard part," he says, trying to calm me.

It works a little bit, and the shivers running through me ebb away.

We dance first, the two princes and their brides, in front of everyone. Another display of strength and power, showing off the two girls who won in front of all the families who lost. Right now it's the last thing I want to do, but it's for the cause. As the electronic music I hate clatters to life, I realize it's at least a dance I recognize.

Maven looks shocked when my feet move into place. "You've been practicing?"

With your brother. "A bit."

"You're just full of surprises." He chuckles, finding the will to smile.

Next to us, Cal twirls Evangeline into place. They look like a king and queen should, regal and cold and beautiful. When Cal's eyes meet mine at the exact moment his hands close around her fingers, I feel a thousand things at once, none of them pleasant. But instead of wallowing, I move closer to Maven. He glances down at me, blue eyes wide, as the music takes hold. A few feet away, Cal takes his steps, leading Evangeline in the same dance he taught me. She's much better at it, all grace and sharp beauty. Again I feel like falling.

We spin across the floor in time with the music, surrounded by cold onlookers. I recognize the faces now. I know the houses, the colors, the abilities, the histories. Who to fear, who to pity. They watch us with hungry eyes, and I know why. They think we're the future, Cal and Maven and Evangeline and even me. They think they're watching a king and queen, a prince and princess. But that's a future I don't intend to let happen.

In my perfect world, Maven won't have to hide his heart and I won't have to hide who I truly am. Cal will have no crown to wear, no throne to protect. These people will have no more walls to hide behind.

The dawn is coming for you all.

We dance through two more songs, and other couples join us on the floor. The swirl of color blocks out any glimpse of Cal and Evangeline, until it feels like Maven and I are spinning alone. For a moment, Cal's face floats in front of me, replacing his brother's, and I think I'm back in the room full of moonlight.

But Maven is not Cal, no matter how much his father might want him to be. He isn't a soldier, he won't be a king, but he's braver. And he's willing to do what's right.

"Thank you, Maven," I whisper, barely audible over the horrible music.

He doesn't have to ask what I'm talking about. "You don't ever have to thank me." His voice is strangely deep, almost breaking as his eyes darken. "Not for anything."

This is the closest I've ever been to him, my nose inches away from his neck. I can feel his heart beat beneath my hands, hammering in time with my own. *Maven is his mother's son*, Julian said once. He couldn't be more wrong.

Maven maneuvers us to the edge of the dance floor, now crowded with swirling lords and ladies. No one will notice we've stepped away.

"Some refreshments?" a servant murmurs, holding out a tray of the fizzy golden drink. I start to wave him off before I recognize his bottle-green eyes.

I have to bite my tongue to keep from shouting his name aloud. *Kilorn.*

Strangely, the red uniform suits him and for once he managed to clean the dirt off his face. It seems the fisher boy I knew is entirely gone.

"This thing itches," he grumbles under his breath. *Maybe not entirely.*

"Well, you won't be in it much longer," Maven says. "Is everything in place?"

Kilorn nods, his eyes darting through the crowd. "They're ready upstairs."

Above us, Sentinels crowd a wraparound landing, lining the walls. But above them, in the carved window alcoves and little balconies near the ceiling, the shadows are not Sentinels at all.

"You just have to give the signal." He holds out the tray and the innocent glass of gold.

Maven straightens next to me, his shoulder against mine in support. "Mare?"

My turn now. "I'm ready," I murmur, remembering the plan Maven whispered to me a few nights ago. Shivering, I let the familiar buzz of electricity flow through me, until I can feel every light and camera blaze through my head. I lift the glass, and drink deeply.

Kilorn is quick to take the glass back. "One minute." His voice sounds so final.

He disappears with a swish of his tray, moving through the crowd until I can't see him anymore. *Run*, I pray, hoping he's fast enough. Maven goes as well, leaving me to carry out his own task at his mother's side.

I head toward the center of the crowd even as the feel of electricity threatens to overtake me. But I can't let it go yet. Not until they start. *Thirty seconds.*

King Tiberias looms ahead of me, laughing away with his favorite son. He looks to be on his third glass of wine, and his cheeks are flushed silver, while Cal sips politely at water. Somewhere to my left, I hear Evangeline's cutting laughter, probably with her brother. All over the room, four people take their last breaths.

I let my heart count out those last seconds, beating away the moments. Cal spots me through the crowd, grinning that smile I love, and starts to come toward me. But he will never reach me, not before the deed is done. The world slows until all I know is the shocking strength within the walls. Like in Training, like with Julian, I'm learning to control it.

Four shots ring out, paired with four bright flashes from the guns high above.

The screams come next.

TWENTY

I scream with them, and the lights flash, then flicker, then fail.

One minute of darkness. That's what I need to give them. The screams, the yelling, the stampede of feet almost break my concentration, but I force myself to focus. The lights flash horribly, then die, making it almost impossible to move. *Making it possible for my friends to slip away.*

"In the alcoves!" a voice roars, yelling over the chaos. "They're running!" More voices join the call, though none are familiar. But in this madness, everyone sounds different. "Find them!" "Stop them!" "Kill them!"

The Sentinels on the landing have their guns aimed while more blur along, barely shadows as they give chase. *Walsh is with them*, I remind myself. If Walsh and other servants could sneak Farley and Kilorn in before, they can sneak them out again. They can hide. They can escape. They'll be fine.

My darkness will save them.

A blaze of fire erupts from the crowd, curling through the air like a flaming snake. It roars overhead, illuminating the dim ballroom. Flickering shadows paint the walls and the upturned faces, transforming the ballroom into a nightmare of red light and gunpowder. Sonya screams nearby, bent over the body of Reynald. The spry old Ara wrestles her off the corpse, pulling her away from the chaos. Reynald's eyes stare glassily up at the ceiling, reflecting the red light.

Still I hold on, every muscle inside me hard and tense.

Somewhere near the fire, I recognize the king's guards hurrying him from the room. He tries to fight them, shouting and yelling to stay, but for once they don't follow his orders. Elara is close behind, pushed on by Maven as they run from danger. Many more follow, eager to be free of this place.

Security officers run against the tide, flooding the room with shouts and stamping boots. Lords and ladies press by me in an attempt to escape, but I can only stand in place, holding on as best I can. No one tries to pull me away; no one notices me at all. *They are afraid.* For all their strength, all their power, they still know the meaning of fear. And a few bullets are all it takes to bring terror out in them.

A weeping woman bumps into me, knocking me over. I land face-to-face with a corpse, staring at Colonel Macanthos's scar. Silver blood trickles down her face, from her forehead to the floor. The bullet hole is strange, surrounded by gray, rocky flesh. *She was a stoneskin.* She was alive long enough to try and stop it, to shield herself. But the bullet couldn't be stopped. She still died.

I push back from the murdered woman, but my hands slide through a mixture of silverblood and wine. A scream escapes me in a terrifying combination of frustration and grief. The blood clings to my hands, like it knows what I've done. It's sticky and cold and everywhere, trying to drown me.

"MARE!"

Strong arms pull me along the floor, dragging me away from the woman I let die. "Mare, please—," the voice pleads, but for what, I don't know.

With a roar of frustration, I lose the battle. The lights return, revealing a war zone of silk and death. When I try to scramble to my feet, to make sure the job is really done, a hand pushes me back down.

I say the words I must, playing my own part in all this. "I'm sorry—the lights—I can't—" Overhead, the lights flicker again.

Cal barely hears me and drops to his knees next to me. "Where are you hit?" he roars, checking me in the way I know he's been trained. His fingers feel down my arms and legs, looking for a wound, for the source of so much blood.

My voice sounds strange. Soft. Broken. "I'm fine." He doesn't hear me again. "Cal, I'm fine."

Relief floods his face, and for a second I think he might kiss me again. But his senses return quicker than mine. "You're sure?"

Gingerly, I raise a silver-stained sleeve. "How can this be mine?"

My blood is not this color. You know that.

He nods. "Of course," he whispers. "I just—I saw you on the ground and I thought . . ." His words trail away, replaced by a terrible sadness in his eyes. But it fades quickly, shifting to determination. "Lucas! Get her out of here!"

My personal guard charges through the fray, his gun at the ready. Though he looks the same in his boots and uniform, this is not the Lucas I know. His black eyes, *Samos eyes*, are dark as night. "I'll take her to the others," he growls, hoisting me up.

Though I know better than anyone the danger is gone, I can't help but reach out to Cal. "What about you?"

He shrugs out of my grasp with shocking ease. "I'm not running."

And then he turns, his shoulders squared to a group of Sentinels. He steps over the corpses, head inclined to the ceiling. A Sentinel tosses him a handgun, and he catches it deftly, putting a finger to the trigger. His other hand blazes to life, crackling with dark and deadly flame. Silhouetted against the Sentinels and the bodies on the floor, he looks like another person entirely.

"Let's go hunting," he growls, and charges up the stairs. Sentinels and Security follow, like a cloud of red-and-black smoke trailing behind his flame. They leave a a blood-spattered ballroom, hazy with dust and screams.

In the center of it all lies Belicos Lerolan, pierced not by a bullet but a silver lance. *Shot from a spear gun, like the ones used to fish.* A tattered scarlet sash falls from the shaft, barely stirring in the whirlwind. There's a symbol stamped on it—the torn sun.

Then the ballroom is gone, swallowed up by the dark walls of a service passage. The ground rumbles beneath our feet and Lucas throws me to the wall, shielding me. A sound like thunder reverberates and the ceiling shakes, dropping pieces of stone down on us. The door behind us explodes inward, destroyed by flame. Beyond, the ballroom is black with smoke. *An explosion.*

"Cal—" I try to squirm away from Lucas, to run back the way we came, but he throws me back. "Lucas, we have to help him!"

"Trust me, a bomb won't bother the prince," he growls, moving me forward.

"A bomb?" *That wasn't part of the plan.* "Was that a bomb?"

Lucas draws back from me, positively shaking in anger. "You saw that bloody red scarf. This is the Scarlet Guard and *that*"—he points back to the ballroom, still dark and burning—"that is who they are."

"This doesn't make sense," I murmur to myself, trying to remember every facet of the plan. Maven never told me about a bomb. *Never.* And Kilorn wouldn't let me do this, not if he knew I would be in danger. *They wouldn't do this to me.*

Lucas holsters his gun, his voice a growl. "Killers don't have to make sense."

My breath catches in my throat. How many were left back there? How many children, how many needless deaths?

Lucas takes my silence for shock, but he's wrong. What I feel now is anger.

Anyone can betray anyone.

Lucas leads me underground, through no less than three doors, each one a foot thick and made of steel. They have no locks, but he opens them with a flick of his hand. It reminds me of the first time I met him, when he waved apart the bars of my cell.

I hear the others before I see them, their voices echoing off the metal walls as they speak to one another. The king rails, his words sending shivers through me. His presence seems to fill the bunker as he paces up and down, his cloak flapping out behind him.

"I want them found. I want them in front of me with a blade at their backs, and I want them to sing like the cowardly birds they are!" He addresses a Sentinel, but the masked woman doesn't even flinch. "I want to know what's *going on!*"

Elara sits in a chair, one hand over her heart, the other clutching tightly to Maven.

He starts at the sight of me. "Are you all right?" he breathes, pulling me into a quick embrace.

"Just shaken," I manage to say, trying to communicate as much as

I can. But with Elara so close, I can barely allow myself to think, let alone speak. "There was an explosion after the shots. A bomb."

Maven furrows his brow, confused, but he quickly masks it with rage. "Bastards."

"Savages," King Tiberias hisses through gritted teeth. "And what about my son?"

My gaze trails to Maven, before I realize the king doesn't mean Maven at all. Maven takes it in stride. He's used to being overlooked.

"Cal went after the shooters. He took a band of Sentinels with him." The memory of him, dark and angry as a flame, frightens me. "And then the ballroom exploded. I don't know how many were still—still in there."

"Was there anything else, dear?" Coming from Elara, the term of endearment feels like an electric shock. She looks paler than ever, her breath coming in shallow pants. *She's afraid*. "Anything you remember?"

"There was a banner, attached to a spear. The Scarlet Guard did this."

"Did they?" she says, raising a single eyebrow. I fight the urge to back away, to run from her and her whispers. At any moment I expect to feel her slither into my head, to pull out the truth.

But instead, Elara rips her eyes away and turns on the king. "You see what you've done?" Her lip curls over her teeth. In the light, they look like glittering fangs.

"Me? *You* called the Guard small and weak, you lied to our people," Tiberias snarls back at her. "Your actions have weakened us against the danger, not mine."

"And if you took care of this when you had the chance, when they *were* small and weak, this would have never happened!"

They rip at each other like starved dogs, each one trying to take a bigger bite.

"Elara, they were not terrorists then. I could not waste my soldiers and officers on hunting down a few Reds writing pamphlets. They did no harm."

Slowly, Elara points to the ceiling. "Does that seem like no harm to you?" He has no answer for her, and she smirks, delighting in winning the argument. "One day you men will learn to pay attention and all the world will tremble. They are a disease, one you allowed to take hold. And it's time to kill this disease where it grows."

She stands from her chair, collecting herself. "They are Red devils, and they must have allies inside our own walls." I do my best to keep still, my eyes fixed on the floor. "I think I'll have a *word* with the servants. Officer Samos, if you would?"

He jumps to attention, opening the vault door for her. She sweeps out, two Sentinels in tow, like a hurricane of rage. Lucas goes with her, opening the heavy doors in succession, each one clanging farther and farther away. I don't want to know what the queen will do to the servants, but I know it will hurt and I know what she will find—nothing. Walsh and Holland fled with Farley, according to our plan. They knew it would be too dangerous for them after the ball—and they were right.

The thick metal closes for a few moments, only to swing open again. Another magnetron directs it: *Evangeline*. She looks like hell in a party dress, her jewelry mangled and teeth on edge. Worst of all are her eyes, wild and wet and streaming with black makeup. *Ptolemus. She weeps for her dead brother*. Even though I tell myself I don't care, I have to resist the urge to reach out and comfort her. But it passes as soon as her companion enters the bunker behind her.

There's smoke and soot on his skin, dirtying his once clean uniform.

Normally I'd be concerned at the ragged, hateful look in Cal's eyes, but something else strikes fear into my bones. Blood stains his black uniform and drips over his hands. It is not silver. *Red. The blood is red.*

"Mare," he says to me, but all his warmth is gone. "Come with me. Now."

His words are directed at me, but everyone follows, pushing through the passages as he leads us to the cells. My heart hammers in my chest, threatening to explode out of me. *Not Kilorn. Anyone but him.* Maven keeps a hand on my shoulder, holding me close. At first I think he's comforting me, but then he tugs me back: he's trying to keep me from running ahead.

"You should've killed him where he stood," Evangeline says to Cal. Her fingers pluck at the red blood on his shirt. "I wouldn't leave the Red devil alive."

Him. My teeth bite my lips, holding my mouth closed so I don't say something stupid. Maven's hand tightens like a claw on my shoulder and I can feel his pulse quicken. For all we know, this might be the end of our game. Elara will come back and shatter their brains, picking through the wreckage to discover how deep their plot goes.

The steps to the cells are the same but seem longer, stretching down into the deepest parts of the Hall. The dungeon rises to greet us, and no less than six Sentinels stand guard. An icy chill runs through my bones, but I don't shiver. I can barely move.

Four figures stand in the cell, each one bloody and bruised. Despite the dim light, I know them all. Walsh's eye is swollen shut, but she seems all right. Not like Tristan, leaning against the wall to take pressure off a leg wet with blood. There's a hasty bandage around the wound, torn from Kilorn's shirt by the looks of it. For his part, Kilorn looks unscathed, to my great relief. He supports Farley with an arm, letting her stand against him. Her shoulder is dislocated, one arm hanging at a strange angle. But that doesn't stop her from sneering at us. She even spits through the bars, a mix of blood and saliva that lands at Evangeline's feet.

"Take her tongue for that," Evangeline snarls, rushing at the bars. She stops short, one hand slamming against the metal. Though she could tear it away with a thought, ripping apart the cell and the people inside, she restrains herself.

Farley holds her gaze, barely blinking at the outburst. If this is her end, she's certainly going to go with her head high. "A little violent for a princess."

Before Evangeline can lose her temper, Cal pulls her back from the bars. Slowly, he raises a hand, pointing. "You."

With a horrific lurch, I realize he's pointing at Kilorn. A muscle twitches in Kilorn's cheek, but he keeps his eyes on the floor.

Cal remembers him. From the night he brought me home.

"Mare, explain this."

I open my mouth, hoping some fantastic lie will fall out, but nothing comes.

Cal's gaze darkens. "He's your friend. *Explain this.*"

Evangeline gasps and turns her wrath on me. "You brought him here!" she screeches, jumping at me. "You did this?!"

"I did n-nothing," I stammer, feeling all the eyes in the room on me. "I mean, I did get him a job here. He was at the lumberyards and it's hard work, deadly work—" The lies tumble from me, each one quicker than the last. "He's—he was my friend, back in the village. I just wanted to make sure he was okay. I got him the job as a servant, just like—" My eyes trail to Cal. Both of us remember the night we first met, and the day that followed. "I thought I was helping him."

Maven takes a step toward the cell, looking at our friends like it's the first time he's ever seen them. He gestures to their red uniforms. "They seem to be only servants."

"I'd say the same, except we found them trying to escape through a drainpipe," Cal snaps. "Took us a while to drag them out."

"Is this all of them?" King Tiberias says, peering through the cell bars.

Cal shakes his head. "There were more ahead, but they got to the river. How many, I don't know."

"Well, let's find out," Evangeline says, her eyebrows raised. "Call for the queen. And in the meantime . . ." She faces the king. Beneath his beard, he grins a little and nods.

I don't have to ask to know what they're thinking about. *Torture.*

The four prisoners stand strong, not even flinching. Maven's jaw works furiously as he tries to think of a way out of this, but he knows there isn't one. If anything, this might be more than we could hope for. If they manage to lie. *But how can we ask them to? How can we watch them scream while we stand tall?*

Kilorn seems to have an answer for me. Even in this awful place, his green eyes manage to shine. *I will lie for you.*

"Cal, I leave the honor to you," the king says, resting a hand on his son's shoulder. I can only stare, pleading with wide eyes, praying Cal will not do as his father asks.

He glances at me once, like somehow that counts as an apology. Then he turns to a Sentinel, shorter than the others. Her eyes sparkle gray-white behind her mask.

"Sentinel Gliacon, I find myself in need of some ice."

What that means, I have no idea, but Evangeline giggles. "Good choice."

"You don't need to see this," Maven mutters, trying to pull me away. But I can't leave Kilorn. Not now. I angrily shrug him off, my eyes still on my friend.

"Let her stay," Evangeline crows, taking pleasure in my discomfort. "This will teach her to treat Reds as friends." She turns back to the cell, waving open the bars. With one white finger, she points. "Start with her. She needs to be broken."

The Sentinel nods and seizes Farley by the wrist, pulling her out of the cell. The bars slide back into place behind her, trapping the rest in. Walsh and Kilorn rush to the bars, both of them the picture of fear.

The Sentinel forces Farley to her knees, waiting for her next order. "Sir?"

Cal moves to stand over her, breathing heavily. He hesitates before speaking, but his voice is strong. "How many more of you are there?"

Farley's jaw locks in place, her teeth together. She'll die before she talks.

"Start with the arm."

The Sentinel is not gentle, wrenching out Farley's wounded arm. Farley yelps in pain but still says nothing. It takes everything I have not to strike the Sentinel.

"And you call us the savages," Kilorn spits, forehead against the bars.

Slowly, the Sentinel peels away Farley's blood-soaked sleeve and sets pale, cruel hands to her skin. Farley screams at the touch, but why, I can't say.

"Where are the others?" Cal questions, kneeling to look her in the eyes. For a moment she falls quiet, drawing a ragged breath. He leans in, patiently waiting for her to break.

Instead, Farley snaps forward, head butting him with all her strength. "We are everywhere." She laughs, but screams again as the Sentinel resumes her torture.

Cal recovers neatly, one hand to his now broken nose. Another person might strike back, but he doesn't.

Red pinpricks appear on Farley's arm, around the Sentinel's hand. They grow with each passing second, sharp and shiny red points sticking straight out of now bluish skin. *Sentinel Gliacon. House Gliacon.* My mind flies back to Protocol, to the house lessons. *Shivers.*

With a lurch, I understand and I have to look away.

"That's blood," I whisper, unable to look back. "She's freezing her blood." Maven only nods, his eyes grave and full of sorrow.

Behind us, the Sentinel continues to work, moving up Farley's arm. Red icicles sharp as razors pierce through her flesh, slicing every nerve in a pain I can't imagine. Farley's breath whistles through gritted teeth. Still she says nothing. My heart races as the seconds tick by, wondering when the queen will return, wondering when our play will be truly over.

Finally, Cal jumps to his feet. "Enough."

Another Sentinel, a Skonos skin healer, drops down next to Farley. She all but collapses, staring blankly at her arm, now jagged with knives of frozen blood. The new Sentinel heals her quickly, hands moving in a practiced fashion.

Farley chuckles darkly as the warmth returns to her arm. "All to do it again, eh?"

Cal folds his arms behind his back. He shares a glance with his father, who nods. "Indeed," Cal sighs, looking back to the shiver. But she doesn't get a chance to continue.

"WHERE IS SHE?" a terrible voice screams, echoing down the stairs to us below.

Evangeline whirls at the noise, rushing to the bottom of the stairs. "I'm here!" she shouts back.

When Ptolemus Samos steps down to embrace his sister, I have to dig my nails into my palm to keep from reacting. There he stands, alive and breathing and terribly angry. On the floor, Farley curses to herself.

He only lingers for a moment and sidesteps Evangeline, a terrifying fury in his eyes. His armored suit is mangled at the shoulder, pulverized by a bullet. But the skin beneath is unbroken. *Healed.* He prowls toward the cell, hands flexing. The metal bars quiver in their sockets, screeching against concrete.

"Ptolemus, not yet—," Cal growls, grabbing for him, but Ptolemus shoves the prince off. Despite Cal's size and strength, he stumbles backward.

Evangeline runs at her brother, pulling his hand. "No, we need them to talk!" With one shrug of his arm he breaks her grip—not even she can stop him.

The bars crack, shrieking with his power as the cell opens to him. Not even the Sentinels can stop him as he strides forward, moving quickly with practiced motions. Kilorn and Walsh scramble, jumping back against the stone walls, but Ptolemus is a predator, and predators attack the weak. With his broken leg, barely able to move, Tristan doesn't stand a chance.

"You will not threaten my sister again," Ptolemus roars, directing the metal bars of the cell. One spears right through Tristan's chest. He gasps, choking on his own blood, *dying.* And Ptolemus actually smiles.

When he turns on Kilorn, murder in his heart, I snap.

Sparks blaze to life in my skin. When my hand closes around Ptolemus's muscled neck, I let the sparks go. They shock into him, lightning dancing through his veins, and he seizes under my touch. The metal of his uniform vibrates and smokes, almost cooking him alive. And then he drops to the concrete floor, his body still shaking with sparks.

"Ptolemus!" Evangeline scrambles to his side, reaching for his face. A shock jumps to her fingers, forcing her to fall back with a scowl. She rounds on me in a blaze of anger. "How *dare* you—!"

"He'll be fine." I didn't hit him with enough to do any real damage. "Like you said, we need them to talk. They can't do that if they're dead."

The others stare at me with a strange mix of emotions, their eyes wide—and afraid. Cal, the boy I kissed, the soldier, the brute, can't hold my gaze at all. I recognize the expression on his face: shame. But because he hurt Farley, or because he couldn't make her talk, I don't know. At least Maven has the good sense to look sad, his stare resting on Tristan's still bleeding body.

"Mother can attend to the prisoners later," he says, addressing the king. "But the people upstairs will want to see their king and know he is safe. So many have died. You should comfort them, Father. And you as well, Cal."

He's playing for time. Brilliant Maven is trying to buy us a chance.

Even though it makes my skin crawl, I reach out to touch Cal's shoulder. He kissed me once. He might still listen when I speak. "He's right, Cal. This can wait."

Still on the floor, Evangeline bares her teeth. "The court will want answers, not embraces! This must be done now! Your Majesty, rip the truth from them—"

But even Tiberias sees the wisdom of Maven's words. "They will keep," he echoes. "And tomorrow the truth will be known."

My grip tightens on Cal's arm, feeling the tense muscles beneath. He relaxes into my touch, looking like a great weight has fallen off him.

The Sentinels jump to attention and pull Farley back into the broken cell. Her eyes stay on me, wondering what the hell I have in mind. *I wish I knew.*

Evangeline half drags Ptolemus out, letting the bars knit together behind her. "You are weak, my prince," she hisses into Cal's ear.

I resist the urge to look back at Kilorn, as his words echo in my head. *Stop trying to protect me.*

I will not.

Blood drips from my sleeve, leaving a spotted silver trail in my wake as we march to the throne room. Sentinels and Security guard the immense door, their guns raised and aimed at the passageway. They don't move as we pass, frozen in place. Their orders are to kill, should the need arise. Beyond, the grand chamber echoes with anger and sorrow. I want to feel some shred of victory, but the memory of Kilorn behind bars dampens any happiness I might have. Even the colonel's glassy eyes haunt me.

I move to Cal's side. He barely notices, his eyes burning at the floor. "How many dead?"

"Ten so far," he mutters. "Three in the shooting, eight in the explosion. Fifteen more wounded." It sounds like he's listing groceries, not people. "But they'll all heal."

He jerks his thumb, gesturing to the healers running among the injured. I count two children among them. And beyond the wounded are the bodies of the dead, laid out before the king's throne. Belicos Lerolan's twin sons lie next to him, with their weeping mother holding vigil over the bodies.

I have to put a hand to my mouth to keep from gasping. *I never wanted this.*

Maven's warm hands take mine, pulling me past the gruesome scene to our place by the throne. Cal stands close by, trying in vain to wipe the red blood off his hands.

"The time for tears is over," Tiberias thunders, fists clenching at his sides. In complete unison, the sobs and sniffles through the chamber die out. "Now we honor the dead, heal the wounded, and *avenge our fallen*. I am the king. I do not forget. I do not forgive. I have been lenient in the past, allowing our Red brothers a good life full of prosperity, of dignity. But they spit upon us, they reject our mercy, and they have brought upon themselves the worst kind of doom."

With a snarl, he throws down the silver spear and red rag. It clatters across the floor with a sound like a funeral bell. The torn sun stares at us all.

"These fools, these terrorists, these *murderers*, will be brought to justice. And they will die. I swear on my crown, on my throne, on my sons, *they will die*."

A rumbling murmur goes through the crowd as each Silver stirs. They stand as one, wounded or not. The metallic smell of blood is almost overpowering.

"Strength," the court screams. "Power! *Death!*"

Maven glances at me, his eyes wide and afraid. I know what he's thinking, because I think it too.

What have we done?

TWENTY-ONE

Back in my room, I rip the ruined dress off, letting the silk fall to the floor. The king's words replay in my head, peppered with flashes of this terrible night. Kilorn's eyes stand out through it all, a green fire burning me up. *I must protect him, but how?* If only I could trade myself for him again, my freedom for his. If only things were that simple anymore. Julian's lessons have never felt so sharp in my mind: *the past is so much greater than this future.*

Julian. *Julian.*

The residence halls crawl with Sentinels and Security, every one of them on edge. But I've long perfected the art of slipping by unnoticed, and Julian's door is not far away. Despite the hour, he's awake, poring over books. Everything looks the same, like nothing's happened. Maybe he doesn't know. But then I notice the bottle of brown liquor on the table, occupying a spot usually reserved for tea. *Of course he knows.*

"In light of recent events, I would think our lessons have been canceled for the time being," he says over the pages of his book. Still, he shuts it with a snap, turning his full attention on me. "Not to mention it's quite late."

"I need you, Julian."

"Does this have anything to do with the Sun Shooting? Yes, they've already thought up a clever name." He points to the dark video screen in the corner. "It's been on the news for hours now. The king's addressing the country in the morning."

I remember the fluffy blond newswoman reporting the capital bombing more than a month ago. There were few injuries then, and still the marketplace rioted. What will they do now? How many innocent Reds will pay?

"Or is this about the four terrorists currently locked in the cells of this structure?" Julian presses on, measuring my response. "Excuse me, I mean three. Ptolemus Samos certainly lives up to his reputation."

"They're not terrorists," I reply calmly, trying to keep myself in check.

"Shall I show you the definition of *terrorism*, Mare?" His tone stings. "Their cause might be just, but their methods . . . besides, what *you* say doesn't matter." He gestures to the video screen again. "They have their own version of the truth, and that's the only one people will hear."

My teeth grind together painfully, bone on bone. "Are you going to help or not?"

"I am a teacher and somewhat of an outcast, in case you haven't noticed. What can I possibly do?"

"Julian, please." I can feel my last chance slipping through my fingers. "You're a singer, you can tell the guards—*make* them do anything you want. You can set the prisoners free."

But he remains still, sipping peacefully at his drink. He doesn't grimace like men normally do. The bite of alcohol is familiar to him.

"Tomorrow they'll be interrogated. And no matter how strong they are, no matter how long they hold out, the truth will be found." Slowly, I take Julian's hand, holding fingers worn rough by paper. "This was my plan. I'm one of them." He doesn't need to know about Maven. It will only make him angrier.

The half lie does its job well. I can see it in Julian's eyes.

"*You?* You did this?" he stammers. "The shooting, the bombing—?"

"The bomb was . . . unexpected." *The bomb was a horror.*

He narrows his eyes, and I can see the cogs turning in his mind. Then he snaps entirely. "I told you, I told you not to get in over your head!" He slams a fist down on the table, looking angrier than I've ever seen him before. "And now," he breathes, staring at me with so much sorrow it makes my heart hurt, "now I must watch you drown?"

"If they escape . . ."

He throws back the rest of his drink with a gulp. With a snap of his wrist, he smashes the glass on the floor, making me jump. "And what about me? Even if I take away the cameras, the guards' memories, anything that could implicate either of us, the queen will know." Shaking his head, he sighs. "She'll take my eyes for this."

And Julian will never read again. How can I ask for that?

"Then let me die." The words stick in my throat. "I deserve it as much as they do."

He can't let me die. He won't. I am the little lightning girl, and I am going to make the world change.

When he speaks again, he sounds hollow.

"They called my sister's death a suicide." Slowly, he traces his fingers across his wrist, dwelling on a long-ago memory. "That was a lie, and I knew it. She was a sad woman, but she never would have done such a thing. Not when she had Cal, and Tibe. She was murdered, and I said nothing. I was afraid, and I let her die in shame. And since that day, I've been working to fix that, waiting in the shadows of this monstrous world, waiting for my time to avenge her." He raises his eyes to me. They sparkle with tears. "I suppose this will be a good place to start."

It doesn't take long for Julian to figure out a plan. All we need is a magnetron and some blind cameras, and luckily, I can provide both.

Lucas knocks on my bedroom door not two minutes after I summon him.

"What can I do for you, Mare?" he says, jumpier than usual. I know his time overseeing the queen's interrogation of servants must not have been easy. At least he'll be too distracted to notice I'm shaking.

"I'm hungry." The rehearsed words come easier than they should. "You know, dinner never happened, so I was wondering—"

"Do I look like a cook? You should've called the kitchens, that's their job."

"I just, well, I don't think now's a good time for the servants to be roaming around. People are still pretty on edge, and I don't want anyone getting hurt because I didn't get dinner. You'd just have to escort me, that's all. And who knows, you might get a cookie out of it."

Sighing like an annoyed teenager, Lucas holds out an arm. As I take it, I glance at the cameras in the hall, making them die off. *Here we go.*

I should feel wrong about using Lucas, knowing firsthand what it's like to have your mind toyed with, but this is for Kilorn's life. Lucas is still chattering when we turn the corner, running smack into Julian.

"Lord Jacos—," Lucas begins, moving to bow his head, but Julian takes him by the chin, moving quicker than I ever thought he could.

Before Lucas can respond, Julian glares into his eyes and the struggle dies before it even begins.

His honeyed words, smooth as butter and strong as iron, fall on open ears. "Take us to the cells. Use the service halls. Keep us away from patrols. Do not remember this."

Lucas, usually all smiles and jokes, falls into a strange, half-hypnotized state. His eyes glaze over and he doesn't notice when Julian reaches down to take his gun. But he marches all the same, leading us through the maze of the Hall. At each turn I wait for the feel of electric eyes, shutting off everything in our path. Julian does the same to the guards, forcing them not to remember us as we pass. Together, we make an unbeatable team, and it's not long before we stand at the top of the dungeon stairs. There will be Sentinels down there, too many for Julian to take care of on his own.

"Speak not a word," Julian hisses to Lucas, who nods in understanding.

Now it's my turn to lead us. I expect to be afraid, but the dim light and the late hour feel familiar. This is where I belong, sneaking and lying and stealing.

"Who is it? State your name and business!" one of the Sentinels shouts up at us. I recognize her voice—Gliacon, the shiver who tortured Farley. *Perhaps I can convince Julian to sing her off a cliff.*

I draw myself up to my full height, though it's my voice and tone that matter most. "My name is Lady Mareena Titanos, betrothed of the prince Maven," I snap, moving down the steps with as much grace as I can. My voice is cold and sharp, mirroring Elara's and Evangeline's. *I have strength and power too.* "And I don't share my business with Sentinels."

At the sight of me, the four Sentinels exchange glances, questioning one another. One, a large man with pig eyes, even looks me up and down in a rude manner. Behind the bars, Kilorn and Walsh jump to attention. Farley doesn't move from her corner, arms curled around her knees. For a second I think she might be sleeping, until she moves and her blue eyes reflect the light.

"I need to know, my lady," Gliacon says, sounding apologetic. She nods to Julian and Lucas, who follow me down. "Goes for you two as well."

"I would like a private audience with these"—I throw as much disgust into my voice as I can; it's not hard, with the pig-eyed Sentinel standing so close—"creatures. We have questions that must be answered and wrongs to repay. Don't we, Julian?"

Julian sneers, putting on a good show. "It'll be easy to make them sing."

"Not possible, m'lady," Pig-Eyes snorts. His accent is hard and rough, from Harbor Bay. "Our orders are to stay right here, all night. We move for no one."

Once, a boy in the Stilts called me a rotten flirt for charming him out of a good pair of boots. "You understand my position, don't you? I will be a princess soon, and the favor of a princess is a *very* valuable thing. Besides, the Red rats must be taught a lesson. A painful one."

Pig-Eyes blinks sluggishly at me, thinking it over. Julian hovers at my shoulder, ready with his sweet words if I need them. Two heartbeats pass before Pig-Eyes nods, waving to the others. "We can give you five minutes."

My face hurts from smiling so widely, but I don't care. "Thank you so much. I am in your debt, all of you."

They tromp away in a single file, their boots scuffing. As soon as they reach the top landing, I allow myself to hope. *Five minutes will be more than enough.*

Kilorn almost jumps at the bars, eager to be free of his cell, and Walsh pulls Farley to her feet. But I don't move at all. I don't intend to free them, not yet.

"Mare—," Kilorn whispers, puzzled at my hesitation, but I silence him with a look.

"The bomb." Smoke and fire cloud my thoughts, bringing me back to the moment the ballroom exploded. "Tell me about the bomb."

I expect them to fall over themselves in apologies, to beg my forgiveness, but instead, the three exchange blank looks. Farley leans against the bars, her eyes on fire.

"I don't know anything about that," she hisses, barely audible. "I never authorized such a thing. It was supposed to be organized, with special targets. We do not kill at random, without purpose."

"The capital, the other bombings—?"

"You know those buildings were empty. No one died there, not because of us," she says evenly. "I swear to you, Mare, this was not our doing."

"Do you really think we'd try to blow up our greatest hope?" Kilorn adds. I don't need to ask to know he means me.

Finally, I nod over my shoulder to Julian.

"Open the cell. Quietly," Julian murmurs, his hands on Lucas's face.

The magnetron complies, forcing the bars into an open O wide enough to step through. Walsh comes out first, her eyes wide in amazement. Kilorn is next, helping Farley fit through the bars. Her arm still dangles helplessly—the healer missed a spot.

I gesture to the wall, and they move soundlessly, mice on stone. Walsh's eyes touch on Tristan's body, still lifeless in the cell, but she stays put beside Farley. Julian shoves Lucas in next to them before taking his spot next to the foot of the stairs, across from the freed prisoners.

I take the other side, pressing myself in next to Kilorn. Even though he's spent the night in the cells, with a dead body for company, he still smells like home.

"I knew you'd come," he whispers in my ear. "I knew it."

But there's no time for pleasantries or celebrations. Not until they're away safely.

Across the open gap of stairwell, Julian nods at me. He's ready.

"Sentinel Gliacon, may I have a word?" I shout up the stairs, laying the bait for our next trap. The shuffle of feet tells me she's taken it.

"What is it, my lady?"

When she reaches the floor, her eyes fly straight to the open cell and she gasps behind her mask. But Julian is too quick, even for a Sentinel.

"You went for a walk. You returned to find this. You do not remember us. Call down *one* of the others," he murmurs, his voice a terrible song.

"Sentinel Tyros, you are needed," she says flatly.

"Now you will sleep."

She drops almost before the last word leaves his lips, but Julian catches her around the middle and lays her gently down behind him. Kilorn exhales in surprise, impressed by Julian, who allows himself a small, pleased smile.

Tyros comes down the stairs next, confused, but eager to serve. Julian does it again, singing his orders in a few whispered seconds. I didn't expect Sentinels to be so stupid, but it makes sense. They're trained from childhood in the art of combat; logic and intelligence are not their highest priorities.

But the last two, Pig-Eyes and the healer, are not complete fools. When Tyros calls out, ordering the skin healer Sentinel to come down, they mutter to each other.

"About finished, Lady Titanos?" Pig-Eyes calls, his voice wary.

Thinking quickly, I shout back to them. "Yes, we're finished. Your companions have returned to their posts, I want to make sure you do as well."

"Oh, have they? Is that right, Tyros?"

With blinding speed, Julian kneels over the fainted Tyros. He pries his eyes open, holding the lids. "Say you've returned to your post. Say the lady has finished."

"Returned to my post," Tyros drones. Hopefully the long stairwell and stone walls will distort his voice. "The lady has finished."

Pig-Eyes grunts to himself. "Very well."

Their boots stamp against the steps, both coming down together. *Two. Julian cannot handle two alone.* I feel Kilorn tense at my back, his fist clenching as he prepares for anything. With one hand I push him back against the wall, while the other grows white with sparks.

The footsteps stop, just beyond the opening. I can't see them and neither can Julian, but Pig-Eyes breathes like a dog. The healer is there as well, waiting just beyond our reach. In total silence, it's hard not to hear the click of a gun.

Julian's eyes widen, but he stands firm, one hand closing around his stolen weapon. I don't even want to breathe, knowing the edge we're all standing on. The walls seem to shrink, boxing us into a stone coffin with no escape.

I feel very calm when I slide out in front of the steps, my sparking hand behind my back. I expect to feel bullets at any minute, but the pain never comes. They won't shoot me, not until I give them a good reason.

"Is there some problem, Sentinels?" I sneer, quirking an eyebrow like I've seen Evangeline do a hundred times. Slowly, I take a step up, bringing the pair of them into view. They stand side by side, fingers itching on twin triggers. "I'd prefer it if you wouldn't point your guns at me."

Pig-Eyes glares at me outright, but it does nothing to faze me. *You are a lady. Act like it. Act for your life.* "Where's your friend?"

"Oh, he's coming along. One of the prisoners has a mouth on her. She needed some *extra* attention." The lie comes so easily. Practice really does make perfect.

Grinning, Pig-Eyes lowers his gun a bit. "The scarred bitch? Had to show her the back of my hand myself." He chuckles. I laugh with him and dream about what lightning could do to his fleshy, pale eyes.

As I move closer, the skin healer puts one hand on the metal rail, blocking my way. I do the same. It feels cold in my hand, and solid. *Easy does it*, I tell myself, pushing just enough energy into my sparks. Not enough to burn, not enough to scar, but enough to take care of them both. It's like threading a needle, and for once, I'm the sewing expert.

Above me, the healer doesn't laugh with his friend. His eyes are bright silver, and, with the mask and fiery cloak, he looks like a demon from a nightmare.

"What's behind your back?" he hisses through the mask.

I shrug, allowing myself one more step. "Nothing, Sentinel Skonos."

The next words are ragged. "You lie."

We react in the same second, blasting into action. The bullet hits me in the stomach, but my lightning blazes up the metal rail, through his skin and into the healer's brain. Pig-Eyes shouts, firing his own gun. The bullet digs into the wall, missing me by inches. But I don't miss him, lashing with the ball of sparks behind my back. They slide past me, both unconscious, their muscles twitching with shocks.

And then I'm falling.

I briefly wonder if the stone floor will smash my skull. I suppose that's easier than bleeding to death. Instead, long arms catch me.

"Mare, you'll be fine," Kilorn whispers. His hand covers my stomach, trying to stop the bleeding. His eyes are green as grass. They stand out in a world fading to darkness. "It's nothing at all."

"Put those on," Julian snaps to the others. Farley and Walsh rush past me to pull on the fire-red cloaks and masks. "You too!"

He yanks Kilorn off me, almost throwing him across the room in his haste.

"Julian—," I choke out, trying to grab him. *I must thank him.*

But he's beyond my reach, kneeling over the healer. He rips open the Sentinel's eyelids and sings, ordering him to wake up. The next thing I know, the healer stares down at me, his hands on my wound. It only takes a second before the world shifts back to normal. In the corner, Kilorn breathes a sigh of relief and pulls a cloak over his head.

"Her as well." I point to Farley. Julian nods and directs the healer over to her. With an audible *pop*, her shoulder snaps back into place.

"Much obliged," she says, pulling the mask over her face.

Walsh stands over us all, her mask forgotten in her hand. She stares at the fallen Sentinels, jaw agape. "Are they dead?" she asks, whispering like a frightened child.

Julian looks up from Pig-Eyes, finished singing to him. "Hardly. This lot will be awake in a few hours, and if you're lucky, no one will know you're gone until then."

"I can work with a few hours." Farley smacks at Walsh, snapping her back to reality. "Get your head on straight, girl, we've got a lot of running to do tonight."

It doesn't take long to slip them through the last few passages. Even so, my fear grows with each passing heartbeat, until we find ourselves in the middle of Cal's garage. The slack-jawed Lucas tears a hole in the metal door like he's ripping paper, revealing the night beyond.

Walsh hugs me, taking me by surprise. "I don't know how," she mutters, "but I hope you become queen one day. Imagine what you could do then? The Red queen."

I have to smile at the impossible thought. "Go, before your nonsense rubs off on me."

Farley isn't one for hugs, but she does pat me on the shoulder. "We'll meet again, and soon."

"Not like this, I hope."

Her face splits into a rare, toothy smile. Despite the scar, I realize she's very pretty.

"Not like this," she echoes, before slipping out into the night with Walsh.

"I know I can't ask you to come with me," Kilorn mutters, moving to follow them. He stares at his hands, examining scars I know better than my own mind. *Look at me, you idiot.*

Sighing, I force myself to shove him toward freedom. "The cause needs me here. You need me here too."

"What I need and what I want are two very different things."

I try to laugh, but I can't find the strength.

"This is not our end, Mare," Kilorn murmurs, embracing me. He laughs to himself, the noise vibrating in his chest. "Red queen. Has a nice ring to it."

"Get on, you fool." Never have I smiled so brightly and still felt so sad.

He spares me one last glance and nods to Julian, before stepping out into the darkness. The metal knits back together behind him, blocking my friends from sight. Where they're going, I don't want to know.

Julian has to pull me away, but he doesn't scold me for my long good-bye. I think he's more preoccupied with Lucas, who, in his dazed state, has begun to drool.

TWENTY-TWO

That night I dream of my brother Shade coming to visit me in the darkness. He smells like gunpowder. But when I blink, he disappears and my mind screams what I already know. *Shade is dead.*

When morning comes, a series of shuffles and slams makes me bolt awake, sitting up in my bed. I expect to see Sentinels, Cal, or a murderous Ptolemus ready to rip me apart for what I've done, but it's just the maids bustling in my closet. They look more harried than usual and pull down my clothes with abandon.

"What's going on?"

In the closet, the girls freeze. They bow, hands full of silk and linen. As I come closer, I realize they're standing over a set of leather trunks. "Are we going somewhere?"

"Orders, my lady," one says, her eyes lowered. "We only know what we're told."

"Of course. Well, I'm just going to get dressed then." I reach for the nearest outfit, intending to do something for myself for once, but the maids beat me to it.

Five minutes later, they have me painted and ready, dressed in odd leather pants and a flouncy shirt. I'd much prefer my training suit over everything else, but it's apparently not "proper" to wear the thing outside of sessions.

"Lucas?" I ask the empty hallway, half expecting him to pop out from an alcove.

But Lucas is nowhere to be found, and I head off to Protocol, expecting him to cross my path. When he doesn't, a trill of fear ripples through me. Julian made him forget last night, but maybe something slipped through the cracks. Maybe he's being questioned, punished, for the night he can't remember and what we forced him to do.

But I'm not alone for long. Maven steps into my path, his lips quirked into an amused smile.

"You're up early." Then he leans in, speaking in a low whisper. "Especially for having such a late night."

"I don't know what you mean." I try for an innocent tone.

"The prisoners are gone. All three of them, disappeared into thin air."

I put a hand to my heart, letting myself look shocked for the cameras. "By my colors! A few Reds, escaped from us? That seems impossible."

"It does indeed." Though the smile remains, his eyes darken slightly. "Of course, that brings everything into question. The power outages, the failing security system, not to mention a troop of Sentinels with blank spots across their memories." He stares pointedly at me.

I return his sharp glance, letting him see my unease. "Your mother . . . interrogated them."

"She did."

"And will she be talking to"—I choose my words very carefully—"anyone else regarding the escape? Officers, guards—?"

Maven shakes his head. "Whoever did this did it well. I helped her with the questioning and *directed* her to anyone of suspicion." *Directed. Directed away from me.* I breathe a small sigh of relief and squeeze his arm, thanking him for his protection. "Besides, we may never find who did it. People have been fleeing since last night. They think the Hall is no longer safe."

"After last night, they're probably right." I slip my arm into his, drawing him closer. "What did your mother learn of the bomb?"

His voice drops to a whisper. "There was no bomb." *What?* "It was an explosion, but it was also an accident. A bullet punctured a gas line in the floor, and when Cal's fire hit it . . ." He trails off, letting his hands do the talking. "It was Mother's idea to use that to our, ah, advantage."

We don't kill without purpose. "She's turning the Guard into monsters."

He nods gravely. "No one will want to stand with them. Not even Reds."

My blood seems to boil. *More lies.* She's beating us without firing a shot or drawing a blade. Words are all she needs. And now I'm being sent deeper into her world, to Archeon.

You won't see your family again. Gisa will grow, until you don't recognize her anymore. Bree and Tramy will marry, have children, and forget you. Dad will die slowly, suffocated by his wounds, and when he's gone, Mom will slip away too.

Maven lets me think, his eyes thoughtful as he watches the emotions rise in my face. He always lets me think. Sometimes his silence is better than anyone else's words.

"How long do we have left here?"

"We go this afternoon. Most of the court is leaving before that, but we have to take the boat. Keep some tradition in all this madness."

When I was a little girl, I used to sit on my porch and watch the pretty boats pass, heading downriver to the capital. Shade would laugh at me for wanting to catch a glimpse of the king. I didn't realize then it was just part of the pageant, another display just like the arena fights, to show exactly how low we were in the grand scheme of the world. Now I'm going to be part of it again, this time standing on the other side.

"At least you'll get to see your home again, if only for a little while," he adds, trying to be gentle. *Yes, Maven, that's just what I want. To stand and watch my home and my old life pass by.*

But that's the price I must pay. Freeing Kilorn and the others means losing my last few days in the valley, and it's a trade I'm happy to make.

We're interrupted by a loud crash from a nearby passage, the one leading to Cal's room. Maven reacts first, moving to the edge of the hall before I can, like he's trying to protect me from something.

"Bad dreams, brother?" he calls out, worried by what he sees.

In response, Cal steps out into the hallway, his fists clenched, like he's trying to keep his own hands in check. Gone is the bloodstained uniform, replaced by what looks like Ptolemus's armor, though Cal's has a reddish tint.

I want to slap him, to claw at him and scream for what he did to Farley and Tristan and Kilorn and Walsh. The sparks dance inside me, begging to be loosed. But after all, what did I expect? I know what he is and what he believes in—Reds are not worth saving. So I speak as civilly as I can.

"Will you be leaving with your legion?" I know he isn't, judging by the livid anger in his eyes. Once, I feared he would go, and now I wish he would. *I can't believe I cared about saving him. I can't believe that was ever a thought in my head.*

Cal heaves a breath. "The Shadow Legion isn't going anywhere.

Father will not allow it. Not now. It's too dangerous, and I'm too *valuable*."

"You know he's right." Maven puts a hand on his brother's shoulder, trying to calm him. I remember watching Cal do the same thing to Maven, but now the crown is on a different head. "You are the heir. He can't afford to lose you too."

"I'm a soldier," Cal spits, shrugging away from his brother's touch. "I can't just sit by and let others fight for me. I won't do it."

He sounds like a child whining for a toy—he must enjoy killing. It makes me sick. I don't speak, letting the diplomatic Maven talk for me. He always knows what to say.

"Find another cause. Build another cycle, double your training, drill your men, *prepare* yourself for when the danger passes. Cal, you can do a thousand other things, and none of them end with you being killed in some kind of ambush!" he says, glaring up at his brother. Then he smirks, trying to lighten the mood. "You never change, Cal. You just can't sit still."

After a moment of harsh silence, Cal breaks into a weak smile. "Never." His eyes flick to me, but I won't get caught in his bronze stare, not again.

I turn my head, pretending to examine a painting on the wall. "Nice armor," I sneer. "It will go well with your collection."

He looks stung, even confused, but quickly recovers. His smile is gone now, replaced by narrowed eyes and a clenched jaw. He taps at his armor; it sounds like claws on stone. "This was a gift from Ptolemus. I seem to share a common cause with my betrothed's brother." *My betrothed*. Like that's supposed to make me jealous or something.

Maven eyes the armor warily. "What do you mean?"

"Ptolemus commands the officers in the capital. Together with me and my legion, we might be able to do something of use, even within the city."

Cold fear steals into my heart again, brushing away whatever hope and happiness last night's success brought me. "And what is that, exactly?" I hear myself breathe.

"I'm a good hunter. He's a good killer." Cal takes a step backward, walking away from us.

I can feel him slipping down not just the hall but a dark and twisted path. It makes me afraid for the boy who taught me how to dance. *No, not for him.* Of *him.* And that is worse than all my other terrors and nightmares.

"Between the two of us, we'll root out the Scarlet Guard. We'll end this rebellion once and for all."

There's no schedule for today, as everyone is too busy leaving to teach or train. *Fleeing* might be a better word, because that's certainly what this looks like from my vantage point in the entrance hall. I used to think the Silvers were untouchable gods who were never threatened, never scared. Now I know the opposite is true. They've spent so long at the top, protected and isolated, that they've forgotten they can fall. Their strength has become their weakness.

Once, I was afraid of these walls, frightened by such beauty. But I see the cracks now. It's like the day of the bombing, when I realized Silvers were not invincible. Then it was an explosion—now a few bullets have shattered diamondglass, revealing fear and paranoia beneath. Silvers fleeing from Reds—lions running from mice. The king and queen oppose each other, the court has their own alliances, and Cal—the perfect prince, the good soldier—is a torturous, terrible enemy. *Anyone can betray anyone.*

Cal and Maven bid everyone good-bye, doing their duty despite the organized chaos. The airships wait not far off, the whir of their engines audible even inside. I want to see the great machines up close, but moving would mean braving the crowd, and I can't stomach the stares of the grief-stricken. All together, twelve died last night, but I refuse to learn their names. I can't have them weighing on me, not when I need my wits more than ever.

When I can't watch any longer, my feet take me where they will, wandering through now familiar passages. Chambers close as I pass, being shut up for the season, until the court returns. *I won't*, I know. Servants pull white sheets over the furniture and paintings and statues, until the whole place looks haunted by ghosts.

It's not long before I find myself standing in the doorway of Julian's old classroom, and the sight shocks me. The stacks of books, the desk, even the maps are gone. The room looks larger but feels smaller. It once held whole worlds but now holds only dust and crumpled paper. My eyes linger on the wall where the huge map used to be. Once I couldn't understand it; now I remember it like an old friend.

Norta, the Lakelands, Piedmont, Prairie, Tiraxes, Montfort, Ciron, and all the disputed lands in between. Other countries, other peoples, all torn along the lines of blood just like us. *If we change, will they? Or will they try to destroy us too?*

"I hope you'll remember your lessons." Julian's voice draws me out of my thoughts, back to the empty room. He stands behind me, following my gaze to the map wall. "I'm sorry I couldn't teach you more."

"We'll have plenty of time for Lessons in Archeon."

His smile is bittersweet and almost painful to look at. With a jolt I realize I can feel cameras watching us for the very first time. "Julian?"

"The archivists in Delphie have offered me a position restoring some old texts." The lie is as plain as the nose on his face. "Seems they've been digging through the Wash and came on some storage bunkers. Mountains to go through, apparently."

"You'll like that very much." My voice catches in my throat. *You knew he would have to leave. You forced him into this last night, when you put his life in danger for Kilorn's.* "Will you visit, when you can?"

"Yes, of course." Another lie. Elara will figure out his role soon enough, and then he'll be on the run. It only makes sense to get a head start. "I've gotten you something."

I'd rather have Julian than any gift, but I try to look thankful anyways. "Is it good advice?"

He shakes his head, smiling. "You'll see when you get to the capital." Then he stretches out his arms, beckoning to me. "I have to go, so send me off properly."

Hugging him is like hugging my father or the brothers I'll never see again. I don't want to let him go, but the danger is too great for him to stay and we both know it.

"Thank you, Mare," he whispers in my ear. "You remind me so much of her." I don't need to ask to know he's talking about Coriane, about the sister he lost so long ago. "I'll miss you, little lightning girl."

Right now, the nickname doesn't sound so bad.

I don't have the strength to marvel at the boat, driven through the water by electric engines. Black, silver, and red flags flap from every pole, marking this as the king's ship. When I was a girl, I use to wonder why the king laid claim to our color. It was just so beneath him. Now I realize the flags are red like his flame, like the destruction—and the people—he controls.

"The Sentinels from last night have been *reassigned*," Maven mutters as we walk along a deck.

Reassigned is just a fancy word for *punished*. Remembering Pig-Eyes and the way he looked at me, I'm not sorry at all. "Where did they go?"

"The front, of course. They'll be attached to some rabble group, to captain injured, incapable, or bad-tempered soldiers. Those are usually the first to be sent in a trench push." By the shadows behind his eyes, I can tell Maven knows this firsthand.

"The first to die."

He nods solemnly.

"And Lucas? I haven't seen him since yesterday—"

"He's all right. Traveling with House Samos, regrouping with family. The shooting has everyone on their heels, even the High Houses."

Relief washes over me, as well as sadness. I miss Lucas already, but it's good to know he's safe and far from Elara's prying.

Maven bites his lip, looking subdued. "But not for long. Answers are coming."

"What do you mean?"

"They found blood down in the cells. Red blood."

My gunshot wound is gone, but the memory of the pain has not faded. "So?"

"So whichever friend of yours had the misfortune to be wounded won't be a secret much longer, if the bloodbase does its job."

"Bloodbase?"

"The blood database. Any Red born within a hundred miles of civilization gets sampled at birth. Started out as a project to understand exactly what the difference is between us, but it ended up just another way to put a collar on your people. In the bigger cities, Reds don't use ID cards but blood tags. They're sampled at every gate, coming and going. Tracked like animals."

Briefly, I think of the old documents the king threw at me that day in the throne room. My name, my photograph, and a smear of blood were in there.

My blood. They have my blood.

"And they—they can figure out whose blood it is, just like that?"

"It takes some time, a week or so, but yes, that's how it's supposed to work." His eyes fall to my shaking hands, and he covers them with his own, letting warmth bleed into my suddenly cold skin. "Mare?"

"He shot me," I whisper. "The Sentinel shot me. It's my blood they found."

And then his hands are just as cold as mine.

For all his clever ideas, Maven has nothing to say to this. He just stares, his breath coming in tiny, scared puffs. I know the look on his face; I wear it every time I'm forced to say good-bye to someone.

"It's too bad we didn't stay longer," I murmur, looking out at the river. "I would have liked to die close to home."

Another breeze sends a curtain of my hair across my face, but Maven brushes it away and pulls me close with startling ferocity.

Oh.

His kiss is not at all like his brother's. Maven is more desperate, surprising himself as much as me. He knows I'm sinking fast, a stone dropping through the river. *And he wants to drown with me.*

"I will fix this," he murmurs against my lips. I have never seen his eyes so bright and sharp. "I won't let them hurt you. You have my word."

Part of me wants to believe him. "Maven, you can't fix everything."

"You're right, *I* can't," he replies, an edge to his voice. "But I can convince someone with more power than me."

"Who?"

When the temperature around us rises, Maven pulls back, his jaw tense and clenched. The way his eyes flash, I half expect him to attack whoever interrupted us. I don't turn around, mostly because I can't feel my limbs. I've gone numb, though my lips still tingle with memory. What this means, I don't know. What I feel, I can't begin to understand.

"The queen requests your presence on the viewing deck." Cal's voice grinds like stone. He sounds almost angry, but his bronze eyes look sad, defeated even. "Passing the Stilts, Mare."

Yes, the shoreline is already familiar to me. I know that mangled tree, that stretch of bank, and the echo of saws and falling trees is unmistakable. *This is home.* With great pain, I force myself away from the rail to face Cal, who seems to be having a silent conversation with his brother.

"Thank you, Cal," I murmur, still trying to process Maven's kiss and, of course, my own impending doom.

Cal walks away, his usually straight back bowed. Each footfall sends a pang of guilt through me, making me remember our dance and our own kiss. *I hurt everyone, especially myself.*

Maven stares after his fleeing brother. "He does not like to lose. And"—he lowers his voice, now so close to me I can see the tiny flecks of silver in his eyes—"neither do I. I won't lose you, Mare. *I won't.*"

"You'll never lose me."

Another lie, and we both know it.

The viewing deck dominates the front of the ship, enclosed by glass stretching from side to side. Brown shapes take form on the riverbank, and the old hill with the arena appears out of the trees. We're too far from the bank to see anyone properly, but I know my house in an instant. The old flag still flutters on the porch, still embroidered with three red stars. One has a black stripe through it, in honor of Shade. *Shade was executed. You're supposed to rip a star off after that.* But they didn't. They held on to him in their own little rebellion.

I want to point my home out to Maven, to tell him about the village. I've seen his life, and now I want to show him mine. But the viewing deck is silent, all of us staring at the village as we come closer and closer. *The villagers don't care about you*, I want to scream. *Only fools will stop to watch. Only the fools will waste a moment on you.*

As the boat continues on, I begin to think the whole village might be made of fools. All two thousand of them seem crowded onto the bank. Some stand ankle-deep in the river. From this distance, they all look the same. Fading hair and worn clothes, blotchy skinned, tired, hungry—all the things I used to be.

And *angry*. Even from the boat, I can feel their anger. They don't cheer or call out our names. No one waves. No one even smiles.

"What is this?" I breathe, expecting no one to answer.

But the queen does, with great relish. "Such a waste, parading down the river when no one will watch. It seems we've fixed that."

Something tells me this is another mandatory event, like the fights, like the broadcasts. Officers tore sick elders from their beds and exhausted workers from the floor, forcing them to watch us.

A whip cracks somewhere on the bank, followed closely by a woman's scream. "Stay in line!" echoes over the crowd. Their eyes never falter, staring straight ahead, so still that I can't even see where the disruption was. *What happened to make them so lenient? What has already been done?*

Tears prick at my eyes as I watch. There are more cracks and a few babies wail, but no one on the bank protests. Suddenly I'm at the edge of the deck, wanting to burst through the glass with every inch of myself.

"Going somewhere, Mareena?" Elara purrs from her place next to the king. She sips placidly at a drink, surveying me over the rim of her glass.

"Why are you doing this?"

Arms crossed over her magnificent gown, Evangeline eyes me with a sneer. "Why do you care?" But her words fall on deaf ears.

"They know what happened at the Hall, they might even agree with it, so they need to see that we aren't defeated," Cal murmurs, his eyes on the riverbank. He can't even look at me, the coward. "We aren't even bleeding."

Another whip cracks and I flinch, almost feeling the lash on my skin. "Did you order them to be beaten as well?"

He doesn't rise to my challenge, jaw firmly clenched shut. But when another villager cries out, protesting against the officers, he lets his eyes close.

"Stand back, Lady Titanos." The king's voice rumbles like faraway thunder, an order if there ever was one. I can almost feel his smug smile when I step away, moving back to Maven. "This is a Red village, you know that better than us all. They harbor these terrorists, feed them, protect them, *become* them. They are children who have done wrong. And they must learn."

I open my mouth to argue, but the queen bares her teeth. "Perhaps you know of a few who should be made an example of?" she says calmly, gesturing to the shoreline.

The words die in my throat, chased away by her threat. "No, Your Majesty, I don't."

"Then stand back and be silent." Then she grins. "For your time to speak will come."

This is what they need me for. A moment like this, when the scales could tip out of their favor. But I can't protest. I can only do as she commands and watch as my home fades out of sight. Forever.

The closer we get to the capital, the larger the villages become. Soon the landscape fades from lumber and farming communities to proper towns. They center around massive mills, with brick homes and dormitories to house the Red laborers. Like the other villages, their inhabitants stand in the streets to watch us pass. Officers bark, whips crack, and I never get used to it. I flinch every time.

Then the towns are replaced by sprawling estates and mansions, palaces like the Hall. Made of stone and glass and swirling marble, each one seems more magnificent than the last. Their lawns slope to the river, decorated with greenwarden gardens and beautiful fountains. The houses themselves look like the work of gods, each one a different kind of beautiful. But the windows are dark, the doors closed. Where the villages and towns were full of people, these seem devoid of life. Only the flags flying high, one over each structure, let me know someone lives there at all. Blue for House Osanos, silver for Samos, brown for Rhambos, and so on. Now I know the colors by heart, putting faces to each silent home. *I even killed the owners of a few.*

"River Row," Maven explains. "The country residences, should a lord or lady wish to escape the city."

My gaze lingers on the Iral home, a columned wonder of black marble. Stone panthers guard the porch, snarling up at the sky. Even the statues put a chill in me, making me remember Ara Iral and her pressing questions.

"There's no one here."

"The houses are empty most of the year, and no one would dare leave the city now, not with this Guard business." He offers me a small, bitter smile. "They would rather hide behind their diamond walls and let my brother do their fighting for them."

"If only no one had to fight at all."

He shakes his head. "It does no good to dream."

We watch in silence as River Row falls behind us and another forest rises up on the banks. The trees are strange, very tall with black bark and dark red leaves. It is deathly quiet, as no forest should be. Not even birdsong breaks the silence, and overhead, the sky darkens, but not from the waning afternoon light. Black clouds gather, hovering over the trees like a thick blanket.

"And what's this?" Even my voice sounds muffled, and I'm suddenly glad for the glass casing over the deck. To my surprise the others have gone, leaving us alone to watch the gloom settle.

Maven glances at the forest, face pulled in distaste. "Barrier trees. They keep the pollution from traveling farther upriver. The Welle greenwardens made them years ago."

Choppy brown waves foam against the boat, leaving a film of black grime on the gleaming steel hull. The world takes on a strange tint, like I'm looking through dirty glass. The low-lying clouds aren't clouds at all but smoke pouring from a thousand chimneys, obscuring the sky. Gone are the trees and the grass—this is a land of ash and decay.

"Gray Town," Maven murmurs.

Factories stretch out as far as I can see, dirty and massive and humming with electricity. It hits me like a fist, almost knocking me off my feet. My heart tries to keep up with the unearthly pulse and I have to sit down, feeling my blood race.

I thought my world was wrong, that my life was unfair. But I could never even dream of a place like Gray Town.

Power stations glow in the gloom, pulsing electric blue and sickly green into the spider-work of wires in the air. Transports piled high with cargo move along the raised roads, shuttling goods from one factory to another. They scream at one another in a noisy mess of tangled traffic, moving like sluggish black blood in gray veins. Worst of all, little houses surround each factory in an ordered square, one on top of the other, with narrow streets in between. *Slums.*

Beneath such a smoky sky, I doubt the workers ever see daylight. They walk between the factories and their homes, flooding the streets during a shift change. There are no officers, no cracking whips, no blank stares. No one is making them watch us pass. *The king doesn't need to show off here*, I realize. *They are broken from birth.*

"These are the techies," I whisper hoarsely, remembering the name the Silvers so blithely toss around. "They make the lights, the cameras, the video screens—"

"The guns, the bullets, the bombs, the ships, the transports," Maven adds. "They keep the power running. They keep our water clean. They do everything for us."

And they receive nothing but smoke in return.

"Why don't they leave?"

He just shrugs. "This is the only life they know. Most techies will never leave their own alley. They can't even conscript."

Can't even conscript. Their lives are so terrible that the war is a better alternative, and they're not even allowed to go.

Like everything else on the river, the factories fade away, but the image stays with me. *I must not forget this*, something tells me. *I must not forget them.*

Stars wait for us beyond another forest of barrier trees, and beneath them: Archeon. At first I don't see the capital at all, mistaking its lights for blazing stars. As we sail closer and closer, my jaw drops.

A triple-layered bridge runs across the wide river, linking the two cities on either side. It's thousands of feet long and thriving, alive with light and electricity. There are shops and market squares, all built into the Bridge itself a hundred feet above the river. I can just picture the Silvers up there, drinking and eating and looking down on the world from their place on high. Transports blaze along the lowest tier of the Bridge, their headlamps like red and white comets cutting through the night.

Both ends of the Bridge are gated, and the city sectors on either side are walled in. On the east bank, great metal towers stab out of the ground like swords to pierce the sky, all crowned with gleaming giant birds of prey. More transports and people populate the paved streets that climb up the hilly riverbanks, connecting the buildings to the Bridge and the outer gates.

The walls are diamondglass, like back at the Hall, but set with floodlit metal towers and other structures. There are patrols on the walls, but their uniforms are not the flaming red of Sentinels or the stark black of Security. They wear uniforms of clouded silver and white, almost blending into the cityscape. *They are soldiers, and not the kind who dance with ladies. This is a fortress.*

Archeon was built to endure war, not peace.

On the western bank, I recognize the Royal Court and the Treasury Hall from the bombing footage. Both are made from gleaming white marble and fully repaired, even though they were attacked barely more than a month ago. *It feels like a lifetime.* They flank Whitefire Palace, a building even I know on sight. My old teacher used to say it was carved from the hillside itself, a living piece of the white stone. Flames made of gold and pearl flash atop the surrounding walls.

I try to take it in, my eyes darting between both ends of the Bridge, but my mind just can't fathom this place. Overhead, airships move slowly through the night sky, while airjets fly even higher, as fast as shooting stars. I thought the Hall of the Sun was a wonder; apparently I never knew the meaning of the word.

But I can't find anything beautiful here, not when the smoky, dark factories are only a few miles back. The contrast between the Silver city and the Red slum sets my teeth on edge. This is the world I'm trying to bring down, the world trying to kill me and everything I care about. Now I truly see what I'm fighting against and how difficult, how impossible, it will be to win. I've never felt smaller than I do now, with the great bridge looming above us. It looks ready to swallow me whole.

But I have to try. If only for Gray Town, for the ones who have never seen the sun.

TWENTY-THREE

By the time the boat docks at the western bank and we're back on land, night has fallen. At home, this meant shutting down the power and going to sleep, but not in Archeon. If anything, the city seems to brighten while the rest of the world goes dark. Fireworks crackle overhead, raining light down on the Bridge, and atop Whitefire, a red-and-black flag rises. *The king is back on this throne.*

Thankfully there are no more pageants to suffer through; we are greeted by armored transports to take us up from the docks. To my delight, Maven and I have a transport to ourselves, joined by only two Sentinels. He points out landmarks as we pass, explaining what seems like every statue and street corner. He even mentions his favorite bakery, though it sits on the other side of the river.

"The Bridge and East Archeon are for civilians, the common Silvers, though many are richer than some nobles."

"*Common* Silvers?" I almost have to laugh. "There's such a thing?"

Maven just shrugs. "Of course. They're merchants, businessmen, soldiers, officers, shop owners, politicians, land barons, artists, and intellectuals. Some marry into High Houses, some rise above their station, but they don't have noble blood, and their abilities aren't as, well, *powerful*."

Not everyone is special. Lucas told me that once. I didn't know he meant Silvers too.

"Meanwhile, West Archeon is for the court of the king," Maven continues. We pass a street lined with lovely stone houses and pruned, flowering trees. "All the High Houses keep residences here, to be close to the king and government. In fact, the entire country can be controlled from this cliff, if the need should arise."

That explains the location. The western bank is sharply sloped, with the palace and the other government buildings sitting at the crest of a hill overlooking the Bridge. Another wall surrounds the hilltop, fencing in the heart of the country. I try not to gawk when we pass through the gate, revealing a tiled square the size of an arena. Maven calls it Caesar's Square, after the first king of his dynasty. Julian mentioned King Caesar before, but fleetingly; our lessons never got much further than the First Divide, when red and silver became much more than colors.

Whitefire Palace occupies the southern side of the Square, while the courts, treasury, and administrative centers take up the rest. There's even a military barracks, judging by the troops drilling in the walled yard. They are Cal's Shadow Legion, who traveled ahead of us to the city. *A comfort to the nobles*, Maven called them. Soldiers within the walls, to protect us if another attack should come.

Despite the hour, the Square bustles with activity as people rush toward a severe-looking structure next to the barracks. Red-and-black flags, emblazoned with the sword symbol of the army, hang from its columns. I can just see a little stage set up in front of the building, with a podium surrounded by bright spotlights and a growing crowd.

Suddenly the gaze of cameras, heavier than I'm used to, lands on our transport, following us as the line of vehicles passes by the stage. Luckily we keep driving, moving through an archway to a small courtyard, but then we pull to a stop.

"What's this?" I whisper, grabbing on to Maven. Until now, I've kept my fear in check, but between the lights and the cameras and the crowd, my wall begins to crumble.

Maven sighs heavily, more annoyed than anything. "Father must be giving a speech. Just some saber rattling to keep the masses happy. The people love nothing more than a leader promising victory."

Maven steps out, pulling me along with him. Despite my makeup and my clothes, I feel suddenly very bare. *This is for a broadcast. Thousands, millions, will see this.*

"Don't worry, we just have to stand and look stern," he mutters in my ear.

"I think Cal has that covered." I nod to where the prince broods, still attached at the hip to Evangeline.

Maven snickers to himself. "He thinks speeches are a waste of time. Cal likes action, not words."

That makes two of us, but I don't want to admit I have anything in common with Maven's older brother. Maybe once, I thought so, but not now. Not ever again.

A bustling secretary beckons us. His clothes are blue and gray, the colors of House Macanthos. Maybe he knew the colonel; maybe he was her brother, her cousin. *Don't, Mare. This is the last place to lose your nerve.* He doesn't spare a glance at us when we fall into place, standing behind Cal and Evangeline, with the king and queen at the head. Strangely, Evangeline is not her usual cool self; I can see her hands shaking. *She's afraid. She wanted the spotlight, she wanted to be Cal's bride, and yet she's scared of it. How can that be?*

And then we're moving, walking into a building with too many Sentinels and attendants to count. Inside, the structure is built for function, with maps and offices and council rooms instead of paintings or salons. People in gray uniforms busy themselves in the hall, though they stop to let us pass. Most of the doors are closed, but I manage to catch a glimpse inside a few. Officers and soldiers look down at maps of the war front, arguing over the placement of legions. Another room spilling with thunderous energy seems to hold a hundred video screens, each one operated by a soldier in battle uniform. They speak into headsets, barking orders to faraway people and places. The words differ, but the meaning is the same.

"Hold the line."

Cal lingers before the door to the video room, craning his neck to get a better look, but it suddenly slams in his face. He bristles but doesn't protest, falling back into line with Evangeline. She mutters to him quietly, but he shakes her off, to my delight.

But my smile fades as we step back out into blinding lights on the front steps of the structure. A bronze plaque next to the door reads *War Command*. This place is the heart of the military—every soldier, every army, every gun is controlled from within. My stomach rolls at the power here, but I can't lose my nerve, not in front of so many. Cameras flash, blinding my sight. When I flinch, I hear a voice inside my head.

The secretary presses a paper in my hand. One glance at it, and I almost scream. Now I know what I was saved for.

Earn your keep, Elara's voice whispers in my head. She glances at me from Maven's other side, doing her best not to grin.

Maven follows her wretched gaze and notes the paper in my shaking hand. Slowly, he winds his fingers around my own, as if he could pour his strength into me. I want nothing more than to rip the paper in two, but he holds me steady.

"You must," is all he says, whispering so low I can barely hear him. "You must."

"My heart grieves for the lives lost, but know that they were not lost in vain. Their blood will fuel our resolve and drive us to overcome the difficulties ahead. We are a nation at war, we have been for nearly a century, and we are not unaccustomed to obstacles in the path to victory. These people will be found, these people will be punished, and this disease they call rebellion will never take hold in my country."

The video screen in my new bedroom is about as useful as a bottomless boat, playing the king's speech from last night in a nauseating loop. By now I can recite the whole thing word for word, but I can't stop watching. Because I know who comes next.

My face looks strange on the screen, too pale, too cold. I still can't believe I kept a straight face while I read the words. When I step up to the podium, taking the king's place, I don't even tremble.

"I was raised by Reds. I believed I was one. And I saw firsthand the grace of His Majesty the king, the just ways of our Silver lords, and the great privilege they gave us. The right to work, to serve our country, to live and live well." On-screen, Maven puts a hand on my arm. He nods along with my speech. "Now I know I am Silver born, a lady of House Titanos, and one day, a princess of Norta. My eyes have been opened. A world I never dreamed of exists, and it is invincible. It is merciful. And these terrorists, murderers of the most evil kind, are trying to destroy the bedrock of our nation. This we cannot allow."

In the safety of my room, I heave a ragged breath. The worst is coming.

"In his wisdom, King Tiberias has drafted the Measures, to root out this sickness of rebellion, and to protect the good citizens of our nation. They are as follows: As of today, a sunset curfew is in effect for all Reds. Security will be doubled in every Red village and town. New outposts will be built on the roads and manned to full capacity. All Red crimes, including breaking of the curfew, will be punished by execution. And"—at this, my voice falters for the first time—"conscription age has been *lowered*, to the age of fifteen. Anyone who provides information leading to capture of Scarlet Guard operatives or the prevention of Scarlet Guard actions will be awarded conscription waivers, releasing up to five members of the same family from military service."

It's a brilliant, and terrible, maneuver. Reds will tear each other apart for such waivers.

"The Measures are to be upheld at all costs until the disease known as the Scarlet Guard is destroyed." I stare into my own eyes on-screen, watching as I stop myself from choking on my speech. My eyes are wide, hoping my people know what I'm trying to say. *Words can lie.* "Long live the king."

Anger ripples through me, and the screen shorts out, replacing my face with a black void. But I can still see each new order in my mind. More officers patrolling, more bodies hanging from the gallows, and more mothers weeping for their stolen children. *We killed a dozen of theirs, and they kill a thousand of ours.* Part of me knows these blows will drive some Reds to the side of the Guard, but many more will side with the king. For their lives, for their *children's* lives, they will give up what little freedom they had left.

I thought being their puppet would be easy compared to everything else. I was so wrong. But I cannot let them break me, not now. Not even when my own doom lingers on the horizon. I must do everything

I can until my blood is matched and my game is over. Until they drag me away and kill me.

At least my window faces the river, looking south toward the sea. When I stare at the water, I can ignore my fading future. My eyes trail from the swiftly moving current to the dark smudge on the horizon. While the rest of the sky is clear, dark clouds hover in the south, never moving from the forbidden land at the coast. *The Ruined City.* Radiation and fire consumed the city once and never let it go. Now it's nothing but a black ghost sitting just out of reach, a relic of the old world.

Part of me wishes Lucas would rap on my door and hurry me along to a new schedule, but he has not returned yet. I suppose he's better off without me risking his life.

Julian's gift sits against the wall, a firm reminder of another friend lost. It's a piece of the giant map, framed and gleaming behind glass. When I pick it up, something thumps to the ground, falling from the back of the frame.

I knew it.

My heart races, beating wildly as I drop to my knees, hoping to find some secret note from Julian. But instead, there's nothing more than a book.

Despite my disappointment, I can't help smiling. Of course Julian would leave me another story, another collection of words to comfort me when he no longer can.

I flip open the cover, expecting to find some new histories, but instead, handwritten words stare up at me from the title page. *Red and silver.* It's in Julian's unmistakable swirling scrawl.

The sight line of my room's cameras beat into my back, reminding me I am not alone. Julian knew that too. *Brilliant Julian.*

The book looks normal, a dull study of relics found in Delphie, but hidden among the words, in the same type, is a secret worth telling. It takes me many minutes to find every added line and I'm quietly grateful I woke up so early. Finally I have them all, and I seem to have forgotten how to breathe.

Dane Davidson, Red soldier, Storm Legion, killed on routine patrol, body never recovered. August 1, 296 NE. Jane Barbaro, Red soldier, Storm Legion, killed by friendly fire, body cremated. November 19, 297 NE. Pace Gardner, Red soldier, Storm Legion, executed for insubordination, body misplaced. June 4, 300 NE. There are more names, stretching over the last twenty years, all of them cremated or their bodies lost or "misplaced." How anyone can misplace an executed man, I don't know. The name at the end of the list makes my eyes water. *Shade Barrow, Red soldier, Storm Legion, executed for desertion, body cremated. July 27, 320 NE.*

Julian's own words follow my brother's name, and I feel like he's next to me again, slowly and calmly teaching his lesson.

> *According to military law, all Red soldiers are to be buried in the cemeteries of the Choke. Executed soldiers have no burials and lie in mass graves. Cremation is not common. Misplaced bodies are nonexistent. And yet I found 27 names, 27 soldiers, your brother included, who suffered these fates.*
>
> *All died on patrol, killed by Lakelanders or their own units, if not executed for charges without base. All were transferred to the Storm Legion weeks before dying. And all of their bodies were destroyed or lost in some way. Why? The Storm Legion is not a death squad—hundreds of Reds serve under General Eagrie without dying strangely. So why kill these 27?*
>
> *For once, I was glad for the bloodbase. Even though they are long "dead," their blood samples still remain. And now I must apologize,*

Mare, for I have not been entirely honest with you. You trusted me to train you, to help you, and I did, but I was also helping myself. I am a curious man, and you are the most curious thing I have ever seen. I couldn't help myself. I compared your blood sample to theirs, only to find an identical marker in them, different from all others.

I'm not surprised no one noticed, because they were not looking for it. But now that I knew, it was easy to find. Your blood is red, but it is not the same. There is something new in you, something no one has seen before. And it was in 27 others. A mutation, a change that may be the key to everything you are.

You are not the only one, Mare. You are not alone. You are simply the first protected by the eyes of a thousand, the first they could not kill and hide away. Like the others, you are Red and Silver, and stronger than both.

I think you are the future. I think you are the new dawn.

And if there were 27 before, there must be others. There must be more.

I feel frozen; I feel numb; I feel everything and nothing. *Others like me.*

Using the mutations in your blood, I searched the rest of the bloodbase, finding the same in other samples. I have included them all here, for you to pass on.

I know I don't need to tell you the importance of this list, of what it could mean to you and the rest of this world. Pass it on to someone you trust, find the others, protect them, train them, for it is only a matter of time before someone less friendly discovers what I have—and hunts them down.

His words end there, followed by a list that makes my fingers tremble. There are names and locations, so many of them, all waiting to be found. All waiting to fight.

My mind feels like it's on fire. *Others. More.* Julian's words swim across my eyes, searing into my soul.

Stronger than both.

The little book sits snugly in my jacket, tucked in next to my heart. But before I can go to Maven, to show him Julian's discovery, Cal finds me. He corners me in a sitting room quite like the one we danced in, though the moon and the music are long gone. Once I wanted everything he could give me, and now the sight of him turns my stomach. He can see the revulsion in my face, as much as I try to hide it.

"You're angry with me," he says. It's not a question.

"I'm not."

"Don't lie," he growls, eyes suddenly on fire. *I've been lying since the day we met.* "Three days ago you kissed me, and now you can't even look at me."

"I'm betrothed to your brother," I tell him, pulling away.

He dismisses the point with the wave of a hand. "That didn't stop you before. What's changed?"

I've seen who you really are, I want to scream. *You're not the gentle warrior, the perfect prince, or even the confused boy you pretend to be. As much as you try to fight it, you're just like all of them.*

"Is this about the terrorists?"

My teeth grit together painfully. "Rebels."

"They murdered people, children, *innocents.*"

"You and I both know that wasn't *their* fault," I spit back, not bothering to care how cruel the words are. Cal flinches, stunned for a moment. He almost looks sick as he remembers the Sun Shooting—and the accidental explosion that followed. But it passes, slowly replaced by anger.

"But they caused it all the same," he growls. "What I ordered the Sentinel to do, was for the dead, for justice."

"And what did torture get you? Do you know their names, how many there are? Do you even know what they *want*? Have you even bothered to listen?"

He heaves a sigh, trying to salvage the conversation. "I know you have your own reasons for—for *sympathizing*, but their methods cannot be—"

"Their methods are your own fault. You make us work, you make us bleed, you make us die for your wars and factories and the little comforts you don't even notice, all because we are *different*. How can you expect us to let that stand?"

Cal fidgets, a muscle in his cheek twitching. He has no answer to that.

"The only reason I'm not dead in a trench somewhere is because you pitied me. The only reason you're even listening to me now is because, by some insane miracle, I happen to be another kind of different."

Lazily, my sparks rise in my hands. I can't imagine going back to life before my body hummed with power, but I can certainly remember it.

"You can stop this, Cal. You will be king, and you can stop this war, you can save thousands, *millions*, from generations of glorified slavery, if you say *enough*."

Something breaks in Cal, quenching the fire he tries so hard to hide. He crosses to the window, hands clasped behind his back. With the rising sun on his face and shadow on his back, he seems torn between two worlds. In my heart, I know he is. The little part of me that still cares about him wants to close the distance between us, but I am not that foolish. I'm not a little lovesick girl.

"I thought that once," he mutters. "But it would lead to rebellion on both sides, and I will *not* be the king who ruins this country. This is my legacy, my father's legacy, and I have a duty to it." A slow heat rumbles from him, steaming the glass window. "Would you trade a million deaths for what they want?"

A million deaths. My mind flashes back to Belicos Lerolan's corpse, with his dead children at his side. And then other faces join the dead—Shade, Kilorn's father, every Red soldier who died for their war.

"The Guard won't stop," I say softly, but I know he's barely listening anymore. "And while they are certainly to blame, you are as well. There is blood on your hands, Prince." *And Maven's. And mine.*

I leave him standing there, hoping I've changed him but knowing those odds are slim at best. He is his father's son.

"Julian's disappeared, hasn't he?" he calls out to me, stopping me in my tracks.

I turn slowly, mulling over what I can possibly say. I decide to play dumb. "Disappeared?"

"The escape left holes in the memories of many Sentinels, as well as the video logs. My uncle does not use his abilities often, but I know the signs."

"You think he helped them escape?"

"I do," he says painfully, looking at his hands. "That's why I gave him enough time to slip away."

"You did what?" I can't believe my ears. Cal, the soldier, the one who always follows orders, breaking the rules for Julian.

"He's my uncle, I did what I could for him. How heartless do you think I am?" He smirks sadly at me, not waiting for an answer. It makes me ache. "I delayed the arrest as long as I could, but everyone leaves tracks, and the queen will find him," he sighs, putting a hand against the glass. "And he'll be executed."

"You'd do that to your uncle?" I don't bother to hide my disgust, or the fear beneath. *If he'll kill Julian, even after letting him go, what will he do to me when I'm found out?*

Cal's shoulders tighten as he straightens, morphing back into the soldier. He will hear no more of Julian or the Scarlet Guard.

"Maven had an interesting proposition."

That was unexpected. "Oh?"

He nods, oddly annoyed at the thought of his brother. "Mavey's always been a quick thinker. He got that from his mother."

"Is that supposed to scare me?" I know better than any that Maven is nothing like his mother, or any other damned Silver. "What are you trying to say, Cal?"

"You're in the open now," he blurts out. "After your speech, the entire country knows your name and face. And so more will wonder who and what you are."

I can only scowl and shrug. "Maybe you should've thought of that before you made me read that disgusting speech."

"I'm a soldier, not a politician. You know I had nothing to do with the Measures."

"But you'll follow them. You'll follow them without question."

He doesn't argue that. For all his faults, Cal won't lie to me. Not now. "All records of you have been removed. Officers, archivists, *no one* will ever find proof you were born Red," he murmurs, eyes on the floor. "That is what Maven proposed."

Despite my anger, I gasp aloud. *The bloodbase. The records.* "What does that mean?" I don't have the strength to keep my voice from shaking.

"Your school record, birth certificate, blood prints, even your ID card have been destroyed." I barely hear him over the sound of my hammering heartbeat.

Once, I would have hugged him outright. But I must remain still. I must not let Cal know he has saved me again. *No, not Cal.* This was Maven's doing. This was the shadow controlling the flame.

"That sounds like the right thing to do," I say aloud, trying to sound uninterested.

But my act can only last so long. After one stiff bow in Cal's direction, I hurry from the room, hiding my wild grin.

TWENTY-FOUR

I spend much of the next day exploring, though my mind is somewhere else. Whitefire is older than the Hall, its walls made of stone and carved wood rather than diamondglass. I doubt I'll ever learn the layout of the whole thing, as it holds not just the royal residence but many administrative offices and chambers, ballrooms, a full training court, and other things I don't understand. I guess that's why it takes the secretary nearly a half hour to find me, wandering through a gallery of statues. But I won't have more time to explore. I have duties to fulfill.

Duties, according to the king's chatting secretary, that apply to a whole range of evils beyond just reading the Measures. As a future princess, I must meet the people in arranged outings, making speeches and shaking hands and standing by Maven's side. The last part doesn't really bother me, but being put on parade like a goat at auction isn't exactly exciting.

I join Maven in a transport, headed for the first appearance. I'm itching to tell him about the list and thank him for the bloodbase, but there are too many eyes and ears.

The majority of the day speeds by in a blur of noise and color as we tour different parts of the capital. The Bridge Market reminds me of Grand Garden, though it's three times the size. In the single hour we spend greeting children and shopkeepers, I see the Silvers assault or aggravate dozens of Red servants, all trying to do their jobs. Security keeps them from all-out abuse, but the words they sling are almost as hurtful. *Child killers, animals, devils.* Maven keeps his grip tight on my hand, squeezing every time a Red is knocked to the ground. When we reach our next stop, an art gallery, I'm glad to be out of the public eye, until I see the paintings. The Silver artist uses two colors, silver and red, in a horrifying collection that makes me sick. Each painting is worse than the last, depicting Silver strength and Red weakness in every brushstroke. The last one depicts a gray-and-silver figure, quite like a ghost, and the crown on his brow bleeds crimson. It makes me want to put my head through a wall.

The plaza outside the gallery is noisy, bustling with city life. Many stop to stare, gawking at us as we head for our transport. Maven waves with a practiced smile, causing the crowd to cheer his name. He's good at this; after all, these people are his birthright. When he stoops to speak with a few children, his smile brightens. *Cal might be born to rule, but Maven was meant for it. And Maven is willing to change the world for us, for the Reds he was raised to spit on.*

I surreptitiously touch the list in my pocket, thinking of the ones who can help Maven and me change the world. Are they like me, or are they as varied as the Silvers? *Shade was like you. They knew about Shade and had to kill him, like they could not kill you.* My heart aches for my fallen brother, for the conversations we might have had. *For the future we might have forged.*

But Shade is dead, and there are others who need my help.

"We need to find Farley," I whisper in Maven's ear, barely audible to myself. But he hears me and raises an eyebrow in silent question. "I have to give her something."

"I have no doubt she'll find us," he mutters back, "if she isn't watching already."

"How—?"

Farley, spying on *us*? Inside a city that wants her torn apart? It seems impossible. But then I notice the Silver crowd pressing in, and the Red servants beyond. A few linger to watch us, their arms banded with red. Any one of them could work for Farley. *They all could.* Even with the Sentinels and Security all around, she's still with us.

Now the question becomes finding the *right* Red, saying the *right* thing, finding the *right* place, and doing it all without anyone noticing the prince and his future princess communicating with a wanted terrorist.

This isn't like the crowds at home, the ones I could move through so easily. Now I stand out, a future princess surrounded by guards, with a rebellion resting on her shoulders. *And maybe even something more important*, I think, remembering the list of names in my jacket.

When the crowd pushes in, craning to look at us, I take my chance and slip away. The Sentinels bunch around Maven, still not used to guarding me as well, and with a few quick turns, I'm out of the circle of guards and onlookers. They continue across the plaza without me, and if Maven notices I'm gone, he doesn't stop them.

The Red servants don't acknowledge me, their heads down as they buzz between shops. They keep to alleys and shadows, trying to stay out of sight. I'm so busy searching the Red faces that I don't notice the one at my elbow.

"My lady, you dropped this," the little boy says. He's probably ten years old, with one arm banded with red. "My lady?"

Then I notice the scrap he holds out. It's nothing, just a twisted bit of paper I don't remember having. Still, I smile for the boy and take it from him. "Thank you very much."

He grins at me, smiling as only a child can, before bounding away into an alley. He bounces with every step. Life has not dragged him down yet.

"This way, Lady Titanos." A Sentinel stands over me, watching with flat eyes. *So much for that plan.* I let him lead me back to the transport, feeling suddenly dejected. I can't even sneak away like I used to. *I'm getting soft.*

"What was that all about?" Maven wonders as I slide back into the transport.

"Nothing," I sigh, casting a glance out the window as we pull away from the plaza. "Thought I saw someone."

We're around a bend in the street before I even think to look at the little paper. I unfold it in my lap, hiding the scrap in the folds of my sleeve. There are words scrawled across the slip, so small I can barely read them.

Hexaprin Theater. Afternoon play. The best seats.

It takes me a moment to realize I only understand half those words, but that doesn't matter at all. Smiling, I press the message into Maven's hand.

Maven's request is all it takes to get us into the theater. It's small but very grand, with a green domed roof crowned by a black swan. It's a place of entertainment, showing plays or concerts or even some archive films on special occasions. A play, as Maven tells me, is when people, *actors*, perform a story on a stage. Back home we didn't have time for bedtime fairy tales, let alone stages and actors and costumes.

Before I know it, we're sitting on a closed balcony above the stage. The seats below us teem with people, many of them children, all of them Silver. A few Reds rove between the rows and aisles, serving drinks or taking tickets, but none sit down. This is not a luxury they can afford. Meanwhile, we sit on velvet chairs with the best view, with the secretary and the Sentinels standing just beyond our curtained door.

When the theater darkens, Maven throws an arm across my shoulders, pulling me so close I can feel his heartbeat. He smirks at the secretary, now peeking between the curtains. "Don't disturb us," he drawls, and he pulls my face to his.

The door clicks behind us, locking shut, but neither of us pulls away. A minute or an hour passes, which I don't know, until voices onstage bring me back to reality. "Sorry," I mutter to Maven, standing up out of my chair in an effort to put some distance between us. There's no time for kissing now, no matter how much I might want to. He only smirks, watching me instead of the play. I do my best to look elsewhere, but something always draws my eyes back to him.

"What do we do now?"

He laughs to himself, eyes glinting mischievously.

"That's not what I meant." But I can't help but smirk with him. "Cal cornered me earlier."

Maven's lips purse, tightening at the thought. "And?"

"It seems I've been saved."

His resulting grin could light the world entire, and I'm seized by the need to kiss him again. "I told you I would," he says, his voice oddly rough. When his hand reaches for mine, I take it without question.

Before we can continue, the ceiling panel above us scrapes away.

Maven jumps to his feet, more startled than I am, and peers into the black space above us. Not even a whisper filters down, but all the same, I know what to do. Training has made me stronger, and I pull myself up with ease, disappearing into the dark and cold. I can't see anything or anyone, but I'm not afraid. Excitement rules me now, and with a smile, I reach down a hand to help Maven. He scrambles up into the darkness and tries to get his bearings. Before our eyes adjust, the ceiling panel slides back into place, shutting out the light and the play and the people beyond.

"Be quick and quiet. I'll take you from here."

It's not the voice I recognize but the smell: an overpowering mixture of tea, old spices, and a familiar blue candle.

"Will?" My voice almost cracks. "Will Whistle?"

Slowly but surely, the darkness becomes easier to manage. His white beard, tangled as ever, comes into dim focus. There's no mistaking it now.

"No time for reunions, little Barrow," he says. "We have work to do."

How Will came to be here, traveling all the way from the Stilts, I don't know, but his intimate knowledge of the theater is even more peculiar. He leads us through the ceiling, down ladders and steps and little trapdoors, all with the play echoing overhead. It's not long before we're belowground, with brick supports and metal beams stretching high above us.

"You people sure like to be dramatic," Maven mutters, eyeing the gloom around us. It looks like a crypt, dark and damp, where every shadow holds a horror.

Will barely laughs as he shoulders open a metal door. "Just you wait."

We tramp through the narrow passage, sloping downward even farther. The air smells faintly of sewage. To my surprise, the path ends in a small platform, lit by only a burning torch. It casts strange shadows on a crumbling wall set with broken tiles. There are black markings on them, letters, but not from any language I can read.

Before I can ask about them, a great screeching sound shakes the walls around us. It comes from a round hole in the wall, rumbling up from even greater darkness. Maven grabs my hand, startled by the sound, and I'm just as frightened as him. Metal scrapes on metal, an earsplitting noise. Bright lights stream out of the tunnel and I can feel something coming, something big and electric and powerful.

A metal worm appears, coasting to a stop in front of us. The sides are raw metal, welded and bolted together, with slit-like windows. A door slides open on shrieking tracks, spilling a warm glow onto the platform.

Farley smiles to us from a seat inside the door. She waves a hand, gesturing for us to join her. "All aboard."

"The techies call it the Undertrain," she says as we shakily take our seats. "Remarkably fast, and it runs on the ancient tracks the Silvers never bothered to look for."

Will shuts the door behind us, slamming us into what feels like nothing more than a long tin can. If I weren't so worried about the under-thing crashing, I'd be impressed. Instead, I tighten my grip on the seat below me.

"Where did you build this?" Maven wonders aloud, his eyes sweeping over the wretched cage. "Gray Town is controlled, the techies work for—"

"We have techies and tech towns of our own, little prince," Farley says, looking very proud of herself. "What you Silvers know about the Guard couldn't fill a teacup."

The train lurches beneath us, almost tossing me from my seat, but no one else even bats an eye. It slides along until it reaches a speed that smacks my stomach into my spine. The others continue chattering, mostly Maven asking questions about the Undertrain and the Guard. I'm glad no one asks me to speak, because I'll certainly throw up or pass out if I do much more than sit still. But not Maven. Nothing gets by him.

He glances out the window, gleaning something from the rock blurring past. "We're heading south."

Farley sits back in her seat, nodding. "Yes."

"The south is radiated," he barks, staring down at her.

She barely shrugs.

"Where are you taking us?" I murmur, finally finding my voice.

Maven doesn't waste any time, moving for the closed door. No one stops him because there's nowhere for him to go. *No escape.*

"You know what it does? Radiation?" He sounds truly afraid.

Farley begins to tick off the symptoms on her fingers, a maddening smile still on her face. "Nausea, vomiting, headache, seizures, cancerous diseases, and, oh yes, death. A very unpleasant death."

Suddenly I feel very sick. "Why are you doing this? We're here to help you."

"Mare, stop the train, you can stop the train." Maven drops in front of me, grabbing me by the shoulders. "Stop the train!"

To my surprise, the tin can squeals around us, coming to a very sharp and sudden stop. Maven and I tumble to the floor in a tangle of limbs, hitting the hard metal deck with a painful thunk. Lights beam down at us from the open door, revealing another platform lit by torches. It's much larger and leads far back out of sight.

Farley steps over the pair of us without so much as a glance and trots onto the platform. "Aren't you coming?"

"Don't move, Mare. This place will kill us!"

Something whines in my ears, almost drowning out Farley's cold laugh. As I sit up, I can see she's waiting patiently for both of us.

"How do you *know* the south, the Ruins, are still radiated?" she asks with a mad smile.

Maven trips over the words. "We have machines, detectors, they tell us—"

Farley nods. "And who *built* those machines?"

"Techies," Maven croaks, "Reds." Finally, he understands what she's getting at. "The detectors lie."

Grinning, Farley nods and extends a hand, helping him off the floor. He keeps his eyes on her, still wary, but allows her to lead us out onto the platform and up an iron set of stairs. Sunlight streams in from above, and fresh air swirls down to mix with the murky vapors of the underground.

Then we're blinking in the open air, staring up at low-lying fog. Walls rise all around, supporting a ceiling that no longer exists. Only pieces of it remain, little bits of aquamarine and gold. As my eyes adjust, I can see tall shadows in the sky, their tops disappearing into the haze. The streets, wide black rivers of asphalt, are cracked and sprouting gray weeds a hundred years old. Trees and bushes grow over concrete, reclaiming little pockets and corners, but even more have been cleared away. Shattered glass crunches under my feet and clouds of dust drift in the wind, but somehow this place, the picture of neglect, doesn't feel abandoned. I know this place from the histories, from the books and old maps.

Farley puts an arm around my shoulders, her smile wide and white.

"Welcome to the City of Ruins, to Naercey," she says, using the old name forgotten long ago.

The ruined island contains special markers around the borders, to trick the radiation detectors the Silvers use to survey the old battlefields. This is how they protect it, the home of the Scarlet Guard. *In Norta, at least*. That's what Farley said, hinting at more bases across the country. And soon, it will be the sanctuary of every Red refugee fleeing the king's new punishments.

Every building we pass looks decrepit, coated in ash and weeds, but upon closer inspection, there's something much more. Footprints in the dust, a light in a window, the smell of cooking wafting up from a drain. People, *Reds*, have a city of their own right here, hiding in plain sight. Electricity is scarce but smiles are not.

The half-collapsed building Farley leads us to must've been some kind of café once, judging by the rust-eaten tables and ripped-up booth seats. The windows have long since disappeared, but the floor is clean. A woman sweeps dust out the door, into neat piles on the broken sidewalk. I would be daunted by such a task, knowing that there is so much left to sweep away, but she carries on with a smile, humming to herself.

Farley nods at the cleaning woman, and she hurries away, leaving us in peace. To my delight, the booth closest to us holds a familiar face.

Kilorn, safe and whole. He even has the audacity to wink. "Long time no see."

"There's no time to get cute," Farley growls, taking a seat next to him. She gestures for us to follow and we do, sliding into the squeaky booth. "I take it you saw the villages on your cruise down the river?"

My smile quickly fades, as does Kilorn's. "Yes."

"And the new laws? I know *you've* heard about them." Her eyes harden, like it's my fault I was forced to read the Measures.

"This is what happens when you threaten a beast," Maven mutters, jumping to my defense.

"But now they know our name."

"Now they're *hunting* you," Maven snaps, bringing a fist down on the table. It shakes the thin layer of dust, sending floating clouds into the air. "You waved a red flag in front of a bull but didn't do much more than poke at him."

"They're frightened though," I pipe in. "They've learned to fear you. That has to count for something."

"It counts for nothing if you slink back into your hidden city and let them regroup. You're giving the king and the *army* time. My brother is already on your trail, and it won't be long until he tracks you down." Maven stares at his hands, strangely angry. "Soon staying one step ahead won't be enough. It won't even be possible."

Farley's eyes glimmer in the light as she surveys us both, thinking. Kilorn is content to draw circles in dust, seemingly unmoved. I fight the urge to kick him under the table to make him pay attention.

"I couldn't care less about my own safety, Prince," Farley says. "It's the people in the villages, the workers and the soldiers, who I care about. They're the ones being punished right now, and harshly."

My thoughts fly to my family and the Stilts, remembering the dull look in a thousand eyes as we passed. "What have you heard?"

"Nothing good."

Kilorn's head jerks up, though his fingers still swirl on the table. "Double work shifts, Sunday hangings, mass graves. It's not pretty for the ones who can't keep up the pace." He's remembering our village, just like I am. "Our people at the war front say it isn't much different up there either. The fifteen- and sixteen-year-olds are being put into their own legion. They won't survive for long."

His fingers draw an X in the dust, angrily marking what he feels.

"I can stall that, maybe," Maven says, brainstorming out loud. "If I convince the war council to hold them back, put them through extra training."

"That's not enough." My voice is small but firm. The list seems to burn against my skin, begging to be let free. I turn to Farley. "You have people all over, don't you?"

I don't miss the shadow of satisfaction cross her face. "I do."

"Then give them these names." I pull Julian's book from my jacket, opening to the beginning of the list. "And find them."

Maven gently takes the book, his eyes scanning over it. "There must be hundreds," he mutters, not looking away from the page. "What is this?"

"They're like me. Red and Silver, and stronger than both."

It's my turn to feel smug. Even Maven's jaw drops. Farley snaps her fingers, and he hands it over without a thought, still staring at the little book that holds such a powerful secret.

"It won't be long until the wrong person figures this out, though," I add. "Farley, you *must* find them first."

Kilorn glares at the names like they offer him some kind of insult. "This could take months, *years*."

Maven huffs. "We don't have that kind of time."

"Exactly," Kilorn agrees. "We need to act *now*."

I shake my head. Revolutions cannot be rushed. "But if you wait, if you find as many as you can—you could have an army."

Suddenly, Maven slaps the table, causing us all to jump. "But we do have one."

"I have many under my command here, but not *that* many," Farley argues, looking at Maven like he's gone mad.

But he grins, alive with some hidden fire. "If I can get an army, a legion in Archeon, what could you do?"

She just shrugs. "Very little, actually. The other legions would crush them on the field."

It hits me like a thunderbolt, and I finally realize what Maven is getting at. "But they won't fight on the field," I breathe. He turns to me, smiling like a crazed loon. "You're talking about a coup."

Farley frowns. "A coo?"

"A coup, a coup d'état. It's a history thing, a before thing," I explain, trying to wave off their confusion. "It's when a small group quickly overthrows a large government. Sound familiar?"

Farley and Kilorn exchange glances, eyes narrowed. "Go on," she says.

"You know the way Archeon's built, with the Bridge, the West side, and the East side." My fingers race along with my words, drawing a rough map of the city in the dust. "Now, the West side has the palace, command, the treasury, the courts, the entire *government*. And if somehow we can get in there, cut it off, get to the king, and *make* him agree to our terms—it's all over. You said it yourself, Maven, you can run the whole country from Caesar's Square. All we have to do is take it."

Under the table, Maven pats me on the knee. He's buzzing with pride. Farley's usual suspicious look is gone, replaced by real hope. She runs a hand over her lips, mouthing words to herself as she eyes the dust-drawn plan.

"This might just be me," Kilorn begins, falling back to his usual snide tone, "but I'm not exactly sure how you plan to get enough Reds in there to fight Silvers. You need ten of us to bring down one of them. Not to mention there's the five thousand *Silver* soldiers loyal to your *brother*"—he glances at Maven—"all trained to kill, all trying to hunt us down as we speak."

I deflate, falling back against the seat. "That could be difficult." *Impossible.*

Maven brushes a hand over my dust map, wiping away West Archeon with a few strokes of his fingers. "Legions are loyal to their generals. And I happen to know a girl who knows a general very well."

When his eyes meet mine, all his fire is gone, replaced now by bitter cold. He smiles tightly.

"You're talking about Cal." *The soldier. The general. The prince. His father's son.* Again I think of Julian, of the uncle Cal would kill for his twisted version of justice. *Cal would never betray his country, not for anything.*

When Maven answers, it's matter-of-fact. "We give him a hard choice."

I can feel Kilorn's eyes on my face, weighing my reaction, and it's almost too much pressure to bear. "Cal will never turn his back on his crown, on your *father*."

"I know my brother. If it comes down to it, to saving your life or saving his crown, we both know what he will choose," Maven fires back.

"He would *never* choose me."

My skin burns under Maven's gaze, with the memory of one stolen kiss. It was him who saved me from Evangeline. Cal who saved me from escaping and bringing more pain upon myself. Cal who saved me from conscription. I've been too busy trying to save others to notice how much Cal saves me. How much he *loves* me.

Suddenly it's very hard to breathe.

Maven shakes his head. "He will always choose you."

Farley scoffs. "You want me to pin my entire operation, the entire *revolution*, on some teenaged love story? I can't believe this."

Across the table, a strange look crosses Kilorn's face. When Farley turns to him, looking for some kind of support, she finds none.

"I can," he whispers, his eyes never leaving my face.

TWENTY-FIVE

As Maven and I are driven across the Bridge, heading back to the palace after our long day of handshakes and secret plans, I wish the dawn would begin tonight instead of tomorrow morning. I'm intensely aware of the rumble around us while we pass through the city. Everything pulses with energy, from the transports on the streets to the lights woven into steel and concrete. It reminds me of the moment in Grand Garden long ago, when I watched the nymphs play in a fountain or the greenys attend their flowers. In that instant, I found their world beautiful. I understand now why they want to keep it, to maintain their rule over all the rest, but that doesn't mean I'll let them.

There's usually a feast to celebrate the king's return to his city, but in light of recent events, Caesar's Square is much quieter than it should be. Maven pretends to lament the lack of spectacle, if only to fill the silence.

"The banquet hall is twice the size of the one at the Hall," he says as we enter the great gates. I can see part of Cal's legion drilling at the barracks, a thousand of them marching in time. Their steps beat like a drum. "We used to dance until dawn—at least, Cal did. Girls didn't ask me to dance much, not unless Cal made them."

"I would ask you to dance," I murmur back to him, my eyes still on the barracks. *Will they be ours tomorrow?*

Maven doesn't answer, shifting in his seat as we coast to a stop. *He will always choose you.*

"I feel nothing for Cal," I whisper in his ear as we clamber out of the transport.

He smiles, his hand closing around mine, and I tell myself it's not a lie.

When the doors to the palace open to us, a wretched scream twists through the long marbled passages. Maven and I exchange glances, startled. Our guards bristle, hands straying to their guns, but they aren't enough to stop me from bolting. Maven keeps up as best he can, trying to match my pace. The scream sounds again, accompanied by a dozen marching feet and the familiar clank of armor.

I break into a dead sprint, Maven right behind me. We burst into a round chamber, a council hall of polished marble and dark wood. There's already a crowd and I almost collide with Lord Samos himself, but my feet stop me just in time. Maven slams into my back, nearly knocking us over.

Samos sneers at both of us, his black eyes cold and hard.

"My lady, Prince Maven," he says, barely inclining his head to either of us. "Have you come to see the show?"

The show. There are other lords and ladies around us, along with the king and queen, all staring straight ahead. I push through them, not knowing what I'll find on the other side, but I know it won't be good. Maven follows, his hand never leaving my elbow. When we reach the front of the crowd, I'm glad for his warm hand, a comfort to keep me quiet—and to pull me back.

No less than sixteen soldiers stand in the center of the chamber, their booted feet tracking dirt over the great crown seal. Their armor is the same, scaled black metal, except for one with a reddish glint. *Cal.*

Evangeline stands with him, her hair pulled back into a braid. She breathes heavily, winded, but looks proud of herself. *And where there's Evangeline, her brother cannot be far behind.*

Ptolemus appears from the back of the pack, dragging a screaming body by her hair. Cal turns away and meets my eyes the moment I recognize her. I can see regret there, but he does nothing to save her.

Ptolemus tosses Walsh to the polished floor, her face smashing against the rock. She barely spares a glance at me before turning her pained eyes on the king. I remember the playful, smiling servant who first introduced me to this world; that person is gone.

"The rats crawl in the old tunnels," Ptolemus snarls, turning her over with his foot. She scrambles away from his touch, surprisingly quick for her many injuries. "We found this one trailing *us* near the river holes."

Trailing them? How could she be so stupid? But Walsh isn't stupid. *No, this was an order,* I realize with growing horror. She was watching the train tunnels, making sure the way was clear for us to get back from Naercey. And while we made it through safely, she did not.

Maven's grip on my arm tightens, pulling me into him until his chest lies flush to my back. He knows I want to run to her, to save her, to help her. *And I know we can't do anything at all.*

"We went as far as the radiation detectors would allow," Cal adds, trying his best to ignore Walsh coughing up blood. "The tunnel system is huge, much larger than we originally thought. There must be dozens of miles in the area and the Scarlet Guard know them better than any of us."

King Tiberias scowls beneath his beard. He gestures at Walsh, waving her forward. Cal seizes her by the arm, pulling her toward the king. A thousand different tortures fill my head, each one worse than the last. Fire, metal, water, even my own lightning, could be used to make her talk.

"I will not make the same mistake again," the king growls into her face. "Elara, make her sing. Right now."

"With pleasure," the queen replies, freeing her hands from her trailing sleeves.

This is worse. Walsh will talk, she'll implicate us all, she'll ruin us. And then they'll kill her slowly. They'll kill us all slowly.

An Eagrie in the crowd of soldiers, an eye with the ability of foresight, suddenly jumps forward. "Stop her! Hold her arms!"

But Walsh is faster than his vision. "For Tristan," she says, before slamming a hand to her mouth. She bites down on something and swallows, knocking her head back.

"A healer!" Cal snaps, grabbing her throat, trying to stop her. But her mouth foams white and her limbs twitch—she's choking. "A healer, now!"

She seizes violently, twisting out of his grip with the last of her strength. When she hits the floor, her eyes are wide-open, staring but not seeing. *Dead.*

For Tristan.

I can't even mourn her.

"A suicide pill."

Cal's voice is gentle, like he's explaining this to a child. But I suppose I am a child when it comes to war and death. "We give them to officers on the line, and our spies. If they're captured—"

"They won't talk," I spit back at him.

Careful, I warn myself. As much as his presence makes my skin crawl, I have to endure it. After all, I let him find me here on the balcony. *I must give him hope. I must let him think he has a chance with me.* That part was Maven's idea, as much as it hurt him to say so. As for me, it's hard to walk the narrow line between a lie and the truth, especially with Cal. I hate him, I know that, but something in his eyes and his voice reminds me that my feelings aren't so simple.

He keeps his distance, standing an arm's length away. "It's a better death than she would get from us."

"Would she be frozen? Or maybe burned for a change of pace?"

"No." He shakes his head. "She would go to the Bowl of Bones." He raises his eyes from the barracks, looking across the river. On the far side, nestled among the high-rises, is a massive oval arena with spikes around the rim in a violent crown. *The Bowl of Bones.* "She'd be executed in a broadcast, as a message to all the rest."

"I thought you didn't do that anymore. I haven't seen one in over a decade." I barely remember those broadcasts from when I was a little girl, years ago.

"Exceptions can be made. The arena fights haven't stopped the Guard from taking hold, maybe something else will."

"You knew her," I whisper, trying to find just one shred of regret in him. "You sent her to me after we first met."

He crosses his arms, like that can somehow protect him from the memory. "I knew she came from your village. I thought that might help you adjust a little."

"I still don't know why you cared. You didn't even know I was different."

A moment passes in silence, broken only by the bark of lieutenants far below, still drilling even as the sun sets.

"You were different to me," he finally murmurs.

"I wonder what could have been, if all this"—I gesture to the palace and the Square beyond—"wasn't between us."

Let him chew on that.

He puts a hand on my arm, his fingers hot through the fabric of my sleeve.

"But that can never be, Cal."

I force as much longing as I can into my eyes, relying on the memory of my family, Maven, Kilorn, all the things we're trying to do. Maybe Cal will mistake my feelings. *Give him hope where none should be.* It's the cruelest thing I can do, but for the cause, for my friends, for my life, I will.

"Mare," he breathes, dipping his head toward me.

I turn away, leaving him on the balcony to think on my words and, hopefully, drown in them.

"I wish things were different," he whispers, but I can still hear him.

The words take me back to my home and my father when he said the same thing so long ago. To think that Cal and my father, a broken Red man, can share the same thoughts makes me pause. I can't help looking back, watching the sun dip behind his silhouette. He stares down at the training army before looking back to me, torn between his duty and whatever he feels for the little lightning girl.

"Julian says you're like her," he says quietly, eyes thoughtful. "Like she used to be."

Coriane. His mother. The thought of the dead queen, a person I never knew, somehow makes me sad. She was taken too soon from those she loved, and she left a hole they're trying to make me fill.

And as much as I hate to admit it, I can't blame Cal for feeling caught between two worlds. After all, so am I.

Before the ball I was anxious, a bundle of nerves dreading the night to come. Now I can't wait for dawn. If we win in the morning, the sun will set on a new world. The king will throw down his crown, passing his power to me, Maven, and Farley. The shift will be bloodless, a peaceful transition from one government to the next. If we fail, the Bowl of Bones is all I can hope for. But we will not fail. Cal will not let me die, and neither will Maven. They are my shields.

When I lie down in my bed, I find myself staring at Julian's map. It's an old thing, practically useless, but still comforting. *It's proof the world can change.*

With that thought in my head, I drift into a restless, light sleep. My brother visits me in my dreams. He stands by the window, looking at the city with a strange sorrow, before turning back to me. "There are others," he says. "You must find them."

"I will," I murmur back to him, my voice heavy with sleep.

Then it's four o'clock in the morning and I have no more time for dreams.

The cameras fall like trees before the ax, each little eye clicking off as I walk to Maven's room. I jump at every shadow, expecting an officer or a Sentinel to step out into the hall, but no one does. They protect Cal and the king, not me, not the second prince. We don't matter. *But we will.*

Maven opens his door a second after I jiggle the handle, his face pale in the darkness. There are circles beneath his eyes, like he hasn't slept at all, but he looks sharp as ever. I expect him to take my arm, to envelop me in his warmth, but there's nothing but cold dripping off him. *He's afraid*, I realize.

We're outside in a few agonizing minutes, walking in the shadows behind War Command to wait at our place between the structure and the outer wall. Our spot is perfect; we're able to see the Square and the Bridge, with most of War Command's gilded roof blocking us from the patrols. I don't need a clock to know we're right on time.

Above us, the night fades, giving way to dark blue. *The dawn is coming.*

At this hour, the city is quieter than I ever thought possible. Even the patrol guards are drowsy, slowly moving from post to post. Excitement trills through me, making my legs shake. Somehow, Maven keeps still, barely even blinking. He stares through the diamondglass wall, always watching the Bridge. His focus is staggering.

"They're late," he whispers, never moving.

"I'm not."

If I didn't know any better, I'd think Farley was a shadow, able to shift in and out of visibility. She seems to melt out of the semidarkness, pulling herself up from a drain.

I offer her my hand, but she pushes herself to her feet alone. "Where are the others?"

"Waiting." She gestures to the ground below.

If I squint, I can just see them, crowded into the drain system, about to retake the surface. I want to climb into the tunnel with them, to stand with Kilorn and my kind, but my place is here, next to Maven.

"Are they armed?" Maven's lips barely move. "Are they ready to fight?"

Farley nods. "Always. But I'm not calling them out until you're sure the Square is ours. I don't put much faith in Lady Barrow's ability to charm."

Neither do I, but I can't say that out loud. *He will always choose you.*

I've never wanted anything to be right and yet wrong at the same time.

"Kilorn wanted you to have this," she adds, holding out her hand. In it is a tiny green stone, the color of his eyes. *An earring.* "He said you'd know what it means."

I choke on my words, feeling a great surge of emotion. Nodding, I take the earring from her and raise it to the others. *Bree, Tramy, Shade*—I know each stone and what they mean. *Kilorn is a warrior now. And he wants me to remember him as he was.* Laughing, teasing me, sniffing around like a lost puppy. I will never forget that.

The sharp metal stings, drawing blood. When I pull my hand back from my ear, I can see the crimson stain on my fingers. *This is who you are.*

I look back to the tunnel, hoping to see his green eyes, but the darkness seems to swallow the tunnel whole, hiding him and all the others.

"Are you ready for this?" Farley breathes, looking between us both.

Maven answers for me, his voice firm. "We are."

But Farley isn't satisfied. "Mare?"

"I'm ready."

The revolutionary takes a calming breath before tapping her foot against the side of the drain. Once, twice, three times. Together, we turn to the Bridge, waiting for the world to change.

There's no traffic at this hour, not even the whisper of a transport. The shops are closed, the plazas empty. With any luck, the only thing lost tonight will be concrete and steel. The last section of the Bridge, the one connecting West Archeon to the rest of the city, seems serene.

And then it explodes in bright plumes of orange and red, a sun to split the silver darkness. Heat surges, but not from the bombs—it's *Maven.* The explosion sparks something in him, lighting his flame.

The sound rumbles, almost knocking me off my feet, and the river below churns as the end section of the Bridge collapses. It groans and shudders like a dying beast, crumbling in on itself as it detaches from the bank and the rest of the structure. Concrete pillars and steel wire crack and snap, splashing into the water or against the bank. A cloud of dust and smoke rises, cutting off the rest of Archeon from view. Before the Bridge even hits the water, alarms sound over the Square.

Above us, patrols run along the wall, eager to get a good look at the destruction. They shout to one another, not knowing what to make of this. Most can only stare. In the barracks, lights switch on and soldiers stir, all five thousand of them jumping out of bed. *Cal's soldiers. Cal's legion.* And with any luck, ours.

I can't tear my eyes away from the flame and smoke, but Maven does it for me. "There he is," he hisses, pointing to some dark shapes running from the palace.

He has his own guards, but Cal outstrips them all, sprinting for the barracks. He's still in his nightclothes, but he's never looked so fearsome. As soldiers and officers spill out into the Square, he barks orders, somehow making himself heard over the growing crowd. "Guns on the gates! Put nymphs on the other side, we don't want the fire spreading!"

His men carry out the orders with speed, jumping at his every word. *Legions obey their generals.*

Behind us, Farley presses herself back against the wall, inching closer to her drain. She'll turn and run at the first sign of trouble, disappearing to fight another day. *That won't happen. This will work.*

Maven moves to go first, to wave down his brother, but I push him back.

"I have to do it," I whisper, feeling a strange sort of calm come over me. *He will always choose you.*

I'm past the point of no return when I step into the Square, into full view of the legion and the patrols and Cal. Spotlights blaze to life on the tops of the walls, some pointed at the Bridge, others down on us. One seems to go right through me, and I have to raise a hand to shield my eyes.

"Cal!" I scream over the deafening sound of five thousand soldiers. Somehow, he hears me, his head snapping in my direction. We lock eyes through the mass of soldiers falling into their practiced lines and regiments.

When he moves toward me, pushing through the sea, I think I might faint. Suddenly all I can hear is my heartbeat pounding in my ears, drowning out the alarms and the screams. I am afraid. So very afraid. *This is just Cal,* I tell myself. *The boy who loves music and cycles. Not the soldier, not the general, not the prince. The boy. He will always choose you.*

"Go back inside, now!" He towers over me, using the stern, regal voice that could make a mountain bow. "Mare, it's not safe—!"

With strength I never knew I had, I grab on to the collar of his shirt and somehow it keeps him still. "What if that was the cost?" I toss a glance back to the broken Bridge, now shrouded in smoke and ash. "Nothing but a few tons of concrete. What if I told you that right here, right now, you could fix everything. You could save *us*."

By the flicker in his eyes, I can see I have his attention. "Don't," he protests weakly, one hand grabbing mine. There's fear in his eyes, more fear than I've ever seen.

"You said you believed in us once, in freedom. In equality. *You* can make that real, with one word. There won't be a war. No one will die." He seems frozen by my words, not daring to breathe. I can't tell what he's thinking, but I press on. *I must make him understand.* "You hold the power right now. This army is yours, this whole place is yours to take and—and to free! March into the palace, make your father kneel, and do what you know is right. *Please*, Cal!"

I can feel him beneath my hands, his breath coming in quick pants, and nothing has ever felt so real or so important. I know what he's thinking about—his kingdom, his duty, his father. And me, the little lightning girl, asking him to throw it all away. Something deep down tells me he will.

Shaking, I press a kiss to his lips. *He will choose me.* His skin feels cold under mine, like a corpse.

"Choose me," I breathe against him. "Choose a new world. *Make* a better world. The soldiers will obey you. Your *father* will obey you." My heart clenches, and every muscle tightens, waiting for his answer. The spotlight on us flickers under my strength, switching on and off with every heartbeat. "It was my blood in the cells. I helped the Guard escape. And soon everyone will know—and they will kill me. Don't let them. *Save me.*"

The words stir him, and his grip on my wrist tightens.

"It was always you."

He will always choose you.

"Greet the new dawn, Cal. With me. With *us*."

His eyes shift to Maven now walking toward us. The brothers lock eyes, speaking in a way I don't understand. *He will choose us.*

"It was always you," he says again, ragged and ruined this time. His voice carries the pain of a thousand deaths, a thousand betrayals. *Anyone can betray anyone*, I remember. "The escape, the shooting, the power outages. It all started with you."

I try to explain, still pulling back. But he has no intention of letting me go.

"How many people have you killed with your dawn? How many

children, how many innocents?" His hand grows hot, hot enough to burn. "How many people have you betrayed?"

My knees buckle, dropping out from under me, but Cal doesn't let go. Dimly, I hear Maven yelling somewhere, the prince charging in to save his princess. *But I'm not a princess. I'm not the girl who gets saved.* As the fire rises in Cal, flaming behind his eyes, the lightning streaks through me, fed by anger. It shocks between us, throwing me back from Cal. My mind buzzes, clouded by sorrow and anger and electricity.

Behind me, Maven yells. I turn just in time to see him shouting back at Farley, gesturing wildly with his hands. "Run! *Run!*"

Cal jumps to his feet faster than me, shouting something to his soldiers. His eyes follow Maven's call, connecting the dots as only a general can. "The drains!" he roars, still staring at me. "They're in the drains."

Farley's shadow disappears, trying to escape while gunfire follows her. Soldiers dart over the Square, ripping away grates and drains and pipes, exposing the system beneath. They pour into the tunnels like a terrible flood. I want to cover my ears, to block out the screams and bullets and blood.

Kilorn. His name flutters weakly in my thoughts, no more than a whisper. I can't think about him long; Cal still stands over me, his whole body shaking. But he doesn't frighten me. I don't think anything can scare me now. *The worst has happened already. We have lost.*

"How many?" I scream back at him, finding the strength to face him. "How many starved? How many murdered? How many children taken away to die? How many, *my prince?*"

I thought I knew hate before today. *I was wrong. About myself, about Cal, about everything.* The pain makes my head spin, but somehow I keep my feet, somehow I keep myself from falling. *He will never choose me.*

"My brother, Kilorn's father, Tristan, Walsh!" What feels like a hundred names explode from me, rattling off all the lost ones. They mean nothing to Cal but everything to me. And I know there are thousands, millions more. A million forgotten wrongs.

Cal doesn't answer, and I expect to see the rage I feel reflected in his eyes. Instead, I see nothing but sadness. He whispers again, and the words make me want to fall down and never get up again.

"I wish things were different."

I expect the sparks, I expect lightning, but it never comes. When I feel cold hands on my neck and metal shackles on my wrists, I know why. Instructor Arven, the silence, the one who can make us human, stands behind me, pushing down all my strength until I'm nothing but a weeping girl again. He's taken it all away, all the strength and all the power I thought I had. *I have lost.* When my knees give out this time, there's no one to hold me up. Dimly, I hear Maven cry out before he too is pushed to the ground.

"Brother!" he roars, trying to make Cal see what he's doing. "They'll kill her! They'll kill *me*!" But Cal is no longer listening to us. He speaks to one of his captains, and I don't bother to listen to the words. I couldn't even if I wanted to.

The ground beneath me seems to shake with every round of gunfire deep below. How much blood will stain the tunnels tonight?

My head is too heavy, my body too weak, and I let myself slump against the tiled ground. It feels cold under my cheek, soothing and smooth. Maven pitches forward, his head landing next to me. *I remember a moment like this.* Gisa's scream and the shattering of bones echo faintly, a ghost inside my head.

"Take them inside, to the king. He will judge them both."

I don't recognize Cal's voice anymore. I've turned him into a monster. I forced his hand. I made him choose. I was eager, I was stupid. I let myself hope.

I am a fool.

The sun begins to rise behind Cal's head, framing him against the dawn. It's too bright, too sharp, and too soon; I have to shut my eyes.

TWENTY-SIX

I can barely keep up the pace, but the soldier at my back, holding my shackled arms, keeps shoving. Another does the same to Maven, forcing him along with me. Arven follows us, making sure we can't escape. His presence is a dark weight, dulling my senses. I can still see the passage around us, empty and far from the prying eyes of the court, but I don't have the strength to care. Cal leads the pack, his shoulders tense and tight as he fights the urge to look back.

The sound of gunfire and screams and blood in the tunnels rumbles in my mind. *They are dead. We are dead. It is over.*

I expect us to descend, to march down to the darkest cell in the world. Instead, Cal leads us up, to a room with no windows and no Sentinels. Our footfalls don't even echo as we enter—soundproof. No one can hear us. And that frightens me more than the guns or the fire or the pure rage rippling off the king.

He stands in the center of the room, dressed in his own gilded armor with the crown on his head. His ceremonial sword hangs at his side again, along with a pistol he's probably never used. *All part of the pageant. At least he looks the part.*

The queen is here as well, waiting for us in nothing but a thin white gown. The moment we enter, her eyes meet mine and she forces her way into my thoughts like a knife through flesh. I yelp, trying to clutch my head, but the shackles hold firm.

It all flashes before my eyes again, from the beginning to the end. Will's wagon. The Guard. Kilorn. The riots, the meetings, the secret messages. Maven's face swirls in the memories, making him stand out against the fray, but Elara pushes him away. *She doesn't want to see what I remember about him.* My brain screams at the onslaught, jumping from thought to thought until my whole life, every kiss and every secret, is laid bare before her.

When she stops, I feel dead. I want to *be* dead. *At least I won't have long to wait.*

"Leave us," Elara says, her voice cutting and sharp. The soldiers wait, looking to Cal. When he nods, they take their leave, departing in a din of clicking boots. But Arven stays behind, his influence still pressing down on me. When the march of boots fades away, the king allows himself to exhale.

"Son?" He looks at Cal, and I can see the slightest quiver in his fingers. But what he could possibly fear, I do not know. "I want to hear this from you."

"They've been part of this for a long time," Cal mutters, barely able to say the words. "Since she came here."

"Both?" Tiberias turns away from Cal, to his forgotten son. He looks almost sad, his face pulling into a pained frown. His eyes waver, reluctant to hold his gaze, but Maven stares right back. *He will not flinch.* "You knew about this, my boy?"

Maven nods. "I helped plan it."

Tiberias stumbles, like his words are a physical blow. "And the shooting?"

"I chose the targets." Cal squeezes his eyes shut, like he can block this all out.

Maven's eyes slide past his father, to Elara, who stands close by. They hold each other's gaze, and for a moment, I think she's looking into his thoughts. With a jolt, I realize she won't. *She can't let herself look.*

"You told me to find a cause, Father. And I did. Are you proud of me?"

But Tiberias rounds on me instead, snarling like a bear. "You did this! You poisoned him, you poisoned my boy!" When tears spring to his eyes, I know the king's heart, no matter how small or cold, has been broken. *He loves Maven, in his own way. But it's too late for that.* "You've taken my son from me!"

"You have done that yourself," I say through gritted teeth. "Maven has his own heart, and he believes in a different world as much as I do. If anything, your son changed me."

"I don't believe you. You have tricked him somehow."

"She does not lie."

Hearing Elara agree with me rips my breath away.

"Our son has always thirsted for change." Her eyes linger on her son. She sounds *afraid*. "He is just a boy, Tiberias."

Save him, I scream out in my head. *She must hear me. She must.*

Next to me, Maven sucks in a breath, waiting for what could be our doom.

Tiberias looks at his feet, knowing the laws better than anyone else, but Cal is strong enough to meet his brother's gaze. I can see him remembering their life together. *Flame and shadow. One cannot exist without the other.*

After a long moment of hot, stifling silence, the king puts a hand on Cal's shoulder. His head shakes back and forth, and tears track down his cheeks into his beard.

"A boy or not, Maven has killed. Together with this—this snake"—he points a shaking finger at me—"he has committed grave crimes against his own. Against *me*, and against you. Against our throne."

"Father—" Cal moves quickly, putting himself between the king and us. "He is your son. There must be another way."

Tiberias stills, putting aside the father to become king again. He wipes away his tears with a brush of the hand. "When you wear my crown, you will understand."

The queen's eyes narrow into blue slits. *Her eyes, they're the same as Maven's.*

"Fortunately, that will never happen," she says plainly.

"What?" Tiberias turns to her but stops halfway, his body frozen in place.

I've seen this before. In the arena, long ago, when the whisper beat the strongarm. Elara even did it to me, turning me into a puppet. Again, she holds the strings.

"Elara, what are you doing?" he hisses through gritted teeth.

She replies with words I cannot hear, speaking into the king's head. He doesn't like her answer at all. "No!" he yells as she forces him to his knees with her whispers.

Cal bristles, his fists exploding into flame, but Elara holds a hand out, stopping him in his tracks. *She has them both.*

Tiberias struggles, his teeth clenched, but can't move an inch. He can barely even speak. "Elara. Arven—!"

But my old instructor doesn't move. Instead, he stands quietly, content to watch. It seems his loyalties lie not with the king but with the queen.

She's saving us. For her son's life, she's going to save us. We bet on Cal loving me enough to change the world; we should've looked to the queen instead. I want to laugh, to smile, but something in Cal's face keeps my relief at bay.

"Julian warned me," Cal growls, still trying to break her hold. "I thought he was lying about you, about my mother, about what you did to her."

On his knees, the king howls. It is a wretched sound, one I never want to hear again. "Coriane," he moans, staring at the floor. "Julian knew. Sara knew. You punished her for the truth."

Sweat beads on Elara's forehead. She cannot hold the king and the prince for much longer.

"Elara, you have to get Maven out of here," I tell her. "Don't worry about me, just keep him safe."

"Oh, don't you fret, little lightning girl," she sneers. "I don't think about you at all. Though your loyalty to my son is quite inspiring. Isn't it, Maven?" She tosses a glance over her shoulder to her son, still shackled.

In response, his arms snap out, pulling apart the metal shackles with shocking ease. They melt off his wrists in globs of hot iron, burning holes in the floor. When he rises to his feet, I expect him to defend me, to save me like I'm trying to save him. Then I realize Arven still has hold of me, and the familiar feel of sparks, of electricity, has not returned. He's still holding me back, even though he let Maven go.

When Cal's eyes meet mine, I know he understands much better than I do. *Anyone can betray anyone* echoes louder and louder, until it howls in my ears like the winds of a hurricane.

"Maven?" I have to look up to see his face, and for a second, I don't recognize him. He's still the same boy, the one who comforted me, kissed me, kept me strong. My friend. *More than my friend.* But something is wrong in him. Something has changed. "Maven, help me up."

He rolls his shoulders, cracking the bones to chase away an ache. His motions are sluggish and strange, and when he settles back on his feet, hands on his hips, I feel like I'm seeing him for the first time. *His eyes are so cold.*

"No, I don't think so."

"What?" I hear my voice like it's coming from someone else. I sound like a little girl. *I am just a little girl.*

Maven doesn't answer but holds my gaze. The boy I know is still there, hiding, flickering behind his eyes. *If I can just reach him*—but Maven moves faster than me, pushing me away when I reach out.

"CAPTAIN TYROS!" Cal roars, still able to speak. Elara has not taken that from him yet. But no one comes running. No one can hear us. "CAPTAIN TYROS!" he yells again, pleading with no one. "EVANGELINE! PTOLEMUS, SOMEONE, HELP!"

Elara is content to let him shout, enjoying the sound, but Maven flinches. "Do we have to listen to this?" he asks.

"No, I suppose we don't," she sighs, tipping her head. Cal's body moves with her thoughts, shifting to face his father.

Cal panics, his eyes growing wide. "What are you doing?"

Beneath him, the king's face darkens. "Isn't it obvious?"

I don't understand at all. I don't belong here. Julian was right. This is a game I don't understand, a game I don't know how to play. I wish Julian were here now, to explain, to help, to save me. But no one is coming.

"Maven, please," I plead, trying to make him look at me. But he turns his back, focusing on his mother and his betrayed blood. *He is his mother's son.*

She didn't care that he was in my memories. She didn't care that he was part of all this. She didn't even look surprised. The answer is frighteningly simple. *Because she already knew. Because he is her son. Because this was her plan all along.* The thought stings like knives running along skin, but the pain only makes it more real.

"You used me."

Finally, Maven condescends to look back at me. "Catching on, are you?"

"You chose the targets. The colonel, Reynald, Belicos, even Ptolemus—they weren't the Guard's enemies, they were yours." I want to tear him apart, lightning or not. I want to make him hurt.

I am finally learning my lesson. *Anyone can betray anyone.*

"And this, this was just another plot. You pushed me into this, even though it was impossible, even though you knew Cal would never betray his father! You made me believe it. You made all of us believe it."

"It's not my fault you were stupid enough to play along," he replies. "Now the Guard is finished."

It feels like a kick in the teeth. "They were your friends. They *trusted* you."

"They were a threat to my kingdom, and they were stupid," he fires back. He stoops, bending over me with his twisted smile. *"Were."*

Elara laughs at his cruel joke. "It was too easy to slip you into their midst. One sentimental servant was all it took. How such fools became a danger, I'll never know."

"You made me believe," I whisper again, remembering every lie he ever told me. "I thought you wanted to help us." It comes out a whimper. For a split second, his pale features soften. But it doesn't last.

"Foolish girl," Elara says. "Your idiocy was almost our ruin. Using your own guard in the escape, causing all the outages—do you really think I was so stupid as to miss your tracks?"

Numb, I shake my head. "You let me do it. You knew about it all."

"Of course I knew. How else do you think you came so far? *I* had to cover your tracks, *I* had to protect you from anyone with enough sense to see the signs," she snarls, growling like a beast. "You do not know the lengths I went to keep you from harm." She flushes with pleasure, enjoying every second of this. "But you are Red, and like all the others, you were doomed to fail."

It breaks against me, memories falling into place. I should've known, deep down, not to trust Maven. *He was too perfect, too brave, too kind. He turned his back on his own to join the Guard. He pushed me at Cal. He gave me exactly what I wanted, and it made me blind.*

Wanting to scream, wanting to weep, I let my eyes trail to Elara. "You told him exactly what to say," I whisper. She doesn't have to nod, but I know I'm right. "You know who I am in here, and you knew"—my head aches, remembering how she played inside my mind—"you knew exactly how to win me over."

Nothing hurts more deeply than the hollow look on Maven's face.

"Was anything true?"

When he shakes his head, I know that is also a lie.

"Even Thomas?"

The boy at the war front, the boy who died fighting someone else's war. *His name was Thomas and I saw him die.*

The name punches through his mask, cracking the facade of cool indifference, but isn't enough. He shrugs off the name and the pain it causes him. "Another dead boy. He makes no difference."

"He makes all the difference," I whisper to myself.

"I think it's time to say your good-byes, Maven," Elara cuts in, putting a white hand on her son's shoulder. I've struck too close to his weak spot, and she won't let me push further.

"I have none," he whispers, turning back to his father. His blue eyes waver, looking at the crown, the sword, the armor, anywhere but his father's face. "You never looked at me. You never saw me. Not when you had *him*." He jerks his head toward Cal.

"You know that's not true, Maven. You are *my son*. Nothing will change that. Not even her," Tiberias says, casting a glance at Elara. "Not even what she's about to do."

"Dearest, I'm not doing anything," she chirps back. "But your beloved boy"—she slaps Cal across the face—"the perfect heir"—she slaps him again, harder this time—"Coriane's son." Another slap draws blood, splitting his lip. "I cannot speak for him."

Thick silverblood drips down Cal's chin. Maven's eyes linger on the blood, and the slightest frown pulls at his features.

"We had a son too, Tibe," Elara whispers, her voice ragged with rage as she turns back to the king. "No matter how you felt about me, you were supposed to love him."

"I *did*!" he shouts, straining against her mental hold. "I do."

I know what it's like to be cast aside, to stand in another's shadow. But this kind of anger, this murderous, destructive, terrible scene is beyond my comprehension. Maven loves his father, his brother—how can he let her do this? How can he *want* this?

But he stands still, watching, and I can't find the words to make him move.

Nothing prepares me for what comes next, for what Elara forces her puppets to do. Cal's hand shakes, reaching forward, pushed along by her will. He tries to resist, struggling with every ounce of strength he has, but it's no use. This is a battle he does not know how to fight. When his hand closes around the gilded sword, pulling it from the sheath at his father's waist, the last piece of the puzzle slips into place.

Tears course down his face, steaming against burning-hot skin.

"It's not you," Tiberias says, his eyes on Cal's wretched face. He doesn't bother pleading for his life. "I know it's not you, son. This is not your fault."

No one deserves this. *No one.* In my head, I reach for the lightning, and it comes. I blast away Elara and Maven, saving the prince and the king. But even that fantasy is tainted. Farley is dead. Kilorn is dead. The revolution is over. Even in my imaginings, I cannot fix that.

The sword rises in the air, shaking in Cal's trembling fingers. The blade is ceremonial at best, but the edge gleams, sharp as a razor. The steel reddens, warming under Cal's fiery touch, and bits of the gilded hilt melt between his fingers. Gold and silver and iron, dripping from his hands like tears.

Maven watches the blade closely, carefully, because he is too afraid to watch his father in his last moments. *I thought you were brave. I was so wrong.*

"Please," is all Cal can say, forcing the words out. "Please."

There is no regret in Elara's eyes and no remorse. This moment has been coming for a long time. When the sword flashes, arcing through air and flesh and bone, she doesn't blink.

The king's corpse lands with a thud, his head rolling to a stop a few feet away. Silverblood splashes across the floor in a mirrored puddle, lapping at Cal's toes. He drops the melting sword, letting it clang against stone, before falling to his knees, his head in his hands. The crown clatters across the floor, circling through the blood, until it stops to rest at Maven's feet, sharp points bright with liquid silver.

When Elara screams, wailing and thrashing over the king's body, I almost laugh aloud at the absurdity of it all. *Has she changed her mind? Has she lost it entirely?* Then I hear the click of cameras switching on, coming back to life. They poke out of the walls, pointing straight down at the king's body and what looks like a queen mourning her fallen husband. Maven yells at her side, one hand on his mother's shoulder.

"You killed him! You killed the king! You killed our father!" he screams in Cal's face. Only a hint of a smirk remains, and somehow Cal resists the urge to rip his brother's head off. He's in shock, not understanding, not *wanting* to understand. But for once, I certainly do.

The truth doesn't matter. It only matters what the people believe. Julian tried to teach me that lesson before, and now I understand it. *They will believe this little scene, this pretty play of actors and lies. And no army, no country will follow a man who murdered his father for the crown.*

"Run, Cal!" I scream, trying to snap him back to life. "You have to run!"

Arven has let me go, and the electric pulse returns, surging through my veins like fire through ice. It's nothing at all to shock the metal, burning it with sparks until the shackles fall off my wrists. I know this feeling. I know the instinct rising in me now. *Run. Run. Run.*

I grab Cal's shoulders, trying to pull him up, but the big oaf doesn't budge. I give him a little shock, just enough to catch his attention, before screaming again. "RUN!"

It's enough, and he struggles to his feet, almost slipping in the pool of blood.

I expect Elara to fight me, to make me kill myself or Cal, but she continues screaming, acting for the cameras. Maven stands over her, arms ablaze, ready to protect his mother. He doesn't even try to stop us.

"There's nowhere for you to go!" he shouts, but I'm already running, dragging Cal along behind me. "You are murderers, traitors, and you will face justice!"

His voice, a voice I used to know so well, seems to chase us through the doors and down the hall. The voices in my head scream with him.

Stupid girl. Foolish girl. Look what your hope has done.

And then it's Cal dragging me along, forcing me to keep up. Hot tears of anger and rage and sorrow drown my eyes, until I can't see anything but my hand in his. Where he leads, I don't know. I can only follow.

Feet pound behind us, the familiar sound of boots. Officers, Sentinels, soldiers, they're all chasing, coming for us.

The floor beneath us steadily changes from the polished wood of back hallways to swirling marble—the banquet hall. Long tables set with fine china block the way, but Cal throws them aside with a blast of fire. The smoke triggers an alarm system, and water rains down on us, fighting the blaze. It turns to steam on Cal's skin, shrouding him in a raging white cloud. He looks like a ghost, haunted by a life suddenly torn away, and I don't know how to comfort him.

The world slows for me as the far end of the banquet hall darkens with gray uniforms and black guns. There's nowhere for me to run anymore. I must fight.

Lightning blazes in my skin, begging to be loosed.

"No." Cal's voice is hollow, broken. He lowers his own hands, letting the flames disappear. "We can't win this."

He's right.

They close in from the many doors and arches, and even the windows crowd with uniforms. Hundreds of Silvers, armed to the teeth, ready to kill. *We are trapped.*

Cal searches the faces, his eyes lingering on the soldiers. *His own men.* By the way they stare back, glaring at him, I know they've already seen the horror Elara created. Their loyalties are broken, just like their general. One of them, a captain, trembles at the sight of Cal. To my surprise, he keeps his gun at his side as he steps forward.

"Submit to arrest," he says, his hands shaking.

Cal locks eyes with his old friend and nods. "We submit to arrest, Captain Tyros."

Run, every inch of me screams. But for once, I cannot. Next to me, Cal looks just as affected, his eyes reflecting a pain I can't even imagine. His wounds are soul-deep.

He has learned his lesson as well.

TWENTY-SEVEN

Maven has betrayed me. *No, he was never on my side at all.*

My eyes adjust, seeing bars through the dim light. The ceiling is low and heavy, like the underground air. I've never been here before, but I know it all the same.

"The Bowl of Bones," I whisper aloud, expecting no one to hear me.

Instead, someone laughs.

The darkness continues to lift, revealing more of the cell. A lumpy shape sits against the bars next to me, shifting with every peal of laughter.

"I was four years old the first time I came here, and Maven was barely two. He hid behind his mother's skirts, afraid of the darkness and the empty cells." Cal chuckles, every word sharp as a knife. "I guess he's not afraid of the dark anymore."

"No, he's not."

I'm the shadow of the flame. I believed Maven when he said those words, when he told me how much he hated this world. Now I know it was all a trick, a masterful trick. Every word, every touch, every *look* was a lie. *And I thought I was the liar.*

Instinctively I reach out with my abilities, feeling for any pulse of electricity, something to give me a spark of energy. But there's nothing. Nothing but a blank, flat absence, a hollow sensation that makes me shiver.

"Is Arven nearby?" I wonder, remembering how he shut off my abilities, forcing me to watch as Maven and his mother destroyed their family. "I can't feel a thing."

"It's the cells," Cal says dully. His hands draw shapes in the dirty floor—*flames*. "Made of Silent Stone. Don't ask me to explain it, because I can't, and I don't feel like trying."

He looks up, eyes glaring through the darkness at the unending line of cells. I should be afraid, but I have nothing left to fear. The worst has already happened.

"Before the matches, back when we still had to execute our own, the Bowl of Bones hosted everything nightmares are made of. The Great Greco, who used to tear men in half and eat their livers. The Poison Bride. She was an animos of House Viper and sent snakes into my great-great-uncle's bed on their wedding night. They say his blood turned to venom, he was bitten so many times." Cal lists them off, the criminals of his world. They sound likes stories invented to make children behave. "Now, us. The Traitor Prince, they'll call me. 'He killed his father for the crown. He just couldn't wait.'"

I can't help but add to the tale. "'The bitch made him do it,' they'll gossip to each other." I can see it in my head, shouted on every street corner, from every video screen. "They'll blame me, the little lightning girl. I filled your thoughts with poison, I corrupted you. I made you do it."

"You almost did," he murmurs back. "I almost chose you this morning."

Was it just this morning? That cannot be true. I push myself up against the bars, leaning just inches away from Cal.

"They're going to kill us."

Cal nods, laughing again. I've heard him laugh before, at me every time I tried to dance, but this sound is not the same. His warmth is gone, leaving nothing behind.

"The king will see to it. We will be executed."

Execution. I'm not surprised, not in the least.

"How will they do it?" I can barely remember the last execution. Only images remain: silverblood on sand, the roar of a crowd. And I remember the gallows at home, rope swinging in a harsh wind.

Cal's shoulders tense. "There are many ways. Together, one at a time, with swords or guns or abilities or all three." He heaves a sigh, already resigned to his fate. "They'll make it hurt. It will not be quick."

"Maybe I'll bleed all over the place. That'll give the rest of the world something to think about." The bleak thought makes me smile. When I die, I'll be planting my own red flag, splashing it across the sands of the massive arena. "He won't be able to hide me then. Everyone will know what I really am."

"You think that will change anything?"

It must. Farley has the list, Farley will find the others . . . but Farley is dead. I can only hope she passed the message on, to someone still alive. The others are still out there, and they must be found. They must carry on, because I no longer can.

"I think it won't," Cal continues, his voice filling the silence. "I think he'll use it as an excuse. There will be more conscriptions, more laws, more labor camps. His mother will invent another marvelous lie, and the world will keep on turning, the same as before."

No. Never the same again.

"He'll look for more like me," I realize aloud. I've already fallen, I've already lost, I'm already dead. And this is the last nail in the coffin. My head drops into my hands, feeling my sharp, clever fingers curl into my hair.

Cal shifts against the bars, his weight sending vibrations through the metal. "What?"

"There are others. Julian figured it out. He told me how to find them, and—" My voice breaks, not wanting to continue. "And I told him." I feel like screaming. "He used me so perfectly."

Through the bars, Cal turns to look at me. Even though his abilities are far away, suppressed by these wretched walls, an inferno rages in his eyes. "How does it feel?" he growls, almost nose to nose with me. "How does it feel to be used, Mare Barrow?"

Once, I would've given anything to hear him say my real name, but now it stings like a burn. *I thought I was using them both, Maven and Cal. How stupid I was.*

"I'm sorry," I force out. I despise those words, but they're all I can give. "I'm not Maven, Cal. I didn't do this to hurt you. I never wanted to hurt you." And softer, barely audible, "It wasn't all a lie."

His head thunks back against the bars, so loud it must hurt, but Cal doesn't seem to notice. Like me, he's lost the ability to feel pain or fear. Too much has happened.

"Do you think he'll kill my parents?" *My sister, my brothers.* For once, I'm happy Shade is dead and out of Maven's reach.

I feel surprising warmth bleed against me, settling into my shivering bones. Cal has moved again, leaning against the bars right behind me. His heat is gentle, natural—not driven by anger or ability. It's *human*. I can feel him breathing, his heart beating. It hammers like a drum as he finds the strength to lie to me. "I think he has more important things to think about."

I know he can feel me crying, my shoulders shaking with every sob, but he doesn't say anything. There are no words for this. But he stays right there, my last bit of warmth in a world turning to dust. I weep for them all. Farley, Tristan, Walsh, Will. Shade, Bree, Tramy, Gisa, Mom, and Dad. *Fighters, all of them.* And Kilorn. I couldn't save him, no matter how hard I tried. I can't even save myself.

At least I have my earrings. The little specks, sharp in my skin, will stay with me until the end. *I die with them, and they with me.*

We stay like that for what must be hours, though nothing changes to mark the passing time. I even doze off once, before a familiar voice makes me jerk awake.

"In another life, I might be jealous."

Maven's words send shivers down my spine and not in a good way.

Cal jumps to his feet quicker than I thought possible and throws himself at the bars, making the metal sing. But the bars hold firm, and Maven, cunning, disgusting, awful Maven, is just out of reach. To my delight, he still flinches away.

"Save your strength, brother," he says, teeth clicking together with every word. "You will need it soon."

Though he wears no crown, Maven already stands with the air of a terrible king. His dress uniform is crowded with new medals. They were his father's once; I'm surprised they aren't still covered in blood. He looks even paler than before, though the dark circles under his eyes are gone. Murder helps him sleep.

"Will it be you in the arena?" Cal snarls through the bars, his hands tight on the iron. "Will you do it yourself? Do you even have the nerve?"

I can't find the strength to stand, as much as I want to rush the bars, to tear away metal with my bare hands until the only thing I feel is Maven's throat. I can only watch.

He laughs dully at his brother's words. "We both know I could never beat you with ability," he says, throwing back Cal's own advice from so long ago. "So I beat you with my head, dear brother."

Once, he told me Cal hated to lose. Now I realize the one playing to win was always Maven. Every breath, every word was in service to this bloody victory.

Cal growls low under his breath. "Mavey," he says, but the nickname holds no love anymore. "How could you do this to Father? To me? To her?"

"A murdered king, a traitorous prince. So much blood," he sneers, dancing at the edge of Cal's reach. "They weep in the streets for our father. Or at least, they pretend to," he adds with a disinterested shrug. "The foolish wolves wait for me to stumble, and the smart ones know I will not. House Samos, House Iral, they've been sharpening their claws for years, waiting for a weak king, a compassionate king. You know they drooled at the sight of you? Think about it, Cal. Decades from now, Father would die slowly, peacefully, and you would ascend. Married to Evangeline, a daughter of steel and knives, with her brother at your side. You wouldn't survive the coronation night. She would do what Mother did and supplant you with her own child."

"Don't tell me you did this to protect a dynasty," Cal scoffs, shaking his head. "You did this for yourself."

Again, Maven shrugs. He grins to himself with a pointed, cruel smile. "Are you really so surprised? Poor Mavey, the second prince.

The shadow of his brother's flame. A weak thing, a little thing, doomed to stand to the side and kneel."

He shifts, prowling from Cal's cell to stand in front of mine. I can only stare at him from the ground, not trusting myself to move. *He even smells cold.*

"Betrothed to a girl with eyes for another, for the brother, the prince no one could ever ignore." His words take on a feral edge, heavy with a wild anger. But there is truth in them, a harsh truth I've tried so hard to forget. It makes my skin crawl. "You took everything that should have been mine, Cal. *Everything.*"

Suddenly I'm standing, shaking violently, but still standing. He's lied to us for so long, but I cannot let him lie now.

"I was never yours, and you were *never* mine, Maven," I snarl. "And not because of *him*, either. I thought you were perfect, I thought you were strong and brave and *good*. I thought you were *better than him*."

Better than Cal. Those are words Maven thought no one would ever say. He flinches, and for a second, I can see the boy I used to know. A boy that doesn't exist.

He reaches out a hand, grabbing at me between the bars. When his fingers close over the bare skin of my wrist, I feel nothing but repulsion. He holds me tight, like I'm some kind of lifeline. Something has snapped in him, revealing a desperate child, a pathetic, hopeless thing trying to hold on to his favorite toy.

"I can save you."

The words make my skin scrawl.

"Your father loved you, Maven. You didn't see it, but he did."

"A lie."

"He loved you, and you killed him!" The words come faster, spilling like blood from a vein. "Your brother loved you, and you made him a murderer. I—I loved you. I trusted you. I needed you. And now I'm going to die for it."

"I am *king*. You will live if I want you to. I will make it so."

"You mean if you lie? One day your lies will strangle you, King Maven. My only regret is I won't be alive to see it." And then it's my turn to grab him. I pull with all my strength, making him stumble against the bars. My knuckles connect with his cheek, and he yelps away like a kicked dog. "I will never make the mistake of loving you ever again."

To my dismay, he recovers quickly and smoothes his hair. "So you choose him?"

That's all this ever was. Jealousy. Rivalry. All so shadow could defeat the flame.

I have to throw my head back and laugh, feeling the eyes of the brothers on me. "Cal betrayed me, and I betrayed him. And you betrayed us both, in a thousand different ways." The words are heavy as stone but right. *So right.* "I choose no one."

For once, I feel like I control fire and Maven has been burned by it. He stumbles back from my cell, somehow defeated by the little girl without her lightning, the prisoner in chains, the human before a god.

"What will you tell them when I bleed?" I hiss after him. "The truth?"

He laughs deep in his chest. The little boy disappears, replaced by the king killer again. "The truth is what I make it. I could set this world on fire and call it rain."

And some will believe. The fools. But others will not. Red and Silver, high and low, some will see the truth.

His voice becomes a snarl, his face a shadow of a beast. "Anyone who knows that we hid you, *anyone* with even a hint of suspicion, will be dealt with."

My mind buzzes, flying to everyone who knew something about me was strange. Maven beats me there, seeming to enjoy listing off the many deaths. "Lady Blonos had to go, of course. Decapitation deals nicely with skin healers."

She was an old crow, an annoyance—and she didn't deserve this.

"The maids were easier. Pretty girls, sisters from Oldshire. Mother did them in herself."

I never even learned their names.

My knees hit the ground heavily, but I barely feel it. "They didn't know anything." But my begging is no use now.

"Lucas will go as well," he says, smirking with teeth bright in the darkness. "You'll get to see that for yourself."

I feel like retching. "You told me he was safe, with his family—!"

He laughs long and hard. "When are you going to realize that every word out of my mouth was a *lie*?"

"We forced him, Julian and I. He did nothing wrong." Begging feels so awful, but it's all I can think to do. "He's of House Samos. You can't kill one of them."

"Mare, haven't you been paying attention? I can do *anything*," he growls. "It's a pity we couldn't get Julian back here in time. I would've liked to make him watch you die."

I do my best to choke back a sob, pressing a hand to my mouth. Next to me, Cal growls deep in his throat, thinking of his uncle. "You found him?"

"Of course we did. We captured Julian and Sara both." Maven laughs. "I'll settle for killing Skonos first, finishing the job my mother began. You know the story there now, don't you, Cal? You know what my mother did, whispering her way into Coriane's head, making her brain crawl." He draws closer, eyes wild and frightening. "Sara knew. And your father, even you, refused to believe her. You let my mother win. And you've done it again."

Cal doesn't respond, resting his head against the bars. Satisfied he's destroyed his brother, Maven turns on me, pacing just beyond my cell.

"I'll make the others scream for you, Mare, every last one. Not just your parents. Not just your siblings. But every single one like you. I'm going to find them, and they will die with you in their thoughts, knowing this is the fate you have brought them. I am the king and you could've been my Red queen. Now you are *nothing*."

I don't bother to brush away the tears coursing down my cheeks. It's no use anymore. Maven enjoys the sight of me broken and sucks on his teeth like he wants to taste me.

"Good-bye, Maven." I wish there was more I could say, but there are no words for his evil. He knows what he is, and, worst of all, he likes it.

He dips his head, almost bowing to the pair of us. Cal doesn't bother to look and grips the bars instead, wearing at the metal like it's Maven's neck.

"Good-bye, Mare." The smirk is gone, and, to my surprise, his eyes look wet. He hesitates, not wanting to go. It's like he's suddenly understood what he's done and what's about to happen to all of us. "I told you to hide your heart once. You should have listened."

How dare he.

I have three older brothers, so when I spit at Maven, my aim is perfect, hitting him square in the eye.

He turns quickly, almost running from the pair of us. Cal stares after him for a long time, unable to speak. I can only sit down, letting my rage seep away again. When Cal settles back against me, there are no more words left to say.

Many things led to this day, for all of us. A forgotten son, a vengeful mother, a brother with a long shadow, a strange mutation. Together, they've written a tragedy.

In the stories, the old fairy tales, a hero comes. But all my heroes are gone or dead. No one is coming for me.

It must be the next morning when the Sentinels arrive, led by Arven himself. With the suffocating walls, his presence makes it difficult to stand, but they force me up.

"Sentinel Provos, Sentinel Viper." Cal nods at the Sentinels when they open his cell. They pull him roughly to his feet. Even now, facing death, Cal is calm.

He greets every guard we pass, addressing them by name. They stare back, angry or bewildered or both. A king killer should not be so kind. The soldiers are even worse. He wants to stop to say good-bye to them properly, but his own men grow hard and cold at the sight of him. And I think that hurts him almost as much as everything else. After a while, he goes quiet, losing the last bit of will he has left. As we climb out of the darkness, the noise of a crowd grows steadily nearer. Faint at first, but then a dull roar right above us. The arena is full, and they're ready for a show.

This started when I fell into the Spiral Garden, a body made of sparks, and now it ends at the Bowl of Bones. I'll leave as a corpse.

Arena attendants, all dull-eyed Silvers, descend on us like a flock of pigeons. They pull me behind a curtain, preparing me for what's to come with brisk movements and hard hands. I barely feel them, pushing and pulling, shoving me into a cheaper version of a training suit. This is meant to be an insult, making me wear something so simple to die in, but I prefer the scratch of fabric to the whisper of silk. I think dimly of my maids. They painted me every day; they knew I had something to hide. And they died for it. No one paints me now or even bothers to brush away the dirt from a night spent in a cell. *More pageantry.* Once, I wore silk and jewels and pretty smiles, but that doesn't fit Maven's lie. A Red girl in rags is easier for them to understand, and to kill.

When they pull me back out again, I can see they've done the same for Cal. There will be no medals, no armor for him. But he has his flame-maker bracelet again. The fire burns still, smoldering in the broken soldier. He has resigned himself to die, but not before taking someone with him.

We hold each other's gaze, simply because there's nowhere else to look.

"What are we walking into?" Cal finally says, tearing his eyes away from mine to face Arven.

The old man, white as paper, looks back on his former students without a flicker of remorse. *What did they promise him, for his help?* But I can already see. The badge over his heart, the crown made of jet, diamond, and ruby, was Cal's once. I don't doubt he was given much more.

"You were a prince and a general. In his wisdom, the merciful king has decided you are to at least die with glory." He smiles as he speaks, showing sharp little teeth. *Rat's teeth.* "A good death, the kind a traitor doesn't deserve.

"As for the Red girl, the trickster." He turns his fearsome gaze on me, focusing harder. The stifling weight of his power threatens to drag me down. "She will have no weapons at all and die like the devil she is."

I open my mouth to protest, but Arven leers over me, his breath reeking of poison. "King's orders."

No weapons. I feel like screaming. *No lightning.* Arven won't let me go, even to die. Maven's words echo sharply in my head. *Now you are nothing.* I'll die as nothing. They don't need to hide my blood if they can claim my powers were faked somehow.

Down in the cells, I was almost eager to step out onto the sand, to send my sparks into the sky and my blood into the earth. Now I shake and shiver, wanting to run away, but my wretched pride, the only thing I have left, won't even allow that.

Cal takes my hand. He quivers like I do, afraid to die. *At least he'll have a chance to fight.*

"I'll protect you as long as I can," he whispers. I almost don't hear him over the tramp of feet and the pathetic beat of my heart.

"I don't deserve it," I mutter back, but I squeeze his hand in thanks all the same. *I betrayed him, I ruined his life, and this is how he repays me.*

The next room is the last. It's a sloping passage, leading up a gentle incline to a steel gate. Sunlight dances through, bleeding down to us along with all the noise of a full arena. The walls distort the sounds, transforming cheers and shouts into the howls of a nightmare. I suppose that's not far from the truth.

As we enter, I see we're not the only ones waiting to die.

"Lucas!"

A guard holds his arm, but Lucas still manages to glance over his shoulder. His face is full of bruises and he looks paler than before, like he hasn't seen the sun in days. *It's probably true.*

"Mare." Just the way he says my name makes me cringe. He's another one I've betrayed, using him like I used Cal, Julian, the colonel, like I tried to use Maven. "I was wondering when I'd see you again."

"I'm so sorry." *I go to my grave apologizing, and it still won't be enough.* "They told me you were with your family, that you were safe, or else—"

"Or else what?" he asks slowly. "I'm nothing to you. Just something to be used and cast aside."

The accusation cuts like a knife. "I'm sorry, but it had to be done."

"The queen made me remember." *Made.* There's pain in his voice. "Don't apologize, because you don't mean it."

I want to embrace him, to show this was not what I wanted. "I do; I swear, Lucas."

"His Majesty, Maven of House Calore and House Merandus, the King of Norta, Flame of the North." The cry rings out in the arena, echoing down to us through the gate. The accompanying cheers make me cringe, and Lucas flinches. His end is near.

"Would you do it again?" The words sting sharply. "Would you risk me for your terrorist friends again?" *I would.* I don't say it out loud, but Lucas sees my answer in my eyes. "I kept your secret."

It's worse than any insult he could throw at me. The knowledge that he protected me, even though I didn't deserve it, gnaws at my core.

"But now I know you're not different, not anymore," he continues, almost spitting. "You're the same as all the rest. Heartless, selfish, cold—just like us. They taught you well."

Then he turns, facing the gate again. He wants no more words from me. I want to go to him, to try and explain, but a guard holds me back. There's nothing more for me to do but stand tall and wait for our doom.

"My citizens." Maven's voice filters through the gate with the daylight. He sounds like his father, like Cal, but there's something sharper in his voice. *He's only seventeen and already a monster.* "My people, my children."

Cal scoffs next to me. But out in the arena, a dead, haunting silence settles. He has them in the palm of his hand.

"Some would call this a cruelty," Maven continues. I don't doubt he memorized a stirring speech, probably written by his witch of a mother. "My father's body is barely cold, his blood still stains the floor, and I have been forced to take his place, to begin my reign in such a violent shadow. We have not executed our own for ten years, and it pains me to begin that awful tradition again. But for my father, for my crown, for *you*, I must. I am young, but I am not weak. Such crimes, such *evil* will be punished."

Up above us, high in the arena, jeers ring out, cheering for death.

"Lucas of House Samos, for crimes against the crown, for collusion with the terrorist organization known as the Scarlet Guard, I declare you guilty. I sentence you to die. Submit to execution."

And then Lucas is walking up the incline, to his own death. He doesn't spare a glance for me. Not that I deserve one. He's dying, not just because of what we made him do but for what I am. Like the others, he knew there was something strange about me. And like the others, he will die. When he disappears through the far gate, I have to turn away and stare at the wall. The gunshots are hard to ignore. The crowd roars, pleased by the violent display.

Lucas was only the beginning, the opening act. We are the show.

"Walk," Arven says, prodding us on. He follows as we begin the slow climb.

I cannot let go of Cal's hand, in case I stumble. Every muscle in him tenses, ready for the fight of his life. I reach out for my lightning in one last attempt, but nothing comes. There's not even a tremor left in me. Arven—and Maven—have taken it away.

Through the gate, I watch Lucas's body be dragged away, leaving a streak of silverblood across the sand. A wave of sickness passes over me, and I have to bite my lip.

With a great groan, the steel gate shudders and rises up. The sunlight blinds me for a second, freezing me to the spot, but Cal pulls me forward into the arena.

White sand, fine as powder, slides beneath my feet. As my eyes adjust, I almost forget to breathe. The arena is enormous, a wide gray mouth of steel and stonework, filled with thousands of angry faces. They stare down on us in deafening silence, pouring their hate into my skin. I can't see any Reds at all, but I don't expect to. This is what the Silvers call entertainment, another play for them to laugh at, and they won't share it.

Video screens dot the arena, reflecting my own face back at me. Of course they must record this, to broadcast it across the nation. To show the world another Red brought so low. The sight gives me pause; I look like myself again. Ratty, tangled hair, simple clothing, dirt falling off me in little clouds. My skin blushes with the blood I've tried so long to hide. If death weren't waiting for me, I would probably smile.

To my surprise, the screens flicker, switching from the image of Cal and me to something grainy—security footage, from all the cameras, all the electric eyes. With a shaky breath, I realize exactly how deep Maven's plan really went.

The screens play it all back, every stolen moment. Sneaking out of the Hall with Cal, dancing together, our whispered conversations, our *kiss*. And then the king's murder in its full, terrible glory. Taken together as one, it's not hard to believe Maven's story. All of it connects together, the tale of the Red devil who seduced a prince, who made him kill a king. The crowd gasps and murmurs, eating up the perfect lie. Even my own parents would have a hard time denying this.

"Mare Molly Barrow."

Maven's voice booms out behind me, and we spin to see the royal fool staring down at us. His own box of seats drips with black-and-red flags, filled to the brim with lords and ladies I recognize. They all wear black, forgetting their house colors in honor of a murdered king. Sonya, Elane, and all the other High House children stare down on me with disgust. Lord Samos stands on Maven's left, with the queen on his right. Elara hides behind a mourning veil, probably to mask her wicked smile. I expect Evangeline to be hovering nearby, content to marry the next king. After all, she only wanted the crown. But she's nowhere to be seen. Maven himself looks like a dark ghost, his pale skin sharp against the black gleam of dress armor. He even wears the sword they killed the king with, and his father's crown nestles against his hair, gleaming in the sun.

"Once we believed you to be the lost Mareena Titanos, another murdered citizen of my crown. With the help of your Red brethren, you deceived us with technological tricks and ruses, infiltrating my own family." *Technological tricks.* The screens show me back in the Spiral Garden, rippling with electricity. In the footage, it seems unnatural. "We gave you an education, status, power, strength—and even our love. For that, you repaid us with treachery, turning my own brother against his blood with your deceit.

"We know now that you are an operative of the defeated Scarlet Guard and are directly responsible for the loss of countless lives." The images flicker to the night of the Sun Shooting, to the ballroom full of blood and death. Farley's flag, the fluttering red rag and the torn sun, stands out against the chaos.

"Together with my brother, Prince Tiberias the Seventh, of House Calore and House Jacos, you are accused of many violent and deplorable offenses against the crown, including deception, treason, terrorism, and murder." *Your hands are no cleaner than mine, Maven.* "You killed the king, my father, bewitching his own son to do the deed. You are a Red devil"—he sweeps his eyes to Cal, now almost igniting in anger—"and you are a weak man. A traitor to your crown, your blood, and your colors." The death of the king plays again, cementing Maven's twisted words.

"I pronounce you both guilty of your crimes. Submit to execution." A great jeer goes up over the arena. It sounds like pigs screaming, howling for blood.

The video screens flip back to Cal and me, expecting us to weep or plead for our lives. Neither of us moves an inch. *They will not get that from us.*

Maven stares over the side of his box, leering, waiting for one of us to snap.

Instead, Cal salutes, two fingers to his brow. It's better than punching Maven in the face, and he draws back, disappointed. He looks away from us, to the far side of the arena. When I turn, I expect to see the gunmen who killed Lucas, but I'm greeted by a very different sight.

I don't know where they came from or when but five figures appear in the dust.

"That's not too bad," I murmur, squeezing Cal's hand. *He's a warrior, a soldier. Five on one might even be fair for him.*

But Cal furrows his brow, his attention on our executioners. They come into sharper focus and fear rolls through me. I know their names and abilities, some much better than others. All of them ripple with strength, in armor and uniforms meant for war.

A strongarm Rhambos to tear me apart, the Haven son who will disappear and choke me like a shadowed ghost, and Lord Osanos himself to drown Cal's fire. Arven as well, I remind myself. He stands at the gate, his eyes never leaving my body.

Don't forget the other two. The magnetrons.

It's almost poetic, really. In matching armor, with matching scowls, Evangeline and Ptolemus stare us down, their fists bristling with long, cruel knives.

Somewhere in my head, a clock ticks, counting down. *Not much time left.*

Above us, Maven's voice croaks out.

"Let them die."

TWENTY-EIGHT

The shield explodes to life above us, a giant purple dome of veined glass like the one in the Spiral Garden. Not to protect us—but to protect the crowd. Sparks of lightning pulse through the monstrous ceiling, teasing me. Without Arven, the lightning would be mine and I could fight. I could show this world who I am. But that is not to be.

Cal shifts, putting out his arm. The air ripples around him, distorted by the waves of heat rolling off his body. He angles himself toward the others, protecting me.

"Stay behind me as long as you can," he says, letting his own heat push me back. The flame maker sparks, and fire crackles between his fingers, growing up his arms. Something in his shirt keeps it from burning, and the fabric doesn't smoke away. "When they break through the wall, you'll have to run. Evangeline's weakest, but the strongarm's slow. You can outrun him. They'll try to drag this out, to make it a show." Then softly, "They won't let us die quickly."

"What about you? Osanos will—"

"Let me worry about Osanos."

The executioners move steadily, like wolves stalking prey. They spread out across the middle of the arena, each one ready to advance. Somewhere, metal scrapes and a piece of the arena floor slides away, revealing a sloshing pool of water at Lord Osanos's feet. He smiles, drawing the water up to him in a menacing shield. I remember his daughter Tirana dueling Maven in Training. She destroyed him.

All around, the crowd jeers. Ptolemus roars with them, letting his famed temper take over. He smacks at his armor, ringing it like a bell. At his side, Evangeline spins her knives, sliding them over her knuckles with a grin.

"This won't be like before, Red," she crows. "No tricks can save you now."

Tricks. Evangeline knows my abilities better than most; she knows they weren't tricks. *But she believes. She ignores the truth for something easier to understand.*

The Haven son, Stralian, grins to himself. Like his sister Elane, he is a shadow. When he flickers out of being, disappearing in the bright sunlight, Cal moves faster than I thought possible, swinging out his arm in a wide arc like he's throwing a haymaker punch.

A roar of flame follows his arm, burning up the sand, separating us from them. But the fire is surprisingly weak. *The sand will barely burn.*

I can't stop myself from glancing back at Maven, wanting to scream at him, only to find he's still staring at me with that insufferable crooked smirk. Not only has he taken away my abilities, but he's limiting Cal as much as he can.

"Bastard," I curse under my breath. "The sand—"

"I know," Cal snaps, igniting more bits of the ground with a wave of his hand.

Directly across from us, the line of flame separates for a second, followed closely by a bitter scream of pain. On the other side of the dying fire, Stralian fades back into sight, batting flames from his arms. Osanos douses him with a lazy gesture, putting out the fire with a wave of water. Then he turns his startling blue eyes on us, on Cal's wall, and in a single motion, draws water across the weak fire like a lapping wave. The water hisses and spits, flash-boiling into thick clouds of steam. Trapped by the glass dome, the steam settles through the arena, shrouding us in a ghostly white fog. It swirls and spins, enveloping us in a white world where every shadow could be our doom.

"Be ready!" Cal shouts, a hand reaching for me, but Ptolemus charges out of the steam in a roar of flesh and steel.

He hits Cal around the middle, knocking him to the ground, but Cal doesn't stay down long enough for Ptolemus to stab out with his knives. The blades dig into the ground seconds after Cal leaps, his hands on Ptolemus's armor. The steel melts beneath his touch, drawing a scream from the berserker. I can only run as Cal tries to cook a man in his own armor.

"I don't want to kill you, Ptolemus," Cal says through the screams of pain. Every knife, every shard of metal Ptolemus raises to stab Cal melts away from his intense heat. "I don't want to do this."

Three sparkling blades cut through the steam, barely flashing blurs. *Too fast to melt in midair.* They hit Cal's back, stinging through his shirt before melting away. He yells in pain, losing focus for a second as three spots of silverblood stain his shirt. The knives were too small to cut deep, but they weaken him still. Ptolemus takes his chance and in the blink of an eye, his knives meld into a single monstrous sword. He slashes, meaning to slice Cal in two, but he dodges in time, earning a scratch across the belly.

Still alive. *But not for long.*

Evangeline appears through the steam, knives swirling around in a glinting display. Cal dips and dodges her blades, throwing blasts of fire to knock her off course. He duels them both, hitting an insane rhythm that allows him to fight off two magnetrons, despite their strength and power. But blood stains his clothes and new wounds appear with every passing second. Ptolemus's weapon shifts, from a sword to an ax to a razor-thin metal whip, while Evangeline's jagged stars keep biting. *They're wearing him down. Slowly but surely.*

My lightning, I think mournfully, looking back to Arven at our gate. He's still there, a black presence to haunt me. A gun hangs at his waist; I can't even try to fight him. *I can't do anything.*

When a massive chunk of concrete sails out of the steam, heading directly for me, I barely have time to dodge. It shatters against the sand where I stood seconds ago, but before I have time to think, another comes hunting, howling through the air. The sky is raining concrete down on me. Like Cal, I find my rhythm, scurrying through the sand like a rat, until something stops me short.

A hand. An invisible hand.

Stralian's grip closes on my throat, choking me. I can hear him breathing in my ear, though I can't see him. "Red and dead," he growls, tightening his hand.

My arm swings out, digging an elbow into what I suppose are his ribs, but he holds firm. I can't breathe and black spots dot my vision, threatening to spread, but I keep fighting. Through the haze, I can see the Rhambos strongarm prowling, his eyes locked on me. *He'll pull me apart.*

Cal still fights the Samos siblings, doing his best not to get stabbed. I can't scream for him even if I wanted to, but somehow he manages to throw a fireball my way. Rhambos has to jump back, stumbling on his massive feet, buying me a few more seconds. Gasping, choking, I dig my nails back, reaching for a head I cannot see. It's a miracle when I feel his face and then his eyes. With a gasping scream, I dig in, thumbs to his eye sockets, blinding him. Stralian roars, letting go of me. He falls to his knees, flickering back into being. Silverblood trails from his eyes like mirrored tears.

"You were supposed to be mine!" a voice screams, and I turn to see Evangeline standing over Cal, her blade raised. Ptolemus has wrestled Cal to the ground, the two of them rolling through the sand with Evangeline haunting over them, her knives peppering the ground around him. *"Mine!"*

It doesn't occur to me that running headfirst into a magnetron might not be a good idea until I collide into her. We fall together, my face scraping along her armor. It smarts and stings and *bleeds*, dripping red for all to see. Though I can't see the screens, I know every one broadcasts the image of my blood through the country.

Evangeline shrieks, lashing out with her dancing blades. Behind us, Cal fights to his feet, blasting Ptolemus away with a blaze of fire. The magnetron collides with his sister, knocking her away seconds before her knives slice through me.

"Duck!" Cal shouts, throwing me to the sand as another slab of concrete flies over us, shattering against the far wall.

We can't keep this up. "I've got an idea."

Cal spits at the sand, and I think I see a few teeth mixed in with the blood. "Good, because I ran out of them five minutes ago."

Another block sails by, forcing us to jump apart, and just in time. Evangeline and Ptolemus return with a vengeance, locking Cal into a chaotic dance of knives and shrapnel. Their powers shake the arena around us, calling up more metal from down deep, forcing Cal to watch his footing along with everything else. Shards of pipes and wires poke up through the sand, creating a deadly obstacle course of metal.

One of them stabs Stralian where he kneels, still screaming over his eyes. The pipe goes straight through him, popping out through his mouth to silence his cries for good. Through the wreckage, I hear the arena crowd scream and gasp at the sight. For all their violent ways, all their power, they're still cowards.

My feet pound through the sand as I circle Rhambos, daring him to attack me. Cal's right, *I'm faster*, and though Rhambos is a monster of muscle, he trips over his own feet trying to chase me. He rips the jagged pipes from the ground, throwing them at me like spears, but they're easy to dodge and he roars in frustration. *I'm Red, I'm nothing, and I can still make you fall.*

The sound of rushing water brings me back, making me remember the fifth executioner. *The nymph.*

I turn just in time to see Lord Osanos part the steam like a curtain, clearing the arena floor. And ten yards away, still dueling hard, is Cal. Smoke and fire explode from him, beating back the magnetrons. But as Osanos advances, the water trailing in a swirling cloak, Cal's flames recede. Here is the true executioner. Here is the end of the show.

"Cal!" I scream, but there's nothing I can do for him. *Nothing.*

Another pipe sails past my cheek, so close I feel the cold sting, so close it makes me spin and fall. The gate is only yards away, with Arven still standing in its mouth, half-shrouded by darkness.

Cal sends a blast of fire at Osanos, but he smothers it quickly. Steam screams from the clash of water and fire, but water is winning.

Rhambos advances, pushing me back toward the gate. *Cornered. I let him corner me.* Rocks and metal break against the wall behind me, enough to shatter my bones. *Lightning,* my head screams. *LIGHTNING.*

But there's nothing. Just the dark smother of dead senses, suffocating me.

All around us, the crowd jumps to their feet, sensing the end. I can hear Maven above me, cheering with all the rest.

"Finish them off!" he yells. It still surprises me to hear such malice in his voice. But when I look up, his eyes meeting mine through the shield and steam, there's nothing but anger and rage and evil.

Rhambos takes aim, a long, jagged pipe in hand. *Death has come.*

Over the din, I hear a roar of triumph: Ptolemus. He and Evangeline step back from a swirling orb of water, and the cloudy figure deep within. *Cal.* The water boils, and his body strains, trying to break free, but it's no use. *He's going to drown.*

Behind me, almost in my ear, Arven laughs to himself. "Who has the advantage?" he sneers to himself, repeating his words from Training.

My muscles ache and twitch, begging for it to be over. I just want to lie down, to admit defeat, to die. They called me a liar, a trickster, and *they were right.*

I have one more trick left up my sleeve.

Rhambos takes aim, setting his feet in the sand, and I know what I must do. He hurls his spear with such strength it seems to burn the air. I drop, throwing myself to the sand.

A sickening squelch tells me my plan has worked and the scream of electricity surging back to life tells me I might win.

Behind me, Arven collapses, a pipe speared through his middle.

"I have the advantage," I tell his corpse.

When I get back to my feet, thunder and lightning and sparks and shocks and everything I can possibly control spits from my body. The crowd screams aloud, Maven above them all.

"Kill her! KILL HER!" he roars, pointing down at me through the dome. "SHOOT HER!"

Bullets dig into the dome, sparking and splintering against the electric shield, but it holds firm. It was supposed to protect them, but it is electric, it is lightning, it is *mine*, and the shield protects *me* now.

The crowd gasps, not believing their eyes. Red blood drips from my wounds, and lightning trembles in my skin, declaring what I am for everyone. Overhead, the video screens go dark. But I've already been seen. They can't stop what's already happened.

Rhambos takes a quivering step back, his breath catching in his throat. I don't give him a chance to take another.

Silver and Red, and stronger than both.

My lightning streaks through him, boiling his blood, frying his nerves, until he collapses in a twitching pile of meat.

Osanos drops next as my sparks run over him. The liquid orb splashes to the ground, and Cal collapses to the sand, spitting up water with hacking coughs.

Despite the jagged metal spikes punching up through the sand, trying to run me through, I break into a sprint, dodging and vaulting over every obstacle. *They trained me for this. It's their own fault. They helped make their own doom.*

Evangeline waves a hand, sending a steel beam flying at my head. I slide beneath it, knees skimming across the ground, before coming up beside her, daggered bolts of lightning in my hands.

She calls up a sword from the swirling metal, forging a blade. My lightning breaks against it, shocking through the iron, but still she duels. The metal shifts and splits all around us, trying to fight me. Even her spiders return to tear me down, but they aren't enough. *She* isn't enough.

Another blast of lightning knocks her blades away and sends her sprawling, trying to escape my wrath. *She won't.*

"Not a trick," she breathes, taken off guard. Her eyes fly between my hands as she backs away, bits of metal floating between us in a hasty shield. "Not a lie."

I can taste red blood in my mouth, sharp and metallic and strangely wonderful. I spit it out for all to see. Overhead, the blue sky darkens through the shielded dome. Black clouds gather, heavy and full with rain. *The storm is coming.*

"You said you'd kill me if I ever got in your way." It feels so good to throw her words back in her face. "Here's your chance."

Her chest rises and falls, heaving with each breath. She's tired. She's wounded. And the steel behind her eyes is almost gone, giving way to fear.

She lunges, and I move to block her attack, but it never comes. Instead, she *runs*. She runs from *me*, sprinting at the closest gate she can find. I pound after her, running to hunt her down, but Cal's roar of frustration stops me in my tracks.

Osanos is on his feet again, dueling with renewed strength, while Ptolemus dances around them, looking for his opening. *Cal is no good against nymphs, not with his fire.* I remember how easily bested Maven was in his own training so long ago.

My hand closes around the nymph's wrist, shocking him through his skin, forcing him to turn his anger on me. The water feels like a hammer, knocking me backward into the sand. It crashes and crashes, making it impossible to breathe. For the first time since I entered the arena, the cold hand of fear clenches around my heart. Now that we have a chance of winning, of living, I'm so afraid to lose. My lungs scream for air and I can't help but open my mouth, letting the water choke me. It stings like fire, like death.

The tiniest spark runs through me, and it's enough, shocking through the water and up into Osanos. He yelps, jumping back long enough to let me scramble free, slipping through the wet sand. Air sears my lungs as I gasp for breath, but there's no time to enjoy it. Osanos is on me again; this time his hands are around my neck, holding me under the swirling foot of water.

But I'm ready for him. The fool is stupid enough to touch me, to put his skin against mine. When I let the lightning go, shocking through flesh and water, he screams like a boiling teakettle and flops backward. As the water falls away, draining into the sand, I know he's truly dead.

When I rise, soaking wet, shaking with adrenaline, fear, *strength*, my eyes fly to Cal. He's slashed and bruised, bleeding all over, but his arms rage with bright red fire, and Ptolemus cowers at his feet. He raises his hands in defeat, begging for mercy.

"Kill him, Cal," I snarl, wanting to see him bleed. Above us, the lightning shield pulses again, surging with my anger. If only it was Evangeline. If only I could do it myself. "He tried to kill *us*. Kill him."

Cal doesn't move, breathing hard through his teeth. He looks so torn, eager for vengeance, consumed by the thrill of battle, but also steadily fading back to the calm, thoughtful man he used to be. The man he *can't* be anymore.

But a man's nature is not so easily changed. He steps back, flames fading away.

"I won't."

The silence presses down, a wonderful change from the screaming, jeering crowd who wanted us dead moments ago. But when I look up, I realize they aren't staring. They aren't seeing Cal's mercy or my ability. They aren't even there at all. The great arena has emptied, leaving no witnesses to our victory. The king sent them away, to hide the truth of what we have done so he can supplant it with his own lies.

From his box, Maven begins to clap.

"Well done," he shouts, moving to the edge of the arena. He peers at us through the shield, his mother close at his shoulder.

The sound hurts more than any knife, making me cringe. It echoes over the empty structure, until marching feet, boots on stone and sand, drown him out.

Security, Sentinels, soldiers, all of them pour onto the sand from every gate. There are hundreds, thousands, too many to fight. Too many to run from. We won the battle, but we lost the war.

Ptolemus scrambles away, disappearing into the crowd of soldiers. Now we're alone in a steadily closing circle, with nothing and no one left.

It's not fair. We won. We showed them. It's not fair. I want to scream, to shock and rage and fight, but the bullets will get me first. Hot tears of anger well in my eyes, but I will not cry. Not in these last moments.

"I'm sorry I did this to you," I whisper to Cal. No matter how I feel about his beliefs, he's the one truly losing here. I knew the risks, but he was just a pawn, torn between so many playing an invisible game.

He clenches his jaw, twisting and turning as he looks for some way out of this. But there isn't one. I don't expect him to forgive me, and I don't deserve it either. But his hand closes over mine, holding on to the last person on his side.

Slowly, he starts to hum. I recognize the tune as the sad song, the one we kissed to in a room full of moonlight.

Thunder rumbles in the clouds, threatening to burst. Raindrops pitter on the dome above us. It shocks and sizzles the rain, but the water keeps coming in a steady downpour. *Even the sky weeps for our loss.*

At the edge of his box, Maven stares down at us. The sparking shield distorts his face, making him look like the monster he truly is. Water drips down his nose, but he doesn't notice. His mother whispers something in his ear and he jolts, brought back to reality.

"Good-bye, little lightning girl."

When he raises his hand, I think he might be shaking.

Like the little girl I am, I squeeze my eyes shut, expecting to feel the blinding pain of a hundred bullets ripping me apart. My thoughts turn inward, to days long past. To Kilorn, my parents, my brothers, my sister. *Will I see them all soon?* My heart tells me yes. They're waiting for me, somewhere, somehow. And like I did that day in the Spiral Garden, when I thought I was falling to my death, I feel cold acceptance. *I will die.* I feel life leaving, and I let go.

The storm overhead explodes with a deafening clap of thunder, so strong it shakes the air. The ground rumbles beneath my feet and, even behind closed eyelids, I see the blinding flash of light. Purple and white and strong, the strongest thing I've ever felt. Weakly, I wonder what will happen if it hits me. Will I die or will I survive? Will it forge me like a sword, into something terrible and sharp and new?

I never find out.

Cal seizes me by the shoulders, throwing us both out of the way as a giant bolt of lightning streaks down out of the sky. It shatters through the shield, sending purple shards down on us like falling snow. It sizzles against my skin in a delightful sensation, an invigorating pulse of power to bring me back to life.

All around us, the gunmen cower, ducking or running away, trying to escape the sparking storm. Cal tries to drag me, but I'm barely aware of him. Instead, my senses buzz with the storm, feeling it churning above me. *It's mine.*

Another bolt strikes down, pounding into the sand, and the Security officers scatter, running for the gates. But the Sentinels and the soldiers are not so easily frightened, and they come to their senses quickly. Even though Cal pulls me back, trying to save us both, they pursue—and there is no escape.

As good as the storm feels, it drains me, leeching my energy away. Controlling a lightning storm is just too much. My knees buckle, and my heart beats like a drum, so fast I think it might burst. *One more bolt, one more. We might have a chance.*

When my feet stumble backward, heels jutting out over the empty chasm that once held Osanos's water weapon, I know it's over. There's nowhere else to run.

Cal holds me tight, pulling me back from the edge in case I might fall. There's nothing but blackness down there, and the echo of churning water deep down. Nothing but pipes and plumbing and black nothing. And ahead of us, the practiced, brutal ranks of soldiers. They take aim mechanically, raising their guns in unison.

The shield is broken, the storm is dying, and we have lost. Maven can smell my defeat and grins from his box, his lips pulled into a terrifying smile. Even from such a distance, I can see the glinting points of his crown. Rainwater runs into his eyes, but he doesn't blink. He doesn't want to miss my death.

The guns rise, and this time they won't wait for Maven's order.

The shooting thunders like my storm, ringing out across the empty arena. But I feel nothing. When the first line of gunmen falls, their chests peppered with bullet holes, I don't understand.

I blink down at my feet, only to see a line of strange guns poking out over the edge of the chasm. Each barrel smokes and jumps, still shooting, mowing down all the soldiers in front of us.

Before I can understand, someone grabs the back of my shirt and pulls me down to fall through the black air. We land in water far below, but the arms never let go.

The water takes me, down into darkness.

EPILOGUE

The black void of sleep ebbs away, giving way to life again. My body rocks with motion, and I can sense an engine somewhere. Metal shrieks against metal, scraping at high speed in a noise I vaguely recognize. *The Undertrain.*

The seat beneath my cheek feels oddly soft, but also tense. Not leather or cloth or concrete, I realize, but warm *flesh*. It shifts beneath me, adjusting as I move, and my eyes open. What I see is enough to make me think I'm still dreaming.

Cal sits across the train, his posture stiff and tense, fists clenched in his lap. He stares straight ahead, to the person cradling me, and in his eyes is the fire I know so well. The train fascinates him, and his gaze flickers now and then, glancing at the lights and the windows and the wires. He's itching to examine it, but the person at his side keeps him from moving at all.

Farley.

The revolutionary, all scars and tension, stands over him. Somehow she survived the slaughter under the Square. I want to smile, to call out to her, but weakness bleeds through me, keeping me still. I remember the storm, the battle of the arena, and all the horrors that came before. *Maven.* His name makes my heart clench, twisting in anguish and shame. *Anyone can betray anyone.*

Her gun hangs across her chest, ready to fire on Cal. There are more like her, tensely guarding him. They are broken, wounded, and so few, but they still look menacing. Their eyes never stray from the fallen prince, watching him as a mouse would a cat. And then I see his wrists are bound, shackled in iron that he could easily melt away. But he doesn't. He just sits there quietly, waiting for something.

When he feels my gaze, his eyes snap to mine. Life sparks in him again.

"Mare," he murmurs, and some of the hot anger breaks. *Some.*

My head spins when I try to sit up, but a comforting hand pushes me back down again. "Lie still," a voice says, a voice I vaguely recognize.

"Kilorn," I mumble.

"I'm here."

To my confusion, the old fisher boy pushes his way through the Guardsmen behind Farley. He has scars of his own now, with dirty bandages on his arm, but he stands tall. And he is *alive.* Just the sight of him sends a flood of relief through me.

But if Kilorn is standing there, with the rest of the Guard, then . . .

My neck turns sharply, moving to look up at the person above me. "Who—?"

The face is familiar, a face I know so well. If I were not already lying down, I would certainly fall. The shock is too much for me to bear.

"Am I dead? Are we dead?"

He's come to take me away. I died in the arena. This was a hallucination, a dream, a wish, a last thought before dying. We are all dead.

But my brother shakes his head slowly, staring at me with familiar honey-colored eyes. Shade was always the handsome one, and death has not changed that.

"You're not dead, Mare," he says, his voice as smooth as I remember. "Neither am I."

"How?" is all I can manage, sitting back to examine my brother fully. He looks the same as I remember, without the usual scars of a soldier. Even his brown hair is growing out again, shaking off the military cut. I run my fingers through it, to convince myself he's real.

But he is not the same. Just like you are not the same.

"The mutation," I say, letting my hand graze his arm. "They killed you for it."

His eyes seem to dance. "They tried."

I don't blink, time doesn't pass, but he's moved at a speed beyond my sight, beyond even that of a swift. Now he sits across from me, next to the still-shackled Cal. It's like he's shifting through space, jumping from one spot to another in no time at all.

"And failed," he finishes from his new seat. His grin is wide now, pleasantly amused by my openmouthed stare. "They said they killed me, they told the captains I was dead and my body burned." Another split second and he's sitting next to me again, appearing out of thin air. *Teleporting.* "But they weren't fast enough. No one is."

I try to nod, I try to understand his ability, his simple *existence*, but I can't comprehend much more than the circle of his arms around me. Shade. Alive and like me.

"What about the others? Mom, Dad—" But Shade stills me with a smile.

"They're safe and waiting," he says. His voice breaks a little, overcome with emotion. "We'll see them soon."

My heart swells at the thought. But like all my happiness, all my joy and all my hope, it doesn't last long. My eyes fall on the Guard bristling with weapons, on Kilorn's scars, on Farley's tense face and Cal's bound hands. Cal, who has suffered so much, escaping one prison for another.

"Let him go." I owe him my life, *more* than my life. Surely I can give him some comfort here. But no one budges at my words, not even Cal.

To my surprise, he answers before Farley. "They won't. And they shouldn't. In fact, you should probably blindfold me, if you really want to be thorough."

Even though he's been cast down, thrown out of his own life, Cal can't change who he is. The soldier is in him still. "Cal, shut up. You're not a danger to anyone."

With a scoff, Cal tips his head, gesturing at the train of armed rebels. "They seem to think otherwise."

"Not to us, I mean," I add, shrinking back against my seat. "He saved me up there, even after what I did. And after what Maven did to you—"

"Don't say his name." His growl is frightful, putting a chill in me, and I don't miss Farley's hand tightening around her gun.

Her words slide out between clenched teeth. "No matter what he did for you, the prince is not on our side. And I won't risk what's left of us for your little romance."

Romance. We flinch at the word. *There is no such thing between us anymore. Not after what we did to each other, and what was done to us. No matter how much we might want there to be.*

"We're going to keep fighting, Mare, but Silvers have betrayed us before. We won't trust them again." Kilorn's words are softer, a balm to try to help me understand. But his eyes spark at Cal. Obviously he remembers the torture down in the cells and the terrible sight of frozen blood. "He might be a valuable prisoner."

They don't know Cal like I do. They don't know he could destroy them all, that he could escape in a heartbeat if he really wanted. So why does he stay? When he meets my eyes, somehow he answers my question without speaking. The hurt I see radiating from him is enough to break my heart. *He is tired. He is broken. And he doesn't want to fight anymore.*

Part of me doesn't either. Part of me wishes I could submit to chains, to captivity and silence. But I have lived that life already, in the mud, in the shadows, in a cell, in a silk dress. I will never submit again. I will never stop fighting.

Neither will Kilorn. Neither will Farley. We will never stop.

"The others like us . . ." My voice shakes, but I have never felt so strong. "The others like me and Shade."

Farley nods and pats a hand to her pocket. "I still have the list. I know the names."

"And so does Maven," I reply smoothly. Cal twitches at the name. "He'll use the bloodbase to trace them, and hunt them down."

Even though the train sways and shakes, twisting over dark tracks, I force myself to my feet. Shade tries to steady me, but I brush his hand away. I must stand on my own.

"He can't find them before we do." I raise my chin, feeling the pulse of the train. It electrifies me. "He can't."

When Kilorn steps toward me, his face set and determined, his bruises and scars and bandages seem to fade. I think I see the dawn in his eyes.

"He won't."

A strange warmth falls over me, a warmth like the sun though we are deep underground. It's as familiar to me as my own lightning, reaching out to envelop me in an embrace we can't have. Even though they call Cal my enemy, even though they fear him, I let his warmth fall on my skin, and I let his eyes burn into mine.

Our shared memories flash before me, parading every second of our time together. But now our friendship is gone, replaced by the one thing we still have in common.

Our hatred for Maven.

I don't need to be a whisper to know we share a thought.

I will kill him.

ACKNOWLEDGMENTS

I'll do this chronologically, to try to include everyone, because I owe thanks to so many people. First and most of all, my ridiculously supportive parents who encouraged me to do anything and everything I wanted. They remain my greatest teachers, and I'm grateful for every gift, especially letting me watch *Jurassic Park* at 3 years old. To my brother, Andrew, who joined in on every game and every joke, and made my fantasy worlds so much bigger and brighter. My grandparents—George and Barbara, Mary and Frank—who gave and continue to give more love and memory than I can understand. Too many aunts, uncles, and cousins to name, not to mention friends and neighbors who tolerated me running through their lives and backyards. Natalie, Lauren, Teressa, Kim, Katrina, and Sam, who stuck with me through the rough teen years and questionable clothing choices. Of course, every English and social studies teacher I ever had, who continuously told me to stop writing novels for essays. And I have to thank the ones who influenced me beyond reason, even though they don't know me. Steven Spielberg, George Lucas, Peter Jackson, J.R.R. Tolkien, J.K. Rowling,

C.S. Lewis. I grew up in a small town, but because of these people, my world never seemed that way.

The University of Southern California and their incomparable School of Cinematic Arts somehow let me slip in, and completely changed the trajectory of my life. My screenwriting professors, every single one of them, pushed me into the writer I am now, and taught me every trick I know. Not only did I begin to believe this storytelling compulsion of mine was a viable pursuit, but I started becoming who I wanted to be. The screenwriting program itself is the reason I got the chance to be a working writer, and I can't thank them enough. I was lucky enough to make amazing friends, some of my closest, at SC—Nicole, Kathryn, Shayna, Jen L., Erin, Angela, Bayan, Morgan, Jen R., Tori, the Chez boys, Traddies, etc.—who made me begrudgingly better (and delightfully worse sometimes).

After college, I faced the terrifying prospect of an impossible career choice. Luckily, I had Benderspink at my back, especially my first manager, Christopher Cosmos, who encouraged me to write *Red Queen*. When I finished the first draft, he sent it along to New Leaf Literary, and set me on another life-changing path. I landed with the best in publishing: Pouya Shahbazian, who continues to guide *RQ* and me through the waters of the entertainment industry; Kathleen Ortiz, my passport to the world and the reason *RQ* continues to travel the globe; Jo Volpe, our fearless captain and wonderful friend; Danielle Barthel, Jaida Temperly, Jess Dallow, and Jackie Lindert, who tolerate my weird requests and are completely indispensable; Dave Caccavo, a fellow George Washington and USA soccer enthusiast, and I'm told he's good at numbers; and sorry guys, I saved the best for last, Suzie Townsend continues to be my literary North Star. *Red Queen* is now a real book because of so many people, but especially her. She's the push, pull, and pat on the head I'll always need.

When Suzie called to tell me we had an offer on *RQ*, I told her I was driving and might crash into a tree. I did not crash, but I did accept the preempt from Kari Sutherland and HarperTeen. As my first editor, Kari held my hand on my journey into the larger publishing world, and turned a manuscript into a novel. I cannot express my unending gratitude to her, Alice Jerman, and the entire Harper team: our dauntless leader and editor-in-chief Kate Jackson; Jen Klonsky, appetizer extraordinaire and fantastic editorial director; production editors Alexandra Alexo and Melinda Weigel; copy editor Stephanie Evans, who wrangles my commas like no other; production manager Lillian Sun; design wizards Sarah Kaufman, Alison Klapthor, and Barb Fitzsimmons, along with cover artist Michael Frost, you've made a truly beautiful book; marketing team Christina Colangelo and Elizabeth Ward, putting *RQ* on the map; Emily Butler, Kara Brammer, and Madison Killen, for making me passable and comfortable on camera, not to mention in frame; the incomparable Gina Rizzo and Sandee Roston, the publicity team working around the clock to spread the world; Ashton Quinn, for sales and great support; the Epic Reads team, Margot and Aubry, who have shimmied their way into my cold heart; Elizabeth Lynch(pin), one of the hardest working people I know; and the joy that is Kristen Pettit, who bravely leads *RQ* and the rest of the series through its journey.

I won't say it takes a village, because that's overdone (but seriously, it takes a village). The rest of mine includes my entertainment team—all the troopers at Benderspink: the Jakes, JC, Daniel, the ever-wrangling David, and too many interns to thank. My lawyer Steve Younger, aka my West Coast dad. Sara Scott and Gennifer Hutchison, the warrior princesses hopefully bringing *RQ* to the big screen. And then there are the people I've never met in real life, who tweet and email and IM me through each day. Publishing and entertainment are very much alive on social media, and I've met so many inspiring and encouraging folks who welcomed me into the fold. Every author, blogger, writer, and fan is so valuable, and I thank you all for your words and support. Particularly Emma Theriault, my Canadian twin, reader, critic, and friend.

I'm a writer, and that means I mostly work alone, but I'm never truly that way. Thank you so much to everyone who stands by me and accepts my weirdness—Culver, Morgan and Jen especially, mind-meld Bayan, the arcane Erin, and #Angela, who never judge me (out loud). And my lifestyle staples that get me through the days—Jackson Market, the barista who never cares about my hobo clothing, Target, fall foliage, Pottery Barn, bookstores, yoga pants, tacky t-shirts, the National Parks System, the Patriots (both football and founding fathers), George R.R. Martin, and Wikipedia. I also have to thank the state of Montana, where I wrote chapter two and decided I was going all in on this book-writing thing.

I apologize for being so gushy, but I'm almost done. Once more to Morgan, my best friend and the kick in the pants I need and never want. I will continue leaving the hall light on. And again to my parents, Heather and Louis. They let me move home and focus on writing a book, which is crazy. They helped me go to an awesome but shockingly expensive university far away, which is crazy. They raised weirdo me into some semblance of a functioning human, which is crazy. And they continue to support, love, sacrifice, and take me down a peg, usually all at the same time. They got me to where I am, and enabled this book, this future, and this life to happen. Which is crazy.

JOIN THE Epic Reads COMMUNITY

THE ULTIMATE YA DESTINATION

◀ **DISCOVER** ▶
your next favorite read

◀ **FIND** ▶
new authors to love

◀ **WIN** ▶
free books

◀ **SHARE** ▶
infographics, playlists, quizzes, and more

◀ **WATCH** ▶
the latest videos

◀ **TUNE IN** ▶
to Tea Time with Team Epic Reads

Find us at **www.epicreads.com**
and **@epicreads**